The Player

the Player

The Wedding Pact
Book Two

DENISE
GROVER SWANK

Chapter One

BLAIR HANSEN HAD ALWAYS HEARD that near-death experiences made people reevaluate their lives. She'd spent nearly thirty years sure about what she wanted in life, but all it had taken for her to start questioning everything was some severe turbulence on a 747.

She picked up her whiskey and took a healthy sip. No girly drinks for her. Blair had forced herself to drink whiskey until she liked it. Being tough—and letting other people know it—was how she'd gotten to where she was in life. Which was currently in a hotel bar in Phoenix, Arizona, waiting to hear if they had a room for her to spend the night.

Of course, she wasn't supposed to be away from home at all, let alone in Phoenix. She was getting married in five days, so her bosses had initially agreed to let her have a short four-day workweek in their office in Kansas City, but then the senior partner had called her on Sunday afternoon with instructions to board a plane to Los Angeles. And that's exactly what she had done—despite the fact that she had a million and one things to do for her wedding. Robert Sisco Sr. didn't want to hear excuses. Sisco, Sisco, and Reece only wanted to hear yes and see lots of dollar signs on checks, and her understanding of that fact was one of the reasons she was so close to making junior partner. They didn't want her wedding to interfere with her work. Even if they were the primary reason she was getting married in the first place. Partners were typically married, which probably had something to do with the illusion of stability and maturity. It was all a bunch of hooey, but Blair Hansen *really* wanted to be a partner.

She took another gulp of her drink, the ice clinking against her glass because of her shaking hand.

The thing was, she'd realized something. Her future life had flashed before her eyes in those awful minutes on board the plane, and she hadn't liked the look of it.

Now she wasn't so sure she wanted to get married after all.

On paper, Dr. Neil Fredrick was perfect for her. Educated, personable, stable. Conservative politically and fiscally. Neil was a firm believer in playing it safe. And stability was exactly what Blair wanted after bearing witness to her parents' chaotic marriage—her father's affairs, her parents' subsequent divorce, and finally her father's death, which had practically bankrupted the family.

But lately, she found herself wanting something . . . more.

She blamed it on her best friend Megan. Megan had gotten married two months ago, though not to her original groom. Their story was the kind of gushy, too-cute-to-be-true, fairy-tale romance that wasn't supposed to happen in real life. But for Megan, the impossible *had* happened. The weekend of her wedding, she'd boarded a plane home to tell her parents that she and her cheating asshole fiancé had broken up. After imbibing several drinks and a large dose of Dramamine on the plane, she passed out and was carried off-board by her gorgeous seatmate, who filled in as her substitute fiancé. By the end of the week, Josh had become her real husband, and the two were still nauseatingly happy.

Gag.

Still, Blair couldn't dismiss the fact that their wild and

crazy love had put a crack in her belief that she had the perfect arrangement—a crack that was starting to spider web. She and Neil had separate apartments, and although Neil had begun spending more time at her place, he remained surprisingly stubborn about keeping his after they were married.

A memory from a couple of months ago intruded on her, tapping directly on that crack in the glass.

"My apartment is closer to the hospital, Blair," Neil had said matter-of-factly, sipping his morning coffee. "It will be easier for the nights I'm on call."

It was hard to argue with his logic—and his stoic logic had always been one of his more attractive traits—but it still seemed . . . wrong. If they were unifying their lives in other ways, why keep separate places? And she knew how it would seem to everyone else.

"But the money—"

"The mortgage on my condo is more than covered by my salary, and the neighborhood is up-and-coming," he had said, his eyes still glued on his newspaper. "If I hold onto it for another five years, there's a chance it will double in value. It makes financial sense to keep it."

At the time, she'd wanted to point out that he could rent it, and anyway, her condo was only twenty minutes from the hospital. He'd already vehemently nixed the idea of sharing his place. According to Neil, the loft was a bachelor pad, and they needed to have a home worthy of entertaining their friends and colleagues. Not that they were known for their dinner parties.

But pointing out those facts would only have instigated an argument. And one of the best parts of their relationship was that they rarely argued. Her job was taxing and full of dissent; when she came home, she coveted peace. And if she were truly honest with herself, a small part of her approved of the living arrangements. Now that he was staying at her apartment on a more consistent basis, she'd begun to find his presence surprisingly suffocating and his previously cute quirks—like the precise way he chewed his food or how he had to have the remote control positioned a very exact way on the coffee table—irritating as hell. But that was normal. As a divorce attorney, she knew better than to expect that marriage would be a roller coaster of excitement.

In fact, if she'd learned anything from her work, it was this: the couples who ended up divorcing after just a year or two were usually the ones who'd been head-over-heels, drawing-hearts-on-everything in love when they approached the altar. Megan's delirious happiness aside, there was no such thing as true love.

If there were, she would still be with Garrett Lowry.

She clanked her now-empty glass on the bar to get the bartender's attention. "Another, please."

He shot her a grin as he poured her drink. "Must have been some kind of Monday."

She grabbed the glass out of his hands. "You have no idea."

The deposition had run nearly two hours longer than planned, and she'd barely made it to LAX in time to catch her plane. Her feeling of relief had been short-lived; the severe turbulence had convinced her and most of the other passengers that they were about to meet their maker. By the time they landed in Phoenix, many of the connecting flights had been canceled or delayed, and Blair discovered she was stuck overnight in Arizona. The airline had sent her to this hotel, but there had been a problem at the check-in desk.

Half her whiskey was gone before she realized it. There were so many things she needed to do in Kansas City, and she wouldn't get back until at least mid-morning, which meant she'd have to rush to get to her morning deposition. To make matters worse, the damn airline hadn't even confirmed her on the six a.m. flight. They'd only made a vague promise to text her around four in the morning to confirm if she had a ticket.

So now she was well on her way to getting drunk in the bar of an Embassy Suites, playing another round of *This Is Your Life, Blair Anne Myers Hansen,* and she wasn't too happy with what she saw.

Practical, pragmatic, sensible Blair wanted a heart-stopping, butterflies-in-her-stomach kind of love.

All that turbulence must have rattled her brains.

But she couldn't deny the fact that she'd been thinking of Garrett a lot over the last two months—much more than the asshole deserved. Truth be told, he was the only man she'd ever loved. And look how that had turned out. Five years later, she could finally admit to the role she'd played in their breakup, but that didn't make it suck any less.

The rift had formed the night Blair had received word of her estranged father's death. Rather than share the news with Garrett when he came over, she had lashed out at him, picking a fight over some nitpicky complaint. Anger had always been her go-to reaction, and Garrett had weathered many a storm, but that night he'd responded with a fire equal to her own. The fight had spiraled out of control, and before she realized what was happening, Garrett had packed the toiletries and clothes he kept at her apartment into a duffel bag. And then he was gone.

She had spent the next day drowning in an emotional fog of dismay, grief, and loss, and even skipping classes—something she never did. After hours of stewing in her turbulent emotions, she had realized she felt an intense ache for Garrett. For the first time ever, she truly *needed* someone. She had decided to swallow her pride and go to him, ready to beg for his forgiveness and ask him to go with her to her father's funeral. Never in a million years would she have guessed the surprise she had found in his apartment.

Jody Stewart, a fellow second-year law student, who'd made no secret of her lust for Garrett, had opened his door wearing cheap superstore lingerie. Neon green, to make matters worse.

Blair had turned around and never looked back, not even when Garrett had run after her. Or when he'd pounded on her apartment door for an hour begging and pleading with her to let him explain. Not even when he'd tried to approach her in class every day for two solid weeks.

When he'd begun to single-handedly plow his way through nearly every available woman in law school the next year, not to mention a couple of not-so-available ones, she knew she'd made the right decision.

Garrett Lowry was a player.

He may have taken a momentary side-stop with her, but he'd wasted no time before jumping back into the game. She was better off without him.

Still, the memories chafed.

Between Garrett's betrayal and her father's bad behavior, it had been easy for Blair to decide what type of law to practice. In fact, she should thank them both. Maybe she'd take daisies to her father's grave when she came back from her honeymoon. He'd always hated daisies.

She was motioning to the bartender to bring her another drink, wishing the hotel staff would finally give her a damn room key, when she noticed him—the man standing in the entrance of the bar, his gaze fixed on her. She did a double take, certain the Embassy Suites was now including hallucinogens in their drinks, because standing in the doorway was the player himself—Garrett Lowry.

She stopped the bartender as he grabbed her glass. "I'm going to need you to make that a double."

Chapter Two

GARRETT LOWRY WONDERED if he should just divorce his family and be done with them. Unfortunately, while he'd seen quite a few unusual divorce cases in his four years of practicing law, he'd never seen anyone divorce his mother and aunt.

All this fuss over a damned one-third carat diamond ring.

There was no disputing that his Great-Grandma Marie had bequeathed her engagement ring to her granddaughter. The trouble was that she hadn't specified *which* granddaughter. Garrett's Aunt Debra claimed that possession was nine-tenths of the law, and since she had possession of the ring, it was, ipso facto, hers . . . or rather, her son's. She had given it to her son for his fiancée six months ago. Garrett's mother felt otherwise, and so the colossal argument had begun. Though he had no real desire to contest his aunt's stance on the issue, Garrett could think of half a dozen legal cases that disputed her claim. But even if he'd felt any familial connection to the round rock on the gold band, surrounded by multiple smaller diamonds, he had no present use for it. He hadn't had a steady girlfriend since law school, when—in a moment of profound idiocy—he'd broken up with the one woman he'd ever loved.

Ever since, he had moved from one fling to the next like a water droplet on a hot skillet. It had been fun at first, but over the last year—with the big three-o on the horizon—Garrett had changed. He was ready to settle down with someone, but none of his relationships seemed to last longer than a couple of months.

The problem was simple, the solution less so: no one could live up to his ex-girlfriend Blair Myers. They'd shared a connection the likes of which he'd never found with anyone else, and he was becoming increasingly convinced that he *wouldn't* find it with anyone else.

Garrett had to admit that it rubbed like hell that his cousin was getting married. The guy had to be the most boring person on the planet, not to mention the most annoying. Garrett assured himself that his bride-to-be was surely some milquetoast woman who was eager to settle with *Dr.* Neil Fredrick in their suburban house with two-point-five kids. He would come home from the hospital talking about which bacteria had given someone the squirts, and his wife would serve up pot roast and boiled potatoes.

But that didn't make Garrett any more eager to take part in the War of the Ring, which had reached a boiling point now that the wedding was only a week away. Too bad Nana Ruby, the family matriarch, had taken it upon herself to assign him the role of peacemaker. Without bothering to consult him first, she'd arranged for him to be a last-minute groomsman in the wedding. He hadn't even planned on going—he'd tossed the ivory invitation into the trash the moment it arrived, knowing he'd only received one at Nana Ruby's behest—and he had plenty of work to do in San Diego. But Nana didn't want excuses; she wanted to know that he would show up in Kansas City with a smile on his face and keep the peace.

And no one said no to Nana.

"I'm leaving the success or failure of this wedding in your hands, Garrett Michael Lowry," the older woman had barked into the phone.

Garrett had snickered in response. "That seems like a huge responsibility, Nana. Are you sure you want to leave that to me? In case you've forgotten, I'm more of an instigator than a peacemaker."

"Ain't your high-falutin' job all about making people come to some kind of agreement? You should be doin' the same for your family." Nana Ruby made no secret that she didn't take much stock in higher education. Born and raised in the Ozarks, she'd gotten a ninth grade education and a doctorate at the University of Hard Knocks, a school she claimed was more beneficial than all those hoity-toity colleges. Garrett had always appreciated Nana's unique charm, so he let her insults roll off his back. Neil, on the other hand, not so much.

"I don't always help them come to an agreement, Nana. Sometimes the judge has to lay down the law." He had paused for a moment before chuckling again. "Kind of like you, when it comes to Mom and Aunt Debra."

"Don't you try sweet talkin' me, you devil child," she'd grumbled.

"Sweet talk *you*? I'd be a fool to try. You'd rather have a cup of vinegar than a pot full of sugar."

"You're damn straight. Now get your ass to Kansas City, and you better have things under control by the time I drive up there on Wednesday."

Garrett had hoped his mother would give him an out. He was her golden child, particularly after his sister's recent out-of-wedlock pregnancy. Never mind that Kelsey was thirty-one years old and an executive sales manager for a national cellular phone service, making a six-figure income. In his mother's eyes —or more importantly, his Aunt Debra's—Kelsey had tarnished the Lowry side of the family. Frankly, Garrett thought Kelsey had dodged a bullet by not marrying her on-again, off-again boyfriend, who seemed incapable of holding a steady job. But all either sister cared about was whether Kelsey's loser ex had put a ring on it.

While Garrett found it irritating that his mother would let his backwoods aunt's attitude sway her, he was opportunistic enough to take advantage of his mother's current desire to keep him happy.

Of course, she'd denied him, insisting that his inclusion in the wedding would be good for family unity.

"*How* will it be good for family unity? It's only going to stir up more shit."

"Language, Garrett," she'd chastised. "You know your aunt can't abide cursing."

"See? All the more reason for me to stay away and not upset the carefully constructed apple cart."

"If your nana wants you to be there, who are we to question it? She knows what she's doing," was all his mother would say.

His mother was up to something, all right, and it sure as hell wouldn't help him play peacekeeper.

The only bright spot was that Neil was probably even more irritated about Garrett's inclusion in the wedding party than he was.

Perhaps their mothers' habitual animosity added fuel to the fire, but the cousins had never gotten along. While Garrett had always loved the two weeks a year he spent on his widowed grandmother's acreage, spending it with Neil had added a partial dark cloud. Nana had taught both boys about the farm— from livestock to gardening—but while Garrett had soaked up the knowledge, reveling in it, Neil had whined so much, Nana had finally agreed to let him stay in the house with a book while she made the farm rounds with Garrett. But the annual visits had stopped in high school—which *might* have also coincided with Garrett playing a practical joke on his cousin involving horse dung. And while Garrett didn't miss his mealy-mouthed cousin, he did miss his one-on-one time with Nana. So, while he technically could have told Nana Ruby no, he respected her so much, he would have done anything she asked of him. Not that he'd ever admit it. So he'd gone to work on Monday, told the senior partners he had a family emergency, and bought a late afternoon ticket to Kansas City.

Too bad Garrett had spilled the slightly amusing, slightly sad tale of what the *emergency* actually was, because as soon as he did, his boss decided to use it to *his* advantage.

Earlier that afternoon, Garrett had been packing his messenger bag when his boss walked into his office looking like he'd won the lottery.

"Since your emergency isn't so emergent, you can do some work while you're there."

Garrett patted his bag. "That's what I'm planning to do, Matt."

Matt shook his head, his grin so wide it was a wonder his face didn't split open. "Nope. Congratulations. You get to take the depositions on the Norfolk case."

Garrett's mouth dropped open. Could this trip get any worse? He shook his head in dismay. "No. *Anything* but that."

His boss only laughed and dropped a huge file on Garrett's desk. "Look at it this way. Now you don't have to take vacation time."

"I'll take the week off without pay to get out of this."

"Too late. It's already been decided by the big guy upstairs." He pointed his finger toward the ceiling. "He figures you'll do a better job than Lopez has done. The client's lost confidence in him, and you have a reputation of being a barracuda, so . . ."

Garrett groaned and picked up the file, flipping through the pages. "Dammit. I hear the attorney representing the wife is a real bitch."

Matt laughed. "You don't know the half of it." He looked over his shoulder at the door, then turned back to Garrett and lowered his voice. "Rumor has it she made Lopez cry."

Garrett started to laugh before realizing he was the one who had to fill Lopez's shoes.

"Lopez's assistant will email you more details about the case, but the file should be enough to get you up to speed. Your first deposition is tomorrow at ten and should get the week rolling."

"*First* deposition?"

His boss laughed. "There are multiple people to depose in this case. The wife. The husband. The girlfriends. Plural."

"I'm flying home on Sunday, Matt. And I supposedly have wedding activities on Thursday and Friday."

Matt headed for the door and called over his shoulder, "Don't come back until they're all done."

The wedding itself had begun to look like a cakewalk.

But now he was grounded in Phoenix for the night, and while he didn't regret missing an early start to the wedding festivities, he didn't want to delay the depositions. He had no desire to stay in Kansas City a minute longer than necessary, and he was pretty sure Nana wouldn't see work as an excuse to get out of forced family fun.

But all thoughts went out the window when he ventured down to the bar at the hotel he'd booked. Because he recognized the woman sitting at the bar.

It was her, the woman who'd ruined all other women for him.

Blair Myers.

He blinked, certain his mind had given up and induced some type of psychosis, but the look of recognition in her own eyes proved she was real.

She was more beautiful than he remembered her. She still

wore her blonde hair long, and it hung loose, though slightly mussed—totally unlike the put-together woman with whom he'd spent nearly a year. She wore a black skirt and a light gray silk blouse that clung to her breasts. Her four-inch black heels rested on the metal footrest attached to the bar. Her clear blue eyes were focused on him.

It took him a full three seconds to come to his senses and another couple to figure out what to do. Did he ignore her? Did he say hello? He knew what *he* wanted to do, but what did *she* want?

In the end, his feet made the decision for him. He found himself moving toward her, and he stopped only a few feet away, his pulse pounding in his head. He couldn't remember the last time he'd been this nervous, and from the way she was clutching the tumbler the bartender had just handed her, so was she.

What did he say? A half a dozen things popped into his head. *I miss you. You look good. Are you happy? There's not a day that goes by that I don't regret what I did.* But the only thing that came out of his mouth was "Hi."

She continued to stare at him, her gaze slightly unfocused.

"Can I sit?" He motioned to the stool next to her.

His question snapped her out of her daze. She gave him a half shrug, then turned to face the bar. "I can't stop you."

He took the fact that she hadn't kneed him in the balls as a good sign. He slid onto the leather stool as she leaned her elbows on the counter, swaying slightly. No one else would ever notice, but he'd spent the better part of a year studying her instead of his law books. The Blair he knew didn't get drunk. "What are you doing in Phoenix?"

"Passing through." She took a sip of her drink.

He was going to need fortitude. He flagged down the bartender. "I'll take a draft beer. You got Coors?"

The bartender nodded and went to get his drink. Blair chuckled, but it was a brittle sound. "You still drink that crap?"

"Crap?" He leaned his forearms on the bar. "It's made from pure mountain spring water."

She laughed, a genuine laugh, and something in his chest seized with a longing that caught him by surprise. He'd missed her, but the ache was even stronger now that she was beside him.

She turned to him, her gaze searching his face. "Are you married?"

He couldn't believe he was sitting with her now. Maybe this was the universe giving him a gift he didn't deserve, or maybe it was some uniquely horrible form of torture. Either way, he'd take it, but he had to tread lightly. He wanted to tell her what an idiot he'd been, but he needed to take this slow or he would scare her off. Every moment he had with her was a gift, and he wasn't about to screw that up. He forced a chuckle. "What do *you* think?" He instantly knew it was a mistake.

"Still footloose and fancy-free, huh?" She waved her glass to accentuate her words.

The bartender handed him his beer, and he grinned. "Since when did you start saying things like 'footloose and fancy-free'?"

"Since I drank three whiskeys, two of them doubles." She lifted her glass in salute and took a sip. "And you didn't answer my question."

He smirked, even if his heart wasn't in it. "You bet I am. You?" He glanced down at her left hand, and his heart sank.

She held up her hand, the better to blind him, flashing a gold ring with multiple diamonds.

He swallowed his disappointment and for a moment actually considered getting up and walking away. He wasn't sure he could sit here and pretend to be happy for her, or that his mind hadn't spun into overdrive with excitement and possibilities the moment he saw her, but he also wasn't sure he could live with himself if he acted that way. After all, he was the one who'd left and hurt her all those years ago. He owed her more than that. "Really, Blair? You don't seem like the marrying kind."

"People surprise you." She grinned, but there was a bitter note in her voice.

He wanted to apologize—every fiber of his being demanded that he apologize. But he couldn't. Despite what she thought, he knew her. The second he apologized, she'd kick his ass—probably physically as well as verbally—and walk away forever. Blair couldn't stomach any sign of weakness, especially in herself. If he let this conversation get even borderline sappy, it was done.

"So tell me about the poor fool you ended up with." He forced a grin.

She lifted her eyebrows. "Why? So you can make fun of him?"

"Depends. You know me. I make fun of anyone who believes in the Hallmark version of love."

She laughed. "We both did."

Yet she'd loved him once. And even though neither of them were sappy, what Garrett and Blair shared had been intense yet fun.

"Remember Anti-Valentine's Day?" she asked, laughing as she watched him.

His breath caught in his throat. Her face was less than two feet away, and he had a powerful urge to lean over and kiss her, but that would ruin everything. He pulled himself together.

"How could I forget Anti-Valentine's Day?" They'd gone out of their way to do the exact opposite of a typical Valentine's Day celebration, opting for Chuck E. Cheese and arcade games and crappy pizza rather than roses and wine. Then Garrett led her to the roof of his three-story apartment building, where he'd set up a telescope, and showed her the star he'd bought for her and named Blazing Supernova. When she argued that the speck of dust he'd bought her wasn't a supernova, he told her she burned brighter than any star in the sky, though of course he teased her too, so it wouldn't come across as sentimental. And he gave her a plastic ring he'd won at Chuck E. Cheese, telling her that someday he'd give her a real ring, but it would be on October 14, because it was the farthest a person could get from Valentine's Day.

Two months later he had ruined everything.

"Remember when we made fun of those idiots who were fighting over the last batch of roses at the grocery store?" she laughed, then finished her drink and motioned to the bartender.

Blair was a social drinker. She only got shit-faced when she was upset. Now he was worried about her. "So does your guy buy you flowers?"

"Hell, no," she scoffed, wobbling on her stool. "He's too practical for that."

"So what *does* he do?"

Her eyebrows lowered, and she spent several seconds deep in thought. To his alarm, tears filled her eyes. "He programed my remote."

He shook his head in mock appreciation. "An admirable gift."

Her attention drifted over his shoulder, and he turned to see a hotel employee walking toward them.

"I'm sorry, ma'am." The skittish woman looked like she was about to bolt. "There aren't any rooms available here at the hotel or any other hotel in a twenty-mile radius. We checked." She cringed. "Twice."

Blair blinked, and her eyes struggled to focus on the

woman. "There are no rooms *anywhere?*" The sentence ended in a shout.

The employee jumped. "No, ma'am. I'm sorry."

"*Ma'am?*" Blair jumped off her stool and nearly fell over as she pointed her finger at the poor woman. "I'm not a ma'am! I could sue you for that!"

Garrett slid off his stool and wrapped his arm around her waist, pulling her back to his stomach. "Whoa, down there, tiger."

She looked over her shoulder and up at him, horror in her eyes. "She called me *ma'am. How could she do that?*"

Garrett gave her a sympathetic look. "Clearly the poor woman needs glasses, but I hardly think it's worth suing over."

Blair twisted in his arms until her chest was pressed against his, and she looked up at him. "There's no room for me in the inn, Garrett."

The seriousness on her face made him chuckle. "I'll find you a stable somewhere, Blazer. Not to worry." His old nickname for her slipped out before he could reel it back in, but thankfully she didn't seem to notice.

"I hate horses," she grumbled, resting her cheek on his chest.

"I know. I'll make sure there aren't any horses."

The poor employee watched them in confusion, then lifted her gaze to Garrett. He winked. "She was joking about suing."

"No, I wasn't," Blair mumbled.

The employee's eyes widened, and Garrett mouthed *run*.

The woman took off, and Garrett helped Blair back onto her stool. The bartender returned with Blair's drink, but Garrett pushed it away before she could see it. "Can you bring a couple of waters and a couple of cheeseburgers, one with extra pickles?"

Blair laid her head down on the bar. "I like pickles."

"I know." He was glad she was too drunk to hear the sorrow in his voice.

Her head jerked up, and her eyes widened. "I have to find somewhere to stay tonight."

"Blair, I've already figured it out. Let's eat, and then we'll talk about it."

She laid her head down on her arm. "Okay."

He watched her for several seconds, wondering what had made her so upset. He'd only seen her this drunk once before— the night she'd learned that her mother was moving from Kansas City to Des Moines. He had been her anchor then.

Now she was a mess, and she literally had nowhere to go. He wasn't about to leave her here. He could spend the rest of his life beating himself up over something that was already done, or he could try to make things right. And other than Blair, Garrett wasn't a man to live in the past and dwell on mistakes. Now was the time to act.

He asked the bartender to have the food sent to his room, and then he helped Blair off her stool. "Come on, Blazer. They found you a room."

She lifted her head slightly. "*They did?*"

"Yeah, your attorney skills must be top notch. All that talk about suing convinced them to find you one." He reached for her. "Let me help you find it."

She sat up and fumbled as she batted his hands away. "I don't need any help. Especially not from *you*."

He lifted his hands in surrender. "Of course you don't. But they asked me to escort you. So there's no further lawsuit-worthy issues."

Her nose scrunched. She was clearly confused, but drunk enough to believe him. She slid off the stool and reached for her overnight bag, nearly tripping when she tugged it off the ground.

He grabbed the bag and slung her purse over his shoulder too.

She shook her head and nearly fell over. "I don't think that bag goes with your outfit."

He grabbed her elbow to steady her. The bag was made of off-white, uber-shiny patent leather with a shiny gold clasp. It had probably cost a fortune. When he compared it to his jeans and pale blue button-up shirt covered in red stains from the Bloody Mary the passenger next to him had spilled during the turbulence, he flashed her a cocky grin. "Really? I thought jeans went with everything."

She looked up into his face, her eyes searching his. "Why do you still have to be funny? And cute?" She slapped his chest, then left her hand there. "Why aren't you fat and bald?"

"Because, Blair Myers, as you and I both know, there's really no such thing as justice in this world." He kept his tone light and teasing, although perhaps this chance meeting proved there *was* justice in the world. He deserved every bit of pain it brought him. That seemed like justice to him.

She lifted her chin. "I'm not sleeping with you."

"I never asked."

She jerked out of his hold and put her hands on her hips. "I'm not good enough for the high and mighty Garrett Lowry?"

"You know me, Blazer. Never go to the same pasture twice." She'd accused him of that once, right before they left law school. It had stung deeper than he'd let on.

"I'm the best lay you ever had, Lowry."

"It's been too long and too many pastures ago to say, Blazer, but I'm sure you make the top five." He knew she was beyond drunk when she had no reply. "Come on, the hotel staff asked me to show you to your room."

He reached for her arm again, grateful when she didn't shrug him off. He led her to the elevator, slightly worried the hotel staff would think he was taking advantage of her inebriation. But Blair's drunken threats seemed to have staved off any such worries. Once they got on the elevator, his thankfulness turned to anger. Anyone could have taken advantage of her. But he knew that wasn't true. Blair Myers was nobody's fool, drunk or not. The fact that she trusted him now told him that she still cared about him. At least on some level.

When they reached his room, he pulled out his key and opened the door, leading her inside.

"There's already a suitcase in here," she said as she wobbled across the room. She kicked off her heels mid-stride.

"It's mine," he said, watching her. "They brought it up here when they asked me to show you to your room." It was utter nonsense, but she was drunk enough to buy it. If he let on that the room had originally been his, there was no way she would stay in it, drunk or not.

"Oh." She sat down on the edge of the bed. "I'm still not sleeping with you." She waved her left hand, the diamonds in her ring catching the light. "I'm not a cheater."

He leaned his ass against the dresser. "I never cheated on you, Blair."

She tilted her head to look at him. "No, I'll give you that. I guess you'd left me before you slept with her." He knew who she was talking about, of course. He *hadn't* slept with her, but this wasn't the time for an explanation. Blair glanced at his suitcase, then back at him. "You don't live in Phoenix?"

"Nope. Looks like we both got stranded here."

"So where are you going to sleep?"

He shrugged. He hadn't gotten that far in this crazy scheme. "After I know you're settled, I can go back to the airport."

She fumbled with the buttons on her blouse, leaving it

gaping open, so that he could see the swell of her breasts in her black bra and the creamy flesh of her abdomen.

God help him, but he was getting turned on by a drunk woman.

But this wasn't just *any* drunk woman. This was Blair. *Blair.* How many nights had he thought of her naked body, the feel of her beneath him as he filled her . . . But it didn't matter what his body—or his mind—remembered. He wasn't about to try anything with her. He respected her more than that.

She settled back onto the bed, her legs curled to the side, and stared up at the ceiling. "You can't go to the airport." She licked her bottom lip and then sighed. "You can stay here."

"It's your room, Blazer. Besides, you already said you weren't going to have sex with me."

She awkwardly reached over and patted the other side of the mattress. "It's a big bed, and I'm a used pasture. You can sleep over there."

He wanted to stay with her, but based on the way he couldn't take his eyes off the curve of her hips in her skirt or her exposed cleavage, he wasn't sure it was a good idea. "That is a very generous offer, but maybe I should head out now that you're settled." He could always grab some food at the airport. God knew, she could probably use both burgers after all the whiskey she'd downed.

She sat up and tears filled her eyes. "You're leaving me again."

Something in her voice ripped his heart to shreds. He'd sooner set himself on fire than make her feel that way again.

"No, Blair," he said softly. "I'm not leaving you." He moved to the bed and sat down next to her, wrapping his arm around her back and pulling her close. "Are you hungry?"

"Yeah." But her eyes sunk closed.

They sat there for five minutes, Blair dozing against him as he cradled her to his chest. He closed his eyes and drank her in —the sight of her, the smell of her, the familiarity of her. The scab on his heart ripped open, leaving him bruised and raw. She only wore an engagement ring. That meant she probably wasn't married yet. Maybe in the morning when she was sober, they could talk, and he could tell her everything—that he was an utter idiot, but he was miserable without her, and he'd do anything to win her back. Literally anything.

Maybe there was hope for them.

Room service knocked on the door, and he gently settled her back onto the bed before he signed for the food. He considered waking her to eat, but she looked so peaceful he couldn't disturb her. He ate his burger while he checked his email and studied for his deposition in the morning, all the while sneaking glances at her. Watching her was surreal. He'd never expected to see her again, let alone have her on his bed. Of course, he'd prefer to have her doing other things in his bed, but the peace and happiness he felt in her mere presence was a telling sign of how he felt.

Soon her draw was too strong. He changed into a T-shirt and a pair of athletic shorts and carefully lay down on the bed next to her, both of them on top of the comforter. She stirred, and he studied her face, taking in every detail and committing it to memory in case she refused to listen to him, which, he realized, was the most likely scenario. Blair was firmly against second chances. The way she'd turned her back on her father was proof enough of that.

She sighed and rolled over again, pressing her back to his stomach. He held his breath, waiting for her to wake up and accuse him of trying to take advantage of her. But she soon stilled, pulling his arm tighter against her stomach. He breathed in her scent, drowning in memories. She still used the same vanilla-scented shampoo.

"I miss you, Garrett," she mumbled, and he froze. If she hadn't said his name, he would have thought she was talking about her fiancé/husband. But she had said *his* name. So he wasn't the only one who still had feelings.

He could make this work. He'd figure out a way. Screw Neil's damn wedding. Screw the Norfolk depositions. He'd stay here with her as long as it took to convince her to give him a second chance.

But when he woke the next morning, the room still dark, he was devastated to find her side of the bed empty.

Blair was gone.

Chapter Three

BLAIR LEANED her head back against the seat on her flight to Kansas City. Tears stung her eyes, making her angry.

What the hell had happened?

She would have chalked it up to an alcohol-induced hallucination, but she was sober when the airline had texted at four-thirty—hung over, yes, but very sober. And there was no denying Garrett Lowry had been in her bed.

She'd panicked, bolting off the mattress and taking stock of her clothing. Skirt and blouse had both been on, if more than a little wrinkled, although the latter had been completely unbuttoned. All her undergarments had still been intact. The only things missing had been her shoes, which had been strewn on the floor. Even Garrett had been dressed in shorts and a T-shirt. She couldn't remember much after seeing him at the bar, just bits and pieces. Something about horses and lawsuits, which made no sense. She vaguely remembered a woman telling her there wasn't a room for her after all. So how had she ended up in a room with Garrett? Oh, God. Had she gotten all nostalgic and begged him to sleep with her?

She was going to die of embarrassment.

Her first mistake had been asking for a second drink. Then a third. And so on. She couldn't hold her liquor, as evidenced by her behavior the night before. Or by how little of it she remembered. She groaned and squeezed her eyes tight. No matter what she'd done—or hadn't done—it chafed her that she'd lost control. Blair did *not* lose control. Ever.

But there was still the question of why he'd spent the night with her. She couldn't help wondering if they'd had sex and then redressed. She couldn't imagine Garrett staying with her otherwise. But if that was the case, she'd cheated on Neil. Regardless of whether anything had actually happened, she couldn't ignore the fact that she still wanted him. Even after all these years and what he'd done to her. She wanted him, and that in and of itself was the same as cheating.

The thought made her want to throw up.

She was just like her father.

She shuddered, and the flight attendant was at her side in moments. One of the perks of business class. "Do you need a blanket, Ms. Hansen?"

Blair smiled up at her. "No. I'm fine. Thanks." Of course, she was anything *but* fine. She prided herself on never falling to pieces, no matter what the situation, but now she felt like a shattered sheet of glass. And she had no idea what to do about that.

Her plane landed after nine, and she checked her phone to see multiple missed calls during the flight from the office and one from Neil. She groaned as she pulled her carry-on bag from the overhead bin. She hadn't called anyone the night before to tell them about being grounded in Phoenix.

She called her assistant as she walked to the terminal.

"Oh, my God, Blair!" Melissa gushed as soon as she answered. "I've been worried sick. I tried to call you last night, and you never answered."

"I'm sorry. I got stuck in Phoenix overnight—gusting winds or some such shit. I just landed, but I'm going to be late. Stall Lopez for the deposition." She chuckled. "That shouldn't be too hard. I doubt he's eager to see me after our last encounter."

"Um . . . Lopez couldn't make it. They've sent someone else from his firm, but he's going to be late too. He says he should be here around eleven."

"They change attorneys last minute, and the new guy can't even bother to show up on time? Never mind." Blair shook her head, getting angry as she maneuvered her rolling bag through the mass of people standing at the gate. She wasn't going to be on time either, but it was the principle of the matter. "Then I'm going home to shower. I slept in my clothes last night, and I don't have a clean change of clothes in my bag."

"But you have an appointment at ten forty-five with Ben Stuart. In his office."

Her heart skipped a beat, and she stopped moving, causing a man to slam into her back. He broke out into a string of curses as she moved to the side. "Wait. Ben? Why?"

"He didn't say, but he told me to keep it secret. Off the books, even."

She sucked in a breath. Ben was a junior partner, and although he'd introduced Blair to Neil two years ago, they rarely spoke, and they *never* had meetings.

She started walking again. If she was meeting with Ben, then she definitely needed a shower and a change of clothes. Something was amiss. "But I was supposed to be in the deposition at ten. When did he request the meeting?"

"He came down here looking for you this morning. He found out about the deposition delay and told me to have you swing by his office at ten forty-five."

"You didn't tell him you didn't know where I was, did you?" she asked in a panic.

"Do you take me for an amateur? No, I covered for you."

True, she'd been in L.A. for a work matter, and she couldn't help the plane delays, but no one at Sisco, Sisco, and Reece liked to hear excuses. And Blair did her damnedest to make sure she never needed one. While Ben was only a junior partner, he still had voting power, and it was rumored he had influence with the senior partner Robert Sisco Sr. himself. "Thanks, Melissa. I owe you," she said as she hurried through the sliding glass doors and out into the August heat.

August was miserable in Kansas City. It was hot *and* humid, and it was landlocked besides, so there was no escaping to the beach. Why Neil's parents had insisted on an August wedding was beyond her, but it wasn't worth fighting over. She wasn't one of those girls who made a huge fuss over wedding frills, although that wasn't to say she wasn't obsessed over the details. The senior and junior partners at the firm were invited to the wedding, and they and their wives would critique every detail, down to the distance between the tines on the salad forks. Blair wasn't about to give them a single reason to deny her partnership.

Melissa lowered her voice. "There are rumors going around that they're about to offer someone a partnership. Maybe the meeting is about that. Just take me with you when you get Rolland's corner office, and we'll call it good."

While Blair hoped it was true, she couldn't see how. A senior partner would be offering her the position, not a junior partner. "You know I wouldn't dream of leaving you behind. I can't function without you. Speaking of the corner office, have you checked with the caterer?"

"Yes, he left a message that they're substituting shrimp for the crab. I plan to call him and let him know there will be absolutely *no* substitutions. His contract says they are part of the menu, and the fact that they've gone up in price isn't our concern."

Blair felt a stab of guilt. Ordinarily, she would have let the crab legs go, but Robert Sr. loved crab legs. She'd heard stories of Robert Sr. walking out of dinners that didn't provide them, and she needed him to stay for at least half the reception. Rumor had it that he was happy if he stayed until the dancing started. She wasn't about to push her luck. "Good. Anything else I should be aware of?"

"Um. . ." She hesitated. "I'll tell you when you get in."

Blair stopped next to her car and dug her keys out of her purse. "No, tell me now. I can't take any more surprises." She liked to be prepared for any outcome, and surprises left her scrambling.

"Dr. Fredrick's mother called. She has another change."

"What? What is it this time?" Blair stopped, her car door half-open. His mother had been nothing short of a nightmare with all her changes and substitutions. Debra Fredrick was a tacky, judgmental, small-town, small-minded woman who had already involved herself in every minute decision involving the wedding. Blair had agreed to some of her suggested changes to keep peace, like putting Neil's brother's fiancée in charge of the guest book to give her a role in the wedding. Or like agreeing to her tacky rehearsal dinner plans. After all, any negotiation was about picking your battles, and it had been much more important to refuse Debra's suggestion that the groom's cake be changed to a clown. Apparently Neil had been one of the only children in the world to love clowns rather than finding them terrifying. Blair shuddered to imagine what the woman wanted, especially since her demands had gotten more and more outrageous the closer they got to the wedding. Just last week she'd nixed Debra's plan of releasing doves with helium balloons tied to the birds' feet. Blair had tried to convince her it was unnecessary since the birds were capable of flight. Nothing had swayed her, so Melissa had made an anonymous call, and Debra had found herself facing the very real threat of PETA picketing outside the church and ruining the wedding.

"She says her mother is switching out Neil's friend Sean for Neil's cousin from San Diego as one of his groomsmen."

Blair threw her purse across the driver's seat. "You have *got* to be kidding me."

"I wish I was." She could practically hear Melissa's cringe.

Blair groaned as she wrestled her suitcase into the backseat. "Unless he's five foot two, he'll never fit in Sean's tux. They'll need his measurements, and he probably won't be here until Friday, and God only knows if they'll even have a tux in his size—"

"I'm on it, Blair. I'll take care of it."

"Thank you." Her voice broke, and embarrassment washed through her. Her encounter with Garrett had affected her more than she liked. She needed to get her shit together. She couldn't afford to look like one of those emotional brides. Even with Melissa. One of the things the partners at her firm liked most about her was that she rarely showed emotion. She wasn't about to start now. "I'll be there by ten forty-five. Make sure Mrs. Norfolk knows the deposition has been postponed, and make sure she has her—"

"Half-caf, soy-milk latte. I know, Blair. Go shower. I'll have everything ready for you when you get here."

"Thanks." She hung up and headed out of the parking lot. As soon as she paid her parking fee, she called Neil, guilt washing through her. Should she confess about her encounter with Garrett? But she had no idea what had even happened. Maybe she should wait and see if she remembered more details as the day went on. Lost in her turmoil, she was surprised when he answered. He was usually tied up with rounds in the morning. She'd expected to leave a message.

"Hey . . . Blair . . ." He sounded distracted. And out of

breath. "How was your trip? What time did you get in last night?"

"You weren't at my condo?" she asked in surprise, scrambling with what to say. "I got stuck in Phoenix. Weather. Sorry I didn't call. Why aren't you at work?"

"I figured you got hung up. It was late when I got off, so I just stayed at my place. I don't have to be at the hospital for another hour. But hey, while I have you, I wanted to make sure you didn't forget about the family dinner tonight."

She shook her head in confusion, even if he couldn't see it. "What family dinner? We're all going to Boulevard Brewery for the tasting and dinner Thursday night."

"Sorry, Blair. Mom's decided to have a pre-wedding festivity dinner tonight at a barbeque restaurant. Just you, me, Mom, and Dad."

"You did *not* tell me that." If he had, she would have nixed it right away. Which was probably why she was only hearing about it now. Blair had no delusions about the real reason Debra Fredrick was in town four days early. This was her pathetic attempt at a power grab over the remaining details of the wedding. She was hoping Blair would be too busy with her job to notice—a job Debra Fredrick hated, but would use to her advantage, nonetheless.

"Well, now you know. And you *have* to go. Mom said she left a message with Melissa, so I'm sure you already heard the news, but my asshole cousin is going to be in the wedding. Mom's about ready to have a seizure."

"If you think he's an asshole, then why the hell are you having him in the wedding?" And why hadn't he told her himself?

"I'm not. And neither is Mom, so don't take it out on her. This change has been decreed by Nana Ruby."

"Well, just tell her no. Your mom needs to get her under

control, Neil." She sounded dismissive and mean, but she was already on edge. She wasn't sure how much more she could take.

"Tell you what. *You* tell Nana Ruby no. You'll get your chance tomorrow night. She's coming early and has declared Thursday to be Family Fun Day."

There was the sound of running water in the background, and she was almost certain she heard a woman's voice. "Is someone with you?" Suspicion had crept into her voice, catching her by surprise. She was obviously deflecting her own guilt.

He paused. "It's the television, Blair. One of those morning talk shows with women hosts. What are you accusing me of?" His voice was tight with anger.

"Nothing. Sorry." She was really losing it. Neil had the libido of a sloth. He was the last person she'd suspect of cheating. It was one of his most appealing traits.

"Mom's going to text you the address of the restaurant. She says to be there by six."

She stifled a groan. The last thing she needed was a night of *fun* with his mother. "I'll try my best."

"There is no try. Only do." His tone was stern, but she heard the hint of teasing.

Blair rolled her eyes, but she felt a stab of nostalgia. He'd been so horrified to learn she'd never seen *Star Wars* that he'd insisted on a six-movie marathon to make up for lost time. That was back at the beginning of their relationship, when they used to have fun. She couldn't remember when that had changed. "Whatever, Yoda. See you later."

As she hung up, she mulled over the fact that they hardly ever said I love you. Megan and her husband said it to each other often enough to make everyone sick . . . but still sort of happy for them. And then there was that other issue. She and

Neil had sex once a week, which was more often than they professed their love. But it had been that way for a while, and she hadn't had a problem with it yesterday morning. Why did it suddenly bother her today? That damn Garrett. He was ruining everything all over again.

Her chest felt tight, and she sucked in several deep breaths. Cold feet. That's all this was. It was normal to feel nervous right before such a life-changing experience. She would have called Megan to talk about it, but the last thing she wanted to hear about right now was Megan's super-happy, crazy-in-love domestic life. It would only make things worse.

Libby. Blair could call her other best friend, Libby.

She pressed the speed dial number and instantly had second thoughts. Megan, Libby, and Blair had been best friends since kindergarten. Even back in grade school Libby was notorious for sleeping late, so there was a chance she would wake her up, but her friend answered after the second ring.

"Hey, Blair!"

"Why do you sound so awake? And chipper?"

"I just dropped Noah off at Megan's dad's office . . . well I guess it's his office now too."

Blair blinked. "Why were *you* taking him to the office?"

"He and Josh are only in town from Seattle for a couple of meetings and the wedding, so they're sharing a rental car to save expenses. Noah and I went out to breakfast this morning, so I dropped him off."

Megan's father's engineering firm had recently merged with Josh and Noah's firm in Seattle. Somewhere in the middle of Josh and Megan's whirlwind courtship, Noah and Libby had become friends. *Close* friends from the sound of things, which wouldn't have been so strange if Noah weren't a serial womanizer and Libby didn't hop from man to man. "Did you finally break up with Mitch?"

Libby was quiet for a moment, but she definitely sounded less happy when she asked, "Why would you think I broke up with Mitch?"

"Libs, you know this is like a record for you, right? How long have you been together? Six months?"

"I'm not getting any younger, Blair. I turn thirty in a few months."

If it had been anyone else, Blair would have figured she was bemoaning her biological clock. But she knew her friend too well for that. "Libby, tell me you're not talking about that damned wedding pact slash curse again."

Libby let out a groan. "You think whatever you like, Blair Hansen, but there's no denying that you're turning thirty in a few months too, and you're getting married in five days."

Blair released a loud sigh. "Libby, please don't tell me that you plan on marrying Mitch because of the pact. We made that pact when we were nine. Hell, you're the only one who still takes it seriously. Megan and I forgot all about it. And I don't want to hear another word about the nonsense that fortune teller told us twenty years ago. Yes, she was right about Megan, but any idiot can win the lottery once. Seriously, not another word."

"And yet you will both be married by your birthdays." She sounded shorter than usual.

"That's purely coincidence, Libs." She softened her tone. "Look, I love you, and I know a lot of the time we don't see eye-to-eye, but I would really hate for you to get married for the wrong reason."

"Because you're getting married for the right reason."

It wasn't a question, nor was there any malice in her tone. So why did it hurt so much? Maybe because she had called to get reassurance from her friend and there was no way she'd confess her concerns now. "I don't want to fight with you, Libby. Especially not this week. I need you."

"I'm sorry," Libby said, her voice softening as well. "I'm here for you. Whatever you need."

"Your friend is all set to photograph the wedding?"

Libby laughed. "Yes, and I've already talked to your assistant about it this morning. Barry's going to do a great job, Blair. He was my intern, and he's fantastic. In fact, I won't trust anyone else to photograph my own wedding when the time comes. Plus I'll take photos of my own at the reception. Relax. I'm going to be personally taking care of this for you."

Out of the three of them, Libby tended to be the most irresponsible, but she took her career very seriously. There was no way she would let Blair's wedding photos turn into a disaster. "Thank God. With all the other issues—"

"What other issues?" Libby asked a little too eagerly.

Why had she said that? She was only feeding Libby's odd obsession with their weddings. "My wedding isn't cursed."

"Of course it's not." She paused. "*You're* cursed."

"Libby! What did I tell you?"

"I have to go, Blair," Libby said, sounding distracted. "Noah's calling me. I'll talk to you later."

Before Blair could ask her anything about her odd friendship with Noah, she hung up.

A little over an hour later, Blair walked into the office wearing a black long-sleeve, scooped-neck blouse, white pencil skirt, and nude pumps, her damp hair pulled up in a neat French roll. She stopped to check in with Melissa, who assured her that Mrs. Norfolk was already in the conference room and drinking her latte.

"Has Mr. Norfolk's attorney shown up yet?" When Melissa shook her head, Blair asked, "And we're sure someone's coming?"

"Yes, he called about ten minutes ago, saying he was almost here. His plane got delayed by the weather too."

Blair sucked in a deep breath at the reminder of Phoenix. More and more pieces of last night had come into memory, and while she was thankful that nothing had happened between her and Garrett, she couldn't ignore the part of her that was disappointed over it. But right now she needed to deal with her meeting and deposition. Her guilt could rear its head later. "Great. Well, I'm off to see Ben."

"Good luck! Maybe I should order out for a celebratory lunch."

Blair put a hand on her stomach to soothe her nerves. "Let's not get ahead of ourselves just yet. This could be about anything."

Melissa flashed her a grin as Blair headed for the staircase that joined the two floors.

When she stopped next to Ben Stuart's assistant's desk promptly at 10:44, she glanced up at her with a questioning glance. "Can I help you?"

Ben appeared in his office doorway and motioned toward her. "Hey, Blair. Why don't you come in and tell me all about the wedding? I haven't talked to Neil in ages."

She tried to hide her confusion. Had he set up this meeting to chat about her wedding? She'd rather be downstairs preparing for her deposition. Hiding her irritation, she followed him into his plush office. He shut the door behind her, and she walked toward his desk, taking in his gorgeous view of the Country Club Plaza.

"Thanks for fitting me in," he said as he gestured for her to sit in one of two leather chairs in front of his desk. "I thought you'd want to hear this."

Now she was curious. She'd rather stand, but she was on Ben's turf, and she suspected he was right; she wanted to hear whatever he had to tell her. She settled into a leather wingback chair while he perched on the edge of his desk.

"We're voting on a new partner next week."

She should have been happy to hear this, but something in his voice was off. "Why am I worried this is bad news?"

He grimaced and leaned forward, lowering his voice. "Listen, you have to swear to me that you'll never say you heard this from me."

She nodded. "Of course."

"It's between you and York."

"George York?" He'd been at the firm longer than she had, but he brought in fewer billable hours. "Why would they choose him over me?"

"Look," he stalled. "This is the sticky part that you can't let on that you know. I'm only warning you because this affects Neil too, but I'll get canned if they find out I said anything."

"I won't tell. I swear. What is it?" How bad could this be?

"Some of the partners are concerned that you're too blunt and direct."

She shook her head in confusion. "How is that possible? Why wouldn't they want me to be blunt and direct?"

He shifted on the desk, looking uncomfortable. "Some of them were born before dinosaurs roamed the earth. Given the choice between a confrontational woman and a mediocre guy, they'll pick the guy." He shrugged. "You know how it is."

She stood, her anger rising. "No. I *don't* know how it is."

He held up his hands in defense. "Hey, don't shoot the messenger."

He was right, but it didn't ease her anger. "What the hell am I supposed to do? Would they rather I play nice and lose cases?"

"No, I think they just want to see you're capable of having a softer side."

"So they want me to bake some cookies and bring them in?" she asked, her voice rising.

"No. I've convinced them to hold off the vote until next week." He paused for a moment. "Until after your wedding."

She looked at him like he'd lost his mind.

"The fact you're getting married is in your favor. They want a married partner, and it's seen as a plus that Neil's a doctor." He cringed. "I shouldn't be telling you any of this."

She waved her hand in dismissal. "You already said that, and I won't tell anyone, I swear. But if they want a married partner, why not go with me? George York isn't married, and if the office rumor mill is to be believed, he isn't even dating anyone."

"Like I said, a few old—but influential—coots are worried you're not feminine enough."

"You've got to be shitting me. That's sexist, not to mention illegal."

His eyes hardened. "I swear to God, Blair, if you file a suit, I'll lie through my teeth and deny it all. You'll lose the case *and* your career."

She put her hands on her hips. "Stop being such a drama king. I wouldn't do that." She knew it would be career suicide, but it didn't mean she didn't wish she could make them pay.

"Listen, it's not all of them, and they *can* be swayed. All you have to do is show up at your wedding in a pretty dress and smile like a demure blushing bride. Then you'll check the marriage box while being sweet and covered in white lace or taffeta or whatever the hell your dress is made from. You'll be a shoo-in. I'll make sure of it."

She had to wonder if she wanted to be a partner. She already knew from personal past experience that some of the partners were sexist, so if the others were really that sexist . . . But she reminded herself that Ben was right—the older partners were in their sixties and seventies. They'd be out soon, one way or the other. She also reminded herself that she and Ben weren't friends, despite his role in introducing her to Neil. He had no obligation to tell her anything. In fact, he was going out on a limb.

"Well, thank you for the heads-up." She glanced at the clock and took several steps toward the door.

"A couple of other things, Blair."

She paused with her hand on the doorknob.

"I think Rob Sisco Jr. might be watching your performance for the rest of the week. And he's looking for reasons to vote against you."

Her mouth dropped, but she quickly recovered. "Thanks. What's the other?"

He grimaced. "If they don't make you partner, they're letting you go."

"*What?*"

His jaw tensed. "You didn't hear it from me."

She nodded as she walked out of his office, shell-shocked.

"Tell Neil I'll see him at the reception," he called after her.

She was momentarily confused before she quickly recovered. "Yeah. He's excited to see you."

She tried to act normal as she made her way back to Melissa's desk, sorting through Ben's bombshell announcement. She should be pissed. She should be ready to fight, but she was too numb to feel anything.

Melissa looked up at her, smiling with excitement. "Well?"

It was nearly eleven, and even if Blair *could* share her conversation with Ben, she needed to process everything first. "Has Lopez's replacement arrived yet?"

"Yes, he's in the conference room with the younger Mr. Sisco." Worry filled Melissa's eyes.

"*Shit.*" So Ben's information had been spot on.

Melissa leaned forward, her face pale. "What's going on, Blair? I take it you weren't offered a partnership."

"I can't get into it right now." She started to feel light-headed, but she couldn't let her job performance suffer now. Now, more than ever, she had to prove she was worth keeping on staff. "I'll tell you about it later. In the meantime, I need you to discreetly find out if any firms are looking for an associate attorney. You can *not* mention my name."

"What?" Melissa's eyes flew open, and Blair instantly regretted mentioning it without more explanation. Not that it would help. The outlook was bad any way she presented it.

Instead, she left the poor woman behind as she hurried down the hall and stopped outside the conference room. She took a moment to put her game face on, feeling more unprepared to deal with this deposition than any she'd had since graduating from law school. Knocking on the door, she walked into the conference room, then nearly passed out when she saw the opposing counsel.

Garrett Lowry.

Chapter Four

GARRETT WAS in a foul mood as he walked into the law offices of Sisco, Sisco, and Reece. He'd been uncharacteristically distraught and surly most of the morning, but he'd assured himself that he might still have a shot with Blair. Perhaps the fact that she'd left like that—without saying anything—meant that she felt something for him. Hell, he'd just use his staff to track her down. Then he'd go to her and present his case. While the first part of his plan would be relatively easy since she was a practicing attorney, the plan for the latter part was sketchy at best. But at least he had a vague hint of a plan. It was enough to put his mind at ease so he could concentrate on the deposition.

He stopped at the front desk, and the receptionist gave him an appreciative stare. "I'm Garrett Lowry here for the Norfolk deposition. Can you let B.A. Hansen know I'm here?"

She made a call to the back, then gave him a friendly smile. "Ms. Hansen's assistant will be with you in a moment to show you to the conference room."

A pretty blonde opened one of the glass doors that cordoned off the back offices. "Mr. Lowry, if you'll follow me." As she started down the hall, he pushed all thoughts of Blair out of his head. If he screwed up this case, then he'd be the laughingstock of the office.

A middle-aged man greeted him outside the conference room. "Good morning, Mr. Lowry. I'm Rob Sisco Jr., one of the partners here, and I'm going to sit in on the deposition."

Ms. Hansen's assistant seemed taken aback by the news, and Garrett was surprised himself. Philip Lopez was no bumbling fool, which meant Ms. Hansen had to be on top of her game. Garrett had to wonder what could have precipitated this supervision.

Rob Sisco pushed the door open and allowed Garrett to enter.

There were two people already seated at the conference table—one was obviously the court reporter, and the other was a woman who looked to be in her mid-fifties. Her blonde hair hung to her shoulders, and while she had a few extra pounds around her middle, she was an attractive woman. She looked up at them, then glanced back at the door. "Where's Blair?"

Good God. Was he so thoroughly haunted by his ex-girlfriend that the opposing counsel had her name? He suddenly felt like Ebenezer Scrooge—forced by the ghosts of his past to face all his wrongs and inadequacies.

Rob Sisco offered her a smile, but it came across as patronizing. "She'll be here in a moment." Then he looked at his watch and stifled a yawn.

Garrett swallowed the urge to ask the guy if he was bored. Instead he sat on the other side of the table, across from Ms. Hansen's client, and pulled out his laptop so he could open the document of questions he'd prepared.

Sisco took a seat several chairs down and started drumming his fingers on the table, not stopping when Mrs. Norfolk shot him an irritated glance.

Garrett glanced up at the clock on the wall. 10:59. Jesus, this was going to be a long week.

He glanced toward the glass door, and his heart skipped a

beat when he saw Blair—*his* Blair—standing in the hall, wearing a long-sleeve black blouse and a white skirt, her hair up in a twist. How could she be *here* of all places? But the dozens of questions running through his head gave way to concern as he studied her. She looked off, like something had upset her. But even as he watched, she steeled herself and shook off whatever was going on. He could tell by the way she straightened her shoulders and turned toward the door with confidence and authority. It burst open, and Garrett stood as she entered, still in shock. Why was she going by B.A. Hansen when she was Blair Myers? A moment of panic washed through him—*could Hansen be her married name?*—but then it hit him. Hansen was her mother's maiden name, and the A was from her middle name—Anne.

He'd found her and he hadn't even tried. They hadn't seen each other since law school, and now they'd been thrown together twice in two days. This had to be the universe telling him to pursue her. He felt more hopeful than he had in years.

She stopped behind one of the empty chairs, her face turning several shades lighter as her eyes searched his face, probably trying to verify that it was indeed him.

"Blair?" Sisco asked. "Is there a problem?"

She gave an involuntary shudder, then forced a smile as she moved to the table. "No. Of course not." She extended her hand to him over the table. "Blair Hansen. I hear you're taking Philip Lopez's place."

He leaned over and shook her hand. So she wanted to play it like they were strangers. He understood the reasoning—he'd probably do the same thing in her situation—but it felt odd to pretend he didn't know her when he'd held her in his arms the night before. "Garrett Lowry."

"Have a seat, Mr. Lowry." She waved toward his chair and waited until he took a seat before she did the same. As soon as she was settled, she placed a legal pad with neatly written notes on the table in front of her. He wasn't surprised. She'd always preferred to handwrite her notes in law school versus using a laptop.

She studied her pad for several seconds, then reached for the water pitcher in the middle of the table and poured a glass. He saw a tremor in her hand as she lifted the glass to her lips. She was obviously shocked to see him, but she'd looked shaken up before she even stepped into the room. Something else had happened, something unrelated to the realization that they'd be sparring partners this week. She needed time to recover, and he was going to give it to her. He turned to the reporter.

"Do you have the physical address and email address of my office in San Diego?"

She looked up in surprise. "Of course."

"Could you read it off to me so I can make sure it's correct? We've recently moved offices."

She rattled off both, then looked up at him with raised eyebrows.

"Thank you." He smiled and caught a glimpse of Blair out of the corner of his eye. Most of her color had returned, and she looked more prepared.

She took a deep breath. "Let's begin."

In many ways, it was a routine deposition. Rowena Norfolk was accusing her husband of philandering with multiple twenty-something-year-old women. Garrett had read Lopez's notes. She was right. Now Mr. Norfolk wanted to divorce the current Mrs. Norfolk and marry version 2.0. The current Mrs. Norfolk wanted to make him pay for his indiscretions, and Blair Hansen was pushing hard to make that happen.

There wasn't much Garrett could do to discredit her story. Hers was the vanilla side of their divorce, and both attorneys knew it. For all intents and purposes, Mrs. Norfolk was the victim. The juicy details would come out when Blair deposed Lopez's client and his girlfriends.

While Rowena Norfolk came across as the victim, it was Garrett's job to find any discrepancies that might discredit her innocence, which meant he had to act like an ass. Fortunately for him, he was fairly good at it. He had a few nuggets to dig into from her answers in discovery. Rowena's husband had suggested his soon-to-be ex-wife had hidden money before the separation, and what was more, had committed an indiscretion of her own. Garrett was fully prepared to weasel the information out of her—if there was any grain of truth to it—but try as he might, his usual tactics didn't work. Blair and Rowena stonewalled him at nearly every opportunity. Blair was protective of the woman, stopping him multiple times when she thought his questions went too far.

Sisco left halfway through the deposition, and Garrett could see some of the tension leave Blair's shoulders. Was this why she'd seemed so upset last night? Was she in trouble at work? He couldn't imagine why. She'd sure as hell convinced Lopez she was a hard ass—the most coveted reputation an attorney could earn. He also knew Blair enough to know she was not the type to break rules or skirt the edges of morality. What could she be in trouble for?

When he finished his questions, he thanked Blair's client and stood to leave. He wanted to talk to Blair, but he couldn't do that in front of Mrs. Norfolk. He walked out of the conference room, taking satisfaction in the way Blair's gaze followed him.

It was a little after noon now, and their next deposition was at three. Maybe he could convince Blair to join him for lunch. The Country Club Plaza was only a couple of blocks away, and they'd have time to talk and get back for the meeting. If Blair was like any other professional, the best way to get in the figurative and literal door was through her assistant. Good thing he knew who her assistant was, even if he didn't know her name.

The short hallway he'd come down had been lined by conference rooms, so he headed down the perpendicular hallway, looking for the woman who'd led him to the conference room. He found an open area with several desks outside a bank of offices and saw her sitting at one of the desks. She had a phone to her ear and was arguing.

"I don't care if you have to fly that crab from Timbuktu— you will have it here for the reception, or we will sue you for breach of contract. Got it?"

He grinned as he listened to her end of the conversation. He could tell Blair had rubbed off on her.

She glanced up at him and her eyes widened. "If there are any more issues, I'll expect you to call me immediately." She hung up and grimaced. "Can I help you, Mr. Lowry?"

"You're Blair's assistant, correct?"

Her guard went up. "Yes, I'm *Ms. Hansen's* assistant."

"Does Ms. Hansen have lunch plans?"

The woman couldn't have looked more surprised. "Uh . . ."

He sat on the edge of her desk and leaned closer, waggling his finger at her computer. "Come on," he teased, knowing he was pouring on the Garrett Lowry charm a little too heavy. "Just squeeze me in there. A quiet little lunch for two."

"That sounds cozy," Blair said, her tone short.

Garrett jerked upright, cursing under his breath. "Blair."

Her eyes narrowed with disgust. She skirted around him and walked into her office. "Well, don't let me stop you. You two have a great time." She slammed the door behind her, and her assistant shot him a death glare.

"I think that's your answer, Mr. Lowry."

Ouch. Garrett stood. "Maybe I should go talk to her."

She reached under her desk and pulled up her three-inch

pump. "You go near the door, and I'll gouge your eye out with my heel." Her jaw clenched with anger.

Her reaction caught him by surprise. While she was admittedly very loyal to her boss, her statement seemed a little strong given the situation, if not unprofessional. Frustrated, he considered threatening to report her, but that would only piss off Blair even more. He needed to regroup and come up with a new way to convince Blair to talk to him. Garrett held his hands up in surrender. "I'm rather fond of my eyes, so I guess I'll go to lunch on my own."

"Good idea."

"I'll go to lunch with you!" a brunette called out from a nearby desk, her voice all sultry promise.

He grinned and pointed his finger at her. "I'm gonna take a rain check, sweetheart."

He walked out angry, but he only had himself to blame. He'd laid the foundation for Blair to believe he was hitting on her assistant, which meant he was back to square one, not that he'd even gotten very far. Blair was a proud woman, and he'd broken her heart five years ago—just as he'd broken his own.

Well, he couldn't change the past. He could only move forward, and if nothing else, Garrett Lowry was a stubborn man. He wasn't giving up that easy. Not this time. Now that she was back in his life—and it was truly starting to seem like this was kismet, even though he and Blair had always laughed at such romantic notions—he was going to try his best to earn another chance.

He went to his hotel and wheedled his way into an early check-in, then grabbed a sandwich before heading back to Blair's office. His phone rang when he was almost there, and he groaned when he saw it was Nana Ruby.

"Hey, Nana. I'm here in Kansas City. Happy?"

"Hell no, I'm not happy. Your mom and your aunt are at it worse than ever."

"You seriously thought making me a groomsman would improve the situation?"

"Your aunt and uncle are having dinner with Neil and his fiancée tonight. You're going with them."

"Nana. No. I have something else I need to do." He had hoped to convince Blair to talk after the deposition, maybe even grab coffee.

"The only thing you need to do is help settle this family war. Suck it up, boy. Your aunt's gonna text you the address. Dinner's at six."

Great. Just what he needed. Dinner with his mouthy aunt, his whipped uncle, his dick cousin, and said cousin's fiancée, who was probably as dull as dirt given her choice of mate. Yippee. He couldn't wait.

He arrived at Blair's office forty-five minutes early and asked for early access to a room so he could have somewhere private to prepare. He had no delusions that the next deposition would go so well. Blair was deposing one of Brian Norfolk's *indiscretions*, and he expected her to bring her A-game and then some.

The receptionist must have heard about his disastrous attempt to secure a lunch date with Blair. She batted her eyelashes and told him she was free for dinner.

"Sorry," he said with a grin. "I have plans."

"Maybe tomorrow?" She sounded hopeful.

"What I really need right now is that room . . ." His words trailed off, and she got the hint.

She stood and opened the door to the back with her keycard. "There's a small room where you can work. I'll show you." Then she led him down a hall and pushed open a door, revealing a table surrounded by four chairs. A phone sat on the table next to the wall. "I'll let Melissa know you're here, and someone will come get you when it's time."

"Do you know if Ms. Keating has arrived yet?"

She shook her head. "She hasn't, but I can bring her back here when she arrives if you'd like."

"Thanks."

He went over his notes until Ms. Keating arrived about twenty minutes later. Between her short, tight dress, her exposed cleavage, and her heavy makeup, she looked like a toss-up between a hooker or a stripper, and neither was a good option for them.

"Did Mr. Lopez not discuss the importance of dressing conservatively?"

She looked herself up and down, batting her eyelashes. "This *is* conservative."

Good God. What did her version of seductive look like? He tried prepping her for possible questions Blair might ask, but it soon became apparent that Brian Norfolk's interest had been in her looks and not in her intelligence.

There was a knock on the door, and Melissa poked her head in. "We're ready for you in the conference room."

The bloodbath he watched unfold in front of him for the next two hours didn't come as a surprise, but it didn't exactly help his ego either. Blair was relentless, and though Tiffany Keating tried to evade Blair's questions, the younger woman was soon spilling her guts, despite Garrett's constant counsel to the contrary.

When Blair finally announced she was done, Garrett figured if there was ever a time she might talk to him, it was now, when he was thoroughly beaten. Perhaps she'd take pity. But she got up from the table and left the room. He would have given anything to follow after her, but he had to deal with Tiffany Keating first.

"Did I do good?" she asked, batting her eyes.

"You answered truthfully," he hedged. "That's the important part."

A grin spread across her face. "Say, do you want to get a drink?"

Garrett forced a friendly smile. "Thanks, but I have plans."

She stood and leaned into him. "How long are you in town?"

"I'm really not sure, but I'm going to be busy the entire time I'm here."

"Well, if you change your mind . . ." She lifted her eyebrows, her voice heavy with innuendo.

He escorted her out to the reception area and saw her off, glad to part ways with her, mostly because she reminded him of one of the flakes he'd dated after he threw Blair away. He didn't deserve a second chance with that powerful, beautiful Amazon of a woman he'd seen in action in the conference room just now, but damned if he wasn't going to try anyway. Tomorrow.

He had another battle to prepare for tonight.

Chapter Five

BLAIR SAT IN HER OFFICE, staring at her blank computer screen. How had her life turned so effectively to shit in less than twenty-four hours? What had Sisco thought of her performance during the deposition? She'd been slower to react than usual. Had he noticed? He'd walked out halfway through. Did that mean she'd done well in his eyes, or had he already decided to vote against her?

"Blair?" Melissa stood in the doorway, worry in her eyes. "I've made some calls in regard to your earlier request. Do you have time for a report?"

One of the things Blair loved about Melissa was the way she always knew when to press a matter and when to leave it. Melissa had no doubt been desperate to ask her questions all afternoon, but she'd waited until she had her own information to share. Of course, Blair couldn't tell her the truth without breaking Ben's confidence.

Blair shook her head and forced a smile. "Yeah."

Her assistant shut the door and stood in front of her desk, lowering her voice. "I talked to a few sources at some of the bigger firms, and no one's looking to bring on associate attorneys. In fact, Morrow and Smith is downsizing."

"And the smaller firms?"

Melissa shook her head. "The only firm that's currently looking is Chester, Williams, and Horn."

Blair rolled her eyes. "They're practically ambulance chasers. So there's nothing?"

"No. Now what's going on?"

Blair tried to ignore the tightness in her chest. "I can't tell you."

"Blair."

She shook her head. "I promised not to tell."

"Are you losing your job?"

She took a deep breath, trying to clear her head. "Of course not." She forced a smile. "It doesn't hurt to put out feelers."

"*Blair.*" Melissa paused and moved forward, crossing her arms over her chest. "I need to know if I should start looking for a job."

Oh God. She'd lose her position too. Blair wanted to tell her everything was okay, but she refused to lie to her. "I don't know. But if you do, I'll write you the best damned reference letter ever written." A lump formed in her throat, and her numbness finally dissolved into anger. It was one thing to screw with Blair, but another to screw with someone she cared about. "I promise you I'll make this right." Her voice shook, and she clenched her fists.

"You can tell me what happened. I won't tell anyone. I swear."

Blair looked at her assistant for a long moment, wishing she could bring Melissa into her confidence. While she knew her assistant wouldn't blab, this was too serious to take the risk. "I'll know something next week. I'll tell you then."

"You'll be on your honeymoon next week."

How could she enjoy herself on her honeymoon if her job hung on the balance? The pins holding her control in place had begun to slip loose. She could *not* flip out now. She cleared her throat. "Now tell me what you found out on the status of Brian Norfolk's side bank account."

"Blair." Melissa's voice was softer than usual. "How do you know Garrett Lowry?"

She turned to look at her assistant, her breath catching in her already tight chest. Just hearing his name sent her heart racing, and that was not good.

"I'm not stupid. I can tell you have a history with that guy."

Blair shook her head. "That's water under the bridge in my *ancient* past." She forced her smile even brighter. "I'm over all that now."

The look on Melissa's face said she didn't buy it for a minute. "For what it's worth, he was using his charm to get me to set up a lunch with *you*."

"Why?" Her stomach dropped to her toes. So he hadn't been trying to get a date with her assistant. The relief she felt from the knowledge was disconcerting.

"He didn't say, but he seemed determined."

Blair steeled her back. "That's out of the question."

"I figured." Melissa hesitated. "But he *is* cute."

Her hand tightened around a pen on her desk. "I'm getting married on Saturday." She hadn't seen Garrett in years, yet now she'd seen him twice in a matter of twenty-four hours, and it was making her question everything. She had to focus on what was important. Her job. Melissa's job. Her upcoming nuptials. Marriage with Neil. She was furious with herself for giving Garrett the power to threaten the world she'd built for herself, simply by walking back into her life, even if it was coincidental. "Melissa. This wedding has to be absolutely perfect."

"It will be."

She frowned. "I need to make sure that absolutely *nothing*

goes wrong with this wedding." She paused, then lowered her voice and stared into her assistant's eyes. "*Everything* is riding on this."

Melissa watched her for a moment, obviously confused as to how a matrimonial ceremony could affect everything. But typical Melissa, she accepted Blair at her word. "And nothing will. It will be perfect. I promise."

Blair knew she could count on her assistant, so she had left many of the wedding details in her capable hands, especially since she had so many other issues on her plate.

She offered her a weak smile. "You've helped me so much, and this completely goes above and beyond anything in your job description—especially since my wedding planner skipped town. Now it's more important than ever. I'll make it up to you. I promise."

Melissa held up her hand. "Please stop. You're the best boss I've ever had, and I'd do anything and everything to help you. And right now, I feel obligated to point out that you have a dinner with your future in-laws in less than twenty minutes."

"Oh shit." Blair groaned. "I really can't face them tonight."

"Maybe you can pretend to have a headache so you can leave early."

Blair perked up. "Great idea."

"I know. I'm full of them. See you tomorrow." She walked out of the office and closed the door behind her.

Blair scanned the mass of files piled on her desk, but instead of cases, she saw women who had been cheated, used, and then dumped. Women like her mother, who'd lost everything in the divorce—her house, her identity, and her dignity. Not to mention the fact that she'd been thrown back into the work force without any experience after nearly twenty years, at her ex's insistence. Her attorney hadn't given two shits about her and had done the bare minimum to settle the case. And then Blair's father had gone and died five years later, leaving nothing to either his ex-wife or his daughter. Blair hadn't wanted anything of his, but her mother had deserved more.

But it was partly because of him that she had her career—a career she loved at the end of the day, in spite of the pettiness and sexism of her bosses. If she lost her job, she'd be forced to start from the beginning and probably in some other city. Neil's practice was in Kansas City, and he'd already let her know he loved his position and had no intention of moving if another opportunity ever came her way. She was stuck.

Neil's mother, Debra, had picked a hole-in-the-wall barbeque joint on the Kansas side of the city. Someplace Blair would feel totally out of place in with her business attire. She considered going home to change, but there wasn't time with rush hour traffic, and besides, this was who she was. Take it or leave it. She was already trying to placate her bosses. There was only so much supplication Blair was capable of in a month, let alone a single day. But she was sure to get an earful of disapproval from Neil's mother. For a woman who sold Tupperware and lived in a double-wide trailer, she was one of the most judgmental women Blair had ever known, and she'd made no secret of the fact she didn't approve of Blair's career. Blair would love nothing more than to tell her off, but she didn't want to make things awkward for Neil. He was caught in the middle enough as it was, what with all the back-and-forth about the wedding arrangements. As an afterthought, she pulled the pins out of her hair and let it tumble down her back. It would definitely be hotter, but she could suffer through some discomfort to appease Debra. Besides, she was already plotting when to execute her headache excuse.

Five minutes after six, she pulled into the parking lot of the restaurant and was blasted by a wave of hot, humid air as she opened the car door, adding to her irritation. Neil's parents had insisted the rehearsal dinner on Friday night take place in the outdoor seating area of a local restaurant. She was going to miss her own wedding due to dehydration from profuse sweating.

Neil and his parents were already seated at a rectangular table when she walked into the room. It was hard not to feel annoyed at the irritated glance Neil gave her as she approached the table.

"There you are. I told you six sharp."

He was being shorter with her than usual, which only added to her brewing annoyance, but she knew he must have caught an earful from his mother. "I've had the day from hell. Then I hit rush hour traffic."

Neil's mother pursed her lips in disapproval. "Language." The woman held a small plastic piggy bank shaped like a cat, with the words "Curse Kitty" handwritten on a piece of copy paper and attached with mailing tape. Coins rattled as she shook the container. "That will be one dollar."

Blair put a hand on her hip and cocked her head. "What the hell is *that?*"

Debra's eyes narrowed. "Now it's two."

Now Neil's expression morphed into an apologetic cringe. His eyes pleaded with her to not flip out. "Mom knows your tendency to swear, and she's bound and determined to make the wedding as stress-free as possible, so she's created a swear jar. She plans to carry it around all weekend."

Blair wanted to point out that it was *her* wedding and curse words *relieved* her stress, but she decided to focus instead on the one point she had a chance of winning. "I only cursed once. My first usage of the word hell was in relation to the location."

Debra shook the jar, making the coins clink. "Now it's three."

"You've got to be kidding me. What am I supposed to call the place where Satan and all his minions reside?" Blair turned to Neil's stoically quiet father. He was studying his menu with an intensity that suggested he'd be given a quiz later.

Debra cringed. "I wish you wouldn't use his name, dear."

"Satan?" Blair asked in disbelief. "Is he like Lord Voldemort? Should we only refer to him as 'you know who'?"

Debra pursed her lips, deep in thought. "I don't know who this Lord Voldemort is, but that's a great idea."

Blair started to tell her that she was being ridiculous, but it was a pointless endeavor. Debra Fredrick was too simple-minded and stubborn for a fair argument. "Never mind." She dug out her wallet and pulled out three ones and stuffed them into the jar.

"Is this some new wedding shower game?" a male voice asked from behind her. "Or have you resorted to panhandling, Aunt Debra? I saw a great corner in downtown Kansas City if you're interested. The homeless guy who sleeps there looked like he'd share his spot *and* his bottle of booze."

Neil's mother gasped and clutched her chest again, looking like she was about to have a heart attack, while Neil's father tried to hide his laughter. It was about the liveliest she'd ever seen him, but she couldn't focus on his transformation because she *recognized* that voice.

Blair spun around in horror. No. It couldn't be . . .

But it was. Standing in front of her was Garrett Lowry.

How was the only word that found its way into her brain. Too dumbfounded to say anything, she simply gaped at him.

The only thing that made her feel better was that the look on her ex-boyfriend's face undoubtedly matched her own.

"I'm glad you regret making such a crass joke," Debra finally said, mistaking his dismay.

"So you really showed up." Neil turned in his seat and glared at Garrett. "That took balls."

"Neil!" Debra said. "A dollar!"

Neil shook his head as he dug a bill out of his wallet.

Garrett Lowry was Neil's cousin? How had this never come up? Neil had told her about his nemesis, the cousin who'd made his every summer a living hell, but he'd never once referred to him by name. He was always *asshole* or *Nana's favorite*. It had infuriated Neil when his nana insisted they invite him to the wedding. Admittedly, Blair hadn't looked at Neil's family's guest list. She'd handed it over to her wedding planner, who had addressed all the invitations before running off to South America with one of her client's grooms.

Garrett recovered enough to say, "Great to see you too, Neil. And I'm here on Nana Ruby's orders. We both know that to defy Nana is to skirt one's own death." His gaze turned to Blair, and his eyes softened. "Trust me. This is the last place on earth I want to be right now."

The pain behind his words caught her by surprise.

"Well . . ." Neil muttered.

Garrett tore his gaze away from Blair and turned his focus to Neil. "So you're marrying Blair . . . Hansen."

There was no mistaking the fact that he didn't sound happy about it. She wasn't sure what to make of that, or of her own elation over the possibility that he might still care for her.

She couldn't trust Garrett Lowry, and she could deal with that. What she *couldn't* handle was that she apparently couldn't trust herself around him. Garrett was bad news, and she needed to steer clear of the man, or she was likely to be susceptible to falling for his charms. She'd fallen for him once; she couldn't afford to do it again. She'd never survive it. But as she stared at him now, an undeniable feeling of longing rose up within her, and she wasn't sure she had the strength to stay away from him.

She needed a drink. And quick.

But Neil must have picked up on something too, because

Garrett had Neil's attention now. Neil stood and wrapped an arm possessively around her waist. "You know Blair?"

One of the great things about Neil was that he didn't pry about her past. Early on, they'd agreed never to talk much about exes, and they'd both stuck to that rule, only exchanging basic information. She planned to keep it that way. "*Mr. Lowry* is the opposing counsel on the case I had depositions for today."

"So you're adversaries?" Neil asked, looking down at her for confirmation. Then he placed a quick kiss on her mouth. "That's my girl."

"I wouldn't say adversaries," Garrett said smoothly, his voice oozing with charm. "More like we have opposing views."

"Semantics." Neil waved his hand. "And I thought the only reason you were here was because Nana Ruby forced you to come."

Garrett's back stiffened. "When my firm found out I was going to be in town anyway, they reassigned the case to me." He gave Blair an appreciative smile. "Your fiancée made mince-meat out of my associate during their last encounter. He didn't fight me for it."

Neil didn't look impressed, and Debra released a disapproving moan. "Blair, that's so unladylike."

Debra's eighteenth century attitude was almost enough to make Blair lose it, particularly on top of the rest of the sexist nonsense that had been thrown at her all day. Debra Fredrick's insistence that Blair quit her job and devote herself to being a wife and mother was easier to dismiss when she was three hours south in McDonald County, Missouri. At least Neil firmly supported her career and didn't want her to quit. But Blair swallowed her pride. She couldn't afford any discord at the wedding. She needed to keep everyone happy to impress the partners and their spouses.

Garrett waved toward the table. "Please, sit down. I don't want to keep you from eating."

Neil pulled out a chair for her, surprising her with his uncharacteristic attentiveness . . . until she noticed Garrett watching them from the other side of the table, where he'd taken a seat next to Debra. Huh. There was some kind of competition between the men.

Neil's mother shifted in her seat and picked up the menu. "I think I'm going to order the pulled pork." She looked up at Blair. "What about you, dear?"

"Uh . . ." Blair's gaze was on Garrett, who was watching her just as intently as she was watching him.

"Why do I think there's something else going on here?" Neil asked, glancing back and forth between them.

What sucky timing for Neil to suddenly become observant.

"I think we're just surprised to see each other in a social setting," Garrett said, something shifting in his eyes before he picked up his menu. "Especially after our last deposition."

"No shop talk," Debra muttered dismissively.

Garrett made a mocking face, and Blair had to stifle a laugh. It was no surprise that Garrett didn't like his aunt. What was surprising was that he and Neil were cousins. Now that she'd had some time to absorb the initial shock, it made sense to her that she'd never discovered the connection. While Neil never really mentioned his nemesis cousin by name, Garrett had never mentioned his cousin at all. And she purposefully steered clear of Facebook, having seen more than one attorney ruin themselves with a poorly planned photo op. One of the associates at her firm had been let go after only a few months on the job. The senior partners didn't have a problem with the associate attorneys posting vacation photos on social media, but they weren't so understanding of the pictures of Byron's vacation to Mexico. While his own photos were mundane, run-of-the-mill vacation pics, his *friend* had posted photos of Byron swinging from a rope in a pair of bikini briefs. He had a bottle of tequila raised to his mouth while bikini-clad women—none of whom were his wife—stuffed money into his briefs. The caption read "Byron plays piñata before some banging of his own later." Blair deleted her own account within the hour.

Garrett's gaze shifted to her hand, which was currently clutching the menu. "That's a very pretty ring," he said. "Can I get a closer look?"

His request was odd, but she saw no reason to deny him. What she didn't understand was why everyone else at the table tensed at his words.

She held it out to him, and he curled her fingers over his hand, leaning over for a closer look at the diamonds.

It was hard to ignore the way his touch sent tingles shooting through her body, but she made a valiant effort. "Neil says it's a family piece." She hoped no one else noticed how breathy her voice sounded, but the look of satisfaction in Garrett's eyes and the way his grip tightened told her he hadn't missed it. It only added to her agony.

Garrett turned her hand so that the diamonds sparkled in the light. "Neil is correct. It belonged to our great-grandmother. However, it wasn't his ring to give." His hold on her hand tightened, and something in his eyes flickered before they hardened. He turned to Neil. "It belongs to my mother, which makes it *mine.*"

"*What the hell?*" Blair asked in astonishment.

"You son of a bitch!" Neil shouted.

"I knew it! You bastard." Debra's chair screeched as she pushed back from the table and turned to look at him.

"About damn time." Neil's father's shoulders shook with suppressed laughter as he grabbed a beer bottle from a passing waitress and took a long chug.

The waitress stopped and gave him an exasperated glare. "Sir, that's not yours!"

"It is now." He took another long sip.

Debra looked torn between addressing her wayward husband or her derelict nephew. Her husband won out. "Gene! What the H-E double hockey sticks are you doing?"

He lifted the bottle. "Seems pretty damn obvious to me."

She put her hands on her hips. "That's the devil's brew."

"And the devil's a-brewing, ain't he?" He took another drink.

Neil's mouth hung open, and Blair suspected it was because he hadn't seen his father defy his mother for years, if ever. Garrett started to chuckle. "Uncle Gene, we should hit up a couple of breweries this week before you go home."

Gene finished off his bottle and grabbed the sleeve of a passing waiter. "I'll take another one of these."

"Get me one too," Garrett said.

The server looked confused. "I'm sorry, but I'm not your waiter." But then he scanned the chaos at the table and patted Gene's shoulder. "Not to worry, sir. Coming right up."

"Gene!" Debra shouted. "Stop this nonsense right now!"

"If Garrett can drink, then so can I."

Debra must have decided her husband was now the lesser of the evils. She picked up the plastic cat and shook it as she swung her attention to her nephew. "You had this in mind all along! You're here to cause trouble! First you claim the ring, then you encourage my poor gullible Gene to drink."

"You can't blame Uncle Gene's newfound independence on me, although I would gladly accept some of the credit, and I'm only here because of Nana. Until now, I didn't care about the ring, but seeing it on Blair's hand has given me second thoughts." His gaze found Blair's. "Now I know what I want, and I intend to fight for it." There was no mistaking the true meaning behind his statement.

A wave of desire washed through Blair, and she fought it back into submission. There was no doubt Garrett was all fire and passion, but she'd found out firsthand how badly it burned. She'd rather take practical and sensible. Safe and reliable were exactly what she needed. So why was she struggling to convince herself?

Chapter Six

THE SHOCK on Blair's face matched his own surprise at his out-of-nowhere declaration.

Nana Ruby was going to kill him.

He'd had no intention of laying claim to the ring, and in truth, he couldn't give a rat's ass about it. But damned if he was going to stand by and let his punk cousin marry Blair, let alone with that ring.

Now, instead of defusing the situation, he'd ratcheted it up to DEFCON 1. Jesus, he had to get things under control.

"I won't rip the ring off the bride-to-be's hand, if that's what you're concerned about," he said, dropping Blair's hand and trying to control his racing heart. "We'll wait for Nana to come tomorrow night. She can help make the decision."

This brought on a new round of shouting and dismay. Whiny Neil tossed out the phrase "you're her favorite." While that was probably true, he doubted Nana could help him get the girl, which was his real goal. That one was all on him.

Blair looked on in confusion, making it abundantly clear they'd kept her in the dark about the questionable ownership of her ring. But soon her bewilderment turned to anger as she narrowed her eyes at him.

"It's time for all of you to pay up," his aunt said, shaking the plastic cat jar. "Blair, you got off easy this time. You only owe a dollar. Neil, you owe two, and you, Gene Neilson Fredrick, must owe at least five between the drinking and the cursing."

Uncle Gene and Aunt Debra had a stare-off for several seconds before Gene caved. He must have decided to choose his battles because he dug out his wallet and sheepishly stuck a five-dollar bill into the jar. Neil put in his money, and Garrett handed over a dollar when Debra shoved the jar in Blair's direction.

His aunt scowled at him. "Surprisingly, you don't owe anything."

Garrett tucked his money into the jar and winked at Blair. "Oh, this is for the bride. Call it an early wedding gift. But if this is for cursing, as the label suggests, you owe some money yourself, Aunt Debra." His eyebrows rose with mock recrimination. "And I do believe I need to have a discussion with my mother about my true parentage. No one ever told me I was a bastard."

Debra's face turned red, although Garrett couldn't tell if it was from embarrassment or anger. Probably both.

He'd earned a scowl from Blair for donating the money on her behalf, but now he could tell she was trying to hold back a grin.

"That was an unfortunate loss of self-control." The woman's face twisted into disgust as she jerked her wallet out of her purse and pulled out one dollar. She screwed an indignant expression on her face. "The Lowrys seem to bring out the worst in me."

Blair tipped her head, her eyes dancing with mischief. "*Actually*, Debra, you owe *two dollars*. One for informing your nephew of his illegitimacy and the second for spelling out the home of *you know who*."

Debra's eyes widened in shock.

"Blair!" Neil cried out in horror.

Garrett knew the Fredricks liked to tiptoe around his aunt's self-righteous attitude. He was glad to see Blair hadn't kowtowed like the rest of them.

"You know who?" Garrett asked in amusement. He couldn't help but take pleasure in riling up his aunt and irritating his cousin. Especially since Blair seemed to find Debra as obnoxious as he did. "Dare I ask who that is?"

Blair lifted her eyebrows. "Why, the prince of darkness himself."

"Lord Voldemort?" Garrett teased, shooting his aunt an amused look.

She wasn't so pleased. "Who is this Lord Voldemort you keep talking about? Do we need to add him to the kitty list?"

Garrett burst out into laughter. He was surprised his aunt didn't already know about the notorious villain.

"No, Mom," Neil said. "He's a character from a children's book, which explains why Garrett is so enthralled with him."

Garrett noticed he left Blair off the naughty list, but it didn't stop him from giving her a look of reproach. She glanced away, trying to hide her grin.

So *his* Blair was still there, lurking below the prim and proper exterior. Just like he'd found her years ago.

Their original waiter appeared with Gene and Garrett's beers—apparently the other guy had wisely handed the task off to the poor man who'd been assigned to them. Gene gave the beer a longing look, but one glance from his furious wife was enough for him to push it to the middle of the table.

Garrett had no such qualms. Taking a drag from the bottle, Garrett wondered if he should leave. An already tense dinner would be all the more so after his bombshell and after the way he'd teased his aunt, but one look at Blair helped him decide. He had five days to win her back, and he was going to make every second count. He asked the waiter to bring him another beer.

"Really, Garrett," Aunt Debra mused, pressing her hand to her chest. "Haven't you done enough?"

Garrett grinned at the waiter. "Make sure it's extra cold."

Neil ordered water, although he gave his father's drink a longing glance, and his mother ordered iced tea. When the waiter turned to Blair, she looked torn, her previous steely presence returning. She cast a glance at Garrett for several seconds, then looked up at the waiter. "Hard lemonade."

Garrett nearly laughed at her order. From the look on her face, it had to be killing her to order something fruity. She was more of a beer and hard liquor kind of girl, but she was obviously trying to make peace with his non-worldly aunt, who would likely miss the fact that she was ordering alcohol.

Neil tensed. "Are you sure you don't want tea? Or water?"

Garrett leaned forward, unable to stop himself. "Let the lady have her lemonade, Neil. I knew you were a stuffed shirt, but I never figured you for a tightwad." He turned his attention to Blair. "Does he make you buy bargain brand toilet paper too?"

Neil's face turned red, and Blair glared at him, but he could tell she was fighting a grin.

"Of course Blair can have whatever she wants."

Garrett's grin spread as he looked up at the waiter. "Then a hard lemonade for the lady it is."

"Lemonade does sound good on a hot day like today," Aunt Debra said, chewing on her lower lip. "Maybe I should change my order."

Blair's eyes widened slightly, but not enough that anyone would notice unless they were watching her closely. Like he was now. A blind man could see the two women didn't get along. This would be one more log tossed onto a fire that Blair now seemed eager to put out. "Maybe I should change—"

"Don't be silly," Garrett said. "Neil just gave you his blessing to spend another dollar or two. But Aunt Debra," he turned to his aunt. "I'm not sure you'd like their lemonade. I hear it's really bitter." He shot the waiter a pointed glance, letting him know not to counter him.

The older woman shook her head and pursed her lips. "I'll get whatever I want, Garrett Michael Lowry." She turned to the server. "Why are you still standing there? Go get our drinks." Then she made a shooing motion.

Garrett tried to keep from laughing. "On second thought, I think a glass of hard lemonade is exactly what you need, Aunt Debra."

Neil shot Blair a look of dismay, then turned his attention to Aunt Debra. "Mother, I think you should get something else."

She gave him a pointed glare. "Why?"

Neil shook his head. "Never mind."

While they waited for their drinks, they all sat stewing in uncomfortable silence. Aunt Debra was fuming, and Uncle Gene was sneaking sips of his second bottle of beer behind his menu. Neil was outright surly, his shoulders tense as he tried to decide whom to shoot angry looks at, Garrett or Blair. Even the always-in-control Blair seemed slightly off kilter now that the dust had settled. Garrett didn't regret throwing down the gauntlet with the ring, but in hindsight, he should have waited until later to do it. He didn't want to cause Blair any additional stress. Since he was the one who'd stirred up this round of conflict, it was on him to make it more bearable.

The waiter brought their drinks and took their food orders, then hurried away. Not that Garrett could blame him after the way Aunt Debra had quizzed him about the various barbeque sauces, wanting to know which ingredients were in each. Thank God she hadn't been so inquisitive about her lemonade.

Blair had started to drink in earnest while Debra gave the waiter the third degree, and her hard lemonade was half gone by the time he scurried off. His aunt eyed her with disapproval. "Really, Blair. That's so unladylike." But she then took a sip of her own drink.

Neil's attention was glued to his mother, and Garrett waited for her reaction. Blair bit her lower lip.

"This is delicious." Aunt Debra took another sip, then glared at Garrett. "Why did you tell me it was bitter? It's actually very sweet and quite refreshing on a hot day."

"My mistake," Garrett murmured, lifting his beer bottle to his lips. "I must have confused this place with another one."

His aunt took another long drink and turned to his uncle. "We should see about having some of this at the rehearsal dinner barbeque."

"Rehearsal dinner *barbeque?*" Garrett asked, trying to keep a straight face.

Blair's brow lowered. "It's a western theme."

Garrett fought to keep from laughing. Blair was hosting a western-themed dinner? "Will there be square dancing?"

Blair's eyes narrowed. "*No.*"

His aunt's mouth pinched with irritation. "As you can see, Blair put her foot down."

"Come on, Blair," Garrett teased. "Everyone loves a good do-si-do or an allemande, right?"

Blair's eyes lit up with challenge. "You know how to square dance, Garrett?"

"Oh, you know me. I like to see the skirts flying."

Neil pounced on his words. "How would she know that, Garrett?"

Something in his tone caught Garrett off guard. It was

almost as if he knew about their past together and was challenging Garrett to admit to it. And he wanted to. But Blair's eyes were wild with panic, so he vowed to himself that he would keep quiet about it, at least for now. He'd stirred up enough trouble for the moment. "Oh, just something from the deposition, right, Blair?"

She looked torn. It was a lie, and she hated lies, preferring omission as her word-weapon of choice. So she gave him a haughty look and took another drink of her lemonade.

Garrett needed to steer the conversation away from Blair. "Neil, Mom tells me that you're a doctor here in town."

Neil studied him for several seconds as if gauging whether he was serious. "I work at St. Luke's in infectious disease."

"So do you spend more time in the hospital or in an office?"

Neil's eyes narrowed. "You just laid claim to my fiancée's ring and now you want to make polite conversation?"

His cousin only had it half right, but then he'd always been an idiot. Garrett had no idea how the guy had managed to fumble his way through medical school. "I said we'd wait for Nana Ruby to help decide. It's about time she got involved in this anyway, don't you think?"

"She says she doesn't want to get involved," Uncle Gene said. Everyone looked over at him in surprise. He wasn't one to give his opinions. Obviously the beer had loosened his tongue.

Aunt Debra frowned. "Yes, Mother says we need to work it out ourselves."

Garrett loved his mother, but she was one of the most stubborn women he'd ever met. His Aunt Debra was a very close second. Nana Ruby was no fool, so it was understandable why she'd tried to extricate herself from the situation.

"Is anyone going to tell me what the hell is going on with this ring?" Blair demanded, fire in her eyes.

He'd expected the question minutes ago, but the Curse

Kitty and the hard lemonade must have distracted her. That, or she'd wanted to wait for her drink before dealing with the mess.

Neil shot Garrett a glare and gave her a condensed version of the story.

"Why am I just now hearing about the controversy over this damned ring?" she asked, her jaw set.

"It wasn't something you needed to worry about, dear," Aunt Debra said, then lifted her jar and shook it. "You owe the jar a dollar."

Blair shot Neil an exasperated glare, then dug out a dollar before flagging down the waiter so she could order another hard lemonade.

"Give me another one too," Debra called after him. "It's really very good."

Their food arrived, and Debra became more and more uninhibited. Garrett had a hard time hiding his snicker, but Neil looked worried.

Neil got in multiple digs at Garrett over the course of the dinner, but it was easy to ignore him, particularly because Blair was at the table. He was dying to find out more about her life. He thought about waiting, but it would be considered normal for him to ask a new acquaintance questions about her career.

"So, Blair," Garrett said as she cut her pork with a knife and fork. "When did you start at Sisco, Sisco, and Reece?"

"Blair is a career woman," Debra said, slurring her words. She leaned her elbow on the table. It slipped on the surface, and she nearly fell face first into her baked beans.

Garrett grabbed her upper arm and helped her upright. "There you go."

She gave him an exaggerated look of confusion as she patted the top of her head. "I'm feeling a bit dizzy."

Neil shot daggers at him across the table. "I blame you for this, Garrett."

Neil's mother shook her head, almost falling out of her chair. "Garrett's being a perfect gentleman, Neilson." Then she added, "For once."

His cousin looked furious.

"Blair doesn't like to keep house or cook," Debra continued. "She *hires* someone to clean." His aunt spat out the sentence as though she'd just declared that Blair drowned puppies for sport.

"After watching Blair in action, I'm certain she's exactly where she needs to be," Garrett said.

Blair's eyes widened at the compliment, but Neil's eyes narrowed with suspicion. "And where's that, Garrett?"

Blair tensed, confusion flickering in her eyes.

"As a practicing attorney, Neil. What else could I be referring to?"

Blair took a deep breath and released it, her resolve returning. "I love what I do and have no intention of giving it up." She gave Garrett a withering glance. "And while Mr. Lowry is trying to appear gracious, I have no doubt that this is just a tactic to throw me off before our depositions tomorrow." Her upper lip curled. "But I can assure you it won't work."

Is that how she saw this? An elaborate attempt to sabotage her strategy? She should know better than to think he'd employ such tactics. He'd always preferred a fair, equal match. It was the only way he could know he'd won fair and square. But he'd let her down in almost every way possible, so maybe she didn't believe him capable of anything good.

He suddenly felt like he was fighting a hopeless battle.

Chapter Seven

GARRETT BACKED off the rest of dinner, and Debra got more and more inebriated. When she ordered her third hard lemonade, Garrett pulled the waiter aside and requested that he deliver her a regular lemonade instead. But she noticed the difference with her first sip.

"This tastes different."

"It's the water," Garrett said.

"The water?" She waved her glass and sloshed her drink over the side onto her hand.

"They ran out of hard water. Thus its name. This batch was made with *soft* water."

"Oh."

Blair grinned when she bought it, but Neil didn't look so amused.

As soon as they were done with dinner, Neil pulled out his phone and sighed. "I have to take this. It's the hospital." He got up and walked toward the front door, his phone pressed to his ear, although from Garrett's angle, his phone had a blank screen—no incoming or missed calls or texts. Not that Garrett would have believed it anyway. The timing was too convenient.

But Garrett decided to take advantage of his absence and turned to Blair. "So how long have you and Neil been together?"

She gave him a frosty gaze. "Two years."

"How did you meet?"

She studied him closely, as though trying to determine if he had an ulterior motive. "At a First Friday." When he gave her a blank look, she shifted in her seat and explained. "Every first Friday of the month, a bunch of the art galleries and restaurants downtown are open to the public, and they feature local bands and artists. We met at an art gallery. One of the associate attorneys in my office introduced us. He's an acquaintance of Neil's."

"Was it a whirlwind romance?" he couldn't resist asking.

Her eyebrows lifted, and she gave him a deathly glare.

"She's lucky to have him," Aunt Debra said, thrusting her shoulders back like a linebacker preparing to tackle. Unfortunately, her normal personality seemed to be returning along with her faculties.

Garrett lifted his second beer and winked. "Seems like it's the other way around to me."

Blair's shoulders relaxed, and he saw a grin tug at the corners of her mouth.

"How long do you think you'll continue working, dear?" his aunt asked her, lifting her glass to her mouth and giving her a sly grin. "You'll want to start having children soon, at your age. The clock is ticking."

Blair tensed again, and Garrett could see she was biting her tongue. She forced a smile. "I'm not going to quit my job. I love what I do. I'm not sure I even want to have children."

Aunt Debra choked on the sip of lemonade she'd just taken, her eyes widening in horror. "*What?*" She started coughing, and she scooted her chair back, the wood screeching on the tiles. She dropped her glass, and it shattered on the hard floor, splattering lemonade on a woman walking behind her.

The young woman shrieked and jumped backward,

landing in the lap of a man who was dining with a group of friends at a nearby table. From their Royals baseball shirts, Garrett figured they were grabbing dinner before the game. The man wrapped an arm around her back to steady her, a surprised grin lighting up his face.

Uncle Gene jumped out of his seat, sending the chair flying to the floor. There was panic in his eyes as he shouted, "Does anyone know the Heil Hitler?"

Blair grabbed Gene's leftover beer and took a long drag.

The older woman was still hacking, but drool was now spilling out of her mouth and down her chin. From the way she was still breathing and as her face was pink instead of blue, it was clear the woman wasn't really choking.

Garrett shook his head as he picked up a napkin and handed it to his aunt, but she batted it away. "It's the Heimlich, Uncle Gene, and she doesn't need it. She's choking on her own self-righteousness."

Neil reentered the restaurant as the manager and waiter rushed over to check on Aunt Debra.

"What in the hell happened?" Neil demanded.

Aunt Debra reached over and picked up the cat jar, shaking it at her son. "Dollar!" she choked out.

The waiter, probably worried about his tip, jerked Debra out of her chair and positioned her back against his chest, but he struggled to wrap his arms all the way around her to form the fist he'd need to give her the Heimlich. Out of apparent desperation, he pressed his palms against her instead and tugged her toward him, his hands cupping each of her breasts.

Garrett tried to keep from laughing as he shot a grin at Blair. "I think the waiter owes the kitty a few dollars for that move."

Aunt Debra screamed and beat at the poor waiter's hands. "I could sue you for that!"

The next couple of minutes were pure chaos as the manager tried to placate Aunt Debra—a task no human was capable of achieving. Neil stood in the mix with his parents and the staff, trying to get the full story of what had happened.

Blair and Garrett remained at the table, Blair sneaking glances at him, then looking away.

"I think Aunt Debra may have unintentionally forged a love connection." He motioned to the woman who had landed in the man's lap. She had moved to a chair, but they were still chatting.

Blair scoffed. "Like you believe in true love."

He gave her a half-shrug. "Maybe I do."

She shook her head. "You never used to."

"People change."

She stared at him for several long seconds, as though measuring the man she saw today against the man she used to know. A sardonic grin lifted her mouth. "No. Not really."

Neil returned to the table but didn't sit down. "I've gotten the situation under control, no thanks to you." He shot Garrett a glare. "I've been called in to the hospital, and I've wasted enough time as it is."

Blair looked up at him with a mixture of irritation and envy.

"We haven't finished our discussion about babies yet," his mother said as the manager walked back to the kitchen.

Blair's jaw tightened, and she shot Neil an angry glare.

"Mom," Neil said, grabbing the back of his chair and waiting until he had his mother's attention. "I can tell from the look on Blair's face that you've given her the grandkids speech again. I told you we'll let you know when we decide to start a family. Blair's career is on the rise. She doesn't have the time or energy to deal with a pregnancy or a newborn right now."

Garrett watched his cousin, stunned. This was the first time all evening he'd defended his fiancée to his mother.

Neil leaned over and planted a chaste kiss on her mouth. "I'll talk to you tomorrow."

Her eyes widened in surprise. "I thought you were spending the night."

"I traded call." He shrugged. "I'm juggling my schedule to accommodate my time off for the honeymoon."

The look she gave him suggested she didn't trust his answer, so Garrett was surprised when she relented. "Okay."

Neil hurried out the door, and Aunt Debra squirmed in place. "After all the commotion, Gene and I should get settled in our hotel room."

Garrett heard a hint of bitterness, and he wondered if she was miffed that she hadn't been invited to stay at Blair's or Neil's.

Relief flickered in Blair's eyes, but she flashed his aunt a polite smile. "That's probably a good idea. We have a busy week ahead of us."

Aunt Debra stood. "Come on, Gene."

He looked confused. "But the waiter hasn't brought the bill yet."

His aunt smiled. "Blair's a career woman, so I'm sure she'll take care of it. Won't you, dear?"

Her jaw tightened. "Of course."

Aunt Debra and Uncle Gene didn't waste any time before heading for the door. Blair turned her gaze on him, and he was suddenly keenly aware of the fact that this was exactly what he'd wanted all day. Time alone with her.

"You can go now." Apparently she had other ideas.

"I'll stay and help cover the tab. It's the least I can do after stirring up trouble."

"Then you must pay for meals right and left," she said dryly. "Stirring up trouble seems to be something you excel at."

He laughed, but he was nervous. "Which means I'm used to it, so you might as well let me. We could have another drink before we go."

She studied him for a moment, and he was struck by her beauty for about the hundredth time today. The bitter thought crossed his mind again: had he not been such a fool five years ago, perhaps she would still be his.

Something flickered in her eyes. "Are you *sure* you don't mind helping me cover the bill?"

Hopeful, he shook his head. "Not a problem."

A wide grin spread across her face as she stood. "Thanks." Then she headed for the door.

Dammit. "Blair!" He jumped up and started after her, but the waiter ran over to block his path.

"Sir! You have to pay for the meal."

Garrett pulled out his wallet. "How much is it?"

The waiter looked frustrated. "I don't know. I still have to print off the bill."

"Then do it. *Hurry.*" Blair was already out the door, and if he didn't get out of here soon, she'd be gone.

The waiter didn't seem to grasp his urgency and checked on another table before getting his bill. Since Garrett only had a twenty-dollar bill in his wallet, he was forced to wait.

Several minutes later, he signed the receipt and ran out the door, sure he'd missed her but desperate to try anyway.

The universe was obviously still rooting for him, because he found her sitting in a sedan, her hands covering her face. He walked over to the driver's door and knocked on the window.

She jumped and lowered her hands. He was relieved to see she wasn't crying, but her eyes were alight with a savage fury he recognized all too well. "Go away!" she shouted, but it was muffled by the glass.

"Open the door, Blair."

"*Go away!*"

He leaned his backside on the car next to hers and crossed his arms.

She rested her hands on the steering wheel and stared out the windshield for several seconds before opening the door. "My car won't start. I need you to figure out what's wrong with it."

He laughed, trying to hide his relief that she was actually talking to him. "Have we met? You know I don't do anything mechanical."

She pressed a button, then got out and walked to the front of her car and lifted the hood.

He dropped his arms and moved next to her. "What are you doing?"

"I'm trying to figure out why it won't start."

"When did *you* become mechanical?" he teased.

She leaned down to look at something around the battery, then stood up. "I'm not. But I figured it couldn't hurt to check." She gave him a withering stare. "I wouldn't put it past you to do something to it. You seem intent on talking to me. And yes, my assistant told me that you were trying to set up a lunch with me when you were at her desk."

Garrett was relieved to know that little mix-up had been handled, but she obviously wasn't any closer to agreeing to have a sit-down talk with him. Still, it was one less strike against him. He walked over and peered down at the engine. "Since we've already agreed that I'm physically—if not mentally—incapable of such an act of vandalism, let's go with general car trouble as the reason your engine won't start." He had to admit that it would have been a great idea if, one, he knew how to do such a thing, two, if he'd known she would be here tonight, and three, if he'd known what make and model of car she drove.

She put her hands on her hips. "Did you arrange to be a groomsman in our wedding?"

"God, no. It's like my worst nightmare come true."

Her eyebrows rose, and her mouth pursed. "Are you saying my wedding is a nightmare?"

He shook his head. "Come on, Blair. Tell me about the last wedding you were in. Did you really want to be in it? Besides, why would I want to be in *your* wedding?" He stopped himself from adding "if I wasn't the groom."

She watched him for a moment, as though scanning him with a bullshit meter. She'd always been good at reading him. He must have passed because her hands dropped from her hips.

His shoulders relaxed. "I honestly had no clue you were Neil's fiancée."

"And what about the Norfolk case? Did you know I was on it?"

He held out a hand toward her. "No, I swear. They told me the attorney was B.A. Hansen. You went by Myers in law school."

"So you would have turned both things down if you'd known?"

Would he? He wasn't so sure. Especially since he'd given so much thought to their relationship over the last year. He would have sought her out if he'd thought there had been any chance she would listen, but now she was forced to endure him, which meant he actually had a shot. There was no denying that fate kept throwing her into his path. He could lie to her, but he'd never done that before. After all the stunts her father had pulled, she couldn't abide liars or cheaters. He had no plans to be either to her. "No."

She seemed to wrestle with herself for a moment, and then, without a word, she walked back to her car door and grabbed her phone out of her purse.

He wanted to stop her or ask who she was calling, but it occurred to him that he was turning into a stalker. So instead he returned to his post next to the car, crossing his arms and waiting for her to finish calling roadside assistance or whatever she was doing. Less than a minute later, she was cursing into the receiver. While Aunt Debra might not appreciate that character trait, Garrett had always thought it was sexy as hell.

"Two *hours*? That's ridiculous," she said in a frosty tone. "I don't have time to wait *two hours*."

"Blair," he said, still resting against the car. "I'll take you home."

She gave him a dirty look and turned her back to him. "If you send someone sooner, I'll pay the driver double." She listened for several seconds. "What good is having a roadside service if you don't show up in a timely manner?" But she hung up before the person on the line had time to answer.

"Blair, stop being so stubborn," Garrett said. "Let me take you home."

She put her hands on her hips and gave him a frosty glare. "Oh, you'd like that, wouldn't you?"

He unfolded his arms. "What do you think I'm going to do? We spent the night together last night, and we didn't do a thing."

She sucked in a breath, her eyes widening. "We really didn't?"

A grin lifted the corners of his mouth. "You don't remember anything from last night, do you?"

She held his gaze, but her confidence faded. "Bits and pieces."

"I was a perfect gentleman. I made sure you got to your room without being accosted."

Relief washed over her face. Had she really thought him capable of taking advantage of her? She quickly regained her composure, then gave him a sarcastic leer. "And of course you stayed."

"I offered to go spend the night in the airport, but you insisted I stay."

Realization replaced the relief on her face. "It was *your* room, wasn't it?"

His voice lowered. "It doesn't matter, Blazer. We slept on the same bed, and nothing happened, which proves I'm trustworthy. Let me take you home."

She flinched at the use of his old nickname for her, and her eyes filled with fire at the word *trustworthy*, but then some of the fight bled out of her. Even back in law school, she'd rarely showed extreme emotion. She had the ability to make most people wither with a mere glance, yet he knew there was more to her. The icy inaccessibility was her wall to keep the world from hurting her any more than it already had. And it was very effective. To his shame, he was sure he'd helped build that wall even higher. The key to Blair's soul was in her eyes. To the casual observer, they were icy blue and full of intimidation, but if you held her gaze long enough, they turned a sky blue that pulled you in deeper. Most people were too intimidated to hold her gaze for long enough to see it. Had Neil?

She released a sigh. "Okay."

He tried not to show his surprise, but her laughter told him he'd failed.

"You didn't expect me to agree?"

He grinned and lifted his shoulders into a sheepish shrug. "I admit that I expected more of a fight."

"Maybe I choose my battles now." She pulled her purse out of her car and locked it. "Let's go."

He led her to his rental car across the parking lot and opened the passenger door for her.

She shot him a sarcastic glance. "No need to waste your gentlemanly manners on me, Lowry. This car ride won't end with you in my bed."

He grinned. "I have no such delusions. I'm merely being a Good Samaritan."

"Trying to earn karma for all the wrongs you've committed?"

And if that wasn't a well-deserved stab in an old wound. "I think it's going to take more than a car ride to right all of my wrongs." Rather than give her a chance to respond, he walked around to the driver's side and slid behind the wheel, then started the car. "Okay. Where to?"

"Get on the highway and head east, and I'll give you directions."

This was his big chance to make some inroads, but he had no clue where to start. He was like a teenager on a first date. His sweaty palms slipped on the steering wheel, and his tongue was heavy in his mouth. He found it ironic that he was known for being able to schmooze anyone, yet now, when the gift of the gab actually mattered, he was tongue-tied. If Blair knew the truth, she'd love every minute of it. Finally, Blair caved to the silence.

"I can't believe you're Neil's evil cousin."

He laughed. "He calls me evil, huh?"

She put her hand on the armrest. "Not in so many words, but I can read between the lines."

"We're cousins all right. We used to spend two weeks together every summer at Nana's farm. Neil hated it."

"I can imagine. And you loved it."

He glanced at her. "What makes you say that?"

"You like the outdoors." She paused. "Or at least you used to."

Her last statement gave him hope after the comment she'd made in the restaurant about people never changing. "Still do. I just don't get out very much anymore. You know how it is to be an associate attorney, always trying to prove your worth, hoping to make partner. You spend most of your time enclosed in glass and metal."

Her easygoing attitude dissolved. "Yeah."

So his earlier assessment had been spot on. Something else was going on with her, something to do with her firm. "How long have you been at Sisco, Sisco, and Reece? You never answered me before."

"Since law school. I did a summer internship there and was offered a position." She tensed. "What about you? Divorce law. I never would have expected it."

He shrugged. "I kind of fell into it. I started out practicing entertainment law, then switched soon after moving out to L.A. With all the high-profile people, not to mention all the alcohol and quickie weddings, there can be some pretty profitable cases."

"And plenty of skinny actresses," Blair said, disgust in her voice.

There was no use denying it. It was one of the reasons he'd moved to the West Coast. But now he was stuck with an awkward silence and no clue how to fill it without saying something else to piss her off. Then an idea hit him. The reason he was here.

"Have you met Nana Ruby yet?" he asked.

"No." Her tone let him know she had no desire to meet her. "I hear she's a tyrant. Debra's bad enough."

"Aunt Debra's something all right, but I think you'll like Nana Ruby."

"I doubt it. She forced you into the wedding party, didn't she? She sounds like a bully."

"Some people might accuse you of the same thing."

Her brow lowered. "I'll never know why men are threatened by powerful women."

"Not just men," Garrett said. "And I know she sounds like a bully, but she usually has a reason for the things she does."

"And what's her reason for doing this?"

"My mother and Aunt Debra have fought over the ring on your hand off and on for over two decades. It used to belong to their grandmother, who left it to her granddaughter. Only no one can definitively prove *which* granddaughter. Aunt Debra claimed ownership because she's had it in her possession most of that time, but my mother threw an epic fit when she found out Neil gave it to you. So Nana Ruby insisted I come and . . ." She was never going to believe him after he'd laid claim to the ring so publicly. But he'd promised himself to be truthful with her.

"And stir up trouble? So your grandmother's an instigator?"

"Believe it or not, she sent me here to keep the peace."

"By announcing that the ring is yours?" she asked in disbelief as she glanced down at the ring on her hand.

"I don't want the ring, Blair," he said quietly.

"Then why the hell did you say that you did? *Especially* if your grandmother wanted you to smooth things over."

He turned and looked at her. This was what he'd been waiting for—this was the time for him to amp up his campaign. The words *I want you* were on the tip of his tongue, but in this moment of truth, he couldn't bring himself to say it. What if she was really happy with Neil? As hard as it was to accept, he didn't want to be the one to screw that up for her. He gave her a lazy grin. "You'd never believe me if I told you."

"Still the same," she said, shaking her head in disgust. "Still the player."

Was he? There was no denying that he'd dated more women than he could count, probably a dozen in the past year alone, but that didn't mean it was what he wanted.

She gave him directions the rest of the way to her condo in Lee's Summit, a suburb on the Missouri side of the city.

"I thought you were a city girl," he teased as he pulled into the parking lot in front of her building. The brick cookie-cutter condos didn't look like her at all. Back in law school, Blair had always insisted that she'd live in the heart of the city after graduation. In fact, she would have probably run off to New York City if not for her mother. She didn't belong in this place.

"It's a good investment."

"I feel like you'd be happier down by the plaza," he said as he parked the car.

She released a sigh. "I *was* renting there, but Neil heard about this place. It was a good deal, so I bought it and moved in six months ago."

"Back when we were together, this wasn't what you wanted."

She looked into his eyes. "We don't always get what we want, now do we?"

An ache squeezed his heart, and without realizing what he was doing, he leaned closer to her. "Sometimes we get a second chance."

He expected her to contradict him or back away, but she did neither. Instead her gaze moved to his mouth.

"You said something to me last night that caught me by surprise."

"Oh?" Her body was tense, and she seemed to have a hard

time concentrating. "I was drunk, so I can't be held accountable for anything I said."

Her words were breathless, and a fire burned in his blood. All he could think about was kissing her and having her in his arms again, but this time not so platonically. He rested his hand on her hand, thankful when she didn't jerk away. In fact, she leaned closer. "You said you missed me."

Her eyes flew open, and the panic he saw there told him she'd meant what she'd said. "Dream on, Garrett."

"Are you happy, Blair?" he whispered. "The woman I knew before wouldn't be happy with this."

She sucked in a breath as he leaned closer still, their faces only a couple of inches apart. "It's called compromise."

"The Blair Myers I knew wasn't capable of compromise."

"I'm told it's necessary for keeping long-term relationships." She licked her lower lip, and he was in agony.

She reached for the door handle. "I have to go." But she didn't open the door, and she didn't look away.

"Blair." Her sky blue eyes held his, and his mind raced for the right words. "For what it's worth, I want you to be happy. Are you happy?"

Her body stiffened. "Five years too late, Garrett." Then she opened the car door, grabbed her purse, and walked into the building.

Chapter Eight

BLAIR LET herself into her condo and barely had the door shut behind her before she began to hyperventilate. She tossed her purse down in a panic as she tried to catch her breath. Being so close to Garrett Lowry unnerved her more than she cared to admit. She'd almost kissed him. Everything within her had demanded that she kiss him. If she had waited a moment longer before leaving, she would have succumbed . . . and she suspected it wouldn't have ended with a single kiss. Now her traitorous body was complaining.

Garrett was a bitter reminder of everything she was giving up to marry stable, reliable Neil.

Too many things were bombarding her at once. Her possible dismissal from the firm. Questioning her relationship with Neil. Her feelings for Garrett.

It had been so much easier to dismiss her feelings for him as sentimentality for the past yesterday morning, but three random encounters in less than twenty-four hours had made her cold feet turn frigid. What were the odds of three coincidental meetings with the man who still stole her breath? And the odds of him turning out to be Neil's cousin . . . How could such a thing happen?

Oh. God. No. A sick feeling spread from her stomach to the rest of her body—it felt a lot like certainty.

She picked up her purse and dug through it, then dumped the contents on her kitchen table when she couldn't find her phone fast enough. Libby answered on the second ring, sounding breathless. "Hey, Blair."

"What are you doing?" Blair asked. "Are you *running? In this heat?*"

"No, Noah and I are walking Tortoise around the pond at the dog park."

Blair shuddered, wondering where to start. "You're walking *a turtle?*"

Libby laughed. "No. Tortoise, my new lab rescue. I told you about him last week, but you were so preoccupied with the wedding you probably forgot. He's been cooped up all day, so Noah and I brought him to the dog park."

"Are you sure you're responsible enough to care for another living animal? You kill plants."

Libby laughed. "Shows what you know. My tomato plants are thriving."

"Wow. You finally kept something alive longer than you usually keep your boyfriends. Hell, you might as well have a kid while you're at it."

Libby's light tone turned serious. "What's going on, Blair?"

"Why do you think something's going on?"

"Because you're talking nonsense."

"Why are you at the dog park with Noah? That's the real question here. Shouldn't Mitch be with you instead?"

"He's at football practice," Libby replied. "You'd be amazed by the hours a high school football coach works."

Blair wanted to ask if Mitch knew she was with Noah, then decided it was Libby's business. She didn't need to act the part of the jealous boyfriend for him. Besides, she had something more pressing to address. "Tell me again about this supposed wedding curse."

"Oh, my God!" Libby squealed. "She was right, wasn't she? Your wedding is cursed! *I knew it!*"

"You don't have to sound so happy about it. Libby, I need this wedding to be perfect. My job depends on it."

"Whoa. Start over and tell me why you think your wedding is cursed."

"Garrett's here. It turns out that he's Neil's cousin, and their grandmother is making him be a groomsman."

"Wait. *Garrett?* You mean your law school boyfriend?"

"Yes, him. And he's messing up everything."

"Wow. What are the chances of that happening?"

"And get this: he just happens to be the opposing counsel in the case I'm deposing this week. That's not even the worst part. If my wedding isn't perfect on Saturday, there's a good chance I'm going to lose my job."

"*What?*"

Blair explained the situation, then waited through several seconds of dead air as her friend mulled it all over.

"Blair, that's totally illegal. You would think attorneys would know better."

"Yeah, well, I'm not supposed to know anything about it, and a couple of the senior partners are old school. Think *Mad-Men*-type sexist. But I can't do anything about the illegality of it. Ben told me in confidence and would lose his job if it ever got out. I can't throw him under the bus."

"So what are you going to do?"

"Get married on Saturday. And that's not the point, anyway. You need to break this curse."

"I never thought I'd hear you say those words. What did you say earlier? That the curse was nonsense?"

"It is! I'm far too logical to believe in that sort of thing, but I'm not taking any chances. Just in case it might be real, I need you to get rid of it."

"I can't."

"What do you mean you *can't?*"

"Blair, the fortune teller at the Santa-Cal-Gon Days festival created the curse. She's the only one who can break it."

"Then go hunt her down, Libby."

Libby laughed. "The first part of the curse says all three of our weddings would be disasters. You know what the second part says, right?"

She did—it was that she'd marry someone else—but there was no way that was happening.

"So Garrett . . . ?"

"Not happening, Libby." Now if only her body would get on board with her mind. Just the thought of how close she came to kissing him made her hot. She told herself it was from embarrassment, not because she was turned on, but the reaction was so strong she had to grip the neck of her shirt and begin fanning herself.

Of course, it wasn't easy to get anything by Libby, who knew her better than most people. "Things would probably go much easier if you would just open yourself to the possibility. At some point you have to stop relying on logic to get you through life and live with your heart. You'll be a whole lot happier if you do."

"See you at the shower tomorrow night, Libby." Then Blair hung up before her friend could say another word. The little part of her that had jumped in excitement at Libby's words scared her. It needed to be reined in. Stat.

Blair flopped down in a stiff chair in her living room, then scooted around trying to get comfortable. Why didn't she have any overstuffed chairs to sink into? Maybe because she never lay around, relaxing. She heaved out of the chair, wondering what was wrong with her all of a sudden. Why was she so unsettled lately? She could blame part of it on Garrett, but she'd been questioning this marriage before he walked into the bar last night. She reminded herself that this was normal. Sane, reasonable people examined life decisions before jumping into them. That was what this was. She was just being cautious.

But she had to admit even to herself that Neil's mother was almost enough to make her take off running. The woman seemed to get worse every time she met her. The only reason Blair had lasted past their first meeting was Neil's insistence that he was nothing like his parents and found his mother's small-minded attitude embarrassing. Thankfully, she'd only needed to deal with her future in-laws on a small scattering of occasions in the two years she and Neil had been together. As long as she could keep future contact to a minimum, she could handle it. All the more reason to seriously consider not having kids.

Blair grabbed her laptop and set it on her dining room table that was covered with papers and files. This was the real reason she didn't sit around in overstuffed chairs. There was always too much work to do. While she might not be working at Sisco, Sisco and Reece after this week, Rowena Norfolk was counting on her to prove her soon-to-be ex was a lying, thieving, cheating bastard.

She pulled out files for the two depositions scheduled for the next day. They were deposing another mistress in the morning—a more important witness than the first, which meant Blair had to be prepared. Rowena was certain her husband had promised to divorce her and marry the mistress . . . and then reneged on that promise to be with mistress number three. Apparently, Mr. Norfolk had been a busy man. Blair was fairly certain mistress number two, Amanda Beasley, was privy to Brian Norfolk's master plan to bilk his wife out of a shitload of money. She was certain he had more money than he'd disclosed in discovery, and Blair was hoping Ms. Beasley would have some knowledge of where all that loot was hidden. It helped that Amanda Beasley was just one more scorned lover. Hopefully, she'd walk in seeking revenge.

But the pièce-de-resistance was Brian Norfolk's own deposition. Blair was hoping he'd take his oath to tell the truth to heart. But scum like him rarely did. She wasn't worried. She'd get him in the end. She always did. He'd thought it was so smart of him to move away to California before filing for divorce, but his fancy San Diego law firm wouldn't save him from her.

It helped knowing that Garrett was his counsel. She had to admit that she'd loved serving him his ass earlier today. But he'd fared a hell of a lot better than his colleague. In fact, he'd fared a lot better than most attorneys she'd gone up against. If he was telling the truth and the case had only been transferred to him the previous day, she had to grudgingly admit she was impressed . . . and remind herself that he'd probably prepare more for the coming depositions, especially now that he knew she was opposing counsel.

She had no reason to doubt his truthfulness. He may have broken up with her, then played the field multiple times over, but he'd never lied. If anything, she had to applaud the fact that he'd owned what—and whom—he'd done. Which made her feelings for him even more pathetic, especially the way her heart had taken off like an Olympic sprinter when he gave her that look in the car ride home—that familiar look that said he was hungry and she was a filet mignon dinner.

Her body betrayed her mind when she was with him, and she found herself longing for more than the vanilla, missionary-style sex she and Neil had every Saturday night. But chemistry had never been an issue with Garrett, so it should come as no surprise she still felt this way. It was physiological. Which was a good thing. God help her if her heart got involved. She wasn't sure she could survive him hurting her a second time.

Still, she couldn't let him see she was affected by him, or he'd take full advantage of her weakness, both in the conference room and out. Yet she knew it was too late for that. She'd sat in his car, practically waiting for a goodnight kiss like a teenager coming home from a first date. Garrett wasn't stupid, and he'd always been able to read her like a book. Based on his questions and observations tonight, it was pretty obvious he still could.

But something bothered her . . . she still couldn't figure out why he'd been so adamant about taking her to lunch. And while it was obvious he'd like another roll in her sheets, he hadn't made a move on her. Far from it—he'd claimed he just wanted her to be happy. Had he meant it? It seemed hard to believe after his attempt to claim the ring.

She stared down at the object of contention—the gold band with a round center diamond and several smaller diamonds clustered on each side. She felt no emotional attachment to the ring. Now she wondered if that was a bad sign. Megan loved the family heirloom ring on her left hand only slightly less than she loved her new husband. But Blair reminded herself that she wasn't like her closest friends. The two of them shared a romantic streak that she'd never possessed. The only person who had ever understood that about her was Garrett. Even Neil had found her lack of sentimentality strange in the beginning.

Maybe she was the type of woman who shouldn't get married at all. While she and Neil were compatible, what if it wasn't enough? She had no desire to be like the women who walked into her office with broken lives and shattered hearts. But she'd never be like those women even if she and Neil ultimately divorced. Because she would have to give Neil her heart to let him destroy it . . . and she hadn't. She wouldn't. She'd done that once. Never again.

There was no denying she'd become jaded over the years. Blair attributed her harshness to her chosen field, but that was only partially true. Her breakup with Garrett had left deep scars, and now she wasn't sure she was capable of loving anyone the way a wife was supposed to love her husband. She couldn't help feeling guilty and had actually confessed her thoughts to Neil after Megan's wedding. Logical Neil had assured her that their relationship was perfect . . . for them.

"That's why we work, Blair," he had said. "Neither of us expects undying love and adoration from the other. We're content with what we have."

She'd agreed at the time, so why was she so uncertain now?

But it was all a moot point anyway. Her entire career hinged on her wedding, so even if she wanted to back out, she was stuck—at least if she wanted to stay at her firm. Idealistic Blair wanted to quit. How could she work for a chauvinistic firm, even if they were closet chauvinists? But pragmatic Blair said to stay the course. She was getting married on Saturday, despite her frigid feet. She'd go through with the wedding, then take it from there.

But the question remained: why was she still hung up on Garrett Lowry? Her reaction to him last night and today shook her to her core. The fact that she had such passionate feelings for a womanizer was sickening. No matter what, there had always been one person she could count on: herself. But now— when she needed to count on herself more than ever—she wasn't sure she could . . . at least not around him. And that shook the very bedrock of her soul.

There was only one solution: she needed to stay as far away from the man as possible, which meant no contact outside the conference room.

That wouldn't be hard to achieve on her end, but would he accept her avoidance? They had no unfinished business from the past. Their break had been clean. Yet he'd been pretty intent on getting some one-on-one time with her.

Then it hit her. Maybe Garrett was only showing interest in her because Neil was her fiancé. The animosity between the two cousins and Garrett's sudden interest in her ring made it abundantly clear that the two men were competitive.

Damn Nana Ruby for throwing her life into chaos. She might not have ever met the woman, but she wanted to snatch her bald the moment she did.

The next morning Blair felt surprisingly energized when she walked into the office. Five hours of sleep had given her a much better outlook. She'd had extra time to prepare for the depositions while the car service took her to work. She and Melissa had the wedding under control. She and Neil had a relationship that ideally suited them and their career goals. The partners would be wowed by her wedding, and she'd be offered a partnership. And Garrett . . . if he wanted the stupid ring so bad, he could have it. She chose to ignore the fact that the ring wasn't his real goal, as she still couldn't possibly fathom what he wanted—beyond annoying Neil, of course. And as for her feelings for him . . . they were a moot point. He'd made his decision five years ago, and if he was interested again, it wouldn't be for anything permanent. She had neither the time nor the inclination for the type of relationship a man like Garrett Lowry had to offer. Sure, he still made her pulse race, but she'd get over it. She was a grown woman, not some hormonal teenager.

"Good morning, Melissa," she said as she stopped at her assistant's desk, sounding more cheerful than usual. "Did you get the text about my car?"

"Yes." Melissa looked at her as though she'd walked in naked. "What happened to *you*?"

"Can't a person be in a good mood?"

"If that person is you, no."

Blair was taken aback. "Am I that much of a bitch?"

"No, of course not. But you're not one of those perpetually happy people either. What's going on?"

She smiled. "I'm feeling optimistic today."

Melissa's eyebrows rose. "So dinner went well last night?"

"No . . . dinner was a disaster, but I've decided to let that go. Is everything set for the party tomorrow night?"

Melissa stared at her for a few moments. "I confirmed the reservation for the tasting room at the brewery on Monday, but I'll call again to verify. And back to your original question, yes, I received your text. I've called the car service, and they've towed your car to the shop. They'll return it to the parking garage, but if it's not ready in time, we'll arrange to get you a rental."

"Perfect," Blair said in a happy tone as she walked into her office.

"I'm calling a doctor. You're having some sort of breakdown."

"Very funny." She shut the door and sat down at her desk to go through her emails.

Several minutes later her door opened, and Melissa walked in with a cup of coffee. "The deposition of Amanda Beasley is still set up for ten, and Mr. Norfolk's for two. And Rowena Norfolk still doesn't want to sit in on either one."

"Okay. Thank you." Blair took the cup from her. "Let me know when Mr. Lowry shows up."

Melissa continued to watch her. "I know you went to law school together."

Blair's gaze narrowed as anger burned to life in her chest. "You're *spying* on me?"

"*No*. I was checking up on *him*." When Blair didn't

respond, Melissa added, "I had to know his connection to you so I could protect you."

Blair clenched her teeth. "I don't need protecting, Melissa. You're overstepping your bounds."

Melissa held her ground. "No. I'm not. You wouldn't tell me, so I had to find out myself. I'm the gatekeeper, Blair. You're depending on me to keep him away from you, and I need to know what I'm facing. That meant finding out how he knew you."

Blair didn't answer.

Melissa sat in the chair in front of her desk. "I'm sorry."

Blair sighed and lightly rubbed her temple. "No, it's fine. I overreacted."

"You two used to date, didn't you?"

Blair shook her head. "It was more than casual dating." She groaned. "We were together for a year, then he dropped me to date every other woman in law school."

"So he's a player," Melissa said in disgust. "Do you think he's trying to go for round two?"

"There's more to it than that. He's Neil's cousin. The groomsman his mother called you about. And I only just found out yesterday."

Melissa gasped. "What?"

"And there's more." Blair found herself spilling out the whole story about the animosity between the two men and the engagement ring, but she left out the part about him taking her home. There was only so much humiliation she could take in one day.

Melissa leaned forward to get a better look at Blair's left hand. "He actually claimed the ring?"

"Neil and his mother just about flipped their shit, and I could tell that Garrett loved every minute of it."

"So he's here to stir up trouble."

Blair nodded slowly. "Looks like it."

"Thanks for trusting me enough to tell me."

"I should have told you yesterday, but I was embarrassed."

"Why?"

"Because I fell for his charm and let him dump me." Although that wasn't quite true. She'd never felt like he was using her or pretending to have feelings he didn't. But that had only made it worse in the end.

"You're not the first person to fall for a smooth-talking, good-looking man, and our very line of work depends on you not being the last. But the fool-you-once adage seems apropos here."

"Agreed," Blair said absently, then she shuddered and looked her assistant in the eye. "Thanks for having my back."

Melissa stood. "What are good assistants for?"

"You're coming tomorrow night, aren't you?"

Melissa looked surprised. "Sure, I can come and make sure everything goes okay if you want."

"No. Not for work. As my friend."

"Oh." Her eyes widened as she stared at Blair.

Blair shook her head. What had she been thinking? A few moments of sharing her emotions and she'd presumed their relationship was more than professional. What if Melissa asked for a transfer now? Especially knowing she might be out of a job next week. "I'm sorry. You don't have to—"

A wide smile spread across Melissa's face. "I'd love to come. Thank you for asking."

Blair's face started to heat up. "Well, I'd give you the details, but it turns out that you know them."

She laughed. "Sure enough." She walked to the door and started to open it before turning around, her hand on the knob. "Thanks, Blair."

Blair's eyes met hers. "Thank *you*." Then she remembered

something else. "Oh, can you get me a stack of dollar bills by the end of the day? At least twenty . . . no, better make it forty."

Melissa's eyebrows rose in amusement. "Planning a racy bachelorette party?"

"Hardly," she grumbled. "A tight-ass wedding shower."

As Melissa walked out of the office, Blair wondered if there were enough bills in circulation to help get her through this weekend.

Chapter Nine

GARRETT LONGED to loosen his tie, but to do so would be, one, unprofessional, and two, it would give Blair the satisfaction of knowing she was getting to him. Not that she didn't already know. The smirk on her face when she shot glances at him between questions was proof enough of that. But he felt like he was choking. He was choking all right—on embarrassment.

He kept reminding himself that Brian Norfolk wasn't really his client. That he hadn't been the one to prep Amanda Beasley for the deposition. But even though Lopez had done a shitty job—so much so that he wished he had the authority to fly back to San Diego and demand his resignation—there was no denying that it was a crap case. If Rowena Norfolk's attorney had been content to just go through the motions, it would have gone smoother, but Blair Myers Hansen didn't understand the concept of *going through the motions*. She was smart, articulate, and ruthless. It didn't hurt that there wasn't an attorney alive who could make Lopez's client look like a saint. Under the circumstances, Garrett was semi-holding his own, but Blair was a barracuda.

Back when they were together, he'd loved to get her riled up. Her eyes always lit up with a righteous fire when she was in the middle of an argument. But their arguments had mostly been over politics and current events—topics they had enjoyed debating. Afterwards, they would laugh together and then take the same passion they'd harnessed for their disagreement to their bed. He hadn't lied to her when he said she was in the top five of the best lays he'd ever had, but he hadn't told her the truth either. No one else had even come close.

"Mr. Norfolk," Blair said, her voice sounding like honey off the comb, but only a fool would fall for it. Garrett was sure her beauty had helped lure Norfolk into complacency. She wore a gray dress today that clung to her curves. Her hair was up again, and she had on a pair of three-inch black patent leather heels. She flipped through the papers in front of her before glancing up at him with those wide blue eyes. "These numbers just aren't adding up."

Brian Norfolk gave her a shit-eating grin. "Maybe numbers just aren't your thing, sweetheart."

The look she gave him would make most men tuck tail and run. But Brian Norfolk was an arrogant fool. Garrett couldn't stand the man. He was a fifty-seven-year-old screenwriter who'd experienced only moderate success until four years ago, when one of his movies suddenly became a blockbuster. The money had gone to his head, and while he'd fooled around on his wife more than once over their twenty-year marriage, he'd decided it was finally time to upgrade. But he'd tried out quite a few women before settling on the woman who was currently living in his San Diego condo, waiting to get her hands on his money. Consequently, he was trying to bilk his wife in every conceivable way. Knowing Blair, she'd sink her teeth into this man like a dog with a bone, and while Garrett would love nothing more than to see her take the prick down a few rungs, his job was to decrease the carnage as much as possible. He'd reluctantly warned Norfolk not to take Blair lightly, but the man was clearly ignoring his advice.

The corners of her mouth tipped up slightly, but he knew that look. She was preparing to go in for the kill.

She pulled a stack of papers from a folder and spread them across the table in front of him. "Mr. Norfolk, these are your tax returns for the last four years. Yes?"

He leaned over and scanned the papers. "Yeah, that's right."

She slid them to the side and pulled another stack of papers from her folder. "These other papers list your assets, investments, and monthly expenses. These were filled out by you, were they not?"

He shrugged. "Yeah."

"So are you very familiar with what's on these sheets, or do you need a moment to look them over?" she asked in a patronizing tone.

His body stilled, and he sat up straighter, turning to look at Garrett. Garrett nodded for him to answer, and he turned back to Blair. "No, I know what's on there."

She tilted her head at him and proceeded to go through the entries in detail, pointing out all the discrepancies. "Maybe you're right and numbers aren't my thing. So how about you save us all some time and tell me where I can find the three million dollars that seem to be unaccounted for? I know you live quite the wild life now, but surely even *you* couldn't have frivolously wasted three million dollars."

He stared at the sheets. "Well, what can I say? I'm in California now. The cost of living is a hell of a lot higher there." He gave her an ugly smile. "But a simple girl like you wouldn't know anything about living on the coast, would you?"

Blair examined him like he was a cockroach she was about to crush with her sexy shoe, then pulled another paper from her folder. "I realize I'm a *simple girl*, so why don't you explain these bank deposits?" She smiled.

He sat up straighter, his body tense.

She slid the paper slowly in front of him, her fingertips still on the sheet as she leaned over, her eyes boring into his. "Multiple large cash deposits were made to a bank account you set up in your father's name. Your dead father, I might add." She stood up and lifted a perfectly teased eyebrow. "Why does your deceased father need one million dollars, Mr. Norfolk? Last I heard, the deceased only need a single coin to travel down the River Styx."

His eyes widened, and his mouth moved several times, forming and discarding words, before he finally said, "How did you find that?"

She gave him a withering smile. "I know. A simple girl like me, stumbling upon your hidden treasure. Maybe I'm not as simple as you think. There's another two million unaccounted for. Where are *those* funds?"

Norfolk's shoulders slumped, and he looked like a balloon that had been pricked with a pin.

She shrugged. "My client is a fair woman. We could bring this matter to the authorities—who would undoubtedly be *very* interested to know that you're committing identity theft as well as tax evasion—since this statement—" she tapped on the paper in front of him, "—*clearly* shows that you are not only depositing money, but withdrawing it as well." She paused and smiled. "But we'll let this go as long as you agree to a new deposition and come clean about everything, and I do mean *everything*, Mr. Norfolk, down to the hangnail you clipped yesterday morning." She leaned closer. "Have I made myself clear?"

"But I'm heading to the airport in an hour," he sputtered.

"Then I guess you'd better reschedule your flight." Blair turned her pointed gaze on Garrett. "Can we adjourn this until tomorrow morning? We obviously won't be able to wrap this up in the next hour, but I will expect those bank account locations, account numbers, and balances by the time you show up tomorrow."

Garrett was so turned on by her right now, and it was becoming increasingly impossible to hide it. *Totally professional, Lowry.* He glanced at his client. "Mr. Norfolk? Can you have the information ready in time?"

The man looked like he was about to jump across the table and throttle Blair. If he tried, it would be the last thing he ever did. But he gave a quick nod instead.

Garrett nodded. "You'll have them."

Blair gathered up her papers and tapped them on the table. "Thank you for your cooperation, Mr. Norfolk. I look forward to seeing you again tomorrow morning." She stood and turned her back as she headed toward the door.

"You bitch," he muttered under his breath.

Garrett's hands fisted, and he gritted his teeth.

Blair stopped and turned around to face him. "Whatever helps you fall asleep at night, Mr. Norfolk." Then she left the room, shutting the door behind her.

The court reporter was packing up her belongings when Norfolk turned his attention on Garrett. "What the hell was that? I thought you were my lawyer, not her assistant."

"Mr. Norfolk." Garrett's shoulders tensed as he forced himself to refrain from letting loose on the man. "If you ever speak to the opposing counsel so disrespectfully again, we will toss your case, along with your ass, out onto the street. Have I made myself clear?"

The man's eyes bulged. "But now I'm going to have to pay the bitch even more money!"

Garrett had had enough of this man. "This is *your* fault. You were required *by law* to provide all of your income and investments, and now that your wife's legal team has realized there were missing funds, you're about to pay out the nose. You would have been better off if you hadn't tried to hide it." The real question was how Lopez had missed it. Garrett had glossed over all the financial paperwork, focusing on the totals, because he'd presumed the fool would have done his homework. He intended to call Lopez as soon as he got rid of the asshole next to him.

Norfolk stood and pointed his finger at Garrett. "You're going to pay for this! I'm talking to your bosses."

"Go ahead. They'll tell you the same thing. That's if they don't fire you for committing illegal activities. We don't represent criminals."

The man's face turned red. "Do they know you want to screw that bitch who just eviscerated me? I saw you salivating after her. What will they say when they find out you let her get away with it because you want to get into her pants?"

Garrett's chest constricted as he stood, but he refused to show a reaction to his douchebag client. "I can assure you that I want to sleep with a long list of women, but I've never let that affect my counsel." He saw movement out of the corner of his eye and saw Blair's assistant in the now-open doorway. *Fuck.*

Her assistant shot him a glare, then moved toward the court reporter and said something in a hushed tone about coming back in the morning.

Norfolk stomped out of the room, and Garrett closed his laptop and stowed it in his bag, taking a deep breath to help himself calm down. He kept the assistant in the corner of his eye. Based on the protective way she'd kept him from Blair's office, he suspected she would run to Blair and tell her everything. Should he try to explain himself? His head told him to let it go, but a little voice inside him said that there was still a chance Blair wasn't happy with Neil. Maybe her assistant could give him some insight. He didn't expect her to spill her guts about her boss, but he was hoping he could read her body language when she answered him.

The court reporter headed out the door, followed by Blair's assistant. He caught up to her just outside the room.

"Melissa, isn't it?"

The woman turned to him in surprise, then her face lost all expression as she waited for him to continue. She reminded him of a slightly younger Blair.

"I feel like we got off on the wrong foot yesterday."

Her eyebrows rose, and her mouth tipped into a hint of a smirk. "No, I think everything happened as it should have."

"I don't know what Blair told you, but—"

"*Ms. Hansen* didn't tell me anything. You are a nonissue, so please don't give yourself any more importance than you deserve."

Ouch. She was good. "Okay, fair enough. But I'm sure she told you that I'm her fiancé's cousin."

She remained icy. "Really? What a coincidence."

"I just don't want things to be awkward this weekend." Damn, he was royally screwing this up. He sounded lame even to himself.

A patronizing smile lit up her eyes. "Don't you worry, Mr. Lowry. You don't have the power to affect anything in regard to Blair's wedding." Then she turned and walked down the hall.

"You got burned by the Ice Princess, huh?" a man behind him said.

Garrett spun around to face him. "What?"

"Melissa." He nodded his head in the direction she'd disappeared. "Her nickname around here is the Ice Princess. She's just as frosty as the attorney she works for—the Ice Queen."

Garrett couldn't believe the arrogance rolling off this guy. "Let me guess, you and half the guys in this office have asked one or both of them out and were turned down."

The guy's confidence wavered. "Well . . . yeah."

"So maybe instead of assigning them sexually degrading names, you should consider the possibility that they actually have good taste."

He stormed out of the office, leaving the stunned man behind. He was furious by the time he reached his car in the parking garage. First Norfolk, then the asshole in the hallway.

Brian Norfolk was sure to call his boss, but no one there would take his claim seriously. Garrett's reputation was too widely known for anyone to believe he'd alter his professional behavior to sleep with a woman. And even though he despised the man, he'd treated this case as he did all the ones he worked on—as if it were the most important one on earth. If anything, once Garrett let his boss know what had really happened, he might not have to worry about Norfolk at all. He hadn't exaggerated about their stance on illegal activity. It was bad timing that Melissa had heard his comment, which would only cement Blair's certainty that he was still a man-whore. But it was what that man had said about Melissa and Blair that burned him the most. Mostly because he'd been guilty of the very same thing in the past.

He put his hands on the top of his car, taking in deep breaths as he tried to calm down. It sucked looking into a mirror and seeing who he really was. And while he'd been sneaking judgmental glances for about a year now, it felt as if he'd just stepped in front of a full-length mirror.

Garrett Lowry was a dick.

Yet, dick or not, he still wanted Blair. He knew that with even more certainty now than he had six years ago, when he first asked her out for pizza on a cold February night in Columbia, Missouri. Maybe he didn't deserve her, but he wanted her nonetheless. He still had no idea what, if anything, to do about it. And then he did.

He pulled his phone out of his pocket and called his sister as he drove to his hotel, which was only a few blocks away.

"Garrett! Why are you calling me at this time of day?"

"Hey, Kelsey. Got time to talk?"

"Yeah, the baby's down for a nap."

"I'm stuck in Kansas City at Mealy Neily's wedding."

"I heard Nana Ruby suckered you into being a groomsman. I'm still not coming down until the rehearsal, so you're on your own." She laughed. "And I forgot about that nickname. I haven't seen him in years. I take it that it still fits?"

"More than ever."

"Well, I suspect you didn't call to gossip about Neil, so what's up?"

"You remember that woman I dated in law school?"

"Blair." Her tone turned serious. "You haven't mentioned her since you were a freaking idiot and broke up with her. What about her?"

"She's here."

"She's in the wedding party?"

"She's the bride."

She was silent for several seconds. "Oh, Garrett. I'm so sorry."

"I'm not sure I can do this, Kels."

"Why?"

"Why?" he repeated. "Because she's my ex."

"Cut the bullshit, Garrett. You and I both know the reason you called me instead of one of your douchebag friends is because you want the truth. Just say it."

Fear coursed through his blood. "Say what?"

"Bye."

"Wait! Okay." He took a breath. "I still love her. I've never stopped loving her. I was a fucking idiot to break up with her. I was an even bigger fucking idiot when I didn't go to her on hands and knees years ago and apologize for being a fucking idiot."

"Now we're getting somewhere." He heard the smile in her voice.

"Look, I've already had enough humiliation in one day without my sister adding to it."

"What else has happened to my wittle baby bwother today?" she said in a baby voice. She had never been one to cut him slack.

"If I'm going to seek advice from you, then that last question will have to be stricken from the record. Otherwise I'll never be able to take you seriously."

She laughed.

"When I told my firm I had to come to K.C. for the wedding, they asked me to handle the depositions for one of our associates' cases."

"Oh, God. She's the opposing counsel."

He'd always known she was smart, which was one of the reasons he'd called her for advice. "And she's fried my ass for two days now."

"I bet she's loving every minute of *that*." She sounded pleased.

"Whose side are you on?" he asked.

"Yours, but you have to admit she's completely entitled to hand you a slice or two of humble pie."

He pulled into his hotel parking lot and put the car into park. "What should I do, Kels?"

"Take it like a man. Don't be like Mealy Neily."

"That's not what I meant."

She was quiet again. "Is she happy, Garrett? I know it's difficult for either one of us to imagine someone being happy with him, but what if she is? Do you really want to take that from her too?"

"No, and I've already considered that. I have to go to this pre-wedding party they're having for family and friends tomorrow night, so I was hoping to talk to her before then. Looks like we have another deposition in the morning. Maybe I can catch her after that."

"You really want to wait that long?"

"I don't know when to talk to her, Kels. I finally got her alone for a few minutes yesterday, and I completely froze up."

"*Mr. Smooth* froze up? You've got it bad."

"Look, I know I do," he said, getting frustrated. "I'm asking for your advice on how to get her back."

"Okay, okay." Her tone was soft and soothing. "I'll help you."

"Thank you."

"First you have to accept that just because you want her back doesn't mean she feels the same. And since we are no longer ruled by caveman philosophy, you'll have to deal with that."

"I know, but I think she still cares about me."

"What makes you say that?"

"I ran into her in a hotel bar in Phoenix on Monday night. We were both stranded there because of the weather. She was drunk . . . and she rarely got drunk when we were together. Only when she was really upset. In any case, they didn't have a room for her, so I let her sleep in mine."

"Oh, Garrett. You didn't." Disappointment was heavy in her voice.

"No. I did *not*. Do people really have that low of an opinion of me?"

"Let's just say it's a reputation earned."

That was sobering. Especially coming from his big sister. He shook his head. "She fell asleep on the bed, and I told her I was going to spend the night at the airport. But she told me to stay. We slept fully clothed, but she pulled me close and said she missed me."

"Oh, my God. Please tell me that you did *not* sleep on top of the covers."

"Kelsey."

"Haven't you seen those news shows, Garrett? They're covered in all kinds of gross germs and bacteria."

"I'm pretty sure those are the same thing. And I need you to focus."

"Okay." She took a deep breath. "This is important. What were the exact words she used? For all you know she was drunk enough to have mistaken you for her dog."

"That is more disgusting than your hotel comforter story."

"You wouldn't say that if you'd seen them use the black light."

"Kelsey. I need you to focus. She said my name. She said, 'I miss you, Garrett.'"

"Wow." She was silent for several seconds. "I guess that means you can move to step two."

"Which is?"

"Proving that you're actually *not* lower than pond scum. The question is how do you pull off that deception?"

"Kelsey."

"Okay, I'm kidding. Kind of. You have to know you've been a slut, Garrett. And honestly, it's pretty gross."

He sighed. "Yeah. I know."

"Hey, admitting you have a problem is the first step, right?"

"Yeah. I guess."

"Are you sure you still love this woman? That was five years ago, Gar-Bear. She's changed. You've changed. And let's not discount that she's with Neil, whom you hate with a passion."

"I don't *hate* him. I just despise him."

"Hate. Despise. Whatever. But you can't ignore that Neil is

marrying your old girlfriend. That is bound to prick your ego, jealousy—whatever you choose to call it. Don't let that blind you."

"I will admit that the thought of her with Neil . . ." His voice trailed off, and he sucked in a breath, not letting his mind go there. "You do have a valid point, but I've been thinking about her for a while now . . . long before I saw her in Phoenix, found out she was Neil's fiancée, and was completely turned on by the way she eviscerated my client today."

"I really hope that was a metaphor, or I'll be forced to call the authorities, brother or not."

"Kelsey." He took a breath. "I've been pining for her since our breakup, and the last year has been even worse. Everyone around me is starting to settle down, which has made me realize that I want to share my life with someone too. So I've been serial dating—not screwing—women for the last year to try and find a partner who comes close to matching what I had with Blair, and it's just not happening. I fucked up when I let her go, Kels, and I'm going to pay for it the rest of my life. I deserve it, but I want her anyway, and as long as she isn't one hundred percent content with Neil, I'm going to try to get her back. Tell me what to do."

"Did you actually use the word *pining?*"

He groaned. "Forget it." His ego was bruised enough by the mere fact that he was asking his sister for help.

"Garrett, I'm sorry. I think you caught me off guard. That's probably the most real thing I've heard you say in a long time."

He paused, then said quietly, "I love her, Kels."

"Then I'll help you. But you have to do what I say."

"Why do I think I'm going to regret this?"

"Because it's going to be painful, but you want the girl, right?"

"More than anything."

"Okay," she sighed. "You two had fun when you were together, right? The weekend I spent with you in Columbia, you both laughed and joked around. Remind her of how much you enjoy each other's company."

He nodded. "Yeah, that's good."

"Prove that you're trustworthy now. You screwed her over, so you have to show her that you won't hurt her again. That one's going to be tricky since you're running out of time."

His chest tightened as he realized just how little time he had left. "Anything else?"

"Show her how much you love her. You two were in love once. Maybe you weren't the typical romantic couple, but it was obvious that you were crazy about her. There's no way Neil can give her that. He's too uptight."

He swallowed a lump of fear. He wasn't sure he'd be able to do all of this before Saturday.

"Good luck, Garrett," she said with uncharacteristic seriousness. "I hope you can pull this off."

"Thanks." He needed all the help he could get.

Thirty minutes later, Garrett pulled into the parking lot of St. Luke's Hospital. He'd already called his boss, who'd told him to go through with the new deposition. Later on, they would have a partner meeting to decide whether to keep Brian Norfolk on as a client. At the moment, he was ready to take his sister's advice.

He'd decided it was time to take a different tactic with Neil and discuss the situation with his cousin like adults. And the sooner the better. If he was convinced Neil really loved Blair— and vice versa—he'd give up his impulsive claim to the ring, beg Nana Ruby to let him out of the wedding, and leave Blair alone. But so far his limited observance suggested otherwise. God help him for hoping he was right.

Garrett had no idea how to find his cousin, so he went to

the information desk and asked for directions to his office. The woman looked up Neil's office number and gave him instructions on how to find it. He took the elevator to the correct floor and found the office without having to go through a receptionist. He raised his hand to knock on the closed door but lowered it when he heard arguing inside.

"You have to choose!" a woman shouted.

"Keep your voice down, Layla," Neil snarled. "Someone's going to hear you."

"We can't keep doing this! You're getting *married*, Neil!"

"Layla." Neil's voice was soft and soothing now. "It's only for a little while, and then we can be together."

"But you're getting married," she said, quieter this time.

"We'll work it out, baby. I promise. Meet me at my apartment later tonight. I'll text you when I leave the hospital."

Fury ran through Garrett's veins, followed fast by horror. Neil was cheating on Blair. It was her worst nightmare come true. Before Garrett could decide whether to bust the door down and punch his cousin out or duck away to reconsider the situation, the door opened.

A young woman with red, swollen eyes gasped as she nearly walked into him. Her hair was tangled, and she reached down to tug on the hem of her shirt. Neil stood behind her, his own hair disheveled, with a shocked look on his face.

"Garrett." The word carried a mixture of horror and surprise. "What are you doing here?"

The woman tried to get past Garrett, but he continued to block the doorway. "Getting more answers to my questions than I expected."

"Layla," Neil said after sucking in a deep breath. "Thank you for bringing those lab reports."

"My pleasure." But her voice suggested she was close to sobbing.

Garrett considered keeping her here, but his beef was with his cousin, not with the nervous woman in front of him. He stepped to the side, and she bolted past him.

"She's a nurse on one of the floors I work on," Neil said.

Garrett fought every instinct within him and went into attorney mode. *No emotion. No reaction. Just let him spill his guts.*

"She was bringing me some lab results."

Garrett remained still.

"How long were you outside the door?"

"Long enough."

"I know it looks bad, but we were discussing a patient." When Garrett didn't respond, he asked, "What are you doing here?"

"Catching you cheating on Blair." He was surprised he sounded so calm. So rational.

Neil tried to look indignant, but did a very poor job of it. "How could you think that?"

"Don't insult me, Neil." His words carried the first note of disgust he'd betrayed.

"I don't know what—"

"Cut the shit." He looked over his shoulder at the hospital personnel hurrying down the hall, then back at his cousin. "Would you like to have this conversation out here, or in your office with the door closed? What would happen to your sterling reputation if word got out that you plan to get married on Saturday *and* keep your girlfriend?"

Two nurses lifted their eyebrows and glanced at them as they passed.

Neil swallowed, his face turning pale. "Let's go inside and close the door." But fear filled his eyes as he ducked into his office. Neil was scared of him . . . or maybe scared of what the others would think of him if they knew the truth.

Good. He should be.

Garrett walked in and shut the door. Neil backed up, moving behind his desk without ever turning away from his cousin. "What difference does it make to you what I do?"

"I couldn't give a flying fuck what you do, but this affects Blair."

"*Blair?* Why would you care about Blair? You have no reason to care about her." Neil bumped into the bookshelf behind him and jumped with fright.

Garrett clenched and unclenched his fists at his sides. "*Wrong.* Blair and I dated in law school." God, what had he done? He was so caught up in the horror of the moment that he'd played his one ace in the hole.

Neil's mouth tipped into a satisfied grin. "*You're* the asshole that dumped her and then slept with half of law school."

Garrett didn't answer.

Neil's shoulders relaxed. "What are you so pissed about? You did the exact same thing."

"Not even close, you dickhead," Garrett seethed, moving closer. "I never cheated on her."

"You think breaking up with her to become the law school slut was any better? Between you and her father, she's messed up in the head. But she's such a cold fish in the bedroom, I can't say I blame you. Why do you think I'm sleeping with Layla?"

Cold fish? God, he really knew nothing about her at all. But his anger quickly turned to guilt and horror. He knew how much her father's philandering had affected her ability to trust men, but could he really have played a part in her unhappiness?

Encouraged by Garrett's silence, Neil continued, "I've convinced Blair that I need to keep my condo so I can be close to the hospital when I'm on call."

"So you can screw your girlfriend."

"Hell, Blair's at the office so long most nights, she'll barely notice that I'm not around."

"Why in God's name are you marrying her?" he asked in dismay.

Neil looked at him like he was insane. "The prestige. The stability. The money."

"The money? You're a doctor!"

Neil shook his head. "I'm an infectious disease physician. I'm employed by the hospital. By the time I've paid my bills and my student loans each month, I barely have anything left. But Blair's a hotshot lawyer on the rise. Do you have any idea how much money she'll make off those cases once she makes partner?" He grinned and sat on the edge of the desk, then waved his hand at Garrett. "You know. You do what she does."

Garrett stared at him in shock.

"Look, I'm not cut out to be faithful. If I'm with a woman for more than six months, I get bored. Hell—" he waved a hand toward Garrett, "—you know what I'm talking about. You move from woman to woman. Maybe it's a genetic trait." Mistaking Garrett's silence for approval, he continued. "Blair won't have a shot at partnership if she's not married, and I'll be taken more seriously here if *I'm* married. I'm doing her a favor. She demands little of my time, and I let her work her crazy hours without complaint. She doesn't really want kids, and neither do I. We'll live our mostly separate lives, and everyone will be happy."

"Except for the part where you're cheating on her."

Neil rolled his eyes in exasperation. "She's too busy to notice, Garrett. And she doesn't want to know. It's not like I'm depriving her of anything. She doesn't have much of a sex drive."

Garrett sucked in several breaths, fighting the rising urge to beat the shit out of his cousin. He was using Blair, and he wasn't even trying to hide it from him, *him* of all people. He'd heard enough. "Let me tell you what's going to happen."

Neil's eyes widened in surprise, then turned to amusement. "Okay."

"You're going to go to Blair tonight and tell her that you have changed your mind. That you aren't worthy of her or you don't love her. Or both. I don't care. But you *will not* tell her that you are cheating on her, or it will kill her."

Neil eyed him with disbelief. "Did you just listen to what I said? Why would I do that?"

"Because it's the decent thing to do."

"Why do you even care?" He gasped. "Oh! This is about the ring. You want me to break my engagement so you can get the ring."

"I don't give ten shits about that damn ring!" Garrett shouted. "Keep the stupid thing!"

A smile of understanding spread across Neil's face, and maliciousness filled his eyes. "Oh, my God. You still love her."

Garrett swallowed his rising nausea. He'd just screwed up big time. Now Neil would use this against him. "Don't do this to her."

"You *do*."

"At least one of us does."

Neil started laughing, and Garrett's anger grew. "I'm not going to break up with her. This is exactly what she wants. What she *needs*."

Garrett shook his head. "She needs someone to love her."

"And that person is *you?*" Neil laughed again. "You showed her how much you cared about her in law school, when you broke up with her and slept around. Besides, she's already told me that she doesn't love me. Not in the matrimonial sense. We care about each other in our own way. This is the perfect solution for both of us."

"You're crazy if you believe that."

Neil crossed his arms. "I really don't care *what* you think. I'm not breaking up with Blair days before her wedding. That would kill her just as much as finding out I'm sleeping with Layla. And if you don't know that, then you don't know her very well after all." Neil hunched over his computer and tapped a few keys, then straightened up. "Now if you'll excuse me, I have to visit a of couple patients before I leave for the day. As you know, I have plans." Then he winked.

Garrett's hands clenched at his sides. "What's to stop me from telling Blair everything you just told me?"

"She won't believe it if you do." Neil grinned. "Not that I have anything to worry about. You won't tell her. You just admitted you don't want her to know I'm sleeping with Layla. The only other thing you have over me is that I've told you I'm not passionately in love with her, and while I've never outright told her so, it wouldn't come as a surprise. Especially after she recently confessed the same thing was true for her."

The words penetrated the haze of his shock: *Blair doesn't love him.*

Neil ushered him out of the office and turned to lock his door. "I presume you'll be at the party tomorrow night."

"Yeah," he said absently. He was busy reworking his plan.

"Then see you later, cousin." Neil winked again, with the assurance of a man who had everything he wanted, then walked down the hall, whistling softly.

Garrett shot daggers at his back. Let Neil think he had the upper hand. He might have practicality on his side, but Garrett had something else . . . something that was certain to win Blair over.

He'd show her what she was missing.

Chapter Ten

THE LAST THING Blair wanted to deal with right now was a bridal shower. She'd found the entire day unnerving. The depositions had gone well, but while she'd savored the chance to give that egotistical prick Brian Norfolk his comeuppance, spending hours in a room with Garrett sitting across from her had nearly driven her insane.

The minute he'd walked in wearing his grey suit and ice blue tie, her heart had begun to race, and her face had flushed. She had spent most of her first deposition trying to convince her traitorous body that she wasn't interested in him. Then she'd spent half of the Brian Norfolk deposition thinking about Garrett naked and all the delicious things he used to make her feel.

She had to put a stop to this. She couldn't afford to be distracted tomorrow. Rowena Norfolk was paying her to make sure she got the best possible settlement—not to fantasize about Garrett stripping off her clothes and—

"Blair?" Melissa asked, standing in the doorway of her office. "The service is dropping off your car in about fifteen minutes. Do you want me to go secure it in the parking garage, or will you be leaving soon? Your wedding shower starts in forty-five minutes."

"Um . . ."

Melissa walked into the office. "Are you okay?"

"Yeah. Why do you ask?" she asked, flustered.

"You look flushed. Do you think you're coming down with something?"

She was coming down with something all right. Her libido was running full throttle after spending years in hibernation. "I'm fine. I'm just thinking about how the deposition went."

Melissa grinned. "You nailed him, huh?"

"He never even saw it coming." She took perverse pleasure in that part. The men always thought they were pulling a fast one on Blair, and she let them think it in the beginning. In fact, she planned it that way. She *wanted* them to underestimate her. It made the look of shock and horror even sweeter when she finally pulled her *gotcha* move. The euphoria of that moment would never get old.

Only today, the horror in Brian Norfolk's eyes wasn't what had made her breathless. It was the raw hunger in Garrett Lowry's eyes after she'd executed her plan to bring Norfolk to his knees.

He still wanted her.

She wasn't sure why she was so surprised. She'd sensed it the night before, particularly during the car ride to her condo. But even then, his desire hadn't been so blatant.

"Well?" Melissa asked.

"What?" She looked up at her with raised eyebrows.

"Your car . . . Are you leaving or staying later?"

To Blair's horror, her face flushed even more. "I'll leave. I need to run home and change before I head to Megan's mother's house."

"Megan's going to be there?"

Blair smiled. "Yeah, she flew in this afternoon."

"I like her."

"Me too." Blair glanced up at her assistant. "What are you doing tonight? You're welcome to come to this thing as well."

Melissa laughed. "Nice try. Showers of any kind give me hives. I'll go to the party tomorrow night, but a shower with games . . . no way."

"*Games?*" Blair asked in dismay. "Good God. We won't have to play any of those, will we?" But then she remembered Megan's mother was planning the party. Knickers was *certain* to have games. "I could force you to go, you know."

Her assistant chuckled. "Now you sound desperate. But don't worry. Libby and Megan will be there to help you through it."

"Yeah, but Neil's mother and sister will be there too. Not to mention Garrett's Nana Ruby."

Melissa's smile fell. "Neil."

Blair shook her head. "What about Neil?"

"You said *Garrett's* nana. Not Neil's."

Oh, shit. She had. "Garrett's nana. Neil's nana. She's the same person. It makes no difference." But it made every difference. What was he doing to her?

Melissa looked even less convinced than Blair, but she didn't call her on it. "Is there anything you need me to do to help you get out of here?"

"You cleared my schedule for the deposition in the morning?"

Melissa flashed a smug grin. "Your ten o'clock meeting has been rescheduled for Friday. It was that or schedule it for after your honeymoon."

"Good call." The meeting was with a potential new client, and she knew she could possibly lose her if she put off the meeting for another week. Women who'd been blindsided by their husbands' infidelity or unexpected divorce papers needed almost immediate reassurance that everything was going to be okay. And while Blair never deceived them, she always assured them that she'd fight for them. And she did. Still, Neil was bound to be unhappy. She'd promised to spend the day with his family, but now she'd have to come into the office for a few hours. Was the fact that she was secretly relieved a bad sign?

"And the court reporter has been scheduled?"

"Before she even left the building." Melissa hesitated. "In fact, before Mr. Lowry left the conference room."

Something in her tone held a sound of warning.

"What aren't you telling me?" Blair asked.

Melissa stared at her for several uncomfortable seconds. "I really like my job, Blair. I love working for you."

Blair released a sigh. She'd tried not to obsess about the threat hanging over her head. She couldn't do anything about it, and worrying about it was wasted effort. Still, the unknown loomed over her like a nuclear bomb's mushroom cloud. "I promise I'm doing everything I can to make sure we both still have a job next week. And if I have to move somewhere else, I'll try my best to bring you with me."

Melissa's jaw went slack. "Are you going to tell me what's going on?"

Oh, shit. She let out a long sigh. If anyone deserved to know, it was her assistant. "You can't tell a soul."

Melissa rolled her eyes. "Please."

Blair gave her a quick version of Ben Stuart's warning, but enough for her to convey the seriousness of the situation.

"So what are you going to do about it?" Melissa asked.

"I'm getting married on Saturday. That should take care of the issue. With any luck, you won't have to worry about your job."

"It's not that." Her mouth twisted as she looked down at her lap, then back up at Blair. "Maybe it would be best if I kept my opinion to myself."

Blair gave her assistant her full attention as warning bells went off in her head. "Your opinion about what?"

"Mr. Lowry."

Oh, shit. The way she'd been mooning over him had to be incredibly obvious. Melissa was a bright and perceptive woman. One of the many reasons Blair loved having her as her right-hand person. She often saw things that Blair didn't. "Go on."

Melissa bit her lower lip, then gave her a half smile. "Mr. Lowry was talking to his client when I went back in to schedule the reporter. He told him that he liked to sleep with quite a few women."

Blair fought the urge to suck in a breath. So Melissa thought she was a fool . . . "I see," she said in an icy tone.

"But in his defense—" Melissa said grudgingly, ignoring her boss's change in demeanor, "he said it after Mr. Norfolk accused Mr. Lowry of going easy on you because he wanted to sleep with you."

Blair cringed. "And what's the point of any of this?"

"I'm not sure really." Melissa clasped her hands together and fiddled with her fingers. "I probably shouldn't have mentioned it at all."

"Yet you did. Why?"

"I think he might have other motives."

Now she had Blair's attention. She leaned her forearm on the desk. "Why do you say that?"

"Because Mr. Lowry caught me in the hallway to try and make up for his attempt to weasel his way onto your schedule yesterday. I quickly shut him down, and as I walked away, Bill Hendricks ribbed him for being turned down by the Ice Princess. He also told Mr. Lowry that you're known as the Ice Queen."

Both women were aware of their nicknames, not that either of them cared. "So?"

"Mr. Lowry blasted him for calling us sexually degrading names."

Blair scowled. "Was he doing it for your benefit? Thinking you'd come back and tell me like you're doing now?"

"No," she said quietly. "I'd already rounded the corner and was eavesdropping. Mr. Lowry's voice was low, as if he was trying not to call attention to himself. He seemed furious."

Blair slowly spun her chair around so she could look out her window. What was Garrett up to? He claimed he hadn't known that she was Neil's fiancée, and maybe she was gullible, but she believed him. So what was his angle? Did he want one last round in bed with her before she married his cousin? "Thanks for the intel. I'll see if I can figure out how to use it to my advantage tomorrow."

"That's not why I told you."

She jerked her gaze up to Melissa.

Melissa's voiced softened. "I think he really cares about you, Blair."

Blair's heart skipped a beat, and she smashed down the hope that bloomed in her heart. Garrett Lowry had *destroyed* her. And here he was turning her life upside down mere days before her wedding. Even if she hadn't been on the verge of getting married to another man, it would have been madness to walk down that path a second time. "Fool me once, Melissa," she said with a bitter tone. "He had his chance, and he blew it."

"You really don't believe in second chances?"

"*No,*" she said with more force than she'd intended, perhaps to convince herself. "And what are you doing advocating that I sleep with him? I'm marrying Neil in three days." Blair stared her down with her iciest glare.

Most people would have crawled out the door, but Melissa

squared her shoulders and held her gaze. "I never said to sleep with him, Blair. Your mind went there on its own. Don't you think it means something?" Her voice softened, and she leaned forward. "I know you were thinking about him when I walked through that door, and you have never *once* looked that way while dating Neil. Not even in the beginning."

Blair shook her head, her chest tightening. Panic flooded her senses. "Our relationship isn't based on hormones. It's built on respect. You *know* that."

"But don't you want love, Blair?"

"I want lots of things, Melissa." Her voice shook, but it wasn't with anger. "I want to eat my weight in chocolate cake, but it doesn't mean I should. In fact, it's quite bad for me." She waved her hand toward her assistant. "Alcoholics crave a drink, but it doesn't mean they should have one."

"Blair."

"*No.* Wanting something doesn't mean you should have it. In fact, it often means you *shouldn't*." Melissa didn't respond, and Blair's panic surged, stealing her breath. "I'm getting married in three days, Melissa," she said again.

Understanding filled her assistant's eyes. "I know."

She shook her head, feeling herself lose control. "I can't trust him. I *don't* trust him. He walked out on me, and he had another woman in his apartment the very next night."

"Maybe it wasn't what you thought."

"*She was in her trashy underwear.*" Blair's voice rose, and her lack of control scared her more than her feelings for Garrett. What in the hell was happening to her?

Melissa was silent for a moment. "Everyone makes mistakes, Blair. Even you. Think about it." Then she stood and walked to the door. "I'll let you know when the car arrives."

The door shut, and Blair sucked in deep breaths, trying to calm down. She was dangerously close to crying, and she couldn't figure out why. She'd shed her tears over Garrett years ago, so she sure as hell didn't want to shed new ones now. Suddenly the room was too small. Her dress was too tight. Her life too confining. She stood and began to pace, chanting a mantra in her head. "I don't need him. It's going to be okay."

It was the very mantra she'd taught herself five years ago.

Tears burned her eyes, but she continued to walk her straight lines, and after several minutes passed, the numbness in her face and head slowly faded. By the time Melissa buzzed in to say her car had arrived, she was relatively calm. By the time she reached the elevator, she had convinced herself everything really *was* going to be okay.

That was, if she survived her wedding shower.

Chapter Eleven

GARRETT HIT his hotel bar as soon as he left the hospital. It was probably the least productive thing he could do, but he needed courage—not to mention inspiration—to go through with his nonexistent plan.

He was on his second beer when he heard a familiar voice behind him. "Do all you lawyers waste your money on fancy beer?"

He turned and a grin spread across his face. An older woman leaned on a four-legged steel cane, the feet covered with neon orange tennis balls. She wore a pair of jeans with a white knit shirt. Her face was covered with the deep wrinkles and brown spots of someone who'd spent most of her life under the sun. He knew for a fact that a few scars on her face were from skin cancer removals. Late seventies or not, she was stronger than anyone he knew. Yet she'd aged quite a bit since he'd seen her last. She looked thinner and more fragile. The cane she was leaning on didn't help. "It's not a fancy beer, Nana. It's Coors. Just like you taught me to drink." He'd give her a hug, but she'd never been big on displays of affection.

A grudging grimace tightened her mouth before she said, "I bet it came with a fancy price."

He couldn't argue with that. "I'm surprised to see you here. I expected you to stay at a Motel 6." Garrett's mother had told him the wedding guests were staying at this hotel, which was why he was here, but he'd never expected his nana to stay somewhere so upscale.

"Neil insisted I stay here, and the fool paid for it," she grumbled. "He's trying to show me how much money he has now. I suppose you're trying to flaunt it too."

He laughed. "You think anything that costs more than fifty dollars a night is too much."

"I don't need my bathroom covered in marble. It's a damn hotel room, not a church."

He chuckled and lifted his bottle in a salute. "How about I get you a fancy beer to drink? I'll waste *my* money."

She pondered it for a moment and moved to the stool next to him. "Why the hell not? I'm going to a damn wedding shower for Neil's bride-to-be. I've never met her, but if she's anything like my pompous grandson, she's bound to be a doozy. I'll need all the help I can get."

Garrett's eyes widened, and several questions ran through his head at once. He latched onto the one that seemed the most important. "Wait? You're going to a wedding shower? Tonight?"

"Ain't that what I just said?" She climbed up on the stool and looked around. "Where's my beer?"

Garrett flagged down the bartender and ordered her beverage.

"You and I need to have a chat." Her tone was hard, which prepared him for what she had to say next. He was lucky she hadn't led with it. "What the Sam Hill you been doin', boy?"

He steeled his shoulders. "Exactly what you asked me to do, Nana." He held out his hands. "I went to the dinner last night. I'm here like a dutiful grandson."

"Bullshit," she barked. "I gave you one assignment, and you blew it to kingdom come."

"Nana, I can explain."

"*Save it.*" She gave him a stern look. "Why do you want the ring?"

What should he tell her? He suspected she'd understand if he told her the truth, but then she'd try and take matters into her own hands. Nana Ruby wasn't known for her subtlety. "I guess Mom's rubbed off on me."

"So how do you plan to get it?"

"I told Aunt Debra and Neil that we'd let you decide."

She stared at him like he'd lost his mind, then started to chuckle. "I want you to take me to the shower tonight."

"*A wedding shower?*" Part of him was horrified, but he also knew Blair would be there, of course. "Okay."

Her eyebrows lifted in suspicion. "No argument?"

Garrett gave her a lazy smile. "I've learned it's pointless to argue with you, Nana Ruby. Besides, I'm already in enough hot water."

"Your mother's gonna be there."

His smile fell. "She said she was coming tomorrow."

Nana shrugged. "She changed her mind."

Well, that changed things. World War III was liable to break out at the party. He really didn't want to be part of it, but he could only imagine how Blair would handle it. It could quickly degenerate into Armageddon, with all three Lowry women pitted against one another. "Are they serving dinner at this thing?"

She pulled an envelope out of her brown purse. "Here. This will tell you everything you need to know."

He pulled the cream invitation out of the envelope and a rose scent hit his nose. The heavy paper was embossed with gold script and covered with flowers.

Nicole Vandemeer cordially invites you to attend a garden party wedding shower for Blair Myers Hansen on August 21 at

7:00 *p.m. Light sandwiches and tea provided. Wear pastel colored clothing to fit in with the theme.*

The bartender brought Nana her beer, and she took a sip. "You think it would taste better at this fancy price."

He grinned. "It doesn't cost that much more, Nana." He waved the invitation. "A garden party? Light sandwiches and tea? That doesn't seem like your kind of party."

"I tried to get out of it, but your aunt had a conniption."

"Why am *I* going?"

"Because I said so."

Maybe this was his punishment for claiming the ring, but if so, he would take it—any excuse to spend more time around Blair. Then another thought hit him. "Wait. Are other men going to be there?"

It would be incredibly awkward if he was the only man around, but he'd live with it if he could somehow get Blair alone.

She shrugged. "Hell if I know. Your aunt and your mother are meeting us there."

"So why didn't you go with *them?*"

"You back-talkin' me, boy?"

He shook his head. "No, ma'am. How did you know where to find me, anyway?"

"Your momma told me you were staying at this hotel along with the rest of the people from out of town, and where the hell else would I find you except at the bar?"

She was covering something up. Part of his job was to discern when someone was lying, and he'd studied his family to the nth degree. His nana rarely lied or dissembled, but whenever she did, her left hand clenched slightly. And right now she was making a loose fist. "I'm not one to typically hang out in bars, Nana, so that seems unlikely. Try again."

Her eyes narrowed to slits. "Don't you worry about the whys of it. Just do what I tell you."

He grinned. "Yes, ma'am. Do you want to get something to eat before we go? Light sandwiches don't sound too filling."

"Hell, no. Why would you want to throw your money away when we're about to get free food?"

He laughed. Nana Ruby was notorious for her penny-pinching. She was a practical woman who lived on several thousand acres of rolling hills and farmland in the Ozarks. She'd been widowed young and raised two girls on her own at a time when farming hadn't been profitable. The land had been in her family for over a hundred fifty years, and as she always said, there it would stay. The only way she'd made ends meet was to become thrifty. And although she had more money now, and the land itself was worth a bundle, she still held her coin purse with a tight grasp.

"Do you mind if I change clothes before I go?" He was still wearing his suit and tie, although he'd lost the coat, and his loosened tie still hung around his neck. "I'm sure you don't want to be seen with a fancy lawyer, and my suit doesn't exactly fit with the theme." He released a chuckle. That didn't sound like Blair at all. He bet she was bristling at the very idea of it.

Nana Ruby frowned, but he could see the hint of a smile on her lips. "Make it quick. I want to get this thing over with."

He hurried up to his room and changed into a pair of jeans and a light blue long-sleeved button-down shirt. Nana Ruby was bound to make some comment about how much time he'd taken with his appearance, but he was in for the fight of his life, and he needed to be prepared.

It was time to pour on the charm.

Chapter Twelve

BLAIR WAS sure she'd been dropped into the middle of hell. "Tell me—why did I agree to this again?" she whisper-hissed.

"Because you're a nice person?" Megan teased.

Libby laughed. "More like you couldn't figure a way out of it."

Blair should have known better. Nicole Vandemeer was known for taking everything to the extreme, and this wedding shower was no different. She'd decided on a garden theme, which for most hostesses might have meant purchasing a couple of pots of flowers, but Megan's mother never did anything half-assed. And while Blair appreciated that character trait more than most people, she was currently caught up in a floral explosion.

The Vandemeers' backyard was a magazine-worthy show-case even without the garden-themed decorations. It consisted of a two-tiered deck that led to an outdoor pool surrounded by a paver stone patio, but Knickers—as Megan and her friends called Nicole Vandemeer behind her back—had gone all out. Tall wooden poles were spaced about six feet apart around the perimeter of the patio. Organza was draped from pole to pole, and Mason glass jars full of fresh-cut flowers covered tables draped with white linen. A large serving table set off to one side was covered with an assortment of small sandwiches, fresh vegetables, and crackers, with wheelbarrows on either side stuffed full of flowers. Mason jars with flickering votive candles hung from the trees around the patio, and hundreds of white and yellow daisies floated in the pool.

"I'm pretty sure those flowers are going to screw up the filter system," Josh McMillan said from behind them as he walked out the back door and onto the deck.

Megan's face lit up, and she turned toward him. "That's what Dad said."

Blair scowled as he put an arm around Megan's waist and pulled her close.

"You weren't supposed to come to this, Josh. It's a *girls'* shower." Blair's relationship with Megan's husband had been rocky from the start. Blair had assumed that Megan, who was too trusting of people, was being taken advantage of by a preda-tor. No one normal would volunteer to be someone's fake fiancé, after all. The fact that Josh had turned out to be the real deal was suddenly irritating as hell. She couldn't care less about who came to her shower, but she didn't feel like seeing Megan and Josh together right now.

"Funny, that's what Knickers said." He laughed, then gave his wife a long kiss.

Without intending to, Blair found herself staring at them. "Yet you came anyway."

He lifted his face, keeping his gaze on his beaming wife. "Megan and I have been apart for two nights and three days. If she's going to be here, so am I."

"But the real reason he's here is because of Dad," Megan added. "Dad was worried about being outnumbered, so he wanted Josh to keep him company."

"Funny," Blair said dryly. "I'm sure Noah's in there too. How much company does your dad need?"

"Neither of them are staying for the shower, Blair," Libby

said, giving Megan a quick glance. "They'll be in the house with Megan's dad. If you want Neil to come over, why don't you give him a call? It's not too late."

"I don't *want* Neil to come." It came out a bit too harsh, but the thought of Neil showing up sounded suffocating.

Megan's eyes widened slightly, and she gave Josh a quick glance.

They must have come up with some secret eye contact language in the few months they'd been together, because Josh nodded and headed for the back door. "I'm going to check on your dad."

That pissed off Blair even more. "For the love of God, can't you two stop the goo-goo eyes for more than two seconds?"

"Blair," Megan said quietly. "What's going on?"

Her heart pounded an uneven dance in her chest as she looked into the earnest faces of her best friends. Could she tell them how Garrett's sudden re-arrival into her life had incited her conflicting feelings? They thought she was cold, calculating, and heartless, and honestly, how could she blame them? She'd spent the better part of ten years convincing them and everyone else around her that she encompassed all of those traits. The only person she'd allowed to see her truly vulnerable was Garrett.

The thought of him made her eyes burn and her chest constrict. *Oh, God.* Why did she have to feel this way? Her relationship with Neil was fine; it was steady, and it was reliable. Sure, the energy between them was lukewarm at best, and they didn't have sex very often, but she was fine with their arrangement. Besides, if Neil wasn't interested in sex, he was less likely to stray. The problem was that an increasingly vocal part of her craved a hot, physical relationship like the one she'd shared with Garrett. Did she really want to live the rest of her life with nothing but mediocre sex?

"Blair, darling," Knickers called out the back door. "Your mother-in-law's here."

Oh, shit. People were starting to arrive. She had to pull herself together. "*Future* mother-in-law," Blair muttered under the breath, then started to panic even more. She wasn't sure she could play nice with Debra Fredrick two nights in a row, let alone for the three more days she had left. Even worse, her mother hadn't been able to get off work, and now Neil's mother was likely to make a big deal of it. "I need a drink."

Something in her tone must have alarmed her friends. They exchanged a quick glance before Libby said, "I'll go get it."

"You better not bring me back some damn girly drink," Blair said, eyeing the punch bowl with radioactive pink liquid on the food table.

Of course, Debra had already slipped out the back door. Without any preliminaries, she reached into her monstrous purse and pulled out the Curse Kitty. "That will be a dollar, Blair."

Libby started laughing as soon as she saw the plastic cat bank. The top corner of the mailing tape had pulled away and was covered in black lint. "What in the hell is *that?*"

"It's the Curse Kitty, of course," Blair said dryly. "See? It's printed as plain as day on the label."

Debra's eyebrows arched as she turned her gaze on Libby. "And you owe me a dollar, too."

Blair sucked in a breath. "Debra, when most people meet someone for the first time, they start off with introductions— they don't extort them for money."

Debra's face flushed, but her mouth was pinched tight with determination.

Blair waved her hand toward Neil's mother. "Debra

Fredrick, these are my best friends, Megan McMillan and Libby St. Clair. This is Neil's mother."

Megan held out her hand. "Nice to meet you, Mrs. Fredrick."

Debra took her hand, beaming. "What a sweet girl you are." She looked down at the wedding ring on her hand. "You're married? That must be why you're so much more civilized than your friends. I keep hoping marriage will make Blair more domestic."

Libby coughed and shot Blair a grin. Thank God she'd thought to warn them about her future monster-in-law.

"How long have you been married?" Debra asked.

Megan smiled, but even a blind man could see it was forced. "Two months."

"Isn't that precious," Debra cooed, oblivious to the tension she was creating. "And when are you having babies? Soon, I hope? Maybe you'll be a positive influence on Blair."

"Debra," Blair scolded. "Megan just got married. She's not in any hurry."

"We're going to wait," Megan said, looking uncomfortable. "We'd like to spend more time together first."

Debra looked over all three women, her mouth pinched into a disapproving frown. "Aren't you girls worried about your biological clocks? You're not getting any younger, you know."

Libby struggled to keep a straight face. "Maybe I should get Blair her drink before we start planning a joint baby shower."

Debra shook the cat jar, the coins rattling against the sides. "Pay your dollar first. You too, Blair."

Libby grinned, trying not to laugh. "I don't have any money on me, so I'll just run inside and get some from Noah. I'm sure he'll appreciate this story." She snickered. "And I'll get you a drink you're guaranteed to like, Blair."

"Oh!" Debra's eyes lit up. "Will you get one for me too? Do

you have hard water? I'd love a hard lemonade." She nodded her head with approval. "I had a few last night, and they were so relaxing."

Libby burst out laughing. After hearing Blair rant about Debra being a teetotaler, she knew the older woman would never knowingly ask for an alcoholic drink. "One hard lemonade coming right up."

Debra held out her cat. "Blair."

Groaning, Blair pulled a dollar from the wad of cash in her skirt pocket and stuffed it into the slot. Everything in her screamed in protest, but she'd promised Neil to try her best to keep his mother happy. If she refused to go along with this damn kitty scheme, she was liable to create family drama. And with the partners watching, it was more important than ever to keep the peace. Thank God she'd asked Melissa to get her more dollar bills. She had a feeling the nine dollars she had left in her pockets wouldn't be enough.

The back door opened again, and a woman who looked remarkably like Garrett walked onto the deck. Debra turned to face the woman, and her face instantly scrunched with irritation. "Hello, Barb. Nice to see you dressed up, but I specifically told you to wear something other than blue and white." The sarcasm was heavy in her voice.

Barb glanced down at her white eyelet shirt and blue capris, then scanned her sister's plain blue and white dress. "Some of us choose *quality*, Debbie Sue. I'm sure that dress came from the Dollar General, while mine came from Target."

"It's *Debra* now," Neil's mother snarled. "How many times do I have to tell you that?" Her jaw tightened as she lifted her chin and gave her sister a haughty look. "And besides, I got this dress at Sears."

"You may call yourself Debra now because you think it'll help you sell more plastic containers for your Tupperware business, but it doesn't mean the rest of us have to follow suit. For heaven's sake, your birth certificate says Debbie Sue."

Debra's face turned red, and she looked like she was about to have a heat stroke.

"I wonder where Libby is with that lemonade," Megan murmured, looking around. "Or where my mother is. Maybe I should go check."

Blair grabbed her arm as she started to walk away, her nails digging into Megan's flesh. "Don't you even think about it."

Megan laughed, but there was a nervous hitch to it.

Barb shifted her attention toward Blair, and she resisted the urge to squirm under her scrutiny. "So *you're* Blair."

"You know who I am?" she choked out. In the year she and Garrett had dated, she'd never met his mother. They'd talked about going to see Garrett's family for Christmas, but they'd visited her mother instead. At Garrett's insistence. He'd claimed it was because his mother and aunt were crazy, but after their breakup, she'd wondered if he'd maybe been ashamed of her.

Megan gave her a concerned glance, and Barb looked at her like she was flat-out crazy. "Well, you *are* the bride." She laughed. "Debbie Sue and I may have our differences, but I know about Neil's fiancée."

"Oh," she mumbled, the blood suddenly rushing from her head. She was totally losing it.

"Blair, are you okay?" Megan whispered. "You don't look like you're feeling well."

"I'm fine."

Barb seemed oblivious to her distress. Turned out the two sisters weren't so different after all. "Debbie Sue says you're a lawyer," Barb said, glancing around the elaborately decorated yard. "My son Garrett is a lawyer too. What type of law do you do?"

"You mean *practice?*" Megan asked, sounding uncharacteristically snippy.

Barb waved her hand back and forth. "Whatever."

Blair's chest felt like someone was tightening a clamp, a quarter turn at a time, until all the air was squeezed out of her chest. Should she admit that she'd dated Garrett? Pretend she'd only just met him? "I . . . divorce law . . ." She wasn't sure she could spend the rest of the evening with Garrett's mother.

"Blair." Megan sounded more insistent. "Let's get you something to eat before the party gets started."

Blair shook her head. "Knickers'll have a fit if we mess up her display."

"Let her." Megan turned to the two sisters, who were currently shooting glares at each other that perfectly punctuated the sharply worded barbs they continued to volley. "If you'll excuse us, I need to get the bride-to-be something to eat."

"Of course. We'll get a chance to chat later," Barb said, then glanced around the yard, already dismissing the two women. "Where's Dena? Is she bringing her ill-behaved children with her?"

Debra bristled at her sister's remark. "Dena will be here soon. The real question is where is Kelsey? Too busy with her poor fatherless baby?"

"And that's our cue . . ." Megan looped her arm through Blair's and tugged her toward the food table, casting another worried look in her direction. "When was the last time you ate something?"

"I don't know. Lunch, I guess, but I didn't eat very much. Nerves."

Megan grabbed a pink paper plate and stacked it with a couple of quartered sandwiches and some raw vegetables. "What's going on, Blair? This is totally unlike you. You're never affected by nerves."

"I'm getting married," Blair said. "I think I'm entitled."

Megan didn't say anything as she handed over the plate.

Even Blair knew she was acting like a bitch. "God, I'm sorry, Megs. I've got a lot on my mind, and I'm taking it out on you."

"Now I'm really scared if you're apologizing." She grinned, but her eyes were full of worry.

Blair took a bite of one of the sandwiches. "This is delicious."

Megan's eyes narrowed. "Cut the crap, Blair. It's not like you to change the subject. You always tell it like it is. What are you hiding?"

The back door banged against the house, and Debra shouted a greeting from the middle of the deck. "Momma, you came! And Dena . . . you brought *him* with you?" Her voice trailed off.

Great. The infamous Nana Ruby was here.

And so were Dena's kids.

"I came across him as he was strolling up to the door," Dena said, speaking in a tight drawl that conveyed her disgust.

Dena was the spitting image of her mother, right down to the way she curled her upper lip when dealing with someone she didn't like, which not so surprisingly included a great many people. Blair still had her back to the deck, but she was certain Dena's lip had curled into her trademark sneer, and she was equally certain she knew who'd put it there. She wouldn't turn around yet. If she kept her back turned, maybe everything would be okay.

The high-pitched screaming of Dena's children made Blair cringe. "Great. Dena did bring her wonder brats. They're the most ill-behaved children I've ever met, but she thinks they're absolutely perfect."

"Blair," Megan reprimanded. "They're children." She eyed

them running all around the deck like a set of wild banshees. "They're bound to have some energy."

"Ha. We'll see if you're still saying that by the end of the evening. Ten dollars says one of them will end up in the pool."

"Only a fool would take that bet," a familiar male voice said from behind her. "And I wager you'd push one of them in to make sure you won."

A chill ran down Blair's spine. She clenched her fists at her sides, her fingernails digging into her palms. Oh, how she wanted to take in the sight of him, but she knew it would be safer if she kept her back to him while she tried to resuscitate her dying self-control.

Surprise filled Megan's eyes as she stared at the man behind Blair. "I didn't know my mother had invited any men to the party."

"Technically, she didn't invite any men," Blair said, wishing Libby would show up with her drink already. Hopefully it would be whiskey. "They just keep dropping in."

"Like that song about raining men." He laughed, a rich warm sound that sent a fire racing through her blood. "That sounds like a single woman's dream come true."

"No," she said, slowly spinning to face him, glad her anger had kicked into gear. It made it easier for her to fight her reaction to him. "Change it to *women*, and it sounds like *your* dream come true. *Player*." The word was jagged and sharp, like a weapon, but she needed the reminder.

He looked even more gorgeous than he had this afternoon. He'd changed into a pair of jeans that hung low on his hips, making her imagination run wild, and a blue button-down shirt. The top two buttons were undone, revealing a smattering of hair on his chest, and his long sleeves were rolled up, showing her that his forearms were just as built as they'd been when they dated.

Her body was about to combust.

"Blair," Megan said, jolting her back to reality. "I take it you know him?" Of course Megan hadn't met him. She'd run off to Seattle by then, running away from her mother.

So Libby hadn't squealed. She'd love to run away and hide from this, but running had never been her style. No need to start now. "Megan McMillan. Meet Garrett Lowry. My ex-boyfriend."

Chapter Thirteen

THE MOMENT GARRETT stepped onto the deck, his eyes instantly found Blair. Her back was to him, but he had no doubt it was her. He ignored the chaos his aunt and mother were creating while Nana watched with narrowed eyes. As far as he was concerned, he'd fulfilled his duty by escorting Nana to the party.

Common sense told him that pursuing Blair at her own wedding shower was a bad idea, yet he was as drawn to her as a plant was to sunlight. She'd changed into a simple peach dress and a pair of white sandals, and her hair hung down her back in loose waves.

The pretty brunette next to Blair watched him closely as he approached, probably wondering why there was a man at a wedding shower. Blair was talking about his cousin's bratty children, so he decided to lead with a joke about her pushing one of Dena's kids into the pool.

Smooth, Garrett.

Instead of stomping off, she introduced him to her friend Megan. The way she did it insinuated she didn't want him there, but he noticed a couple of things, both in his favor. One, the way she moved a little bit closer when she turned to him, as if she felt as helplessly drawn to him as he did her, and two, her eyes had turned that enthralling shade of sky blue.

But he was struggling to stay focused on the conversation. She was gorgeous in peach. It brought out the color in her pale skin and made her eyes even bluer.

He could tell her friend—Megan—had already heard about him, not that he was surprised. Blair had told him plenty about her two best friends. "Garrett from law school?" the woman gasped.

Blair's lips pinched as she slightly stuck out her leg and crossed her arms. "The one and the same."

Megan lowered her voice to a hiss. *"What's he doing here?"*

"Stirring up shit. What he does best."

"That's not entirely true," Garrett said. Her words didn't faze him—he knew that every second she continued to talk to him was a second in his favor. "I'm here because Nana insisted I bring her to the shower. You know me, Blair. The last thing I would choose to do with my night is play *what's in your purse* with a bunch of women."

"The fact you know a shower game is a bit frightening."

He shrugged. "I'm a wealth of information."

A sardonic smile lifted the corners of her lips. "Looks like you've done your duty. I'm sure you're free to leave."

He shook his head and gave her a smug grin. "No can do. Nana says she owns me for the night." He scanned the food table. "Got anything to drink besides that pink punch on the table? Is it spiked? I think we're all gonna need it if we're going to endure a couple of hours with my mother and my aunt."

He glanced over his shoulder at the argument still raging behind him. The hostess was probably regretting throwing this party right about now. Or at least inviting those two.

"You still haven't explained how *he* ended up here," Megan said, addressing them both.

Blair sighed, rolling her eyes. "It's actually very convoluted."

"Oh!" a woman exclaimed from behind him. "I arrived just in time. I love convoluted stories."

Blair's eyes narrowed, and if possible, she tensed up even more. "You already know the story, Libby."

The woman came to a stop at his side and handed Blair a red plastic cup. "I had to sneak that out of the house. The red clashes with Knickers' party colors, and I'm pretty sure whiskey doesn't fit in with the food theme."

"God bless you." Blair snatched the cup and took a generous sip.

And this was another sign in his favor. Blair had never needed a crutch to get through adversity—hell, she thrived on it—but now she was acting like she needed alcohol to get through the evening. Sure, Libby had left to get her a drink before he arrived, but he knew it wasn't his argumentative and judgmental relatives who were affecting her.

Blair only relied on alcohol when she was scared.

His relatives wouldn't scare her. Not Blair. He suspected she'd tolerated his aunt the evening before in an attempt at compromise. Something else scared her, and God help him, he hoped she was scared of what she felt when she was close to him.

"I also gave Neil's mother her lemonade. I know there's a story there, which I'm dying to hear, but this one gets my attention first." The black-haired beauty turned her dark chocolate eyes on him, looking him up and down like he was an amusing street corner act.

He would have known this newcomer was Blair's other best friend even if she hadn't been identified by name. Blair had always told him that men were drawn to Libby's exotic beauty and vivacious personality, so he kept his attention on Blair, smiling at her as though she were the only woman in the world. After all, as far as he was concerned, it was true.

"Aunt Debra is a fundamentalist teetotaler, and I suspect last night was her first encounter with alcohol, even if she didn't realize it," he explained. "It will be interesting to see if she gets as loopy as she did last night."

"I still don't know why you're here." Megan stared at him and planted her hands on her hips. "Somebody better start talking."

Blair gave him her iciest glare, but he grinned, undeterred. "I'm Neil's cousin."

"What?" Megan gasped, then tilted her head as she turned her attention to Libby. "Why don't you look just as surprised as I do?"

Libby shrugged, looking like a kid with a big secret.

"Oh, for God's sake," Blair groaned. "Now is not the time to get jealous of who knew what when. The important part is that Garrett has weaseled his way into our wedding and is now a groomsman."

Libby tapped her foot, wearing a smug expression. "He's also claimed the ring on her hand."

"*What?*" Megan gasped loud enough to draw the attention of some of the newly arrived shower attendees.

"I don't have time to deal with this." Blair took another healthy sip of her whiskey, then lowered the cup and shuddered, as though trying to lodge the practical, no-nonsense part of herself back into place. "It's a family ring. Garrett has claimed it belongs to him. His grandmother is supposed to sort it out." She took a deep breath and glanced down into her cup. "I suppose I'd better go meet her and break up the scuffle over *who wore it best*." She started to hand her cup to Libby, then hesitated and took another gulp before relinquishing it. "Hide this."

"I'm going to exchange the waffle iron I got you for your wedding for a flask," Libby teased.

Blair started to walk away, then turned around and pointed her finger at Libby. "You better not have gotten me a waffle iron."

Libby burst out laughing as Blair swung back around and started across the patio. Garrett was about to take off in pursuit, but Libby blocked his path. "I don't think so."

"Look," Garrett said, lowering his voice, "I know you want to grill me, and I promise to answer any questions either of you throw at me—later." He glanced over at Megan and nodded. "But right now I need to get over there and try to defuse a pending nuclear war."

Libby studied him for a moment, her eyes narrowing as she scrutinized him. "Fine. But I get to read your palm later."

Megan snorted.

"*What?*" He shook his head, sure he'd heard her wrong. "Sure. Whatever." Garrett would have agreed to anything so long as she willingly let him go. If they were still her best friends—and the way they hovered around her assured him they were—he knew they had influence over her. He was desperate enough to recognize he needed all the help he could get. "Done."

Libby made a shooing motion toward him. "Go."

He hurried after Blair, ignoring the adversarial conversation between the two sisters. He reached her just as she stopped in front of his grandmother.

"Nana," he said, as she stuck out her hand to the elderly woman. "This is Blair Myers Hansen. Blair, this is Nana Ruby. The *true* instigator of all the trouble in this family." He winked at the older woman. "She taught me everything I know."

Blair shot him an irritated glare before returning her attention to his nana, who cracked a grin.

"So you're the bride everyone is making such a fuss about." She looked Blair over.

Blair bristled, and her eyes turned frosty. "I need this wedding to go off without a hitch, so let's get this ring issue sorted out as quickly as possible. And if we need to replace the ring before the ceremony, I'd prefer to know sooner rather than later."

Nana laughed, and Garrett was surprised to hear it was genuine. Blair gave her a look of uncertainty.

"You're not what I expected," Nana said once she'd settled down.

"And what did you expect?"

"Some hoity-toity, dainty woman who thinks the world revolves around her."

"Is that how Neil painted me?"

Rather than answer, she gave Garrett an inscrutable glance. "I like you," she said, turning back toward Blair. "Do you want the ring?"

Blair blinked in surprise. "I . . ." She swallowed. "It's Neil's."

But not hers. Garrett was certain his grandmother had picked up on her peculiar wording too, because she studied Blair for several moments. "I haven't decided that yet."

Blair groaned. "Why does this family have to be so difficult?"

As if to punctuate her statement, the argument between Nana Ruby's two daughters rose in pitch. Nicole Vandemeer, the woman who had greeted Garrett and Nana at the door, was standing between the women trying to get them to reach a truce. Her eyes were wild with frustration.

Nana put two fingers in her mouth and released a loud whistle that filled the air and stopped everyone mid-word or mid-movement. "That's enough nonsense, Debbie Sue and Barbara Mae," Nana shouted. "I raised ya better than that.

You're guests here." She waved to Nicole. "You get on with what you need to do, Mrs. Vandemeer."

"It's Debra," his aunt grumbled.

Nicole smoothed back her hair and took a deep breath. "Oh, dear. Why doesn't everyone help themselves to some refreshments, and then we'll start the games."

Nana hobbled over to the food table, muttering about needing a Coors, and everyone else followed, leaving Blair alone with him on the deck.

"Games?" Blair groaned under her breath. "Shit."

Garrett chuckled. "How bad could it be?"

She gave him a baffled look, as if he'd just claimed to be a Martian. "What are you doing? Why are you here?"

"I told you, Nana Ruby made me come."

"So why don't you go inside with the men?"

"What men?" A shot of worry worked through his veins. Was Neil here after all?

She groaned. "Megan's dad and her husband Josh. And for some reason, Noah, Josh's brother, came along. He follows Libby around everywhere she goes, even though she has a—" Letting the sentence break off, she shook her head. "Never mind. I don't know why I'm telling you anything."

"If you're marrying Neil, that means we'll be seeing each other at family functions. That typically involves small talk." He hadn't considered it before, but it was true. If he did lose her to Neil, he wasn't sure he'd be able to sit around making small talk with her on Thanksgiving.

"I don't have time to small talk with you. I need to socialize." Yet she didn't move from her spot. Not that he was surprised. She had always hated this kind of thing.

"This doesn't seem like you, Blair. A wedding shower? We used to make fun of this shit," he teased.

She released a long sigh. "I tried to get out of it, but Knickers is relentless."

He laughed. "Knickers?"

"Nicole. Megan's mom. We nicknamed her Knickers back when we were kids." She glared at him. "But she doesn't know, so don't you dare call her that."

He grinned. "Wouldn't dream of it."

"Good." She scanned the twenty people covering the patio. "We're grown-ups now, and apparently this sort of thing goes with the territory."

"And your wedding? It's not at a courthouse like you always said you wanted. Nana said it's going to be in a big fancy church."

"You should have gotten an invitation with all the details," Blair said. "Debra insisted on inviting everyone she knew to the wedding of her doctor son and his lawyer fiancée."

He cringed. "I saw Neil's name on the invite and tossed it into the trash before reading anything else. Including your name." He worried about delving into dangerous water, but nothing risked, nothing gained. "You really didn't realize it was me when you sent it out?"

"I didn't address them. My now-absentee wedding planner did. Debra sent her a very long list, which I didn't really inspect."

"So a big, fancy wedding, huh?"

She stiffened slightly. "The partners expect it."

To anyone else, it might have gone unnoticed, but to him that statement filled in a missing puzzle piece.

"Blair!" a young woman called out as she came through the back door carrying a small pink box topped with a large white ribbon. "I haven't seen you in ages."

Blair smiled, but Garrett could see it was forced. "Ashley. I think it was our five-year reunion."

Ashley gave Garrett a thorough once-over and beamed. "It looks like you've done very well for yourself. You two make a striking couple. I wholeheartedly approve."

"What?" Blair asked in confusion that quickly turned to alarm. "Oh, no. This is Garrett Lowry. The cousin of the groom. Neil isn't here."

"Oh, that's unusual." Ashley's mouth twisted. "And unfortunate. Unless the groom is even better looking." She winked.

Blair glanced down at her friends. "Libby and Megan are over there. You should go say hi."

Garrett leaned into her ear and whispered, "She thinks we look good together."

Blair turned her head to look up at him, her mouth closer to his than seemed appropriate. Conflict raged in her eyes before they hardened. "A relationship needs to be based on far more than looks."

God, it was hard to be this close to her without touching her, but he was sure she'd bolt if he did, not to mention the whole issue of this being her wedding shower for her marriage to another man. "I agree. But I think there's more to it than compatibility."

"You mean sex?" she asked. It was obvious she was trying to sound disgusted, but her words came out breathless at the end.

Jesus, from the way her eyes dilated, he could tell she was thinking about them in bed. He had to steer the conversation in a different direction soon, or he'd embarrass himself. He shifted his weight slightly. "Well, yeah, amazing sex is a given, right?"

"Not necessarily."

He was tempted to let her statement pass, but he just couldn't. "I suppose that could be true for people who aren't very sexual, but some people have a natural fire, don't you think?" Then, before she could counter, he shifted the topic.

"But I didn't just mean sex, anyway. There are other important considerations in a relationship."

"Like what?" she asked without sarcasm.

He forced himself to rein in his hope. "The two people should know each other's hopes and dreams. The little things that make each other happy. They should share inside jokes and secrets. And love." He tacked it onto the end, making it sound like an afterthought.

"Love," she scoffed.

"Of course love." He kept his tone light. "Love is the foundation on which the entire relationship is built. A relationship is *nothing* without love."

Sadness flooded her eyes, and she looked close to crying for a moment. Then her body stiffened. "I think we need ice." And with that, she bolted for the back door.

He considered letting her go. He'd clearly struck a nerve, and he didn't want to agitate her too much at a party that was being held in her honor. But time was running out, and now that he'd peeled back a section of her protective layer, he needed to keep digging if he hoped to get through to her.

He went through the back door and found her in front of the sink holding onto the counter, panic in her eyes.

"What do you know about love, Garrett Lowry?" she said, looking at the side yard through the window. "You found our love so disposable you were willing to toss it aside to sleep with someone the very next night."

He gave up all pretense of playing it cool and spanned the room in four footsteps to stand at her side. "I didn't sleep with her, Blair. I swear to God. I was an idiot the night I walked out and an even bigger idiot when I got so drunk with my buddy that I couldn't drive. I let Jody take me home."

"I don't believe you."

He held out his hands. "Why would I lie now? Why not

just own up to it? I won't deny I slept with quite a few women afterward, so why would I lie about that?"

"I don't know." Her voice cracked.

Time to go for broke. "I've spent five years regretting both of those nights. If I could give up everything I've achieved in the last five years to go back and live that first night over again, I'd do it."

She shot him a look of indecision.

"I was too stupid to see that you were lashing out because something had happened. I'd gotten a bad grade on my paper—the one I'd worked on relentlessly for two weeks—and I was mad and upset. All the way to your apartment I kept thinking about how much I wanted to see you. I knew you'd help me put everything in perspective. Then I walked in, and you got pissed because I hadn't picked up laundry detergent for you, and the next thing I knew we were both yelling, and before I could even process what was going on, I'd packed my things and left."

"I didn't know," she whispered as she turned to face him.

They were inches apart, and without thinking, he reached for her face and cupped her cheek. "And I didn't know about your dad. Oh, God, Blair. You have no idea how devastated I was when I heard."

She closed her eyes and leaned into his palm.

He wrapped his other hand around her back and slowly pulled her to his chest. "Nothing happened with Jody. I swear to you. She brought me home. I stumbled inside my apartment, and before I knew what happened, she kissed me and then stripped off her clothes before I pushed her away."

"How can I believe you?"

"If I wanted to break up with you, why would I have run after you? Why would I have stood outside your door half the night, begging you to let me explain?" His thumb stroked her jaw, and he couldn't believe she was in his arms again. Could it be this easy? "I was crushed, Blair. I didn't have a clue how much I really loved you until I lost you. I had this gaping hole in my heart. I knew you'd never give me another chance, so I tried to find other ways to fill it. But no one ever came close to you."

Her eyes fluttered open, and she looked at him with such longing it stole his breath.

"I love you, Blair. I *never* stopped loving you."

She lifted her hand behind his neck and kissed him, her lips soft on his, hesitant. His tongue slid along her lower lip, and her mouth parted. Her grip on his neck tightened, and her tongue joined his as she dropped her guard and lost herself to the moment.

The fire that swept through his body caught him by surprise, and he pulled her closer, his hand sliding from the small of her back down to her ass and pulling her against his pelvis.

She groaned, and he felt her free hand grabbing his own ass, pulling him closer.

The sound of a doorbell barely registered in his head, but the voice he heard several seconds later sent ice water through his blood.

Neil was at the front door.

Chapter Fourteen

WHAT THE HELL had she done?

She heard Neil at the front door. "Hey, Josh. I didn't know you were here," he said. "I thought I'd crash the party."

Shit.

Blair froze in Garrett's arms and tried to jerk away from him, but he held her tight.

Josh answered, "Bart invited me over to hang out in the basement and watch a game. He was feeling outnumbered. Noah's here too."

Panic flooded her, and she pulled against Garrett's vise-like grip. "Let me go!" She couldn't let Neil find her like this. Oh, God. What had she done?

He dropped his hold, and worry filled Garrett's eyes as she took several steps backward.

"You have to break off this wedding, Blair," he insisted in a whisper. "Tell him when he comes in. We can tell him together."

Lifting a hand to her temple, she shook her head. "This is all happening too fast. I have to think." She couldn't just throw away a two-year relationship over a hot kiss—and from a man who'd slept with half the women in law school after their breakup. This was ridiculous. She was getting married in three days.

But her panic increased, stealing her breath. How could she face Neil after what she'd just done?

"They're out back," Josh said, and moments later, Neil stood in the doorway with Megan's husband.

"Oh, hey, Blair," Josh said in surprise. "I didn't know you were in here. Look who just turned up."

Neil surveyed the both of them. He smiled, but his eyes were cold as his gaze swung from her to Garrett and back.

"What are you doing here?" Blair asked, placing her hands on the kitchen island to steady herself, her peripheral vision darkening. She wasn't a fainting kind of girl, but the situation seemed to warrant it.

Neil's eyes pinned hers. "Funny, I was wondering what *Garrett* was doing here."

Garrett gave him a lazy grin. "Nana made me come with her."

"So I see all the guys are here," Neil said, his jaw tightening. "Why didn't you ask me to come, darling?"

She knew that look. He was pissed.

Suddenly Noah appeared behind Josh. "Bart needs another beer," he said, slapping a hand on his brother's shoulder. His eyes widened as soon as he sensed the tension in the kitchen. "Whoa."

"Noah, how about you go out back and grab Megan for me." Josh tried to sound casual, but no one in the room was fooled. "Hey, Neil," he said. "There wasn't any mal-intent here. Bart invited me and Noah today, and Garrett's grandmother insisted that he come."

"She's *my* grandmother too." Neil's voice was tight. He walked around the island toward Blair.

Several feet now separated her and Garrett, but she could still feel him tense up.

Neil stopped next to her, leaving a foot between them.

"Where's my kiss hello, darling?" He wrapped an arm around her back and leaned down to kiss her, but she couldn't bear to kiss him after the way she'd just thrown herself at Garrett. She turned her head at the last moment, and his mouth skimmed the corner of her mouth.

"It wasn't intentional, Neil," she said, trying to keep it together. "Why did you stop by?"

"I was missing you, of course."

Her gaze shot up to him in surprise. That was a bald-faced lie. He rarely told her he missed her, and even then, it was only after a separation of multiple days. But he took the opportunity to plant a lingering kiss on her lips. His mouth felt rough and possessive against hers, as if he were staking his claim. She resisted the urge to pull away, and part of her wondered why she even *felt* that urge. Was it because his kiss left her cold compared to Garrett's fire? Or was it out of guilt?

"Is my cousin bothering you?" Neil murmured after he lifted his head, still looking down into her eyes.

Her face burned under his scrutiny.

"I can have him kicked out. I *am* the groom."

Garrett crossed his arms over his chest. "I thought you had *other* plans tonight, Neil."

Neil's nostrils flared, and some unnamable emotion glowed in his eyes. *Oh, God.* He either knew or suspected she'd behaved inappropriately with Garrett. "My plans fell through. Besides, I know where my true priorities lie."

"Funny how quickly they've changed. What spurred that?"

Blair glanced from one of them to the other, trying to understand their secret exchange, but the room was spinning and she could hardly stand, let alone form a rational thought.

Garrett took a step toward them, his hands fisted at his sides. "Don't be so sure of yourself. There's something we need to tell you."

Neil's eyebrows rose. "*We?*" Then he looked down at her, demanding an answer.

She pulled free of his hold and took a deep breath. In her office and in the courtroom, she was the epitome of confidence and control. Where was that woman now? But everything felt jumbled and out of sorts in her head. For the first time in her life, she literally had no idea what to do. "I . . ."

The back door opened, and Libby and Megan hurried through, worry in their eyes. Noah trailed behind them. "Blair, there you are," Megan said, rushing over to her. "It's time to open presents."

Libby intercepted Garrett. "I think you two should hang out with the guys. What do you think, Noah?"

"Yeah." Noah nodded. "There's a Royals game on."

"Sure, he should join you," Neil said, his anger unmistakable. "But I'll be staying with *my fiancée.*"

"Oh, I don't know." Megan smiled, but it was forced. "It's girls only, Neil."

His jaw tightened. "If Nana insisted that Garrett come, I'm sure she'd want her other grandson here too."

Megan looked from Neil to Josh, her eyes wide.

Some of Blair's senses began to return, and she realized she had to get things under control. "Megan's right, Neil." She looked up at her fiancé. "There's a whole bunch of women out there along with your sister's two kids. But if you'd rather come outside and play stupid shower games, then by all means, feel free."

"*Blair.*" The disbelief in Garrett's voice sent a stab of pain through her chest, but it wasn't enough to get her to react. She couldn't do this right now. She couldn't spontaneously make a decision that would affect the rest of her life. Not when the future of her job depended on this wedding. The very fact that she was prepared to consider calling it off after one mere kiss scared the shit out of her.

She let Megan lead her outside and was surprised to see that everyone was sitting at the small tables around the pool now, eating and drinking. Presents and cards covered a small table to the side of the food table.

"Blair's going to open gifts now," Megan announced as her shoes clacked across the patio.

Knickers was shifting the food around on the platters, but she bolted upright at Megan's declaration. "The presents aren't until after the games."

Megan released her hold on Blair and pulled a chair over to the presents table. "The schedule's changed. She's opening them now."

"Neil!" Debra squealed as she glanced up and saw her son trailing behind the two women. She shot out of her seat and nearly tripped on the chair leg. "Thank goodness you're finally here."

Blair wanted to kill the woman. She was obviously the reason Neil had shown up. She hadn't been able to accept the fact that Garrett was present and Neil wasn't. *She* was the reason Neil had almost caught her in a compromising situation. But that wasn't really true, and she knew it.

Blair was a cheater. And she wasn't sure she could live with that title.

To make matters worse, that damn kiss kept replaying over and over in her head, and try as she might, she couldn't banish it to the dungeon with all the other thoughts and feelings that had threatened to consume her over the last ten years since her father had abandoned her mother. Her mind was still reeling from the events of the last ten minutes, trying to sort through the mess of emotion. Give her facts and she could cut through them like a world-renowned surgeon with a scalpel. But feelings?

Did Garrett really still love her? And if so, what did it mean?

All she could process at the moment was that her world was toppling over like a tower of blocks, and she had no idea how to stop it.

Nana Ruby's eyes narrowed as she glanced up at her grandson. "What are *you* doing here? Where's Garrett?"

Neil slid next to Blair. When he spoke, his voice was tight. "He's in the house. Where he belongs." He wrapped an arm around Blair's waist and pulled her hip against his. "I'm here to open presents with my bride." He leaned over and kissed her again, setting off a round of oohs and awws from the gathered audience. Blair just stood next to him, still in shock. He was showing more public displays of affection than usual, which was throwing her off almost as much as everything else that was going awry in her life.

"Garrett's here somewhere," Debra said, trying to untangle herself from a purse handle.

"I know," he said coolly as his hand dug tighter into her hip. It was meant to show her that he was still there—seething but still there. She found it suffocating.

"Garrett's in the house drinking a beer with Noah," Josh said, walking up behind Neil. "Not to worry. He's still here."

Blair shot him a look, surprised by his confrontational tone.

"Debbie Sue," Nana barked. "Sit down before you fall into the pool."

Debra began to giggle, and Dena gave her a strange look before turning her attention to her restless children.

Clearly determined to single-handedly defuse the situation, Megan walked over and grabbed Blair's wrist. "Present time," she said, pulling Blair away from Neil and leading her over to the chair she'd set out.

When Neil started to drag a chair over to her, Megan held up her hand.

"Oh, no. You get to sit with all the other women."

Josh dragged over two chairs and pointed to one of them. "Here you go, buddy."

"But they're my presents too. Don't I get to help open them?" He flashed a charming smile to the gathered women.

"That's not how showers work," Josh said, pushing Neil into the chair. "It's all about the woman. You wouldn't want to steal Blair's limelight, would you? You want her to be happy, don't you?" The questions were barbed enough to surprise Neil into compliance. He sat down; Josh sat next to him.

"Isn't that sweet?" one of Blair's former high school classmates asked. She couldn't even remember the woman's name. Why had she been invited? Then again, this was Knickers's party, not hers, so it made sense that Megan's mother had invited the most perfect, and perfectly coiffed, people she knew —excluding Neil's family, of course. Ordinarily, Blair would stand at the periphery and laugh at a spectacle like this, but she was stuck firmly in the middle of it, along with her confusion over Garrett and how to handle Neil, and she wasn't laughing at all. Her brain was currently too stunned to process anything.

She was completely out of her perfectly organized comfort zone.

What was perhaps most startling of all was Megan's behavior. While Blair had always been the natural leader of the trio, Megan was the take-charge girl in a crisis, and she was clearly in disaster recovery mode at the moment. What had Noah said to make her take control? Had her . . . *indiscretion* with Garrett been so obvious that everyone could tell? She was about to die of embarrassment, an emotion she found strangling.

She looked up at Megan with pleading eyes. "I don't think I can do this, Megs," she whispered. The quiver in her own voice frightened her.

Megan squatted a few inches. "You can. And you will. If we cancel the party, it's going to raise red flags. We'll get through it as quickly as possible, and then we'll figure everything out. Okay?" The understanding and love in her friend's eyes was probably the only thing that could have soothed her. She found herself nodding like a puppet whose strings had been pulled. The thought of being weak and malleable provided a spark of anger. She was familiar with anger. Anger was an old friend who'd kept her company more than half her life. Anger she could use. She grabbed hold and held tight before it slipped under the current of her other emotions.

Megan watched her face, then slowly shook her head and whispered, "Don't you dare lash out at people, Blair. You'll only make things worse. Libby and I are going to get you through the next hour—then when we're alone, you can call the two of us every nasty name you have tucked in a file in your brain." She smiled. "Trust me. Okay?"

Placing her trust in another person felt unnatural to her, and she could honestly say she never had. Not even with Garrett all those years ago. But she was drowning, and Megan was offering her a lifeline. Megan and Libby had been her best friends since kindergarten. They loved her and would do everything in their power to help her.

As if sensing her thoughts—and her need—Libby came out the back door, her face a study in determination. She'd gone into defense mode too. Yes, it was time to rely on her friends. After all, if she couldn't trust her two best friends, who could she trust?

"Okay."

Megan's eyes softened. "Thank you." Then she grabbed a

gift bag off the table and handed it to Blair. "Mom, do you want to keep the list of gifts?"

Megan's mother glanced around, looking even more flustered when she realized the party-goers were watching Blair in silent curiosity. "But I need to get the board to make her bow bouquet."

"Bow bouquet?" Blair asked in alarm.

"*No bow bouquet*," Megan said, picking up a pad of paper and a pen from the gift table. "Start writing."

Blair went out of her way to avoid showers of any kind, but it didn't take a fool to realize the present opening was proceeding at a much faster clip than it did at most parties. She knew she had her friends to thank for that. As soon as Blair opened the last gift—a twenty-dollar Target gift card from the high school friend she couldn't remember—Knickers looked up at the group and beamed.

"Time for games!"

Shoot me now.

Chapter Fifteen

GARRETT WATCHED in shock as Blair walked out the door and returned to her wedding shower, leaving him standing there.

"We need to chat," Libby said, grabbing his arm and dragging him to the breakfast table.

He resisted her tug. "No. I need to get out there."

"Hey, Libs. I've got this." Noah clapped a hand on Garrett's shoulder. "Why don't we go outside for a minute?"

"I don't think so," he said through gritted teeth and took a step toward the back door. He had to put a stop to this.

Noah blocked his path. "Trust me, dude. If you want the girl, you don't want to do this right now."

Garrett blinked in surprise.

Noah smirked. "It's not that obvious to anyone else . . . yet. But if you go over there now, everyone in the whole damn party will know. And that's not how you want this to play out. And I *know* that's not how Blair wants it to play out." He grabbed two beer bottles out of the refrigerator, then motioned to the door to the living room. "Come on."

Garrett studied both of them, unsure of their motives, but his mind was spinning too fast for him to think clearly.

"Do you still care about her?" Libby demanded, hands on her hips.

"What?" He blinked. So much was happening at once, he wasn't sure he should answer. He felt like any hope of getting Blair back had just been yanked out from under him.

Josh, who'd been standing at the periphery of the room for most of the last five minutes, stared out one of the back windows, his jaw tight. "I don't trust that prick, and I don't want him out there with my wife." Then he stomped out the door.

Garrett could only presume the *prick* was Neil, which eased some of the tension from his shoulders.

Without warning, Libby snatched Garrett's right hand and pulled it closer, her thumb brushing his fingers open.

He considered pulling free until he remembered her earlier demand to read his palm.

Her index finger traced his hand, following lines for several seconds until she looked up into his face. "When you love, you love for keeps. Is she the one?"

Noah chuckled as his brother disappeared out the door. "Libby, just look at him and you've got your answer. Let me handle this."

She studied him for another second before dropping his hand. "Okay."

With a grin, Noah handed one of the beer bottles to Garrett. "Libs, go out and keep an eye on things—Josh included. This might take a little bit, but come get me if you need me."

Libby gave them both a once-over, then pointed a finger in Noah's face. "You better not screw this up."

He laughed, completely unthreatened, then clapped an arm around Garrett's shoulders and led him through the living room and out the front door.

"This some elaborate ploy to kick me out?" Garrett asked, half-joking.

"Nah. Josh and I could have easily kicked your ass out the door. We wouldn't need a ploy." He settled onto the top step and opened his bottle, then took a long drag.

Garrett sat next to him, putting his hands behind his head. He wasn't sure what Noah's purpose actually was. He had one, Garrett was sure of that, but he wasn't about to let down his guard. Now that Blair had kissed him with that same fiery passion he remembered, he wasn't backing down. Not a chance in hell.

Noah leaned his elbows on his knees and tilted his head to look at him. "So you love her, huh?"

Was it so obvious? "Yeah."

"Do you think she loves you?"

Garrett didn't answer, sorting through his thoughts. From the way she'd kissed him back, he thought there was a definite possibility. But she'd walked out on him no more than a couple of minutes later. "I don't know. This morning I would have said no. I broke her heart five years ago. I definitely don't deserve her. But now . . ."

"Hey, who does deserve the love of a good woman?" Noah asked, but it sounded self-deprecating. "But it doesn't mean you should give up. Otherwise hardly anyone would get married. So what are you going to do about it?"

Garrett sighed and ran a hand over his head. "My sister told me to show her I'm not an ass anymore, but I'm under a tight deadline here. That plan might work if I had a month or two. So I tried to apologize to her in the kitchen . . ." He wasn't sure he should confess that she kissed him first. He knew her, and he suspected she was in agony over the thought that she'd just cheated on Neil. "I know she still feels *something* for me."

"You need to step up your game, dude."

Garrett took a long sip of his beer and lowered the bottle. "I think I may have just pushed her away."

They sat in silence for a minute before Noah said, "I don't know Blair very well, but I know she likes to act like a hard ass. From what Libby says, she resists letting anyone get close to her."

Garrett shook his head. "You're not telling me anything I don't know."

"Okay then, Mr. Know It All. How do you get to her?"

He groaned. "Persistence. Patience. Things I don't have time for." He motioned to the house behind him. "She's out there opening wedding gifts with my asshole cousin." Should he give up? Let her go? But he knew she wasn't happy with Neil, and said asshole was cheating on her. He just had to make her realize he really loved her, and he'd do his damnedest never to hurt her again.

Noah's brow lowered in concentration as he stared out into the street. "So what you need is an accelerated plan. Sometimes a chemical reaction speeds up when heat is applied."

Garrett's eyes widened.

Noah chuckled. "I'm an engineer, and contrary to what my younger brother thinks, I did pay attention in a few of my college courses."

"Heat, huh?" He might be right, but he still needed a plan.

"Are you going to their party tomorrow night?"

"Yeah. Nana's insisted that I attend all of the wedding functions, but I would have been there anyway. I'm going to take every opportunity I can to see her. In fact, we have a deposition together tomorrow."

"We'll come up with something by the party. Just keep trying to charm her in the meantime."

Noah was being a little too friendly—why was this total stranger so gung-ho to lend his assistance? "Why are you helping me? We're plotting to break up a wedding."

He grinned. "Instigating trouble is something I'm good at,

and Libby's a perfect partner in crime. The two of us made sure Josh and Megan were officially married, and if we managed to do that, we can definitely break up Blair and Neil's wedding."

Garrett's hand tightened around his beer bottle. "So this is all some game to you?" His voice rose with his anger.

Noah shook his head. "Hell, no. I'm doing it because there's no way she's happy with that dickhead."

Garrett's gaze jerked up to his. "How do you know?"

"I spent time with them a couple of months ago at Josh's wedding. The guy's a total douchebag. Blair might come across as a bitch—no offense, dude—"

He shrugged. He knew how she came across. "None taken."

"—but she doesn't seem like the type to tolerate a guy like him for very long."

Garrett took a long drink. "And yet she has . . . she is." Could their arrangement be as practical as Neil had suggested?

"Look, I don't know you, man, but I saw my brother with Megan in June. When he thought he was going to lose her, he was totally messed up. I can't imagine what would have happened if he hadn't taken a chance." He paused, twisting the bottle in his hand. "If you love her, win her over. You still have a couple of days, and the two of you have history. Josh had less than that with Megan. Hell, the two of them met on the plane on her way to her wedding." He flashed a grin. "But I bet beating the crap out of Blair's fiancé in front of her friends isn't going to win you any favors. Not with a pistol like her." He laughed at the surprise on Garrett's face. "Yeah, it was pretty easy to see your intention."

Garrett grinned. "Yeah, you're right."

Noah's smile widened, and he held out his hands. "Why can't more people see that?"

His grin morphed into a laugh. "Won't your girlfriend be looking for you soon?"

Noah took sip of his beer, then lowered his bottle. "Libby's not my girlfriend. She's just a friend."

Garrett studied him for a moment. Given the way those two acted around each other, he was pretty sure Noah might need a straight talk of his own.

"Libby's worried about her and would do anything to protect her. That's why she and Megan were so quick to jump in when Neil showed up."

That got Garrett's attention. "Blair's not the type to tolerate people hovering and taking care of her. She's too independent for that. I can't believe she let Megan drag her off like that."

"Blair hasn't been acting like herself lately, and like I said, they're worried about her. They think she's making a mistake but is too scared to admit it. If they push too hard, she'll do it anyway just to prove them wrong."

Garrett suspected they were right.

"I'm sure the way Neil was acting in the kitchen hasn't done much to set them at ease." Noah drained his bottle, then stood. "Let's go out there and keep an eye on the douchebag. Libby doesn't trust him, and neither do I."

Though the last thing he wanted to do was watch Neil parade around with Blair, he forced himself to rise from the stoop. If he truly wanted a chance with her, what choice did he have? Maybe it was time to tell her that Neil was cheating on her. Perhaps it would ease the guilt she was sure to be feeling. But he worried it would harden her heart against love even more, or worse, she'd accuse him of lying about her worst fear in a desperate attempt to win her back.

He'd sit on the information and hope he could win her over his way. He only hoped his way didn't take too long.

Chapter Sixteen

BLAIR DIDN'T HAVE a lot of experience with showers, but this had to be the strangest one she'd ever attended. After the gifts, Knickers divided the attendees into three teams and set them to work draping one team member with toilet paper in an attempt to create a wedding dress.

Knickers insisted that if Josh and Neil were going to sit in on the shower, they had to join a team. So Josh was sent to Megan and Libby's group with a couple of other partygoers, and Neil joined forces with his mother and sister and a few others. Of course, Neil's mother decided it would be cute if Neil was the bride, and soon he was draped in long ribbons of paper. He shot a grin at Blair, who was waiting by the food table. Her job was to judge at the end. She was sure his amusement was supposed to give her warm fuzzies or fill her with reassurance after the kitchen debacle, but all she felt was disgust, directed at both Neil and herself.

Libby was the model for their group, and Megan and the others wasted no time before slapping toilet paper on her in a haphazard manner.

Dena's kids were out in the yard, each with a roll of toilet paper, throwing streamers up into the trees. Knickers watched in dismay, gnawing on a knuckle. "Oh, dear."

The back door burst open, and Megan's grandmother let

out a shout. "Ho, boy! You're playing dress-up. I wanna play." She was dressed in a hot pink bowling shirt, paired with silver sparkly leggings and orthopedic shoes. Her gray hair was accented with pink streaks, and her arms were wrapped around a present wrapped in purple paper. She set the gift on the presents table and hurried over. "Is the theme Vegas-style weddings? I want to be the bride." She started to lift up her shirt.

Knickers cringed. "Mother, stop! There are children present."

Her mother looked taken aback. "What's that got to do with anything?"

Several people laughed, much to Knickers's chagrin.

"You can be on our team, Gram," Libby said, grabbing her wrist and pulling her closer. "Where have you been? It's not a party without you."

"It's bowling night. I couldn't let my team down, but I decided to come home early." She pinched Libby and Megan's cheeks. "I couldn't miss my girls."

Megan gave her grandmother a hug. "I've missed you, Gram."

"Then you and Josh need to get your hienies back in K.C. I'm not getting any younger."

Blair was surprised by the sorrow that crept into her as she watched the exchange. The only real family she had left was her mother, and she hadn't expected to miss her so much, especially at her stupid wedding shower. In fact, her mother had been more upset than Blair that she was missing it. Blair had truthfully assured her it was no big deal, so she was shocked at the sudden realization that she now felt very alone.

Gram looked over at Blair and reached for her, pulling her into a bear hug. "You think you're getting out of some lovin'?"

Blair found herself hugging the woman back. Gram held

tight and whispered in her ear, "You got a lot of people who love you, girl, me included. Don't you ever forget it."

Blair leaned back and looked up into her face. Gram had been around as long as the three women had been friends. And while she and Libby were much closer, Blair had always loved her antics. Still, she'd never guessed that Gram was so sentimental about her. "Thank you," she whispered. It was as if Gram had known exactly what she'd needed to hear.

Gram winked. "Now someone make me a bride!"

Megan laughed and handed her a roll.

Neil's grandmother sat close to his group, of which she was technically a member, but she didn't participate. She watched everything around her with an expressionless face, and Blair couldn't help but wonder what the older woman was plotting. She was definitely the polar opposite of Megan's grandmother.

"Hold still, Neil!" Debra cried out, stumbling as she tried to wrap the toilet paper more firmly around his chest. "I think the patio must be uneven. I can't seem to stay upright."

Neil rolled his eyes, then turned his attention to Blair. "Do we get to play-act the wedding ceremony, Blair?" There was a huge grin on his face as he held out his arms so his sister could give him sleeves. "We can practice our kiss."

"Only if you win!" someone in the third group shouted.

Blair watched him, wondering what in the hell she was doing. Neil wasn't fireworks and rollercoaster feelings, but did she really want that? There was no doubt she and Garrett still had chemistry, but a fire could only burn so long before it became a pile of ashes—a lesson she'd already learned the hard way.

And as she watched Neil good-naturedly play along with the game, she realized he really was a great guy. He had a respectable career. He was responsible. He was good-looking. And he was capable of adapting to social situations. Neil wasn't a stupid man. He had to know something had happened between her and Garrett, and yet here he was making an effort to have fun.

Was she really willing to throw away everything they had together? And for what? A few months with Garrett before he changed his mind again? She needed stability and respect, and she got both of those things from the man she was engaged to marry in a few days.

"You can have one now." It went against her nature to show public displays of affection, but she wanted to offer him an olive branch. She walked over and lifted her mouth to his, expecting a brief kiss. But Neil glanced over her head as she moved to kiss him. Something flickered in his eyes, and his arms snaked around her back, pulling her tight against him, his kiss all teeth and tongue, catching her off guard. When she tried to pull loose, he held her close for a couple seconds longer before finally lifting his head.

Several of the women squealed and tittered, but Blair's face burned with embarrassment.

"Neil!" his mother shouted, throwing up her hands in disgust. "Look what you've done! You've gone and ruined your dress."

"But I got the girl," he said smugly, glancing back toward the deck again. "That's all that really matters."

It was only then that Blair realized Noah and Garrett were on the deck. They'd seen the whole thing. Garrett's body was rigid, but he let Noah lead him to the patio area.

Neil had staged the entire thing to prove a point to Garrett. They saw her as the prize for a competition. Was that why Garrett was pressing her so hard? To get one up on his cousin? Anger simmered below the surface, but guilt rose above it, catching her by surprise. Sure she had reason to feel guilty over her kiss with Garrett, but strangely enough, her guilt was over the way Garrett was watching her now. He didn't look like besting Neil was his end goal.

"Hot damn!" Gram shouted. "Somebody needs to hose that boy down!"

Debra gasped, grabbing her cat and shaking it. "One dollar!"

"WTF?" Gram asked, walking toward her.

"Gram!" Megan gasped, but she couldn't stop herself from laughing.

She looked back at her granddaughter. "What? Isn't that what you kids say?"

Libby giggled. "Do you even know what WTF means, Gram?"

"Yeah. Wild turkey fun."

The women burst out laughing. But Knickers was wringing her hands as she assessed the situation.

One of Blair's old friends groaned. "What's the point of doing this if Blair's just going to pick her fiancé anyway?" Then, as if in agreement, everyone stopped decorating their models.

Knickers's eyes were wild with dismay. She was used to running things her way, and everything she'd planned was going to shit. "Well, okay . . . We can move to the next game."

Blair stifled a groan. She wasn't sure how much more of this evening she could take. Especially with the way Neil was clinging to her.

Knickers grabbed several trash bags and handed them out. "Let's clean up, and then we'll start." She turned to look at the new additions and frowned. "Even the men can play this one."

The toilet paper was cleaned up within minutes, and now that everyone was listening to Megan's mother, she seemed much more self-assured. She picked up a shallow bowl filled with small pieces of paper and pens. "Everyone sit down and take two pieces of paper and a pen." She walked around with the bowl, allowing each guest to pick his or her own slips. "Answer the questions you've selected, and then we'll put them into the bowl. I'll read the answers out loud, and Blair will have to guess who wrote them."

Blair couldn't restrain her groan this time. This sounded like pure torture. She hadn't seen half the women in this group since high school and early college, and she'd spent as little time as possible with Neil's family.

Knickers heard her sound of dismay and flashed her a toothy smile. There was no way she was getting out of this. Part of Blair couldn't help wondering if this was Megan's mother's way of seeking revenge for all the shit the three of them had given her over the years. Truth be told, Blair probably deserved it.

She sat dutifully in the tall stool Knickers had assigned her, watching as everyone scrawled down their responses. Some finished quickly, and Blair took note of who they were, hoping it would give her a better chance at guessing who had written the short answers. Neil kept looking up at her with playful eyes that caught her off guard. What was he doing? Their relationship had been many things over the last two years, but it had never been playful. Megan and Libby looked tense, splitting their attention between their assigned task and the two men who were vying for Blair's attention.

Garrett. Her gaze landed on the man who made her want to forget about responsibility and just say to hell with it all. But she was scared. Garrett Lowry was about the furthest thing from a safe bet, and while Blair might play high stakes with her work, she always thought through every move carefully before making it, even if she appeared to do otherwise. There would be no safety net with Garrett. Yet watching him now, bent over his paper, still writing when everyone else had finished and handed their papers to Knickers, part of her wondered . . . what if?

Finally, Garrett looked up and handed his sheets to Megan's mother. His eyes met hers, and she could feel her resolve weaken, but then her gaze shifted to Neil, and she knew he'd seen it all.

Her chest tightened, squeezing the air from her lungs until her head felt fuzzy.

"Blair, dear," Knickers said, putting a hand on her shoulder. "Are you okay?"

No. She was nowhere near okay, but Blair Anne Myers Hansen never showed signs of weakness. She lifted her chin, defiance filling her and easing the clamp on her lungs. "Of course. I'm fine."

Her two best friends didn't believe her, but she could tell they weren't sure what to do about it.

Knickers reached into the bowl and handed her a paper. "Let's get started!"

Sucking in a deep breath, Blair reached into the bowl and pulled out a slip, then opened it and read out loud, "When did you first meet Blair?" A slow smile spread across her face. "The first day of kindergarten. I was crying after my mom dropped me off, and Tim Eagers called me a crybaby. Blair walked in with her blonde curls and blue dress, headed straight over to Tim, and told him she'd beat his ass if he ever talked shit to her best friend again." Blair looked up, surprised by the burning in her eyes. What the hell was going on with her? All this sentimental shit was coming out of nowhere. "Megan."

Megan laughed. "And that's exactly how it happened. You got sent to the principal's office the very first day for cursing."

Neil gave her a disapproving look, but Garrett was beaming.

Debra cleared her throat. "That's two dollars, Blair." She

passed the kitty to her daughter, who leaned forward and reached it out toward her.

Blair chuckled and pulled two dollars from her pocket and stuck them in the jar. Then she winked at Megan, who was wiping her eyes. "Best two dollars I ever spent."

Hopefully most of the questions and answers wouldn't be like that—otherwise, Blair was doomed to embarrass herself with tears. Blair grabbed another question.

"What is Blair's idea of a fun night?" She looked over the one-sentence answer, then read it out loud. "Working in her office." She glanced up. "Debra." Even if she hadn't known, the tight loopy handwriting would have given it away.

Debra's mouth pinched into a frown. "You really need to get a hobby, dear. Like quilting or couponing . . . so you'll have something to occupy your time when the babies come."

Garrett looked like he was going to combust, but Josh and Noah now sat on either side of him, and they each grabbed hold of him.

Gram's mouth twisted with worry. "Maybe I should take my present back if you're already pregnant. It's a box full of edible underwear and lotions."

"I am *not* pregnant," Blair said, vehemently shaking her head.

Libby giggled and patted Gram's arm. "And even if she were pregnant, she could still eat it . . . I mean wear it." She and half their friends broke out into hysterical laughter.

Blair might have joined them if she wasn't about to bolt out of the chair.

Knickers patted her shoulder. "Maybe we should read another question."

Blair went through several more papers, most of them easy to guess. And even if she couldn't guess who'd written the answer, all she had to do was keep an eye on the group as she read the paper. She was used to reading people, and the person usually gave himself or herself away without realizing it.

After about ten minutes, the crowd was getting restless, so Knickers handed her the bowl and said, "Last one, Blair. Make it a good one."

She opened the paper and automatically read, "Your first impression of Blair." Then she stopped when she saw the words that followed. Her heart sped up, and she glanced up at Garrett, his eyes dark and intense.

"Go on," Knickers encouraged.

The words swam on the page through her tears. Oh, God. She couldn't believe what he'd written, and she definitely didn't have the strength to read it out loud.

Before she knew what was happening, Knickers pulled the paper from her hand and started to read. "I was blown away by her confidence. Most of us were anxious, but not Blair. She walked into class like she owned the place and let everyone know she was the one to follow. I could see she held people at a distance, afraid to let them close. But that first day, as she walked past me, I looked into her eyes—something everyone else was too intimidated to do—and she held my gaze for a mere second, but it was long enough for me to see she was just as nervous as the rest of us. She was only better at hiding it. It took me six months to work up the courage to ask her out for pizza and beer. And when she sat across from me that first night, I lost my heart to her forever."

Blair's skin prickled and panic swam through her head as she glanced up at Neil's furious face.

Knickers pulled the paper to her chest and sighed. "Neil, that is so romantic."

The other women in the crowd gushed over him, and he forced a smile. "What can I say?"

Garrett glanced at his cousin in disbelief as Debra said, "I didn't know you had any classes with Blair. I thought you were introduced by a friend."

Blair could feel herself losing her tenuous grasp on control. She slid out of the chair, desperate to escape.

Megan jumped out of her seat as though someone had shot her in the ass. "Time for cake!"

Knickers shook her head. "But I have another game."

"But everyone wants cake, Mom." Then she pulled Blair's arm and tugged her toward the back door. "We'll go get it. Libby too."

"Megan!" Knickers called after her. "You can't make the bride get her own cake!"

"She wants first pick!" Libby said as she hurried after them into the house. "And she has a really hard time making up her mind, so this might take a while. We'll be out when she's done."

"But there's only one flavor," Megan's mother called after them.

Megan shoved Blair through the door, and when Libby entered, Megan shut the door and locked it.

Blair began to pace and sucked in deep breaths of air, feeling dangerously close to losing it.

"Blair," Megan said, "talk to us."

She shook her head. "There's nothing to talk about." She just had to whip herself into shape, go back out there, and finish this party. Then she could go home and sleep.

"How about starting with why you're so upset," Libby suggested.

"I'm perfectly fine!" she practically shouted.

"Okay . . ." Megan said, lifting her hands in surrender.

"Please," Blair begged. "Just give me a minute to catch my breath."

She continued to pace while sucking in deep breaths. What should s s he do? She had finally composed herself after getting caught in the kitchen, but then Garrett had written that damn answer . . . Part of her desperately wanted to talk to him, but based on the way she seemed to lose all sense of reason when she was near him, she suspected there wouldn't be much talking. She couldn't risk it.

The fact was that she had to stay as far from Garrett Lowry as possible. She only had to make it through the week. Then he'd be gone, and everything would go back to normal.

But her heart wanted more. Then the faces of her clients filled her head—women who had crawled into her office, shards of their former selves, all because they had given too much of themselves away in the name of love.

Blair had lived through the pain of a broken heart once, and once was enough.

No, she'd thought long and hard about marrying Neil. It made perfect sense, so there was no point in reconsidering now.

Finally, Megan sighed. "Blair, talk to us."

"About *what?*"

Megan opened her mouth, but Libby interrupted before she could say anything. "Girl talk. When was the last time we had a good chat?"

"Are you insane?" Blair nearly shouted. "There are a dozen women out there who never cared much for me in high school. They would just love to find every little flaw I have and shove it in my face. Then there's Neil's family, who wouldn't know fun if it bit them in the ass. We can't leave those wild hyenas with your mother so we can *chat.*"

Megan grinned. "I left a family dinner before my wedding to run off with Josh. You can afford to give your friends a few minutes. Besides, Gram can entertain them until we go back out there."

"Blair, you're overwhelmed, and it's okay. It's your party, so you can cry if you want to," Libby teased.

"I don't cry!" Blair pointed a finger in her face. "And I don't need any help! I can do it myself!"

"Of course you can, Blair," Megan said softly. "No one is questioning that. But you've got a lot on your plate right now with all the fuss about the ring, not to mention your job hinging on the wedding." She gave Blair a sad look. "And Garrett." When Blair opened her mouth to ask her how she knew about her job, Megan gave her a weak smile. "Libby told me. You should have called me."

Blair shook her head, irritated by the tears burning behind her eyes. "I can handle it." But there was no force behind the words.

"We know you can," Libby said quietly.

"What do you want me to say?" she asked defensively.

There was a knock at the back door. "Megan?" Knickers called through the door. "Is everything okay in there? I thought I heard shouting."

"We're all excited over this cake!" Libby said.

"Oh . . . okay. Are you coming out soon?"

"Yes," Blair said, heading for the door.

"Not yet!" Megan yelled, blocking the door. "We're still working on the cake."

"Well, okay . . ."

They heard her clomp off and Libby hopped onto a barstool. "The sooner we get our answer, the sooner we'll let you out of here. Why don't you start with what's going on between you and Garrett?"

Blair's preservation instinct sprang into action before she even realized what she was doing. "You want to do the sharing thing? How about we start with what's going on with *you* and *Noah?*"

Her friend folded her hands on the table and rolled her eyes. "Fine, if you want to start with me, we will, but you have to agree to answer our questions too."

Blair put her hands on her hips. "Fine." She figured she'd badger Libby with enough questions to exasperate her into giving up her witch-hunt. "Now tell us about Noah."

"Quit trying to make something out of it that's not there. We're just friends."

"A friend who spends the night?" Megan asked.

"He sleeps on the sofa," Libby protested good-naturedly. "*That's* not the topic of discussion. And don't help her deflect, Megan."

"Why not?" Blair asked, leaning against the bar counter. "I thought we were having *girl talk*."

Megan shot a glance out the back windows, her brow wrinkling with worry. Despite all her posturing, Megan would soon cave to the societal demand to appease her mother and her guests. Blair crossed her arms, feeling a bit evil. Better to feel evil and in control than on the verge of a panic attack.

Suddenly she realized how much the three of them had changed. Once they'd known everything about each other. It made sense that their friendship had changed—they all had their own lives, their own careers—but both Megan and Libby had found close relationships with other people. Blair had been stuck in the same place for years: alone.

The thought of being alone forever was suddenly terrifying, but then she reminded herself she wouldn't be alone. She'd have Neil. Why didn't that make her feel better?

Libby groaned. "I don't expect you two to understand, which is why I haven't told you much about it. I knew you'd react exactly this way." She shrugged. "We're friends, end of story. Other than this week, we haven't seen each other since last month when he was here for business."

"And Mitch is good with this?" Blair asked, intentionally sounding judgmental.

Libby gave them a tight smile. "Mitch trusts me, while you two obviously don't." Strangely enough, she didn't sound offended. It was more as if she were stating a fact. Then she turned her attention on Blair. "But it's easier to focus on my relationships than your own, isn't it?"

Blair lifted her chin. "There's nothing to discuss, and there is no plural 'relationships.' Just the one."

"What's going on with Garrett?" Megan asked.

She waved her hand in frustration. "Nothing you don't already know. He's Neil's cousin, so he's a groomsman now, thanks to their domineering grandmother . . . who, by the way, creeps me out. She watches everything like a damn eagle. What woman drags her grandson to a wedding shower? And why did he agree to come?" Her voice rose, and she knew she was losing control once more.

Megan leaned forward. "We all know his grandmother dragged him here. That's not why we're hiding in my kitchen while Neil's niece and nephew destroy my parents' backyard. How do you *feel* about him being here?"

She kept her voice cold. "I'm unhappy about it, and I have every right to be. What woman wants her ex-boyfriend at her wedding shower?"

"Blair," Megan protested. "Josh told me it was pretty obvious there were some major sparks between you and Garrett. You can't ignore that. Especially since you and Neil have none."

Her eyes narrowed. "We have sparks."

"Oh, please!" Libby snorted. "We all saw that kiss with Neil. Talk about awkward. If we counted on your chemistry to start a fire in a blizzard, we'd freeze to death. There is *nothing* there."

"He caught me off guard," Blair said in defense. "Besides, there's more to a relationship than sparks."

"Surely you don't believe that," Libby said softly. "Why won't you tell us how you *feel?*"

"Again with the *feelings*," Blair moaned. "Why do we have to discuss *feelings?*"

Megan frowned. "Because no matter what front you present to the world, you are not a cyborg. We're your friends; we know you are actually capable of emotion."

Blair lifted her eyebrows. "Cyborg?"

Megan shook her head and made a dismissive gesture with one hand. "Josh's influence, but so not the point."

"But it is the point," Blair protested. "It's *exactly* the point." She put her hand on the counter and leaned forward. "Since when have you ever paid attention to anything the least bit sci-fi?" She turned to Libby. "And when did you start having guys as friends?" She waited for a moment, then pressed on, as if delivering a rousing closing statement in court. "You two have relationships I don't understand. Have I been judgmental?"

"Yes," both of her friends said simultaneously.

"Okay," she agreed. "I have. But you still have them anyway, right? Live and let live—isn't that your motto, Libby?"

She grimaced. "Not exactly . . ."

"Close enough. But isn't it hypocritical of you guys to judge me when you're doing exactly what you want? Why can't I?"

They exchanged exasperated looks, then Megan turned to Blair. "You're right, in a way. But we're both happy. You're not."

"I am—"

Megan's eyes narrowed. "Please don't insult us. We know you too well for that."

Blair sighed and stood upright. "Just because Neil and I

don't hold hands and make out in public doesn't mean I'm not happy. Everyone has their own definition of happy."

"And what's yours?"

She'd never really asked herself that question before. "Winning every case and making partner."

"And?"

She shrugged. "Probably buying a house and doing some traveling."

Megan's eyes pierced hers. "Where does Neil fit into this?"

Blair groaned. "He's part of it."

"Yet you made no mention of him." Megan held up her hands when Blair started to protest. "Do you love him?"

Blair didn't answer. She knew Megan and Libby didn't understand her feelings for him, but she wasn't like them. She didn't expect them to understand.

Megan looked hopeful. "And what about Garrett?"

Blair's back stiffened. *"Why are we back to him?"*

"Even if Josh hadn't caught you guys in this kitchen, it's plain as day he's still interested in you. And I can tell you still feel something for him. So can Libby." Megan continued to stare at her, waiting for some sort of response. "What are you going to do about it?"

A molten core of anger erupted in her then. "I'm not going to do a damn thing about it. I'm getting married, Megan, in case you didn't get the clue from the gold embossed invitation and the taffeta bridesmaid dress."

Libby exchanged a look with Megan before turning toward Blair. "We want you to rethink this wedding."

"Why?" she asked, sounding snotty. "Because you don't approve of the way I reacted to Neil's kiss?"

"Blair," Libby sighed.

She shook her head. "Our relationship isn't based on passion and hormones. I've already told you that. Many times."

"And each time I keep hoping you're pulling my leg. That's no kind of relationship at all."

"I've done the whole *can't eat or sleep, let the guy consume your every thought* relationship, and look how that turned out."

"Blair," Megan said, lowering her voice. "You can't give up on love because you got your heart broken one time."

"Yes, I can."

Silence and tension hung heavy between them.

"You never told us much about Garrett," Megan said. "You were busy in law school. Libby was in graduate school. I was out in Seattle. All we knew was that you were dating this really awesome guy, and then he dumped you to play the field."

Blair shrugged. "What more is there to say?"

"Surely there's more to it."

"What do you want me to say, Megs? That I must be a bad lay?"

"Blair!" Megan gasped. "No."

"Look," Libby said. "I think what Megan is trying to say is that the guy is still very interested in you. He couldn't keep his eyes off you the entire evening."

Blair tilted her head back and groaned. "He's only acting like that because Neil's my fiancé. They hate each other. Garrett Lowry doesn't do relationships. Remove Neil from the equation and he's gone."

Megan looked into Blair's eyes. "So remove Neil from the equation."

Her body stiffened. What if she *did* remove Neil from the equation? What if she said to hell with it all? So, she'd lose her job. She'd earned a reputation she could use to her advantage. True, it wouldn't be in Kansas City, which would mean she'd have to move. It wasn't the end of the world. But the moment she let herself really consider it, paralyzing fear overcame her.

To cancel the wedding now would humiliate her in front of everyone. And Blair couldn't willingly risk humiliation.

This was beyond ridiculous. A week ago she was perfectly content with her life. Wasn't that proof enough to leave things the way they were?

Her jaw tightened as she stared at her friends. "I'm getting married this weekend. My career depends on this wedding going smoothly. This is *not* up for discussion."

"Your *job* depends on this wedding, not your career. You can go somewhere else, Blair," Libby said, echoing her thoughts of a moment ago. "In fact, maybe you should. What kind of company forces their employees to get married in order to make partner?"

Blair took a step backward. "I know you two don't understand, but I ask that you support my decision. Can you do that?"

Both women looked up at her with sadness and sympathy, which killed her even more. Sympathy meant they saw her as weak. Weak meant vulnerable. She couldn't afford to be either.

"Yes," they finally said in unison.

"We're here for you, no matter what," Megan added.

"Thank you." Blair picked up the cake on the counter and headed for the back door. "Now it's time to go back to the party." And back to the nightmare that had become her life.

Chapter Seventeen

GARRETT WATCHED the three women practically run into the house. Maybe he'd gone too far.

Noah patted his arm and tilted his head toward the back door, chuckling. "That's a good thing."

Was it? He knew he had to knock Blair out of her comfort zone to reach her, but it killed him that he was hurting her in the process. If he only had more time . . . but he didn't.

Lost in thought, it took him a moment to realize that Neil was standing in front of him, his eyes dark with anger. "We need to talk."

Garrett rose from his chair and stood face to face with his cousin. "I agree."

Josh and Noah got to their feet as well. "I'm not sure that's such a good idea," Josh said.

"No," Nana Ruby barked. "You two go talk out your differences."

"Oh, for goodness sake," Dena groaned. "Please tell me that you two aren't going to duke it out over that stupid ring."

Neil's eyes hardened. "We're fighting over something, all right."

Josh glanced around the yard, worried. "Maybe you should go in the front."

"I think by the shed is good enough," Neil said with a toothy grin. "I want to be here when Blair comes out."

"Sounds good to me," Garrett forced out, stomping over in that direction.

Neil followed him, and as soon as they rounded the corner, he lost all pretense of playing the nice guy. "What the hell do you think you're doing, Garrett?" he asked in a low voice. "What are you *really* doing here?"

"I already told you. Nana made me come."

"Bull shit. Nana didn't make you write that answer."

"At least I was being truthful. And what would your answer be? That you saw her and got dollar signs in your eyes?"

Neil rolled his eyes. "There's more to us than that."

"You don't love her, you prick. You don't deserve her."

Bewilderment covered Neil's face. "And now you think you do? You're only hurting her more." He swallowed, his eyes turning cold. "What happened in the kitchen before I walked in, Garrett?"

"Why don't you ask Blair?"

"Because I'm asking you."

Garrett refused to answer.

Neil poked Garrett's chest. "You keep your hands *off* my fiancée."

"How would you notice? You're too busy screwing other women to give her the attention she deserves." He fisted his hands at his sides. "I intend to make sure she knows she has a *choice.*"

"With you?" Neil laughed. "You're delusional if you think she'd go back to you." He shrugged. "If you want to break us up so badly, why don't you just tell her about Layla?"

Garrett gritted his teeth. Despite what Neil had told him earlier—and his own gut feeling—he'd thought about it. He knew it was a potential grenade that could blow up in his face, but he absolutely could not let her marry Neil. He had to tell her. So why couldn't he make himself do it?

One more day. He'd give her one more day.

"If you don't break it off by tomorrow night, I'll tell her."

Neil chuckled. "Do what you think is best." His smirk told him that Neil still thought there wasn't a chance in hell Blair would believe him.

"Just let her go, Neil. Please."

Neil watched him with amusement. "I like watching you squirm."

"*What?*"

"I kissed her because I saw you coming out the door. I kissed her to show you that she's mine." Hate filled his eyes. "For once I have something you want but can't have. How does it feel?"

White-hot rage rushed through Garrett's body. "Oh, my God. So this is *revenge* for you? You're doing this to hurt *me?*"

Neil's grin turned evil. "I'm marrying Blair for the reasons I told you earlier. But I have to admit that making you suffer is a very nice bonus." He swallowed. "There's no way I'll break up with her now, because I will *never* let you have her."

Jesus, Garrett had only made things worse.

"Now if you'll excuse me, I'm going to go find my fiancée and take her home and screw her." He winked and started to walk back to the party, then looked back over his shoulder. "I'll be sure to give you all the details tomorrow."

Garrett lost it.

Neil had just reached the patio next to the pool when Garrett tackled him, sending them both into the water. They both came to the surface, and Garrett grabbed Neil's shirt and slammed his fist into his cousin's eye.

Several of the guests began to scream.

"Garrett!" his mother shouted.

"Neil!" Debra moaned. "Barbara, your son is attacking my boy! Make him stop!"

Neil tried to pull out of Garrett's grip, but Garrett held tight. "You're going to tell her tonight, you piece of shit."

"That's a dollar!" Debra shouted, waving her jar around like a maniac.

Neil backed up, trying to break free from Garrett's hold, then ducked abruptly, leaving Garrett with a ripped shirt in his hand.

As soon as she saw Neil standing in the pool naked from the waist up, Gram shouted, "It's a topless pool party!" She stripped off her shirt, revealing that she hadn't been wearing a bra, and proceeded to hop into the pool with a large splash.

"Mother!" Nicole shouted in horror. "Get out of the pool!"

"Enough!" Nana Ruby shouted in a loud boom. Everyone stopped, including Gram, who wore a frown of disappointment.

Garrett pointed his finger at his cousin, who had waded backward toward the steps. "You think this is a contest, you asshole? Game on."

"Go ahead and try," Neil said in a deadly tone. "I will enjoy every moment of watching you lose."

Garrett's gaze was drawn to the deck. Blair stood between Megan and Libby, holding a sheet cake. The look of astonishment and betrayal on her face sent a cold jolt of shock through him.

What had he done?

Blair stomped down the steps as Neil scrambled out of the pool, panic in his eyes. "Blair, I know how that sounded."

She stopped in front of him, her eyes an icy blue. Her gaze swept from Neil to Garrett and back. "Am I the prize or the goddamned ring?"

"You took the Lord's name in vain!" Debra shouted. "Five dollars for the kitty."

"Take your goddamned kitty and shove it up your ass," Blair hissed.

Debra's eyes flew wide, and she grasped her chest in shock. "Well, I never."

"Well, maybe you *should.*" Blair turned her attention back to Neil. "Which is it, Neil? Me or the ring?"

"Blair," he pleaded.

Garrett watched in horror.

"All this fuss over a silly ring," Dena murmured.

Blair cocked her head. "You know, Dena, you're right. All this damn fuss over a fucking ring." She glared at Neil. "Here, hold this." Then she dumped the cake on top of his head, smashing it down. Globs of cake fell onto the pavement.

"I wanted a piece of that," Gram said with a pout.

"You want your stupid ring?" Blair asked, pulling it off her finger. "Here's a new contest for you." She pulled her arm back and threw it into the deep end of the pool. "The first one to find it wins."

Neil pulled the cardboard cake base off his head and tossed it into the water, huge hunks of cake falling to the bottom. He glanced over to the pool as though torn over whether he should go find the ring or try to win her over.

"Oh, dear," Nicole said. "That's definitely bad for the filter."

Blair took several steps backward, her body stiff.

"Blair." Neil started after her. "Let me explain."

She pointed her finger at him. "You stay away from me."

Garrett watched in horrified silence, unsure what to say.

Megan and Libby stood at the bottom of the deck steps and tried to reach for her as she stomped past them. She lifted her hands into the air and cringed. "Don't touch me." She strode to the back door and flung it open, banging it into the side of the house as she disappeared inside.

Her friends looked torn between going after her and heeding her demand.

Garrett knew how they felt . . . only he was certain he felt a hundred times worse. What the hell could he do now?

Nicole looked around the chaos, tears in her eyes. "Oh, dear."

Barb walked over to her and patted her arm. "It was a lovely party, Nicole. Thank you for having us."

Of course his mother would bail first.

"Neil!" Debra shouted. "Go get the ring before your cousin gets it."

Garrett shook his head, fighting the urge to cry. "It's all yours," he said, sloshing out of the water.

"All of it?" Neil asked with too much glee as he waded back into the pool.

Garrett shook his head in disgust. "You still think you have her?" His voice rose as his anger resurfaced. "You think you're still *marrying* her after that?"

He heard a splash behind him, and Noah grabbed his arm and tugged him toward the steps, but Garrett resisted.

Neil grinned. "Blair is, if nothing else, practical. She'll come to her senses tomorrow. Especially after I talk reason into her."

Garrett had never hated anyone in his entire life as much as he hated his cousin in that moment. He moved toward his cousin in the pool, wading through the waist-deep water. He stopped when they were face-to-face, then whispered, "My only consolation right now is knowing you won't be screwing her tonight after all." His mouth lifted into an ugly grin.

Neil swung a punch at Garrett, which he tried to dodge. The water slowed his movement, and his cousin's fist caught him in the mouth. His lip split, and he lunged for Neil just as Noah tried to drag him back.

The women on the patio released shrieks of dismay.

Josh jumped in behind Neil and pulled his arms behind his back.

"Stay away from my fiancée!" Neil shouted as Garrett started to climb up the steps, his wet jeans dragging him down.

"She's not your fiancée anymore!" Garrett said, shaking his head in disgust. "In case you didn't notice, she returned your fucking ring." Not that she'd probably ever speak to Garrett again.

He felt like he was going to be sick.

One of the guests shook her head as she tsked and turned to the woman next to her. "And this is why you shouldn't let men come to wedding showers."

He started up the steps to the deck, then turned to Megan's mother. "Mrs. Vandemeer, I apologize for ruining your party. I'll be happy to cover any damages. Just send me a bill." Then he moved past Blair's stunned and angry best friends, feeling heartbroken all over again.

"Garrett," Nana Ruby called after him. "Where do you think you're going?"

He turned around, ashamed to face her. Neil was splashing around in the pool, diving for the ring.

"Don't you dare leave without me. Now go stop that lip from bleeding."

"Yes, ma'am," he said, sounding like a chastised five-year-old, but that's exactly how he felt. Jesus, he'd really fucked things up.

Noah bounded after him. "Hold up. Let me get you a towel."

Garrett followed him into the kitchen. He grabbed a paper towel and wet it, then dabbed his lip. Less than an hour ago, he'd held Blair in his arms and kissed her in this very room. And now she was probably lost to him forever.

Noah disappeared down the hall and returned half a minute later with a towel. "So what happened?"

Garrett patted at his wet jeans and shook his head, too sick to repeat the sordid mess.

"Okay, it's done. The real question is, what are you going to do about it?"

"She hates my guts. There's nothing I can do."

"You're seriously going to give up?" Noah asked in disbelief.

"Look," Garrett said, his anger returning. "Why do you even *care*? What's in this for you?"

"I already told you."

"Well, I know her, and it's too late. My only consolation is that I've saved her from him. Especially after I found out he's ch—" Garrett stopped, horrified that he'd almost let his secret slip.

Noah's eyes narrowed. "He's what?"

"It doesn't matter now."

The back door opened, and Nana hobbled in. "You're ready to go?"

He tossed the bath towel onto the counter. "Yeah."

They drove back to the hotel in silence. He spent the twenty-minute drive expecting her to berate or lecture him. The silence was convicting enough. He pulled into the parking lot in front of the hotel and turned off the engine.

"Nana, I . . . I don't know what to say."

She narrowed his eyes. "Bullshit. You *do* know what to say."

He swallowed. "You have no idea how sorry I am."

"I'm not."

His gaze jerked up. "Excuse me?"

"You deaf? I'm not sorry."

He shook his head, certain he'd heard her wrong. "Excuse me?" he said again.

"That punch was a long time coming."

He blinked. *"What?"*

"You think I'm stupid?"

He grinned, his lip stinging. "No, ma'am. Never."

"I know my grandkids. I know that boy's a weasel."

He sighed. "I did more harm than good."

"True." She chuckled. "But I confess I liked seein' you deck him."

"Don't be telling Aunt Debra that. She might have you committed into a home."

"Over my cold dead body."

"I'd never let that happen, Nana. Either one."

"I know," she sighed, sounding weary. "I told you I know my grandkids." She paused. "Which is why I'm giving you my farm in my will."

He turned to her in shock. "What?"

"I don't trust that boy with it, and I sure don't trust his momma."

"I don't know what to say."

"Tell me you'll take care of it. Keep it in the family."

"I'm not a farmer, Nana."

"You don't have to be. Rent it out. Sell off part of it. Just promise me you'll keep the house and the barn."

A lump filled his throat. "I promise."

She patted his hand, which was still on the steering wheel. "You're a good boy, Garrett. I don't say it much, but it's true nonetheless."

He grinned again. "You're getting sentimental. Maybe you *are* going senile."

She laughed, then sighed again. "Just old. Now on to the next part."

He looked at her expectantly.

"What are you going to do about the girl?"

"Blair?"

"Of course, Blair. I don't see you making goo-goo eyes at anyone else."

He cringed. So it was that obvious? Hell, of course it was. He and Neil had brawled in the pool over her. The entire neighborhood knew. "There's nothing to do. She thinks I'm only pursuing her to win some contest with Neil. She hates me, and I can't say I blame her."

"Bullshit. I didn't set this all up for you to give up now."

His eyes narrowed. "What are you talking about?"

"I didn't put you in the damn wedding to mess with Debra and Neil." She grinned and shrugged. "That part was a bonus."

"Then why did you make me a groomsman?"

Her eyes flew open in exasperation. "And you just called me senile. I know who she is, Garrett Michael Lowry. I know she was the one who broke your heart back in law school."

"What? How?"

"I read the damned invitation, you fool. It said Blair Myers Hansen. I knew she was an attorney. It wasn't hard to figure out."

He shook his head. "You set this up for me to see her again?"

She whacked him in the head. "I did this for you to win her back, you fool."

He stared at her in shock, rubbing his head. "I had no idea you could be so devious. It's not usually your style."

She grinned. "Sometimes you have to mix it up a little." Then her eyes narrowed. "Now what are you going to do to fix this?"

He wished to God he knew.

Chapter Eighteen

BLAIR WALKED into the office the next morning knowing that she looked like shit. She wasn't a crier, but she had shed more than a few tears the night before. She felt duped by both Neil and Garrett, but it was Neil's behavior that had really shocked her. It seemed so out of character. She walked past Melissa's desk without acknowledging Melissa, so she wasn't surprised when her assistant followed her into the room and shut the door.

"What happened?"

She set her purse and laptop bag on her desk, and then sat in her chair. "I don't want to talk about it."

Melissa perched in the chair in front of her desk. "O-kay." She paused. "The caterer called to confirm the crab legs."

"Shit." Why had she not considered this part? There were a ton of details to deal with now. She took a deep breath and let it out. "I called off my wedding last night."

"You did *what?*" she gasped. "What happened?"

Blair rubbed her forehead, trying to ease the pounding in her head. "I can't deal with this right now."

"Do you want me to . . ." Melissa was flustered. She had never once seen Blair like that, not in the four years they'd known each other.

"No," Blair sighed. "Let's wait until after the deposition,

and we'll deal with it together." The deposition. She'd considered stalling it, but she'd already made Brian Norfolk delay his trip home. She couldn't very well cancel it and reschedule, particularly since she wasn't sure how much more time she had with the firm.

She leaned back in her chair, tears pricking her eyes again. What would happen to all her clients?

"Do you want me to get you something?" Melissa asked, sounding worried. "Water? Coffee? Something for your headache?"

Blair was about to ask Melissa how she even knew about the headache, but Melissa always knew everything, anticipated everything. And now she was going to lose her.

"Blair?"

How did her life turn to shit in so short a time?

Blair sat up in her seat and took several deep breaths. A cold sweat broke out on her forehead, and she felt like she was suffocating. "The deposition is in twenty minutes. I need to get it together."

"Maybe we should postpone." Her voice faltered as though she expected Blair to dress her down.

"I can't." And to her dismay, her voice broke.

Melissa leaned forward. "Blair, there's no shame in needing personal time. This is a big deal."

She blinked her tears away. "I can't. If I want to be the one who takes this deposition, it has to be today. Otherwise someone else will be doing it, and I don't know that they'll fight for Mrs. Norfolk like I will." Her nerves pinged, and she stood and moved to the center of the room, needing space, needing something . . . if only she knew what. "I'm going to lose my job." That was the biggest bitch of all. Marry an asshole or lose her job.

"You don't know that for sure."

Blair stopped moving, and her gaze pierced her assistant. "Melissa. Neither one of us hides from the truth. It's not the time to start."

Melissa stood. "I'll get us both a glass of water."

Blair knew she should be getting ready for her deposition. She should be preparing to face Garrett in the conference room, but all she could do was relive her kiss with him in the Vandemeer kitchen. How she'd thrown herself at him. How he'd been just as eager to kiss her. But that was before she'd overheard him and Neil fighting over who would win the contest. Was that his true motivation? So why had he told her he still loved her? To try to earn points in some pissing contest with his cousin? She knew they had a rivalry, but this . . .

Her office door opened, and Melissa walked in with a huge bouquet of flowers. "These were just dropped off." Her eyes flashed with anger as she set them down on Blair's desk.

"Who are they from?"

Melissa hedged. "I didn't open the card."

Blair stomped over and snatched the card from the middle of the flowers. It was a beautiful bouquet of red roses and white lilies. They were her wedding flowers, so she knew who'd sent them before she even read the card.

Blair,

I'm gutted. Please let me explain.

Forever yours,

Neil

"Blair?"

She spun around to see him looming in the doorway, a wary expression on his face.

Melissa hurried over and began to shove him out of the room with a surprising amount of strength for someone so slight. "I told you that you can't come in here."

Blair sighed and shook her head. "He can come in." No

matter the outcome, she needed to talk to him. There were too many complications to walk away without ever seeing him again. Melissa left the room, but she gave Blair one last significant glance before shutting the door behind her.

"Blair." Neil rushed to her and tried to pull her to his chest, but she pushed him back.

"No."

He took several steps backward and raised his hands in surrender. "Okay. Your rules, Blair. Just tell me what to do so I can fix this."

She shook her head. "I don't even know where to start."

"Can I explain what you saw? Please?"

"I have a deposition in fifteen minutes, Neil. Fifteen minutes."

"Blair." He reached for her hand. When she didn't pull away, he continued. "I know things got out of hand last night, and you have no idea how sorry I am. I confronted Garrett about cornering you in the kitchen and . . . Let's just say I couldn't stand by and let him insult you like that." His brow lowered with indignation.

"What are you talking about?"

"He was bragging about how he could win you from me." He took a deep breath. "He was rude and disgusting about how he planned to go about it, and I refused to listen to him talk about you that way."

"What way?"

He moved closer to her and slowly slid an arm around her back. "Darling, don't make me tell you. I had enough trouble listening to him say it. So I hit him."

Neil had to be one of the most non-confrontational people she'd ever met. She had a hard time picturing him throwing a first punch, yet she'd clearly seen them scuffling in the pool, and there was no denying the bruise under his eye now.

"I really don't have time for this. I have to be ready for this deposition. Now more than ever."

He slowly ran his hands up and down her bare arms. "Darling, we were both angry last night, and things got out of hand. But we're getting married in two days. All I ask is that you think things through before you make any hasty decisions you'll regret."

She didn't respond. Perhaps he had a point.

"I know you have a lot on your mind. The last thing you needed was for my cousin to turn up and try to humiliate you. And then there's Nana Ruby." Her name rolled off his tongue as though it imparted a bitter taste. Then he looked into Blair's face. "But there's something I didn't tell you." He lowered his eyes. "The reason I'm putting up with her shit."

She gave him a look of irritated disbelief. This sounded a lot like a con job. "Go on."

"Her inheritance." He licked his lower lip. "She has thousands of acres right outside the Springfield city limit. Her land is probably worth millions, though she hardly acts like a woman of wealth and class. If I piss her off, she'll cut me out of the will."

Blair's eyes narrowed. "That seems unlikely."

"You don't know her like I do. You didn't spend every summer watching the two of them huddled together over horses and literal shit in the barn, while they pretended I didn't exist."

She backed up and put her hands on her hips. "And thus your need to best him."

His face softened. "No, Blair. It's not like that." He was quiet for a moment. "Garrett's a player, through and through. He assesses a situation and tries to figure out the best way to milk it to his advantage. He's only close to Nana Ruby because he wants the land all to himself. And the best way to do that is

206 DENISE GROVER SWANK

not only to get into her good graces, but to alienate her from me."

She shook her head. "That seems like a stretch."

"You knew him before, right? He was the boyfriend who broke your heart in law school. He tried to rekindle your relationship last night in the kitchen."

Guilt swam in her head, making her dizzy. The kiss. "How did you—?"

"He told me, Blair. He came to my office yesterday before the shower and laughed about how he was going to get you to cancel the wedding to get back at me. It's all a game to him."

"So you admit to there being some weird competition between you two?"

"On his side, not mine." When she didn't answer, he cocked his head. "But Blair, let me ask you this. If he wants you so badly—" a sympathetic smile spread across his face, "—why did he wait until *now* to try to win you back? Why didn't he resurface in your life before we met? Why is he only showing up now, the week of our wedding?"

He was asking questions she'd been asking herself all night long while she tried—and failed—to sleep.

"Garrett's always been competitive. I'm sure you saw that side of him during the year you were together."

It was true. He hated to lose, just like she did, but it had always been a healthy trait. Not destructive. The man Neil was describing to her was not the man she knew. She glanced up at the clock on the wall. "Neil. I have to get to my deposition."

"It's with him, isn't it?" Hatred filled his eyes.

"Yes." There was no reason to deny it. "But it's work. It's my job."

"I know. I know." He pressed the heel of his palm to his forehead. "I just hate that you're going in there with him before

I've had the chance to convince you how sorry I am. Please at least give me that opportunity, Blair."

She groaned. "I don't know what to believe, Neil, and I don't have time to sort it out right now. I have a client who is depending on me to go in there and do my job." Irritation laced her words.

"I know. I'm sorry." He sounded desperate. "Have you called anything off yet?"

"No." The word came out harsher than intended. Before he could read too much into it, she added, "Nothing is open yet."

He pushed out a sigh of relief. "Then don't. Please, Blair. Just wait and let's talk this through before you do anything hasty. Let me take you out to lunch. Then, if you still want to call it off, we will."

Did she really want to take the time to meet with him? Canceling a wedding this size was going to be a logistical night-mare. She and Melissa needed to get on it right away.

"Blair, darling. *Please.* I'm begging you."

A couple of hours weren't going to make much difference at this point. And she supposed she owed him this. "Fine. Now I have to get ready."

He moved closer and put his hands on her shoulders, searching her eyes. "I'll make this up to you, I swear." He leaned down to give her a kiss. She turned her head, and he planted it on her cheek. "If you call it off, I'll be devastated. But don't leave me for him. I don't want that asshole to hurt you twice. So please, when you see him today, ask him if he came to see me at the hospital yesterday. When he says yes, you'll know I'm telling the truth."

"*Neil.*" She didn't have time for this.

"It will be proof that I'm telling you the truth about him. You know he and I aren't friends. Why else would he come to see me?"

She scrunched her eyes closed. She wasn't sure how much more stress she could take.

He kissed her temple, his lips lingering as his hands slowly slid down her arms. "Thank you for listening." Then he turned around and walked out the door.

She couldn't help noticing that his plea hadn't included any heartfelt professions of love. But that's what she wanted, right? Emotions were messy things to add to the mix. They broke hearts, caused fights. Last night was proof enough of that.

Maybe she was better off spending her life alone.

Chapter Nineteen

GARRETT WALKED into the office of Sisco, Sisco, and Reece looking like a defeated man. And while that was exactly how he felt, he couldn't let his client see him that way. Especially after Brian Norfolk had accused him of letting Blair win because he wanted to get into her panties.

The receptionist called Blair's assistant for him, and a minute later, Melissa opened the door. She studied him for a good long moment, no doubt taking in his swollen lip, then stood to the side and motioned him into the hall. "Do you want a room to prepare?"

"Yeah." He nodded. He needed to clear his head and get his shit together, but all he really wanted to do was go home and lick his wounds.

She led him to the small room he'd used before, but rather than leave him there, she followed him in and shut the door. His head jerked up in surprise.

She stood in front of the closed door and lifted her chin. "Do you love her?"

"*What?*" That was probably the last thing he'd expected her to ask.

"Do you love her? It's a simple question with a simple answer. Yes or no."

He nodded, feeling the first spark of hope since last night. "Yes. Definitely yes."

"Did you cheat on her when you were together?"

Her assistant was asking him personal questions that she had no right asking. They were both crossing a line if he answered, but he was desperate, and besides, he could tell that she was much more to Blair than just an assistant. "No. I swear to you, I didn't." He ran his hand through his hair. And just like that, he found himself telling Melissa the whole sordid story.

She just stood there and listened, nodding in all the right spots.

"The worst part was when I found out why she'd picked a fight with me that night," he finished, his voice choking. He looked up at her with tear-filled eyes. "Her father had just died."

She closed her eyes and released a soft groan. They stood in silence for several seconds before she opened her eyes. "She said she broke off the wedding."

More hope flooded into his battered heart. "She did?" Though he'd watched her toss the ring into the pool, he'd worried she would second-guess her decision in the cold light of day.

"But Neil's in her office with her right now, trying to get her to change her mind."

He tried to bolt for the door, but she blocked his path. "Stop. You know that's not the way to get to her."

He backed up, scrubbing his hand over his head. "Yeah, you're right."

"Blair doesn't fall for bullshit, but for some reason she has blinders on for him. I think she sees him as safe."

"He's not. There are sides to him you don't know about."

"I've suspected as much. But there's another threat you don't know about—one that might encourage her to go through with the marriage anyway." She paused until she knew she had his attention. "The partners are considering offering her partnership, but it all hinges on her wedding. They tend to prefer married partners, and they also want to see that she's not all sharp edges, that she's capable of a softer side. If they like what they see, they'll offer her partnership. If they don't, she loses her job."

"*They'll fire her?*"

She nodded.

It seemed unlikely, but it wasn't the first time he'd heard a story like that. "They told her this? They could lose millions if she chose to sue."

"A junior partner confided in her and told her they're voting next week. If she tells anyone, he'll deny the story up and down."

He grunted his frustration. "Damn."

"She doesn't love Neil, but she loves her job, and she's very loyal to me." Melissa took a deep breath. "She's already had me put out a feeler for other jobs in the Kansas City area, and there aren't any good ones. She'll have to move, which she can do, but it's very doubtful I'll end up with her."

This was going from bad to worse. "So you're worried she'll marry him to keep her position and you."

"Yes. If he can convince her." She reached for the door. "I've already said too much. I don't want her to marry him, and while I've hinted to her that I see issues in her relationship, as her employee, I can't outright tell her. But I can see you've shaken her up. Even if she's pushing you away, she still cares about you."

He smiled and immediately regretted it when his lip stretched and tugged on his cut. "Thank you."

Then her eyes narrowed and pierced his. "But if you hurt

her again . . ." The threat was unfinished, but it still held weight.

"I want to protect her, just like you do."

"Then you better work fast." She opened the door and stepped into the hallway. "The conference room is down the hall when you're ready." Then she turned and headed toward the back offices.

Garrett heard Neil's voice in the hall outside the room.

"Melissa, I know we've had our differences," Neil said. "But Blair won't be canceling the wedding, no matter what she says at the moment, so I would appreciate it if you kept that busy work on the back burner until she gives you official word that the wedding's back on."

Melissa's voice was clear and direct. "I take my direction from my employer, Dr. Fredrick. Not from you."

Garrett headed to the doorway and spotted the two several feet down the hall. If Blair cared about her assistant half as much as he thought she did, he had a feeling she'd call off the wedding solely based on the condescending look on Neil's face.

"Just remember you're her *assistant*. Don't overstep your bounds." He brushed past her and stopped when he saw Garrett in the doorway. He glanced back at Melissa, who was still watching him, and then shifted his gaze to Garrett. "So the two of you are colluding?"

Garrett leaned his shoulder against the doorframe, feeling more confident than when he'd walked into the office minutes ago. "I think you've watched one too many episodes of *House of Cards*, Neil. I'm here for a deposition. Quit making everything into a conspiracy plot."

Neil's face twisted into an ugly glare. "You've always thought you were smarter than me. I'm about to prove you wrong." Then he grinned and strutted down the hall and out the office door.

That statement scared Garrett more than he was willing to admit.

He headed into the conference room, where the court reporter was already setting up in the corner. There was no sign of his client. They still had five minutes, but Brian Norfolk's attitude the previous night didn't bode well for how things were about to go down. If he didn't show . . . well, the joke would be on Norfolk. Garrett almost hoped he didn't show. It would help Blair's client, and it would give Garrett's firm sufficient grounds to drop the sleazebag as a client.

Garrett was pouring himself a glass of water when Blair appeared in the doorway, just as beautiful as ever, albeit clearly exhausted. Today she wore a cream-colored dress with a black trim. Her hair was pulled up, and his gaze pivoted to the curve of her neck, then rose to her lips, making him think of the night before.

She'd kissed him. She'd made the first move. It gave him more confidence, and God knew he needed as much as he could get.

"Good morning, Mr. Lowry," she said briskly.

"And to you, Ms. Hansen."

"I see your client hasn't arrived yet." Her words were crisp and tight.

"I expect him shortly."

She approached the table and rested her hands on the back of the chair across from his. "I am a very busy woman, Mr. Lowry. I can't afford to waste time waiting for fools."

He had no delusions regarding her true meaning. "Sometimes fools rush in, Ms. Hansen, but their intent blinds their judgment and incites rash behavior."

The court reporter glanced between them, trying to figure out what she was missing.

"We still have two minutes before the deposition is

supposed to start." Garrett forced himself to sound nonchalant. "You'd waste more time going to your office and back than if you stay here and wait."

He knew Blair hated to be seen as reactionary, and if she stomped off now, that's exactly how it would appear. A rush of relief washed through him when she sat down in her chair.

The reporter cringed. "Would you mind if I take a restroom break? I had some spicy tuna rolls last night . . ." Her voice trailed off.

A flash of irritation flickered in Blair's eyes, but then it softened. "No. Of course."

The woman hurried out the door, leaving Blair and Garrett alone.

Her eyes narrowed into angry slits. "Did you encourage her to do that?"

"No, Blair," he said sadly. "I didn't. But I won't lie and tell you that I'm not happy she left. We need to talk."

Her shoulders tensed. "There's nothing to talk about."

"There's *everything* to talk about, from our kiss in that kitchen to Neil's reasons for marrying you to what you heard when you came out of the house last night."

Her eyes turned a cold, clear blue. "I told you I won't waste my time on fools, and I meant it."

He put his hands on the table. "You think calling me a fool is an insult? I *am* a fool. I've never denied it. Not now and not five years ago when I camped out on your doorstep for half the night begging you to let me explain."

She sucked in a breath, and though he hated that he was picking at her old wounds, he had to make her see that this wasn't some stupid competition to him. This was his heart in his hands. "Go out on a date with me."

Her head jutted back, and she looked at him like he was crazy. "I can't go out on a date with you. I'm engaged."

"Not anymore." He pointed to her now bare hand.

She reached absently for her ring finger, rubbing at the empty spot.

"That ring was never right for you anyway. A traditional, heirloom piece? That seems more like your friend Megan's style."

A slight grin tipped the corners of her lips. "Good call. Josh gave her his grandmother's ring. She loves it."

"You're more contemporary. Probably a square diamond solitaire, large but not too large."

She smirked. "For a guy, you know more than you should about engagement rings."

He lifted an eyebrow. "That's a sexist statement." But it was true. He hadn't known jack crap about engagement rings up until last night. He'd spent one of his many sleepless hours searching for the ring that would best suit her if he ever got the opportunity to propose. "Am I right? Would that be more your style?"

She didn't answer, which was an answer in itself.

"So go on a date with me. How about lunch?"

Her grin faded. "I'm having lunch with Neil."

"I see."

Anger flashed in her eyes. "Do you?"

He put his hand on the table and leaned forward. "No, Blair. I honestly don't. You don't love him. And I know you think he's safe, but I'm not sure why."

"That is none of your business."

"Okay, fair enough, but answer me this." He kept his tone soft and comforting to cushion the barbs he was about to sink. "When did *you* start running away? That's not like you at all."

She slammed her hands on the table. "What the hell are you talking about? When did I ever run away? You're the one who left me!"

"You're pretending that marrying a man you don't love is the logical decision. If that's not running away, I don't know what is."

"How in God's name is that running away?"

"Because you're running away from love."

"What the hell do you know about love, Garrett Lowry? You took what we had and destroyed it."

"I know." His voice broke. How many times would she have to say it to purge it from her system? What if the number was infinite? "I'll regret it until the day I die, but I loved you, Blair. I still do." He reached over the table and grabbed her hand. "I meant every word I said last night. I've never stopped loving you."

She looked away, but she didn't pull her hand away. It was something. "So what exactly are you proposing here?" She glanced back at him. "A date?"

He tried to hold back his excitement. "Yeah. A date."

"Where would we go?"

He took a shallow breath. "Pizza. Some place where we could get a beer and talk. Then we'd go to a piano bar, like we always loved doing, and make fun of all the cheesy love songs."

Sadness filled her eyes, and she slid her hand out from under his. "We've both grown up since law school."

"Sure, but not completely. Are you telling me that doesn't sound like something you'd want to do?"

She didn't answer, which meant she was considering it. He wondered what her dates with prissy Neil were like, but he didn't dare ask, and part of him didn't want to know.

"Why now, Garrett? After all these years, why now?"

He sighed. "I told you, Blazer. I was too scared to approach you after all this time. But then when I saw you in Phoenix . . . and then here. Call it whatever you like—fate, kismet, or coincidence—but to me it was the universe telling me to man up and go after you."

Her gaze pierced his. "And where does Neil fit into this?"

"Hopefully, Neil doesn't fit *anywhere* into this."

"How can you say that?"

Understanding hit him, and he groaned. "There is no contest, Blair. You're not some inanimate object to be fought over. I only want you to be happy, but I hope to God it's with me."

Garrett glanced up in time to see Brian Norfolk walk through the door.

Blair sat upright in her seat, but her eyes were still locked onto Garrett's—like she was performing some kind of human lie detector test—as she waited for the jerk to sit next to him.

"Mr. Norfolk," she said. "How wonderful of you to finally join us."

"Hey, I'm only five minutes late." He plopped down in the chair next to Garrett's.

Blair gave him a condescending glare as the court reporter entered the room behind him and took her seat. "Mr. Norfolk, I'm sure your attorney has told you this, but I feel compelled to reiterate that when we win—which we will—you will end up paying us by the hour. If you waste any of my time, you will end up paying for it handsomely." She flashed him a smile. "So thank you."

He muttered a curse word under his breath, and Blair shot him an evil smile before beginning her questions. Garrett had to hand it to her. Now that she'd made him admit to his hidden money, she knew exactly what follow-up questions to ask to find everything else he'd squirreled away. Frankly, Garrett was surprised there was that much money left. He'd seen Norfolk's expenses.

The entire matter took less than three hours, and Norfolk

slunk out as quickly as he could, leaving Garrett in the conference room with the court reporter and Blair. He could see she was stalling, shuffling her papers in her folder. It was another hopeful sign that she was hanging back to talk to him.

He stood to leave, and she did as well, keeping her gaze on the door. Once they were both in the hall, she glanced up at him.

"Did you go see Neil at the hospital yesterday?"

"Neil told you?"

Her eyes flew open in surprise. "So it's true?"

Why would Neil confess such a thing? Garrett suspected it couldn't be good, but he wouldn't lie to her. "Yes, it's true."

Her eyes turned icy again. "Then you're wasting your time and mine, Garrett. Go back to California where you belong." She turned her back to him and started down the hall.

"Blair!"

He followed her, and she turned back to him, fear and anger in her eyes. She reminded him of a trapped wild animal. "Stay away from me."

What in the hell had just happened?

Chapter Twenty

"BLAIR, PLEASE," Megan pleaded over the phone. "Rethink this decision."

Blair leaned her head against the back of her office chair. Good God. How many people had pleaded with her over the last twenty-four hours? It was exhausting. "I've made up my mind. I don't want to hear any more about it."

"Even after what happened last night?"

"Neil and I discussed it over lunch. I accepted his explanation. There's nothing to rethink."

"And what about Garrett?"

"What *about* Garrett? He's from my past. We had our chance. It's gone. Neil is my future." She'd been telling herself that all afternoon. She was starting to believe it. At least a little.

"Oh, Blair."

"We've decided to call off the party tonight, especially after everything that happened last night."

"You mean so no one can talk you out of the wedding?" Megan snorted. "Was this his idea?"

"It was a mutual decision." But Neil had been the one to suggest it.

"So you don't have plans tonight?"

"Neil and I are going out to dinner."

"You'll be spending every day with Neil after Saturday, but

I'm going back to Seattle. Come out with Libby and me tonight.
We'll make it a bachelorette party."

"I thought you didn't want me to marry Neil," Blair said in
a haughty tone.

"Blair, you're a grown woman. We've stated our opinion,
but it's ultimately your decision. Now let's have a girls' night
out." She paused. "If Neil will let you, that is."

Her back stiffened. "Neil doesn't own me, Megan. We
don't have that kind of relationship."

"Then it's a plan?"

Neil would likely be upset. At lunch, he had taken the
blame for their broken relationship and had suggested they
spend more time together to rekindle the connection they'd
shared in the beginning, although Blair could admit to herself
that it had never been even close to what she'd shared with
Garrett. He gave her back the ring and said he wanted to start
tonight with a special dinner. But Megan was right. They had
the rest of their lives to spend together. She had no idea when
she would see Megan again. Besides, she couldn't think of the
last time the three of them had all just hung out and talked.
"Yes, but I have some work to do before I take off."

"Good." Megan sounded smug. "Then meet us for dinner.
You pick when and where. We can meet close to your office to
make it easier for you."

"Okay. Seven o'clock at O'Malley's."

"At least *try* to sound excited about it."

"I'm excited." And she was. She just needed to tell Neil
first. "I've got a lot on my mind."

"A wedding will do that to you. See you at seven."

Blair was caught by surprise when Neil's phone didn't go to
voice mail.

"Blair? Miss me already?" he asked in a teasing tone.

His response was so unlike him, she was shocked into silence. "Uh . . ."

"I can't wait until our dinner tonight. I've come up with the perfect restaurant. I was just about to text you the location."

"Actually, that's why I'm calling . . ." Why was she so nervous? She'd never had trouble telling him what she wanted before. "I need to cancel our plans tonight."

He paused. "Blair. I thought we agreed to focus more on *us*. Starting *tonight*."

"I know, but Megan and Libby want me to go out with them. I can't even think of the last time all three of us went out to dinner."

"Darling, they want to convince you to break off the wedding." He sounded worried.

Her temper flared. "You think I'm incapable of making up my own mind?"

"No. Of course not." He sounded taken aback. "But—"

"Then there's no discussion. I'm going out with my friends."

"I'll miss you."

Now she was really suspicious. "Don't lay it on too thick, Neil."

"Due to my own stupidity, I almost lost you last night. It's made me realize that I've taken you for granted." His voice lowered. "I love you, Blair. I know I rarely say it, maybe because you never do, but I *do* love you."

He was right. She rarely said it, but she hated lying. "I'll call you tomorrow."

Melissa came in about an hour later, set a file on Blair's desk, and then spun around to leave. She wasn't acting like herself, and Blair was worried. It occurred to her that she'd piled a lot of her own personal tasks onto her assistant, especially since she'd asked her to take care of canceling tonight's party.

"Did you have any problems with the cancellation?"

Melissa turned to face her, crossing her arms. "None at all."

"Melissa, is everything okay?"

Her eyes were guarded. "And why wouldn't it be?"

Blair knew a deflection when she saw one. She stood and walked around her desk. "I know I've asked you to do a lot of personal errands for me lately."

Melissa sucked in a breath and stared her down. "I'm your assistant. It's my job."

"No, it's not. Not really." She moved closer. "I don't tell you often enough how much I appreciate everything you do."

Her assistant looked down and then back up, still on guard. "I know you do, Blair. Thank you." And with that, she left the room.

Blair considered going after her, but she had enough on her hands. She'd deal with whatever was bothering Melissa later.

Megan and Libby were waiting for her in the restaurant when she arrived several minutes after seven. She prepared herself to be berated for being late, but they just smiled and held up their drinks.

"We started without you," Libby said.

Blair cracked a smile. "So it would seem."

"We're still waiting for our table," Megan added. "Let's get you something."

"Just water. I have a busy day tomorrow and a meeting with a potential new client in the morning."

They both knew she wasn't supposed to be in the office on Friday, but neither woman commented on it.

Libby took a sip of her wine. "I guess you don't have to worry about your job now, huh?"

She thought about defending herself, but she doubted

Libby meant it as a jab. She was just being sensitive. That thought almost made her snort out loud—when had Blair Myers Hansen become *sensitive?*

The hostess approached them a few minutes later and led them to their seats. They spent the next hour and a half talking about their jobs, their mutual friends, Megan and Josh's life in Seattle, and a new photography project of Libby's. The conversation steered clear of all topics even peripherally related to Neil, Garrett, and the wedding. Which left Blair with very little to discuss.

"I've heard this place has amazing cheesecake," Libby said, taking a sip of her wine. "Want a slice?"

Blair laughed. "No way. I have to fit into my dress on Saturday."

"One piece of cheesecake won't hurt," Megan teased.

Blair stuck to her guns. "Nope. I have enough things to worry about without adding the fear of being unable to zip up my dress."

"Well, in that case," Libby said, flagging down the waitress. "Let's pay the bill and head over to the bar down the street and get a drink."

Blair shook her head. "I can't. It's a work night."

"Come on, Blair." Megan tilted her head and gave her a pouty face. "It's too early to call it a night. Who knows when we'll be able to hang out again."

She only had one meeting scheduled, so she could afford a later start than usual. Especially since it was officially her day off. "Okay."

They left the bar and were heading down the street when a woman emerged from a doorstep and grabbed Blair's arm.

She stared up at Blair with intense brown eyes. "Your fortune for five dollars."

Blair tried to pull free, but the woman's grip was like a vise.

Her first thought was that the panhandlers in this part of town had gotten significantly more aggressive, but the woman didn't look homeless. In fact, she was clean and fairly well dressed in a long flowing skirt and shirt. Tight black ringlets framed her face.

"I don't think so."

"I'll pay," Libby said, rummaging through her purse and pulling out a bill. "Come on. You have to admit you of all people need your fortune read."

Blair's body tensed. "You know I don't believe in that crap."

"Humor us." Libby handed the money to the woman. "I'm paying for it. Consider it my bridesmaid's gift.

"*Fine*." She held out her hand to the woman, palm up. "Read it."

The woman took it and shook her head. "I don't read palms. I read souls."

Blair didn't hide her amusement. "By all means. Read my soul." Her grin widened. "If you can find it."

The woman's eyes held Blair's for several uncomfortable seconds before she spoke. "You are at a crossroads both professionally and in love."

Blair's smile fell.

"You've been cursed."

Blair tried to jerk her hand free, but the woman's fingers dug into her flesh. "Now this is just bullshit," Blair said.

"It's up to you to break the curse. Everything depends on making the right choice," the woman said, releasing her hold. "You don't have much time." Then she smiled. "For twenty-nine dollars, I can give you a tarot reading. If you'll just come into my office . . ." She motioned to the door behind her, and Blair realized they were standing in the awning of her psychic shop.

Blair turned to give Libby a scathing glare. "You set this up."

Libby lifted her hands in defense. "No. I swear."

Megan flashed the psychic a smile. "Thank you, but we're going to pass." She grabbed Blair's arm and tugged her away.

"That was bullshit, Libby." Blair felt her cheeks grow hot, which only made her angrier.

"How could I set this up, Blair?" her friend asked. "You picked the restaurant. I never come down to Brookside. I didn't even know this place was here."

"Come on," Megan said. "Let it go."

Blair dug her heels into the sidewalk. "I think I should just go home." Though she'd die before admitting it out loud, the fortune teller had scared her. Blair reminded herself that the psychic had thrown out general terms in a fishing expedition, looking for a topic to narrow in on based on her reaction. But while her head knew this, the unreasonable part of her considered going back for some answers.

She had finally lost her mind. What if she was making the wrong choice? "Fine."

"Great!" Megan exclaimed, ignoring her short response.

The bar was a short walk away, and as soon as Blair got through the door, she ordered a whiskey.

"Don't you want to find a table first?" Megan asked.

"No."

Libby ordered a glass of wine and Megan a beer, and once they had their drinks, they found an empty table in the back of the bar.

They'd barely gotten settled when Libby looked at Blair's left hand and asked, "So you're wearing the same ring?"

The panic rose out of nowhere, and she wasn't even sure why. "Yeah," she forced out. "It's practical." She took a sip, trying to hide her shaking hand.

"Yes," Libby murmured. "It is practical."

Blair took another sip. "Just say it, Libby. Say what you've been dying to say all night."

She shook her head. "Blair, we really do just want you to be happy. You don't look happy."

"How could I be happy when you two won't accept my choices?"

"Enough, Libby," Megan said, taking a big gulp of her beer. "Change the topic."

The three women sat in silence until Megan finally said, "Blair, we stand by you no matter what. Right, Libby?"

Libby nodded. "My lips are sealed."

Still, their mood—already dampened from the encounter on the street—was grim.

"Maybe we should just call it a night," Blair said.

"No," Megan protested, anger darting into her eyes. "Not yet. We used to have fun together, *and we're going to have fun, dammit!* We'll stay here all night if we have to!"

The two women looked at her and burst out laughing. Megan joined them and ended up laughing the hardest of all of them.

"I've missed this," Blair confessed.

Libby grinned. "Me too."

"See?" Megan countered. "We all miss this, and it's wonderful that we're here together. Let's make the most of it."

They ordered another round of drinks, and Blair felt her panic retreat. Maybe this was what she needed—a night of fun with her friends.

They'd finished their second drinks, and Megan ordered another round. Blair knew she probably shouldn't drink any more, but she picked up the drink and took a sip as soon as it was placed in front of her.

"Oh, crap." Megan's eyes widened.

"What?" Libby and Blair asked in unison.

"I think we should go." Megan turned to her, her forehead wrinkled with worry. "We didn't do this, Blair. *I swear.*"

"Do what?" Then she glanced at the front door, and her face instantly flushed when she saw who'd just walked into the bar.

Garrett.

Not just Garrett. The McMillan brothers were behind them. The way Josh and Noah had taken to Garrett, Blair wouldn't be surprised if they sent out an adoption announcement officially changing Garrett's last name to theirs.

Blair narrowed her eyes. "Are you kidding me?"

"We didn't plan this," Libby said, looking worried. "Josh and Noah were supposed to meet Garrett in his hotel bar, which is right around the corner. There was no way they knew we'd be here."

Garrett looked around, and his eyes found Blair. Though she could hardly believe this was a coincidence—particularly after all of the other coincidences that had been piled into her lap lately—the shock in his eyes was undeniable. And like a moth to a flame, he came right to her. Her eyes were so laser-focused on him, she barely registered that the McMillan brothers were following him.

He stopped in front of her table. "Blair."

She couldn't believe he had the nerve to come over to her after admitting he'd gone to Neil's office. "Go away, Garrett."

He swallowed, looking nervous. "Give me one dance."

She looked around the bar, incredulous. "No one's dancing, Garrett."

"I don't care. Dance with me."

She lifted her chin and held up her left hand. "I'm engaged."

"So I heard. I rented a tux today. Black with a red tie. Classic. Good choice. I think I'm standing on the end of the line."

She jumped off her stool and stumbled around Libby to stand in front of him. "You've got to be kidding me! You're still in the wedding?"

He smiled, but his eyes were sad. "Nope. Nana Ruby still insists."

She poked her finger into his chest. "Then grow a pair of balls and tell her no!"

"No. I won't. But Neil can." His eyebrow rose. "Did you know that? He could tell her no, but he hasn't. Why not?"

She knew, but she wouldn't admit it to him.

"You obviously don't want me to be in your wedding. Have your fiancé kick me out."

"How about you do the right thing?"

His face spread into a slow lazy grin. "I *am* doing the right thing."

"Then quit."

"Dance with me."

She tried to sort it through in her head, but her mind was fuzzy from the alcohol. One dance and he'd quit the wedding. It seemed safe enough, even if the thought of dancing with him spread a pool of heat between her legs. She reached across the table and took a big gulp of her drink before turning back toward him. "Okay."

He looked surprised by her easy acceptance. Maybe she should have negotiated for more.

He took her hand and interlaced their fingers as he pulled her away from the table. A distant part of her mind realized Libby and Megan and the brothers McMillan were gaping at them in surprise. Her hand tingled from Garrett's touch, and she wondered what else he could make her feel. If it would be even half as good as it had been in the past. Based on her current reaction, she was sure it would be a thousand times better.

He tugged her around a booth and led her into a dark corner with two empty tables, giving them privacy from the rest of the patrons. He stopped and looked down into her eyes, making no move to touch her other than their still-linked hands.

"I thought we were going to dance," she murmured, her gaze drifting to his lips.

He grinned. "We are, but not yet."

"Why not?"

"It's the middle of a song. I want my full dance."

"So we're just going to stand here and wait, looking like idiots?"

"No one can see us, Blair. I'm the only one who can see you right now, and I definitely don't see an idiot."

"Why are you doing this, Garrett?" Her voice hitched as she said it, and she just wanted to slap herself silly.

The song ended and a new one started, a nineties ballad with cheesy lyrics. Blair barely heard it. He took a step toward her, making her hyper-aware of how close they were.

His hand reached for her waist, slowly skimming her dress before coming to rest on the small of her back, his eyes holding hers. He stepped even closer, leaving barely an inch between them. Her skin tingled, and she automatically lifted her hand and rested it on his shirt. His chest rose and fell under her hand.

"Just a dance," she whispered, his eyes captivating hers.

He smiled and pulled his other hand free from hers so he could rest it on the rise of her hip.

"Were you really scared to ask me out?"

His grin spread, and he leaned down toward her ear. "More than you could ever know," he whispered. "You still scare me."

"How do I scare you?"

Rather than answering, he lowered his face to the nape of her neck, his breath hot against her sensitive skin. Shivers shot down to her toes. She cupped the back of his neck, her breath coming in short pants.

"Do you have any idea how sexy you are in a deposition?" he asked, moving his mouth to her jaw, his breath fanning her cheek.

"No." She could barely think, barely breathe—all she knew was that she needed him.

"You're like a panther, slowly circling its prey, looking for any sign of weakness. And then when you strike . . ." His teeth skimmed her jaw, lightly nipping. "It's so damn sexy."

Her toes curled, and she pressed against him, trying to get closer.

"I want you." He pulled her tighter to him, leaving her with no doubt of how much he meant the words. "I want you more than I've ever wanted anyone." His mouth hovered over hers.

She could smell beer on his breath, and she was sure he could smell the whiskey on hers, yet he didn't kiss her . . . and it was driving her crazy.

"I've tried so hard to forget you, but you're burned into my brain, imprinted on my heart." He placed kisses at the corners of her mouth, and her body felt more alive than ever before, each nerve ending pinging and begging for release. "Give me another chance, Blair. We'll get it right this time."

She turned her head, trying to capture his mouth, but he lifted it millimeters from hers. "Garrett," she pleaded, and he groaned, drawing her lower lip between his teeth and nipping lightly. She tugged on his neck, trying to pull him closer, but he resisted.

"You are the sexiest woman I have ever met, and I want you, Blair. I need you."

She rose on her tiptoes and captured his mouth, and he

released a deep groan, his kiss devouring her. He pressed her back against the wall, one hand skimming up her waist and to her breast. His thumb brushed her nipple, sending a jolt of electricity through her, and she wrapped her leg around his and pulled his erection tighter against her.

"Blair. Wait. Stop." He pulled back, his chest rising and falling, his eyes hooded with desire.

Her back was still against the wall, her hands on his chest, as the horror of what she'd just done washed over her. She tried to break loose, but he held her still.

"I'm sorry. Just listen to me."

Everything had a weakness. With enough pressure, even the hardest metal bent and twisted. Garrett Lowry was hers. She'd been drawn to him, coaxed to the edge of surrender. She had completely lost control. And Blair could not afford to lose control.

Panic raged through her like wildfire. "I have to go."

His hands held her waist. "It's okay, Blazer. We'll figure this out together."

The song ended, and her eyes flew open. "One dance. You said one dance and you'd quit the wedding."

"Blair, I love you, and I think you love me too. But I'm damn sure he doesn't love you."

She shook her head. "You don't know that."

"Do you love *him*? Tell me that you love him."

Tears stung her eyes. "Garrett."

"How can you marry him if you don't love him?"

She shoved against him. "I have to leave."

He held on tighter, his eyes begging her to listen. "How can you deny this thing between us?"

She wanted him so much it hurt, but she couldn't do this. She couldn't take such a risk. "It's not real, Garrett. If it were real, we would have lasted the first time."

He shook his head. "No, that's not true."

"It is. You do what I do, so you see the same parade of people. They flow into your office too. They all loved each other once—most of them were head over heels when they married. Hate is the opposite of love, Garrett, and only a fine line separates them. One minute you're in love and the next . . ." Her voice broke. "We love each other too much. We would *destroy* each other."

"You don't know that! We don't know that we'll break up."

Sadness filled her with an ache that made it difficult to breathe. "But we don't know that we won't."

His eyes hardened. "The Blair Myers I knew never ran from anything."

"You already told me this morning that I do. Why should it come as such a surprise now?" She jerked free from his hold and took a step to the side. "I can't risk it. I'm marrying Neil."

"You're really going to throw us away?" he demanded in disbelief.

"There *is* no us! We were done five years ago!"

He shook his head, anger burning in his eyes.

"I gave you a dance. Now call your grandmother and tell her you're not in the wedding."

His jaw tensed. "No. There was no deal."

Her mouth dropped. "What are you talking about?"

"I only asked you to dance with me. I never agreed to bow out of the wedding in exchange. You concocted that one. I just didn't correct you."

Rage rushed through her. She shoved at his shoulders, but he barely budged. "You bastard! Why are you doing this to me?"

His eyes were wild. "Because I love you, Blair. *I love you*, and I can't let you marry him."

"You *can't?*" she shouted, her voice drowned out by the

music overhead. "When did you get the power to *allow* me anything?"

"*Dammit!* That's not what I meant!"

His hold loosened, and she gave him another shove. He stumbled back several steps, and she bolted for her friends, panic making her clumsy.

Megan spotted her first, and she slid off her stool and rushed toward her. Libby's eyes widened in concern and she followed.

"Blair?"

"I have to go." She grabbed her purse from her chair as she passed it.

"Okay." Both women flanked her as she hurried for the door, leaving behind the McMillans.

When they reached the sidewalk, Libby grabbed her shoulder and spun her around. "Blair, slow down. Tell us why you're crying."

"I'm not crying!" But when she reached up to touch her face, her cheeks were wet.

"What happened?" Megan asked softly.

And that was what pushed her over the edge. Megan's kindness. She couldn't handle softness, not now. She choked on a sob but swallowed it back down. "I have to go."

"We'll go with you," Megan said.

Blair glanced at the entrance to the bar. It surprised her that Garrett hadn't followed her out. In truth, it disappointed her too. The thought sent a new wave of terror through her, and she felt the desperate need to be alone.

"No." She took a deep breath, forcing all the escaped emotions back into the cracks from which they'd oozed. Only they wouldn't go back. Now that they were loose, they refused to be tamed.

An empty cab turned the corner, and Blair flagged it down.

She had to get away. She had to escape from her friends' sympathy. It was unbearable.

The taxi stopped, and she opened the door, pausing only to glance back at her stunned friends. "I have to go. I'll see you both tomorrow night."

"Blair."

Blair climbed into the car and shut the door.

"Where to?" the driver asked.

Where to, indeed. There was only one place on earth she wanted to be, and she wasn't willing to take the risk. Which meant she had nowhere to go at all.

Chapter Twenty-One

MELISSA TOOK one look at Blair's swollen eyes the next morning and brought her a cup of coffee, shutting the door behind her. Still, typical Melissa, she set the cup on her desk and ignored the elephant in the room. "The only thing on your schedule today is your consultation. Do you want to leave at noon and join Neil and his family?"

"No." That was the very last thing she wanted to do. "I think I'll stick around and work."

Melissa nodded. "You'll need to go home and change for the rehearsal. Do you have a dress picked out?"

"For the hoedown?" she snorted. "Yes."

Melissa left without comment, and Blair got to work. She became so engrossed in her computer that she was caught off guard when Melissa buzzed to tell her that her consultation had arrived.

"Send her in."

Blair hadn't been expecting a young woman. Her clients were typically in their forties and fifties, but the woman entering her office had to be in her late twenties or early thirties.

Blair stood and walked around the desk. "Mrs. Cooper. Please, come in." She met the woman in the middle of the room and held out her hand. "I'm Blair Hansen."

"I expected you to be older," the woman said, looking Blair up and down.

Blair smiled. "And I could say the same about you. How did you hear about me?"

"You represented my mother. She said you fought tooth and nail for her. When I suspected Thomas . . ." She paused. "I knew who I had to call."

Blair motioned her toward her small conference table. "Thank you for the confidence. Why don't we sit, and you can give me your side of things."

The young woman told her story, and Blair took notes. In many ways, it was similar to her other cases. The couple had started out young and in love, but for the past several months, Leslie Cooper had suspected her husband of cheating on her. As Blair listened, a cold chill washed over her. Leslie was a beautiful, intelligent woman. Why would her husband cheat on her?

"So did you catch him?" Blair asked.

"No."

Blair glanced up. "Do you know who he's having an affair with?"

"No."

Blair set down her pen. "What did he say when you confronted him?"

"He swears he didn't do it. That he loves me."

"So why do you think he's lying?"

She looked sad. "He's just so cold. So distant."

"Is he working out more? Putting more care into his appearance?"

"No." She looked confused. "No more than usual."

"Is he having trouble at work?"

"Yeah, he has issues with his boss."

Blair took a deep breath. "Leslie, I would be happy to represent you should it come to a divorce, but I think what you need is a private investigator or a marriage counselor."

"But..."

"We'll need names and some type of proof he's cheated on you to build a stronger case. And if your only hint that he's been unfaithful is that he's acting distant, I suspect he's merely preoccupied with the possibility of losing his job."

Leslie looked surprised.

Blair rested a forearm on the table. "Do you still love him?"

Tears filled her eyes. "Yes."

"Then fight for your marriage. Don't give up on him so easily." Like she'd done with Garrett five years ago. "But if you do find proof or you decide you still want a divorce, come back and I'll help you in any way I can."

"Thank you." Relief washed over her face.

Blair watched her walk out of her office, and Melissa came in several minutes later. "Do you have a new client?"

"No. I told her to hire a private investigator or a marriage counselor."

Her eyes widened. "The marriage counselor bit is new."

She shrugged. "Her suspicions were flimsy. And she still loves him."

Melissa moved toward the door, but instead of leaving, she surprised Blair by shutting the door and moving back toward her. "So you're still getting married?"

Caught off guard, Blair looked up at her. "Well... yeah."

Melissa grabbed the chair Leslie had used and moved it in front of Blair. Blair watched in silence as her assistant sat in front of her.

"Blair, we've been together for four years. I think I know you pretty well by now, wouldn't you say?"

Blair sat rigid, wondering where Melissa was going with this. "Of course."

She took a deep breath. "Sometimes the relationship you and I have is difficult."

Pain twisted in her gut. "You don't like working for me?"

"What?" Melissa asked in horror. "No! I love working for you. What I meant is that you're my boss, but we're also friends, so I sometimes struggle with knowing when not to cross that line."

Blair nodded, her anxiety ratcheting up.

"But I decided to risk my relationship as your employee today to approach you as your friend."

"Okay."

"I don't think you should marry Neil. He doesn't love you, so why does he want to marry you?"

Blair expected to feel anger, but she felt exhausted instead. "We love each other in our own way. I know you don't understand. No one does, and I get it. It's different. But let's face it, I intimidate most men . . . and even those who aren't afraid of me wouldn't tolerate my schedule. Besides, I might not believe in happily ever after, but I think it will be nice to be married and have a partner for special events and vacations. Plus we both know it will help my job."

"None of those are good reasons, Blair," Melissa said bluntly. "What about love?"

"I've spent all night thinking this over. It's simple. I can either go with emotion or with reason. Emotion is not to be trusted. At least I know what I'll be getting with Neil."

"Do you?" she asked. "Are you sure?"

Blair's eyes narrowed. "Why do you say that?"

"He doesn't like me, and while that sounds petty on my part, I don't get why he sees me as a threat."

"Surely you've misunderstood."

"No. You know I don't misunderstand."

She was right. Melissa was excellent at reading people. "What else?"

"He hates Mr. Lowry."

"Well, that's to be expected. Even more so now."

"I'm certain that he wants to marry you to hurt Mr. Lowry. I don't trust him, Blair."

She knew that had to be part of his motivation now, but he didn't know Garrett was her ex-boyfriend until the shower, so that certainly hadn't been his motivation to propose. She nodded. "Okay."

"You're not angry?"

Blair shook her head. "No. But I admit I probably wouldn't have listened to you before now."

"So what are you going to do?"

"I don't know."

"Your rehearsal's in six hours."

"I know. For now, we'll leave it as it stands."

Melissa stood and took several steps before turning around. "I know you want to keep your job, but don't do this to save me. I couldn't live with the guilt." Then she walked out.

Blair sat there thinking about it. She had three choices. Marry Neil. Give Garrett a chance. Or be alone. If she chose one of the latter two, she would need to make sure Melissa was protected. But how could she do that without letting on that Ben Stuart had told her about her potential partnership and its unique conditions?

Five minutes later, she knocked on the door to human resources, but even as she did, she knew it was a mere formality. The door was always open, and Mary, the one-person department, was always welcoming.

"Blair! What are you doing here? You requested the day off for your wedding."

She smiled. "Oh, you know work . . ."

Mary grinned. "I do. But don't let the important things slip by."

"Thanks, Mary. I'll remember that."

"So what can I do for you?"

"Um . . ." She'd worked up a story of sorts. "Neil got word that he might be offered a position in Dallas. Now, we're not at all sure what decision he'd make, but I would go with him if he went."

Her eyes widened. "Oh! I know they'd miss you around here. Why, Mr. Sisco Sr. himself was raving about you just last week."

"Really? Mr. Sisco Jr. sat in on one of my depositions this week. I was worried they found my work unsatisfactory."

She waved her hand. "Standard performance review. He didn't tell you?"

"No." Had Ben lied to her? But then again, the partners probably wouldn't have informed Mary of their intentions. "So . . . if I were to move to Dallas with Neil, what would happen to Melissa?"

Mary smiled. "Oh, aren't you a sweet girl. She's a wonderful employee. We'd find a place for her."

"So she wouldn't lose her job?"

"Good heavens, no. Half the attorneys here would duke it out over who gets to work with her."

"Thank you, Mary." She turned to leave, then asked, "If it comes to that, promise me that you'll make sure to put her with someone who will be good to her. Not Mark Garter. He's an ass." Her voice tightened. She couldn't handle Melissa working for that jerk.

"Blair. You two are as thick as thieves. I know you care

about her." She lowered her voice. "I'd sooner quit than put her with Garter."

"Thanks."

So Melissa was covered. That only left herself. What the hell was she going to do?

Chapter Twenty-Two

AT 6:05 P.M., Garrett stood in the Presbyterian Church, trying to swallow his nausea. Blair was sequestered in a corner with Libby and Megan, glancing around the church as she counted off who was missing. Neil stood nearby with a couple of his friends. He crossed his arms and shot Garrett a smug grin. The bruise on his cheek and under his eye gave Garrett minimal satisfaction.

Blair was still going through with it.

Noah had arrived with Josh and Megan, and Garrett had wondered why until Libby showed up a few minutes later holding hands with another man, presumably her boyfriend Mitch. He was bigger than Noah, a beefy-looking guy with oversized muscles, and he seemed protective of Libby. Garrett would have found it amusing if he weren't so miserable. Of the two women in his acquaintance who least needed protection, Blair ranked first with Libby at a close second.

While the ladies pow-wowed near the church door, Mitch was hanging out with Josh and Noah. Given the amount of time Noah had spent with Libby over the past week, Garrett was surprised by the apparent lack of tension between the two men. Still, Noah didn't look disappointed when Garrett pulled him into a side aisle so they could chat without being overheard. "Is Blair okay?" he said in an undertone. "Did Libby get a chance to talk to her?"

Noah just shook his head. "I don't know. Blair never returned her or Megan's calls. But she texted them around noon to say she was fine and that they should come to the rehearsal."

Garrett ran his hand through his hair. "I screwed up last night."

"Libby's not so sure about that. But it was a gamble." He clapped a hand on his back. "Hey, she's not married yet. You still have about twenty-four hours."

True, but while they were talking, Blair and Neil had walked up to the altar and started talking to the minister who was scheduled to marry them the next afternoon. The sight didn't fill him with a lot of confidence.

Blair looked over her shoulder, and Garrett's eyes met with hers. He expected to see anger or derision there, but instead he found sadness.

What was he going to do? He *had* to convince her not to make this colossal mistake. It was time to tell her about Layla, even though he knew it would be the kiss of death to any chance of a relationship between them. He just hoped she believed him.

Garrett's parents had arrived, and his mom and his aunt wasted no time in picking a nothing argument. This time it was over the faded lines in the parking lot.

"You think I had control over that?" Aunt Debra demanded.

His mother gave her a haughty look. "Well, if this were Kelsey's wedding, I'd make sure everything was perfect."

"Oh, isn't that something," his aunt sniped. "Kelsey's too busy putting the cart before the horse to even consider getting married."

Garrett looked around the church for a glimpse of his sister. For once, he was grateful that she was notoriously late. Otherwise the bickering between his mom and his aunt would probably turn into an all-out brawl.

Everyone stood around, twittering anxiously over the argument until Nana Ruby finally stepped away from the back wall and whistled loud enough to get everyone's attention.

"Debbie Sue and Barbara Mae! That's enough!" Then his grandmother lasered him with a pointed gaze that let him know how disappointed she was that he hadn't yet managed to steal his cousin's bride. If he had succeeded, she wouldn't have needed to tolerate this madness.

"Let's get this started!" Nana Ruby shouted. "There's a rack of ribs waiting for me."

Aunt Debra cringed. "We don't have ribs. Just pulled pork and ham."

"Well, what kind of barbeque is *that?*"

Garrett took his place at the front of the church, standing at the end of the wedding party, next to one of Neil's fraternity brothers. His cousin Dena, Libby, and Megan all strolled down the aisle pretending to hold bouquets while a pianist played a classical piece.

"And then the music changes," the minister said from his perch on the altar after all the bridesmaids had taken their places. "And the bride comes down the aisle."

Blair stepped into the doorway, and while he'd already seen her today, she looked somehow different as she stood there in the threshold. She wore a fitted blue and white print dress, and her long, dark blonde hair fell in soft waves down her back and over her left shoulder. The V-neck of her dress dipped low enough to expose a small amount of her cleavage, and the hem hit just above her knee, exposing her shapely calves. He was sure she'd never looked more beautiful.

Garrett's gaze was glued to her, and she stayed in place for a few heartbeats, as if trying to decide whether to turn around and run away. She glanced in his direction, and their eyes locked. Her lips parted, and her eyes filled with a softness that told him her iron-clad resolve was on the verge of weakening, that she wanted to walk down that aisle toward him one day, not Neil, but then she sucked in a breath, steeled her back, and started down the aisle.

She came to a stop beside Neil and looked up at the minister.

"Since you walked down the aisle alone," the minister said, "I presume no one will be giving you away."

Blair looked over her shoulder before returning her attention to the minister. "No. My mom is late, but she won't be giving me away."

"Blair's too independent for that," Neil added, only it sounded more like a dig at her character than a compliment. Or perhaps Garrett was too sensitive. But one glance at Libby confirmed he wasn't alone in his opinion.

The minister continued. He had reached the vows part of the ceremony when Kelsey walked in through the back door. She took one look at Garrett and sighed. It was a relief to see her.

She walked down the aisle and sat in the front pew on the groom's side of the church, eyeing Blair before returning her attention to Garrett. She pursed her lips and gave him a mischievous wink.

The minister explained when the rings would be exchanged, then smiled at the couple. "All that's left is the kiss."

Blair gave a forced smile, and Neil leaned in and planted a kiss on her that lasted several seconds.

The minister cleared his throat. "Now you two walk down the aisle together, and the bridal party will file out after you."

Neil looped his arm through Blair's, and they walked toward the back door as the groomsmen and bridesmaids paired up. Garrett was on the end, and when he walked down the steps, Kelsey cut in front of their cousin and grabbed his arm before Dena could.

"Good of you to join us, Kels."

She grinned. "Traffic's a bitch." She leaned closer. "So the siren's still going through with it, huh?"

He shrugged, feeling uncomfortable. "I wouldn't call her a siren."

"She's captured the attention of my man-whore brother. She must be."

"Shh." He looked around and pulled her into a pew, worried someone had overheard them, but no one seemed to be paying attention. "Where's the baby?"

"Drake's watching her at the hotel."

"*Drake?*"

She shrugged with a frown. "I know. Drake's so irresponsible he can barely be trusted with a goldfish. But he's her father, and he's threatening to sue for visitation rights. If I let him play house, maybe he'll be too lazy to pursue it."

Drake was a worthless piece of scum who happened to contribute his DNA to Kelsey's baby. "You know I'll help you with any kind of custody battle."

"In California?" Her eyebrows lifted in a humorless smirk. "Besides, it's for less than an hour. Drake's bringing her to the picnic."

He groaned. "Damn Aunt Debra. I hear she's having a softball game too."

Kelsey laughed. "Mom'll love that. She only knew about the barbeque. It's likely to cause a fight."

"They've already had one that registered 6.5 on the Richter scale. And your ears must have been burning."

She beamed. "I love being the center of attention. Tell me what they said."

"Nope. That's what you get for not being here to have my back."

"Mom'll tell me."

Probably. His mother loved to complain about his aunt.

As if on cue, Aunt Debra leapt to her feet and approached the altar. "We'll have to do it again. You didn't practice lighting the unity candle."

Blair headed back into the sanctuary, followed so closely by Neil it was a wonder he didn't step on her shoes. "We're not lighting a unity candle."

Debra put her hands on her hips. "And why on earth not?"

Clearly gunning for a battle, Blair stopped in the middle of the aisle, her hands on her hips. "Because we chose not to have one."

"How could you not have a unity candle?" his aunt asked, as though it were the most preposterous idea in the world. "Don't you want your marriage to be unified?"

"Of course we want our marriage to be unified, but lighting a damn candle won't make a bit of difference."

Debra gasped and rushed over to her big purse, pulling out the cursing jar. One of the plastic ears had caved in, and the cat's belly was bulging, presumably from all the money stuffed inside. "I can't believe you cursed in the Lord's house!" She held it out in front of her and shook it, causing the money to rattle around inside. "That's five dollars!"

"What in God's name is that?" Kelsey whispered.

"Aunt Debra at her best."

Blair shook her head and pointed at the kitty. "I'm not putting five dollars in that damn jar!"

Debra gasped, her eyes flying wide. Her face turned red, and she spat out, "I've resigned myself to Neil marrying a foul-mouthed woman, but the least you could do is try to watch your tongue in church. Your mother should have raised you better."

Blair's body tensed, and Garrett dropped Kelsey's arm and took an instinctual step forward. As protective as Blair had always been toward her mother, this was bound to end badly.

"Mom," Neil warned.

"Why are you marrying her, Neil?" she demanded. "Why can't you find a nice girl who will take care of you and give you babies?"

"Mom!"

"Where's her mother, Neil? She couldn't even bother to show up for her daughter's rehearsal. If she were any kind of mother at all, she'd be here washing her daughter's mouth out with soap."

Blair took several steps toward the woman, her face frozen into one of her most intimidating looks. The older woman had the sense to take a step back.

Blair's eyes were cold as ice. "You can say whatever you like about me, but don't you dare talk about my mother in a derogatory manner ever again. Have I made myself clear?"

The woman nodded, her body shaking.

Blair spun around and stomped out of the sanctuary.

Neil clenched his fists. "If you ruin this for me, I'll never forgive you, Mother." Then he spun around and hurried out of the church. "Blair!"

Kelsey moved next to Garrett. "He loves her, Garrett," she whispered. "You need to let this go."

"That's where you're wrong, Kels. He thinks the two of them are going to be some sort of power couple, and he's already counting the future money he hopes she'll make. Add to that the fact that she doesn't require much of his time and attention and the reality that he'll be taking the woman he knows I want, and he's become like a rabid dog who won't let go," he snarled under his breath. "Love doesn't compute in that equation at all."

"What an ass." Her words weren't very loud, but they bounced around in the silent sanctuary.

Debra's eyes narrowed. "Kelsey Lowry, you're just as vile as that girl who's trying to steal my boy."

Kelsey laughed. "You don't scare me, Aunt Debra. And if you don't like Blair, then I know I'm gonna love her."

"She's lowlife trash, and I'm gonna put a stop to this."

While Garrett appreciated her goal, he was livid over her assessment of Blair's character. And he wasn't the only one.

"*Excuse me?*" Libby demanded, stalking down the aisle toward the woman. "Did you just call Blair *lowlife trash?*" Her eyes were wild, and her hands had fisted at her side.

Megan rushed after her and put her hand on her shoulder. "Libs, she's not worth it. Let's go."

Libby shook her off and gave Debra her full attention. "You have no idea what Blair's been through. Her family had money until her father divorced her mother to marry one of his mistresses and left his family destitute."

"I wasn't even talking about her money. I was talking about her filthy mouth." The older woman lifted her chin. "But if her father was a cheater, then all the more reason for Neil not to marry her. Cheating runs in her family's blood."

Megan gasped, and Libby's eyes filled with rage.

"*Are you kidding me?*" Libby raged.

"Libby." Garrett's firm voice cut her off. "Go find Blair."

She sucked in several short breaths as she continued to stare his aunt down.

"Come on, Libs. Don't do this to Blair," Megan said, grabbing Libby's arm and tugging. "Garrett's right. Let's go find her."

Mitch looked baffled as he watched the scene, but Noah

knew exactly what to do. When Libby continued to refuse to let Megan drag her out of the church, he walked over to them and stared her down. Finally she let Megan turn her toward the door, and Noah murmured comforting words to her, coaxing her down the aisle. He looked back at Neil's mother. "If Blair's smart, she'll run far and fast to get away from you."

She gasped. "Well, I never . . ."

"Do you think she will?" Kelsey asked Garrett.

"Not a chance. Blair loves a good fight. She'll marry him for the sake of pissing her off."

Aunt Debra had probably made his mission ten times harder.

Chapter Twenty-Three

BLAIR PACED BACK and forth in the parking lot, stomping her feet so hard her soles hurt. "I can *not* believe her."

Neil leaned against the trunk of his car as he watched her. "Blair, I'm sorry."

"Who the hell does she think she is?"

He stood and moved in front of her, grabbing her shoulders. "You have to know I don't approve of what my mother said."

She studied his face, where she saw undeniable frustration.

"Blair." He lowered his voice. "I'll tell her she can't come to the wedding."

Her brow rose as some of her anger faded. "You would do that?"

"For you? Yes."

He wasn't acting like himself again, which only caused her anxiety to rise. He'd been trying so hard to prove himself to her, but while that should relieve her fears, it was sending her into a near panic attack.

"I love you, Blair." He sounded desperate. "You have to know that." She gave him a tight smile, but she let him pull her into his arms. He stroked the back of her head. "I don't want to lose you."

If the situation were reversed, she knew she wouldn't have

pled with him like he was doing with her. Was that another sign she didn't really love him, or was it just a character flaw?

"I know things with my family have been unbearable. I'm sure Garrett throwing himself at you hasn't helped."

She couldn't handle discussing Garrett, but she had no trouble discussing Debra. She pulled loose. "How long have you known that she hates me?"

"She doesn't hate you."

"Okay, strongly dislikes me."

He sighed.

"Lying serves no purpose, Neil. She made her feelings perfectly clear. I can only presume she's felt this way all along. I only need you to confirm it."

He leaned his ass against the trunk of the car. "She's old-fashioned. I have no control over her behavior. Just like you had no control over your father's."

Anger burned in her chest. "Don't you bring him into this."

"Why not? Isn't he part of the reason we're standing here in the parking lot arguing instead of inside with our family and friends?"

She shot him a glare. "We're out here arguing because of your mother's bitter tongue."

"And that's our only problem? At least we only have to visit my mother from time to time. Your father is haunting us from his grave. Isn't he part of the reason you're so cold and unfeeling?"

She gasped.

"Deny it."

She couldn't. Everything he'd said was true.

"I know your faults, yet I'm still here." He stood and moved closer to her. "Why can't you just admit it? You need me."

She shook her head.

"It's not a weakness to need someone."

He was wrong. It was the worst kind of weakness.

"I don't *need* you, Neil. We have a relationship based on mutual respect and companionship. That's all this has ever been. It's all we've ever needed."

He stared at her, anger darkening his eyes. "Sometimes you can be such a bitch, Blair."

His words drew blood on her already aching psyche. She clenched her hands into fists and stared into his eyes. "You've just now figured that out? Where the hell have you been the last two years?"

They stood in silence. Anger rippled across his face.

"Maybe we should just call this all off," she finally said.

"You've said you don't need me, but that's not entirely true, is it? If you don't go through with this wedding, you'll lose your job." He took a step toward her and looked down at her with cold eyes. "So maybe you need me more than you think you do." He stated it like a threat, and in that moment, she felt she really didn't know him—that maybe this was her first sight of the real Neil.

"Go to fucking hell, Neil."

He cursed under his breath and stomped over to his car. Then, without a backward glance, he got in, backed his car out of the parking space, and took off, his tires squealing on the pavement.

"Blair?" Megan called out her name, sounding panicked.

Her eyes sank closed. She loved Megan and Libby like the sisters she'd never had, but the last thing she could handle right now was their hovering and mothering. She spun around to face them as they strode toward her.

She crossed her arms over her chest. "I'm fine."

"Like hell you are." Libby looked furious, but Blair knew her friend's anger wasn't directed at her. Still, when Libby reached for her, she ducked her embrace and took several steps back.

"No."

"Blair," Megan pleaded. "Let us help you."

"I don't need any help!" Her shouts echoed in the parking lot, and the guests pouring out of the church could hear her hysterics. Her brewing panic was close to exploding, inflamed by the knowledge that she was about to make a spectacle of herself. "I have to get out of here." She looked around. "Where's my purse?"

Megan gave her a patient look. "We'll get it. Or we can take you to get it."

"Blair." Garrett's voice broke through the rest of the noise like a beacon, and then she saw him, making his way across the parking lot toward her.

She froze, tears burning her eyes, waiting for his pity or contempt, but neither of those emotions were apparent on his face or in his voice.

Her chest tightened, and she fought to catch her breath. "I have to get out of here," she whispered raggedly.

"You need a ride?" he asked, walking past her two best friends. He glanced over at them, and they both nodded. "Let me take you."

"You helped get me into this mess," she choked past the lump in her throat.

His face softened. "I know. All the more reason for you to let me give you a ride."

"This doesn't mean I'm sleeping with you."

He forced a smile and held his hands up in surrender. "I can live with that." Then he motioned toward his car. She walked past him, opened the passenger door, and climbed in, knowing her friends would take care of her purse.

The driver's door opened, and he settled into the seat and started the engine. "Where to?"

"Just drive."

He did as she'd asked, driving toward the entrance to the parking lot. Blair heard Neil's mother shouting her name, but both of them ignored her. She leaned her elbow on the door and rested her forehead in her hand.

Garrett drove for ten more minutes, then pulled into a parking lot and shut down the engine.

Blair's head jerked up, and she started to laugh. "Chuck E. Cheese? Really?"

He shot her a grin. "It seemed somehow appropriate. Rumor has it I can get a beer here."

"You're going to need more than one to survive all the kids' birthday parties." She opened her car door and moved around to the back of the car.

Garrett met her there, still wearing his grin. "I like a challenge."

"I'm not taking it easy on you in Skee-Ball, Lowry," she said as she walked to the entrance, her mood lightening. This was the last place she was supposed to be and with the last person on earth she should be with, but it felt so completely right that she decided to just go with it.

"God, I should hope not."

"I don't have any money, so you'll have to spot me."

He grinned. "I've got you covered."

He opened the door and followed her inside. The noise from the games and screaming children was deafening.

The teenager at the entrance gave them a strange look as he stamped their hands with invisible ink.

"I'm hungry," Garrett said. "Let's get a pizza."

She shook her head and laughed as he ordered a pepperoni and mushroom pizza, two beers, and got a cup full of tokens.

She picked up the number for their order and found a table for them, then walked to the edge of the arcade. "Are you going to give me half those tokens?"

"No way. You have to earn them."

"I already said I wasn't sleeping with you."

A mother with a baby on her hip walked past them at just the wrong moment and gave her a disapproving glare.

"Look at you. You're in Chuck E. Cheese for less than five minutes, and you're already making friends," Garrett laughed. "And I never said I wanted to sleep with you."

He might not have said it, but they both knew it. Correction: they wanted to sleep with each other, and the electricity in the air between them still scared the shit out of her. The panic hit again, and she took big gulps of air.

Garrett put his hands on her shoulders and squatted down so they were face to face. "Blazer. I would never try to convince you to do anything you didn't want to do. You know that, right?"

She nodded. The night they'd spent together in Phoenix was proof enough of that.

"I promise you that I won't make any moves on you at all tonight. No pressure. Just fun, okay?"

She nodded again, still trying to catch her breath.

"Everything's going to be okay. Forget about everything else —except that you claim you can beat my ass in Skee-Ball. But I've been practicing, so I'm about to give you a run for your money." He handed her the cup of tokens, but he didn't let go of it. "Time to show me what you're made of, Myers."

She narrowed her eyes, but a grin tugged at her lips. "It's Hansen now, and it's time for you to kiss your ass goodbye."

They carried their beers with them and headed for the Skee-Ball game. True to his word, he beat her in their first round.

"Lucky break, Lowry," she said, putting another token into the machine. "I was just warming up."

He gave her an ornery grin. "Bring it."

Two boys who looked to be around eight years old picked the two lanes next to Garrett.

Blair leaned forward. "You boys any good at this game?"

They gave her a wary look. "Kind of."

Garrett picked up his beer cup and took a sip.

"See this guy here?" She motioned her thumb toward Garrett. "He thinks he's some kind of Skee-Ball king, and he's offered to give five tokens to any kid who can beat him."

Garrett choked on his beer, and Blair burst out laughing. "What's the matter, Lowry?" she asked, slapping him on the back. "Afraid of a little healthy competition?"

"No way," he grinned. "I can take 'em."

The two quickly made mincemeat out of Garrett, and word got out that some old guy who wasn't very good was holding a Skee-Ball contest. A line formed, and he ran out of tokens within ten minutes.

"So much for your mad Skee-Ball skills," Blair teased, leaning against the basketball shooting game with her arms crossed. "You should demand a refund from your instructor."

He laughed. "I think he fled to Mexico."

"I can see why." She waggled her eyebrows. "How about a basketball challenge?"

"Depends on who's asking. You or every kid in this building?"

"I'll go easy on you. Just me." She winked.

"We need more tokens."

She tapped her foot. "Get your ass moving. I'm not getting any younger."

She beat him on the first round, and he beat her on the second before word spread through the building that the old

Skee-Ball loser had moved on to basketball. He had to fend off a horde of power-hungry children as they moved away from the game.

Garrett pointed to the table. "The pizza's ready."

"Likely story," Blair said. "Admit it, you need some time to lick your wounds."

His eyes turned wicked. "Something like that," he said with a grin.

"Hey, guy." A little girl tugged on his shirt. "I want to win five tokens too."

Blair laughed. "Come on, Lowry. Can you really turn her down?"

Garrett groaned and snatched the plastic cup from Blair. He dug out five tokens and handed them to the girl. "Let's just save us both some time."

"That old guy just gave me some tokens!" she shouted as she ran away. A low rumble instantly spread through the crowd.

"Look what you started," Garrett said.

The small hint of fear in his voice was enough to send Blair into a fit of hysterics. "I never told you to just hand them out."

A group of kids had already surrounded him and pushed Blair to the side in their quest for free tokens.

"Hey, are you like Santa Claus?" a kid shouted.

"Naw, his belly's big, but not big enough," a boy told him.

"Hey!" Garrett protested, good-naturedly. "No tokens for you."

Blair watched him handle the kids, passing out the coins as he took their teasing and dished it back in return. She couldn't remember the last time she'd had so much fun. And then she remembered. It had been with him.

Nostalgia swept through her, hot and sweet, reminding her that chemistry wasn't the only thing she missed about their relationship. It was his good nature, his healthy competitive streak, his kindness and compassion, and his intelligence. And most of all, it was his ability to ground her. He had always been the one person who could help her calm down after a less-than-perfect test score or some tiff with her friends.

She missed *him*.

He grinned at her above the heads of the kids, and she realized Garrett Lowry was the whole package. Looks, brains, and personality. Besides, she would wager the kid who'd made the belly comment a whole cup of tokens that he was wrong. She'd felt his torso under her fingers the other night, and it was all muscle.

Garrett dumped the cup upside down and shook it. "I'm tapped out, guys. Go thug roll some other old dude."

Blair laughed as he approached her.

"You were loving every minute of that, weren't you?"

"Thug roll?" she teased. "Is that even a thing?"

He gave her a goofy grin. "Not everyone can be hip to the lingo. Don't be a hater, Blair."

They had almost reached their table when Blair saw the whack-a-mole game. "Oh, I'm not passing this one up." She grabbed his arm and pulled him to a halt.

"I'm fresh out of coins."

She pulled one out of her pocket. "Good thing I saved a couple."

"You've been holding out on me."

"Hey, can you blame me? You keep giving them all away."

His smile faltered. "I should have saved some for you. I can get more."

She shook her head and picked up the mallet, getting a good grip on it. "I had more fun watching you with the kids."

"Whose head are you planning to whack?"

She drained the last of her beer and handed him the empty

cup before placing her token in the machine and picking up the club. A mole popped up, and she smashed its head. "That's Neil." Another mole's head rose, and she hit that one too. "Robert Sisco Sr." And another. "Rob Sisco Jr." She hit the empty hole even harder. "Jack-wipe."

She continued to beat the moles, naming them all before she slew them. She named the last one Garrett.

"I guess I deserve that," he murmured.

She put another coin in the machine and played another round, drawing a crowd of kids as she smashed the heads with more enthusiasm than in the first round. She clipped one on the side, and the mole's head dented on the lip of the hole.

"Oops."

Two of the other heads stopped popping up, presumably broken, and the game finally ended when the mallet shattered into three pieces. When she looked up, panting, he was staring at her, and it was enough to make her lose her breath all over again. He leaned against the machine, his beer in his hand and his eyes on her. A wave of heat washed through her, and she knew she wanted him. God help her if he tossed her away again, but she wanted him for as long as she could have him.

He grinned and stalked toward her, pushing through her fan club of admiring eight-year-old boys and lifted her hand into the air. "And there you have it, kids. The mole champion!"

The kids cheered as he led her to the table, hand in hand. Tingles raced along her skin where it was joined with his.

"I think I probably owe Chuck E. Cheese about two grand, but I guess you'll have to cover that too. I'm probably the most expensive date in history." She gave him a mischievous grin.

His eyes were hungry when they met hers. "Worth every damn penny."

They sat across from each other and ate for a few minutes

in silence before Blair said, "I never heard from my mom. And I don't have my phone."

"Do you want to call her?"

"I need to tell her what happened."

"What *did* happen, Blair?"

She took a deep breath and looked into his eyes. "I don't think I'm getting married anymore."

Relief swept across his face as he handed her his phone.

She punched in her mother's number and typed in a quick text message telling her that she was fine and would call her later and explain, then she handed the phone back to Garrett. "Thanks."

He took the phone and slid it back into his pocket. "Finish up. It's almost time for our next stop."

She fake groaned. "Dear God, please tell me we're not going to the park for the softball game."

He laughed, his eyes lighting up. "I'm not a masochist. I have something else in mind."

She picked up another slice of pizza. "Should I be scared?"

"Terrified."

She laughed again and took a bite, wondering how she could feel this content after all the ugliness of the day and her run-ins with Neil and his mother. For once, she decided not to question it.

Chapter Twenty-Four

GARRETT COULDN'T REMEMBER BEING this nervous on a date since high school. He wasn't sure Blair really meant it when she'd called it a date, but he was going to pull out all the stops to prove to her that he still loved her and was worth the risk.

"Are you going to tell me where we're going?" she asked as he led her out to the car.

"Nope. It's a surprise." *He* was surprised when she didn't push him for an answer. She hated surprises.

After spontaneously asking her out on a date the other night, he'd done some research about where he wanted to take her if he managed to convince her to give him a chance. Now he was glad he'd done his homework.

He drove down to Brookside and parked his car, then walked around the car quickly enough to help Blair out of it. He held her hand after shutting the passenger door, and his pulse picked up when her fingers curled gently around his. She looked up at him with parted lips and soft eyes. Some of her hard exterior seemed to have flaked away, which he found surprising after the scene at the church. This was his Blair, the Blair he'd uncovered years ago after months of patience. And here she was, the woman he'd longed for since that stupid night five years ago, and he cursed his impetuous announcement earlier that he wouldn't touch her tonight. He wanted her to see that she was so much more to him than a roll in bed, although he desperately wanted that too. So he held onto her hand as he led her down the sidewalk to their next destination.

That afternoon he'd constructed a plan to convince Neil to break off the engagement. The legal papers were in the works, waiting for the final details. He figured he'd eliminate the Neil problem and then concentrate on winning Blair back. He knew it was a lot of money, but he didn't care. He'd gladly give it up for her. Never in a million years had he expected he'd be spending the evening with her. He wasn't about to screw it up.

He stopped outside the building's entrance and looked into her eyes, seeking permission as the music streamed through the door.

"So we really are going to a piano bar?" she asked with a teasing glint in her eyes.

"I promised, didn't I?"

They entered the dark bar that consisted of a baby grand piano in the back corner and about twenty tables spread throughout the room. It was still early on a Friday night, but the place was half full, and he had to lean into her ear so she could hear him. "Let's go in the back."

She nodded, and he moved his hand to the small of her back, amazed by how natural it felt, as if they hadn't been apart for five years or even for five days. She sat on the bench seat along the wall, and Garrett had a moment of indecision as to whether he should sit by her or in the seat across from her. But she looked up at him expectantly and patted the seat beside her, making the decision for him. He slid in, grateful to be close to her, even if it made it a thousand times more difficult for him to keep his promise.

A man sat at the piano playing a Barry Manilow song. Blair

looked up at Garrett and laughed. "I want to hear Billy Joel." She gave his arm a shove. "Go request it."

"I see some things never change. You're as bossy as ever."

"And you used to love it, if I recall." A teasing glint filled her eyes.

Desire shot straight to his crotch. *Damn*. He knew what she was talking about and it wasn't requesting songs in a piano bar.

Her eyelids lowered, and her grin turned sexy, but her voice still held a teasing tone when she said, "Now go request a Billy Joel song."

He wasn't going to be able to get up from the table if she kept this up. He forced himself to be playful. "Only if you promise to sing."

"Ha! My singing hasn't gotten any better since we were together."

"Neither has mine. We can sing it together."

"Then I'm going to need a drink first."

"Deal." He got up and wrote his song request on a piece of paper and stuck it in the glass bowl on the piano with a couple dollars.

He stood at the bar and ordered their drinks, watching her while he waited. She looked more relaxed and at peace than she had all week. What had happened between Blair and Neil in the parking lot? According to her, the wedding seemed to really be off this time. He hoped it was true, but he needed to put his insurance policy into place just in case.

He slid his phone out of his pocket and pulled up Neil's number, and then typed out a text.

We need to talk. Omni Hotel. Room 678. 10:00 a.m. I'll make it worth giving up Blair.

Neil still hadn't answered by the time the bartender returned with their drinks, but if Garrett knew him at all, he would come. Still, he wouldn't rest until this scenario had played out—until he knew there was no chance Blair was actually marrying the guy.

Blair glanced up at him and smiled. He was suddenly overwhelmed by his good fortune. He couldn't believe he was here with her tonight, that he was possibly getting this second chance with her. Grinning, he carried the drinks back to their table. He handed her a glass as he sat down next to her.

She took a sip and looked amused. "Whiskey?"

"If I'm making you sing, I figure the least I can do is provide liquid courage. Beer didn't seem to be enough."

She laughed and glanced at his glass. "But *you're* still drinking beer."

"I'm less inhibited than you."

Something flickered in her eyes, and he thought he'd lost her, but she grinned and took another sip. "What did you request?"

He waggled his eyebrows. "It's a surprise."

"Now I'm scared."

"You should be. When he starts to play the song I requested, remember that you *promised* to sing."

She laughed. "Now I'm *really* scared."

He scooted closer to her on the upholstered bench, close enough that their thighs pressed together. He watched her face to see if she was bothered by the contact, but she rested her chin on her hand as she watched the pianist belt out a Britney Spears song.

It was still early, not quite nine o'clock, but the bar was already busy and more people were coming in the door. Blair was finishing her drink when the pianist pulled out a slip of paper and groaned after he read it. "Really?" he asked, looking up and searching the crowd. "'Piano Man' by Billy Joel. Who requested this?"

Garrett grabbed Blair's hand and lifted it into the air. She tried to pull loose, but he held on tight while he shouted, "She did!"

The pianist turned the spotlight on them. "Can't you come up with something else? It's such a cliché."

Garrett put his arm around Blair's shoulders, pulling her close as he squeezed. "It's her favorite."

The musician turned on his bench and played a few notes before stopping. "'Piano Man' is your favorite, huh?"

Blair glanced up at Garrett with a look that said he was going to pay for this later. She gave the entertainer a dazzling smile. "You have no idea."

"Okay . . ." He shook his head, grinning. "I'll only do this if you sing."

Garrett held up his beer bottle in salute. "Oh, she plans on singing."

The crowd broke into applause as the pianist started to play the first notes of the song. "I'm going to play a Billy Joel medley, so make sure you sing all the parts."

"Oh, shit," Blair said under her breath. "I don't know many Billy Joel songs."

He leaned into her ear. "Should have thought of that before you requested him."

The pianist started singing the first lines of the song, and Blair joined in as best she could, stumbling over the words. But instead of getting irritated, she laughed and looked up at him, her eyes pleading with him for help.

He joined in, his arm still tight around her back, and she made no move to get away.

They sang the chorus, and then the pianist moved into "Only the Good Die Young." Blair knew this one better, and she looked up into his face from time to time as both of them sang, laughing when they both stumbled over a line. The rest of the bar had joined in by the time the song merged into "Just the Way You Are."

Blair's smile faded, but she continued to sing, and Garrett picked up her hand and held it to his chest. He gave her a grin, and her playfulness returned. The entire bar was singing with them now and drowning them out.

When the song ended, the crowd burst into applause and someone shouted, "You've gotta kiss her, man!"

"They're right, dude," the piano player cajoled Garrett. "Give the crowd what they want."

Blair's back stiffened, but she searched his eyes, and her body softened. "Well?"

He lifted his free hand to her cheek, and her eyes fluttered closed as he pressed his lips gently to hers. She leaned into him, and he fought the urge to deepen the kiss—a herculean task after the taste of her last night and considering how much he'd dreamed of doing more than this over the last week. Hell, the last several years. But Blair had never been a fan of public displays of affection, and he didn't want to push her boundaries too far. Baby steps.

He lifted his face and searched her eyes while the crowd cheered and catcalled all around them. She smiled, her eyes lighting up. She looked happy, and his heart burst with joy at the knowledge that he'd played a part in that. His thumb brushed her cheekbone before he dropped his hand and captured hers again.

The pianist had moved on to a Keith Urban song, and the crowd's attention moved on to someone else.

She leaned her head on his shoulder, and he was scared to move in case it would be just the jolt she needed to change her mind. But several minutes later, she turned and looked up at him, her eyes hooded. "Let's go."

He hesitated, worried that he'd gone too far and that she'd

changed her mind about him. Worried that she'd run from him once they left the bar.

She got up, and he followed her out the door, ready for the debate of his life. But as soon they walked out into the summer night, she turned to him and pressed her lips to his. He froze for fear he'd ravage her in public.

When she pulled back, she looked up at him with her sexy eyes. "Take me to your hotel."

He wondered how fast he could get there.

Chapter Twenty-Five

BLAIR MYERS HANSEN wasn't impulsive. Every move was carefully thought out and executed. So on the surface, asking Garrett to take her to his room seemed impulsive. But she had no doubt that it was the best idea of her life.

She'd spent most of her time in the piano bar trying to talk herself out of it, but no argument had stuck. Ultimately, she believed Garrett's account of their breakup. And if he hadn't cheated on her and she was now single, what was keeping them apart?

The speed with which Garrett was ushering her down the sidewalk to his car was amusing. "It's not a race, Garrett."

"Says you," he muttered, looking down at her shoes. "Can't you go any faster?"

She laughed. "No. I'm not frolicking off to have sex with you. This isn't some cheesy movie."

"Then you aren't properly motivated." He grabbed her hand and tugged her into an alley. He pushed her back against the brick wall and kissed her roughly, his hands grabbing her hips and pulling her to him. When he lifted his head, he looked down at her panting. "Did that help?"

She was grateful the wall was at her back to hold her up. "What was the question?"

He kissed her again, and she clung to him, pulling him flush against her.

Garrett backed away. "If we don't stop, I'll have to ask you how you feel about sex in public, which was something I never considered before this moment."

She grinned up at him. Oh, yes, she'd forgotten this part—the passion and the fun. "You've made me dizzy. I may walk even slower now."

"Are you trying to manipulate me into carrying you?" A grin spread across his face. "Because I'll do it."

"Ha." She laughed. "I suspect you've gone soft in the office. All those late hours working on briefs."

"Remember when we worked on that group project for our Evidence class?" He nuzzled her neck, sending shivers down her back. "I still found time to work out then."

"Sex doesn't qualify as a workout, Garrett."

He shot her a wicked look. "I think some of *our* sessions did." He kissed her again, and her memories of their shared passion only made her hotter.

She pushed him away. "Let's go before we get arrested for public indecency."

He laughed and stepped away from her, snagging her hand in his. She was amazed by how familiar he still felt, how right.

Soon they were in his car, en route to his hotel, and even though they didn't talk, she didn't feel awkward. When he pulled up to the valet, he got out and met her on the other side, grabbing her hand to help her out of the car.

"Nice hotel," she murmured as they crossed the lobby.

He looked down at her with hooded eyes. "I hadn't noticed." He pushed the elevator call button and groaned when he saw it was on the eleventh floor. "I would consider the stairs, but those shoes of yours will never make it."

"What's the hurry?" she teased. "Afraid I'll change my mind?"

Fear flickered in his eyes. "Yes."

She wrapped a hand around the back of his neck, pressed her chest to his, and looked up into his eyes. "I'm not going anywhere."

The elevator dinged and the doors slid open, allowing an older couple out of the car. Garrett snaked his arm around her waist and held her close to him as he backed into the elevator, already lowering his face to hers.

She sucked his bottom lip between her teeth—a move she knew drove him crazy. He groaned, his hand sliding down over her ass and pulling her firmly against him. White-hot lust rushed through her, and she was suddenly beyond impatient to get to his room.

The elevator doors opened, and she heard voices. Garrett dropped his hand and lifted his head, but he kept her snugged against his chest as two other couples entered the car.

She turned to face the wall, embarrassed that they'd almost been caught. Prim and proper Blair Myers had never been so prim and proper with Garrett when it came to sex. He made her lose all reason. Was that a good thing or a bad one?

The elevator chimed again, and the doors opened. Garrett turned her around, ushered her into the hall, and led her to a room at the end of the hall.

She suddenly felt nervous as she followed him into the room, especially when he shut the door behind them. If she chose to do this, she knew it wouldn't be just sex. It would mean entrusting him with her heart.

"Blair, turn around."

She slowly spun to face him, expecting to see lust in his eyes. It surprised and disarmed her to see adoration instead. He closed the distance between them and rested his hands on her hips. "I love you, Blair. Let me prove it to you."

Her back stiffened. "Don't break my heart again, Garrett."

He smiled. "I won't. I swear. I'm yours."

Chapter Twenty-Six

UNCERTAINTY FLICKERED IN HER EYES, but she must have accepted his answer because she grabbed the sides of his face and pulled his mouth to hers. His resolve to hold back, to give her more time, evaporated. His lips and tongue devoured hers, while his hold on her hips tightened, pressing her against his growing erection.

His hand found the zipper on the back of her dress and tugged it down, sending the straps of her dress slipping off her shoulders.

She pulled her arms out of the sleeves so the top of her dress pooled at her waist, exposing her plain beige bra. She glanced down self-consciously. "I'm not wearing anything sexy."

He tipped her chin up so he could look into her eyes. "You're beautiful, Blair. You could wear an old, holey T-shirt covered with stains, and I'd still think so."

She smiled and didn't look away from his eyes as her fingers made quick work of the buttons on his shirt. She pushed it off his shoulders, her fingers trailing over his bare shoulders and arms. A bolt of desire shot through him, and he pushed her dress and panties over her hips and down to her feet, and then tugged her over to the bed and pulled down the covers.

He pulled her to his chest and kissed her, his hands

roaming her body and stopping at the clasp of her bra. He quickly undid it and then slid the straps over her shoulders. He moved back, letting it drop to the floor as he took a step back to look at her.

She had his belt unfastened in seconds, but she got hung up on his button.

"You're taking too long." His hands tried to brush hers away, but she grinned and swatted them.

"Patience."

He groaned. "I've waited five years for this. I'm done with being patient." He took over and dropped his pants and underwear.

He reached for her, but she gave him a sexy smile and took a step back so she could sit on the bed. She slowly tumbled onto her back, her hair pooling around her on the sheets. This was Blair's playful side—rarely released, but oh so beautiful to see. Then the look in her eye—that teasing glint—faded, replaced with raw need. He wanted to touch her, to give her the pleasure she needed from him, but he took a moment to enjoy the sight of her.

"I thought you were done with patience."

"I could have a million years, and it wouldn't be long enough." He lay beside her and leaned over to capture her mouth with his as his hand roamed her body.

She reached for him, and he groaned as she circled his erection with her soft, lithe hand. He shifted so he could grab her wrist, then pinned it to the bed over her head. "I won't last one minute if you keep that up."

"Is that your final answer?" She laughed.

"Yes." His mouth skimmed her neck, trailing kisses down her chest and brushing her nipple, causing her chest to rise and fall in rapid succession. His free hand slipped between her legs and into her folds. Her back arched, and her eyelids closed.

"This hardly seems fair," she forced out as his tongue traced her areola. "You have me captive, and I can't do anything to you."

"You're doing plenty to me just the way you are," he said in a low growl, torn between taking his time getting reacquainted with her body and ravaging her. He moved his attention to her other breast as he plunged his finger inside her and rubbed her mound with the heel of his hand.

"Garrett." Her voice was impatient as she squirmed underneath him.

"What do you want, Blair?"

"I want you, and I want you now."

He tortured her for several seconds more, taking delight in her groans of frustration before he lifted his head to study her face, his hand moving in slow circles between her legs. "Are you on birth control?"

Her eyes flew open. "What?" But then the question seemed to sink in. "No. Please God, tell me you have a condom."

He grinned, his hard-on aching as he studied her swollen lips and hooded eyes. "And if I said no?"

She grinned back. "You'd have to wear a pair of loose gym shorts and a long T-shirt to the nearest pharmacy."

He sat up and pulled a small box out of the drawer, opening the flap to remove a package. "Good thing I have this."

"A new box," she murmured.

He turned his attention to her, wondering what she would read into his next words. "I bought them for you."

Her body tensed, and her eyes were guarded. "You thought you'd be having sex with me?"

"Honestly, Blair? No. I only wanted you to give me a chance. I never expected that we'd be doing this. Hoped? God, yes." He leaned over her, placing a soft kiss on her full lips and resisting the urge to devour them. He looked into her eyes. "I *hoped* I'd have the chance again, because there's never been anyone like you. Every other experience I've had has been hollow and empty. It has only made it alarmingly clear what I really need." He kissed her gently again. "I need *you*."

She reached up and kissed him with a fire that consumed him, and then pulled away to take a package out of the box and rip it open. Just the feeling of her rolling it over his erection was about to do him in. "I need you too," she finally said.

He rested his elbow next to her head, kissing her while his hand skimmed between her breasts, slowly glided down her abdomen, and ended up between her legs once more. Within seconds she moaned and lifted her hips to him.

"Garrett."

"Not yet," he murmured against her lips, moving his mouth over her jaw and down to her neck.

"I thought you were impatient."

"I was impatient to touch you."

His mouth found her breast again, his tongue and teeth making her squirm.

She gasped, her nails digging into his shoulders. "Now I'm impatient. I want you *now*, Garrett."

He sat up and moved between her legs, getting to his knees. Lifting her ankle behind his back, he looked down at her, appreciated the beautiful strong lines of her body. "I'll give you anything, Blair. You only have to ask." Then he entered her in one stroke as she arched up to take him in.

Her eyes sank shut, and her chest rose. He reached for her breast, his thumb softly brushing her nipple, reveling in the way she writhed beneath him. When he pulled back and entered her again, she lifted her other leg and locked her ankles, clinging to him.

She reached for him, but he laced his fingers with hers and placed her hands on either side of her head as he leaned over her, pushing deeper. He kissed her deeply, his tongue mimicking his thrusts.

As soon as he felt her tighten around him, he shifted slightly, eliciting a soft cry from her. He moved his mouth next to her ear as he released one of her hands and tilted her pelvis up, concentrating on her needs, wanting more than anything to push her over the edge. She arched up again and released a low guttural sound before moaning his name.

The sound of his name on her lips, like this, was his undoing. He plunged into her harder, needing to get deeper. Her hands grabbed his ass, helping him with his goal. He rocked against her, and she came again, and her soft sounds as she tightened around him pushed him over the edge. He pushed into her with several more grunts before collapsing on top of her. He could make love to her from now until forever, and he would never have enough of her.

She moved beneath him. Realizing he was crushing her, he rolled to his side, taking her with him.

For a moment she didn't say anything, and he worried she was feeling regret, but then she opened her eyes and stared at him with amazement. "I don't remember it being that good."

"It's only going to get better."

Uncertainty filled her eyes, so he kissed her. At first it was just to show her he wasn't going anywhere, but with her naked body pressed against him, her leg still slung over his hip, he found himself getting hard again.

She laughed against his lips and leaned forward to rake her teeth over his lower lips. "Again?"

His hand moved to her breast, and he grinned. "Blazer, we're only getting started."

Chapter Twenty-Seven

BLAIR WOKE up to sunlight filtering through the cracks of the hotel room's drapes. Today was her wedding day, and here she was in a tangle of sheets and limbs with another man.

Guilt practically choked her as she pushed up, letting the sheet pool at her waist.

"Blair?" Garrett's voice was groggy with sleep as his arm tightened around her waist. "Come back."

"I have to go." The words were delivered in a wobbly voice, and he was instantly awake.

He bolted into a sitting position. "Why? What's wrong?"

Tears burned her eyes. "I have to talk to Neil."

His eyes flew open wider with alarm. "Why?"

"We're still engaged, Garrett. Him calling me a bitch and stomping off didn't officially break us up."

His jaw clenched, and his eyes turned dark. "He called you a *bitch*?"

She gave him a tight smile. "I probably deserved it."

"I don't think so. I want to talk to him too."

She laughed softly. "Admitting that I'm turned on by you going slightly caveman seems wrong, especially since it theoretically sets women's rights back a few decades." She gave him a kiss. "But nevertheless, I don't need you to talk to him. I'm perfectly capable of talking to him myself."

He shook his head, his jaw set. "I don't want you talking to him at all."

"Garrett. A little caveman goes a long way. Now is not the time for jealousy."

"It's not jealousy, Blair." He swallowed and picked up her hand in his. "He doesn't love you. I'm worried he'll do something to hurt you."

She shook her head in disbelief. "Neil would never hit me."

"There are other types of pain besides physical violence."

She narrowed her eyes. What did he know that he wasn't telling her? "Garrett, I still have a wedding scheduled for five o'clock this evening. I have to deal with this situation."

"But you're not still marrying him, right?"

She gestured to the mussed covers. "After this? I would never have slept with you if I still intended to marry Neil."

His eyes closed, and his shoulders sank. "Thank God."

"You really thought I'd go back to him?" she asked in disbelief.

His eyelids flew open, and he gave her a wry smile. "No, but I just got you back." He picked up her left hand and twisted the ring on her finger. "And you're still wearing his ring."

Oh, God. She was. Did that make her a cheater after all?

"I'd like to think of it as you wearing *my* ring."

Her gaze lifted to his, confusion in her eyes.

"My mother is the eldest daughter. Legally, the ring belongs to my mother. Not Aunt Debra."

"It's an *engagement* ring, Garrett."

His eyes searched hers as his fingers tightened on the band. "I know, and I'll get you another one if you'd like. One that's more like you." He clambered around her and off the bed, and then dropped to one knee beside her. "Blair, I love you, and I don't want to spend another day without you. Marry me."

She grinned. "Did you seriously just propose to me on one knee—*naked?*"

He lifted his shoulder and smirked. "Full disclosure. Literally."

Her smile fell. He was serious. "Garrett . . ."

He rose to sit on the side of the bed, then cradled the back of her head and pulled her mouth to his. His tongue parted her lips and ignited another fire of desire inside her. She had no doubt that she loved him, and no one had ever made her feel the way Garrett did, but . . .

She pushed against his chest, pulling back. "It's so sudden. Where would we live? How would this work?"

He cupped her cheek, looking up into her eyes. "For once in your life, go with your heart, Blair. Not with your head."

"But my job—"

"Fuck Sisco, Sisco, and Reece. Why would you want to work for them after the sexist stunt they pulled on you?"

"So I give up my job—and you just keep *yours?*"

"From what you said, if you're not getting married tonight, you won't have a job to give up." He said it matter-of-factly, but not without sympathy.

Oh, God. He was right.

He held her hand. "I'll quit mine too. We'll both start over. I don't care where we live, Blair. As long as it's *together.*"

This was crazy. They had both changed in five years. They needed more time. But looking into his eyes now, she knew she could wait five minutes or five more years, and she'd still want the same thing. She'd want him.

For once she was going to listen to her heart.

"Yes."

He tackled her onto the bed, capturing her mouth and showing her what she had to look forward to as his wife.

A half hour later, she lay in his arms with her head nestled against his chest. His fingers stroked her back, and she looked up at him. "Garrett, I still need to see to Neil."

"Why don't you just call him?"

She pushed up on one elbow. "I can't end this on the phone. That's nearly as bad as breaking up with someone in a text message."

"I know, but it was worth a shot." He grinned, but the expression faded quickly. "At least you're seeing him with *my* ring now."

She sat up and sighed. "I need to go home and change. But my car's still at the church. And I have to find out who has my purse."

He sat up, snatched his phone off the nightstand, and handed it to her. "I'll drive you home, but why don't you call him to set up a time? I'm sure there are arrangements that need to be canceled."

She cringed, overwhelmed by the enormity of the task.

He smiled at her and gave her a kiss. "It's going to be okay. I'll help you. I'm sure Megan and Libby will help too."

She nodded. "Thank you."

He put the phone in her hand and stood. "I'll go into the bathroom and give you some privacy, but come join me in the shower when you're done."

"Okay."

She watched him walk into the bathroom and shut the door. When she heard the water come on, she took a deep breath to steady her nerves as she placed the call.

"Where is she, Garrett?" Neil answered. The obvious hate in his voice caught Blair off guard.

"It's not Garrett," she said. "And I'm right here."

"Blair." His tone softened. "God, I've been so worried about you."

"I'm fine."

He paused, and his voice was cold when he spoke again. "I'm sure you are, since you're calling me at nine in the morning on our wedding day from your ex-boyfriend's phone."

She cringed but didn't respond. It was deserved. "I need to see you, Neil."

"It's bad luck to see your groom on your wedding day."

She rested her elbow on her knee and pressed her hand against her forehead. "*Neil.*"

"Okay. I'll meet you."

"Thank you."

"You know I love you, Blair. If you need reassurance, and I'm sure you do after your . . . night—I'll be more than happy to give it to you. Do you want me to come to the condo?"

"I'm not there."

"I see." He paused. "Can you come to my loft?"

Something in his voice sounded off, not that she blamed him. He was handling it better than she would have if their situations had been reversed. "I'd rather meet somewhere neutral."

He was silent for several seconds. "Garrett's staying at the Omni, and I know for a fact your car is still at the church. There's a bakery a block away from the hotel, close enough for you to walk there. Can you be decent in a half hour?"

She cringed again, but she deserved that too. "Yes. I'll meet you then."

"I know you're worried about sparing my feelings, but I fully expect you to show up in the dress you wore last night." His voice broke. "So don't worry about changing. I just want to see you. I can overlook what you're wearing."

"Neil," she forced past the lump in her throat. "I'm sorry."

"It's going to be fine, Blair. Just come see me."

She hung up and set the phone on the nightstand. It dinged, so she picked it back up.

There was a text on the screen from BD: *The contract still needs some work. We'll try to have it done in time.*

She cringed when she realized she'd read a professional text. Then it dinged again, and a new one popped up.

That's a lot of money to give up for a woman. I hope she's worth it.

Was that text about her? What money was he giving up?

Garrett found her sitting on the bed when he got out of the shower. He pulled her up and into his arms, his body still damp.

"Blair? Are you okay? Did he—"

Her mouth twisted to the side. "He was more understanding than I would have been." She paused, then looked into his eyes. "Why did you go to see Neil at his office?"

He swallowed. "I'm not sure what bullshit he told you, but from your reaction when I confirmed going there, it couldn't have been good. But I promise you, I only went to find out if he really loved you."

"And?"

His jaw tightened. "I was unsatisfied with his answers. Do you believe me?"

She wanted to ask about the texts too, but she worried she'd come across as defensive or snooping. Bottom line, she trusted him or she didn't, and she wholeheartedly did. "Yes."

He cradled her head to his chest. "So you and Neil are done?"

She pulled away to look at the clock on the nightstand. "No. I have to meet him in twenty minutes, and I still need a shower. I can't meet him smelling like you."

"If he knows, then you don't need to see him."

She slid off the bed. "I do. It's the right thing to do."

He stood up and stared into her eyes. "I love you, Blair. I'll do anything I can to help you. Just tell me what you need."

She shook her head. "This part I have to do alone. Then when I'm done, we'll figure out the rest together."

"You might not have to do it at all."

Blair groaned. "I just told you that I did."

"No. He might end it without you going."

She narrowed her eyes. "I just talked to him on the phone, Garrett. He knows I called from your phone, and he very much still wants to get married."

His face contorted with anger. "He's up to something. Let me go with you."

"I'm a big girl. I can handle myself."

He looked torn, but he pulled her close and gave her a soft kiss. "Okay."

She took a quick shower and dried her hair before putting on her dress. Garrett gave her privacy, but he was waiting for her when she emerged from the bathroom.

He pulled her into his arms. "Are you sure you want to do this? At least let me walk you there."

She pushed him away and broke free. It didn't feel right to let him hold her before she went to see Neil. "I don't want to do it, but I *need* to do it. And I have to hurry, or I'm going to be late."

Worry filled his eyes. "I wish you had your phone."

A low laugh escaped her, and she forced a smile. "I'm walking all of a block to see a mild-mannered man. What do you think is going to happen to me? Physically, I'm perfectly safe. Emotionally, I deserve everything I'm going to get."

"Blair. Don't say that. You don't deserve the stress he's putting you through."

"Why not? I knew I didn't really love him. Not like this. The relationship wasn't fair to him. And now we're both paying the price."

"Neil is hiding something from you. Something big." Indecision flickered in his eyes. "Make him tell you what I found out when I went to see him."

She shook her head. "What are you talking about?"

He gave her a soft kiss. "You're a good person, Blair. No matter what you believe right now. Make him confess, and you'll realize you've made the right decision, even if you take me out of the equation."

That sounded ominous. "What is he hiding, Garrett?"

He shook his head. "I want him to be the one to tell you."

Five minutes later she made the walk of shame to the bakery and found Neil sitting at a table, two cups of coffee in front of him.

He stood when he saw her, wariness in his eyes. "You came."

"I said I would."

He gave her a soft smile. "You're a woman of your word. I've always loved that about you."

She sat in the chair across from him. He sat back down and slid one of the cups toward her. "I got you a vanilla latte. No whip. Just the way you like it."

She grasped the cup with a shaking hand. She wished she were more confident, but was that a positive character trait when you dumped your fiancé on your wedding day? "Thank you."

"I know that about you," he said in a low voice. "Just like I know you hate wearing socks in the winter, and you like to eat mac and cheese with a spoon instead of a fork."

She swallowed, fighting back tears. "Neil."

He leaned forward and grabbed her hand. "We've been together for two years now, Blair. That's more time than you spent with him."

She looked up at him. "But I don't love you."

"You keep telling me that, but I think you've confused love

with lust." He shook his head, his eyes pleading with her. "Remember when I had the flu last year? You took off work and stayed at my loft for three days to take care of me. *That's* love. And when you pick up those cheese crackers at Trader Joe's, just because you know I love them—*that's* love."

"Neil."

He shook his head. "No, Blair, it's true. What you had with Garrett last night is lust, and lust fades," he said. "Where will you be when that happens?"

Her cheeks burned with shame.

"Darling, I understand that you got scared last night. Especially after my mother's tirade and my temper. I don't blame you for running off, and I'm not surprised Garrett took advantage of your vulnerability."

She thought about telling him he ran off before she did, but there was no point. Still, there was no way she'd allow him to treat her like she was a biddable and naïve woman incapable of making her own decisions. "Garrett didn't take advantage of me. I'm a grown woman. I made my own choice."

"I called you a terrible name. I hurt you, and I'll never forgive myself for that. But Garrett saw an opportunity and took it. He's an opportunist."

She remained silent, telling herself it was pointless to argue with him.

"What about your job, Blair? If we don't get married, you're going to be fired."

"I know."

His face turned red, and he took several deep breaths before continuing. "So you're going to throw *everything* away after one night with the man who broke your heart? You're going to regret this decision when he leaves you for some other woman. And we both know he will."

He was giving voice to the fears that niggled at the back of her brain. But the night she'd spent with Garrett had only pointed out all the inadequacies of her relationship with Neil. Deep down she'd always known she was settling, and now she had the proof.

"Blair. I still love you," Neil pleaded, tears in his eyes. "I'm begging you to think this through. I can't stand back and let him do this to you." He paused, his eyes searching hers. "I'm willing to overlook your indiscretion. I understand why you did it, and I forgive you. I still want to marry you today."

She groaned. "How can you say that? I wouldn't be so understanding if it were the other way around. I'd be handing you your ass on a platter."

"I know. It only proves how much I love you."

"I can't marry you, Neil."

He took a breath and looked at her with eyes full of understanding. "Darling, don't make a decision of this magnitude based on *one* night with a man who is determined to break us up. How can you be sure that this isn't part of his plan?"

"He wouldn't do that." She pushed on. "In fact, Garrett said you're hiding something from me."

He paused. "What exactly did he say?"

"He said you were hiding something big."

Neil paused and then shook his head. "If he's talking about Layla, that's his story to tell. I won't hurt you that way." When she started to protest, he said, "You're still wearing my ring."

She glanced down at her hand. This ring had been nothing but trouble. She'd gladly take it off and give it to Neil, but according to Garrett, it belonged to him, not Neil. Which meant it wasn't hers to return.

"Why are you still wearing the ring, Blair? Why not just take it off and give it to me?"

"I can't."

He grabbed her hand and held tight. "Because you really

do love me, even if you can't admit it. You still want to marry *me*."

"Garrett says the ring is his."

"And yet you're still wearing it." His tone was harsh.

She took a deep breath, her voice wavering. "I'm sorry."

"He asked you to marry him and you said yes? *After one night?*"

She cringed. "Yes."

His face reddened, his hand holding hers tighter. "You made me wait months to propose—you said you weren't ready. Yet you accept his proposal *after one night?*"

"Neil." Her voice broke. She might not love him, but it still killed her to hurt him like this. "I'm sorry."

He released her hand and sat back in his chair, staring out the window for several seconds before pulling out his phone and glancing at the screen. He stuffed the phone back into his pocket and gave her a soft smile. "All I want is for you to be happy. If this is what you want, you have my blessing. You're sure?"

"Yes."

"Then I wish you the very best. Both of you."

Her mouth dropped open.

"Don't look so surprised. I care about you . . . and despite everything, Garrett is my cousin. He's family."

There was no way he could be handling this so well. What was he up to?

"Why don't you let me walk you back to his room, and we can sort this all out."

She shook her head. "I don't think that's a good idea." Was that why he was taking it so well? Did he want to go over to confront Garrett?

He grimaced. "Blair, this entire situation is incredibly awkward. Not only are we canceling a wedding, you're planning to marry my cousin. The least you can do is help come up with some kind of story that will allow me to save face with my family." When she didn't answer, he added, "This affects Garrett too. If you really don't care about how this is going to affect me, at least consider *him*."

"I really think this is a terrible idea, Neil."

"I'm trying to be the bigger person here, and I'm willing to let bygones be bygones. Are you really going to refuse me?"

He was right. This *would* be awkward. If they could come up with some kind of understanding now, it would go a long way toward keeping their family from being torn apart. Over her.

"Okay." She looked into his face. "Thank you." She still wasn't certain it was the right decision, but she had to admit he was being reasonable. Still, she hated springing this on Garrett. She now wished she had brought his phone so she could warn him by calling the hotel room phone.

Neil stood and looked impatient as he waited for her, ushering her toward the door. "Thanks for being reasonable, Blair. I'm sure you'll appreciate it later."

She only hoped Garrett saw it that way.

Chapter
Twenty-Eight

GARRETT HAD NEVER BEEN SO nervous in his life. He knew Neil wouldn't let Blair go without a fight, and Blair had gone to meet him without knowing everything. How stupid could he be? Now Neil could spin an elaborate web of lies, especially since Garrett had fed her that vague line about Neil's secret. But Garrett just hadn't been able to bring himself to tell her something that would hurt her . . . even though he wasn't the perpetrator.

What bothered him even more was that Neil hadn't returned his text. He'd been purposely vague in an attempt to pique his interest. Maybe Garrett had underestimated Neil's intentions. But Blair was breaking up with Neil, which made it a moot point. So why didn't that reassure him?

He'd turned on the TV to try and take his mind off his nerves, but he couldn't quell his anxiety. Something told him that things were about to go very, very bad.

Dammit.

He walked over to the window and looked down at the street, eager for a glimpse of her.

She had only been gone for twenty minutes when a knock sounded at the door. He wondered why she was knocking if she had the room key. But she didn't have a purse, so there was the possibility that things had gotten tense and she'd left it at the coffee shop.

When he opened the door, he was surprised to see Layla, the woman he'd found in Neil's office.

"Garrett?" she asked, looking nervous.

"Uh . . . yeah . . ." He blinked.

"Can I come in?"

He blocked the entrance, still in shock. "What are you doing here? How'd you know how to find me?"

"Neil got your message."

"So why are you here instead of Neil?"

"Can I come in?" Tears filled her eyes. "Please."

He swung the door open, and she walked past him into the room, looking around and taking in the sight of the mussed bed.

Garrett stood at the still-open door. He didn't feel comfortable with her in the room, and he definitely didn't trust her or her motives. "Did Neil send you?"

"No."

Why was she here? When he thought about it, Layla most likely had the same goal Garrett had—prevent the wedding. He still didn't understand why it wasn't Neil at his door instead of his girlfriend.

"Can you shut the door?"

He heaved out a breath and looked into the hall. "I think I'll leave it open. Why don't you just get to the point?"

She sat down on the bed and grasped her shaking hands.

"Look, if you're upset about Neil marrying Blair, you don't have to worry. She's breaking up with him as we speak."

She shook her head, a tear sliding down her cheek. "There's something you have to know."

"What?" She didn't respond, and he wondered why she was there. The only reason he could come up with was that she wanted Neil to ditch Blair so she could have him. "Neil's free now. Or he will be in a few minutes. You can run off and be together."

"There's more to it. Please. I think you're the only one who can help me." Tears streaked down her face. Garrett's room was at the end of the hall, giving them a complete view all the way to the end. A door opened several rooms down, and a couple emerged into the hall. They looked down at the woman crying on his bed and gave him a dirty look.

With a groan, he shut the door. "Okay, you're here. I'm listening. What do I need to know?"

"Neil's not who you think he is."

He released an annoyed grunt. "I've known the man for nearly thirty years, and I'm not a fan, so I'm not sure there's anything you can tell me that will surprise me right now."

She stood and moved toward him. "You seem like a nice man."

"Layla, spit it out already. What do you want?"

She stopped in front of him. "I've met Blair before, you know."

The very thought made him livid. "You mean at the hospital?"

"No. Before that. When she and Neil first started dating."

His fists clenched. "Were you and Neil already having sex then?"

She looked up at him, defiance in her eyes. "It's not like that. It's not that crass."

"Then what's it like? Because he was going to marry her and have sex with you. Sounds pretty crass to me."

"No. He only realized he loved me after he proposed to her." She shrugged. "But he has to marry her so we can be together. She's got a huge trust fund. After they're married for a year, he can divorce her and get half her money."

"Is that what he told you? You really bought that bull-shit?" He shook his head in disgust. Could she really be that gullible? But then again, maybe that was part of her appeal. Neil had said he couldn't stay with one woman long. So his choices made sense. Marry the respectable woman. Sleep with the not-so-bright ones, feed them a few lines to string them along, and then find a replacement mistress once the relationship had run its course. "There is no trust fund. Blair's father left her and her mother penniless. He's lying to you."

Layla's eyes widened, and fresh tears filled her eyes. "No. He wouldn't do that."

"He's a doctor, Layla. Why would he need her money to be with you? Why not ditch her and marry you?"

"Why do you even like her?" Layla asked. "She's such a cold bitch."

He took a step back, the hair on the back of his neck standing on end. "I think you should go."

"Why would Neil want to be with someone like that unless he wanted her money?"

"Layla, I can't help you. You need to talk to Neil about this."

"Do you know how they met?"

Why wasn't she leaving? He'd given her the information she wanted, so why hadn't she just left? But then again, she hadn't actually told him what she wanted. "What does it matter? Layla, what do you want?"

"A guy from Blair's office set them up. He told Neil that she was a hotshot lawyer on the rise with a multi-million-dollar trust fund. The rest is history." She reached for the bottom of her shirt and tugged it over her head, revealing a purple bra.

"What the hell are you *doing*?"

She tossed her shirt onto the floor and moved toward him,

unfastening her pants. "You think Neil's stupid, but he's actually very, very smart."

He backed up toward the door. "I need you to leave."

"Neil is much more calculating than most people give him credit for." Her pants dropped to the floor next, and she backed him into the door, pressing her nearly naked body against him. All he felt was disgust and revulsion.

He moved away from her, heading into the middle of the room. "You need to go. *Now.*"

"Not yet." She moved toward him. "I know you don't believe it, but I know the trust fund exists. I love him, and we'll be together soon enough. It's just not time yet."

He heard voices outside the door, and he froze in place as panic washed over him.

Layla put her arms around his neck and smiled. "Trust me. You'll thank me for this later. She's a bitch." And then she kissed him, locking her fingers around his neck.

Garrett was trying to pry her off him when the door flung open. Garrett's heart ripped open when he heard Blair's gasp.

Layla leaned back and turned toward the door. "Garrett, why are those people in your room?"

Blair's mouth dropped open, and she stumbled backward.

Garrett tore free of the clinging witch and shoved her aside. "Blair!"

She shook her head, tears filling her eyes. "You lying son of a bitch."

"I didn't do this, Blair. I swear. This is Neil's doing."

She shook her head again and flung her hand toward Layla, who stood in the middle of the room, wearing nothing but her bra and panties. "How can this be *Neil's* doing? This looks like it's all *you*, Garrett."

He pointed at Neil, barely keeping his anger in check. "He

sent her here! He'll do anything to keep you." He turned to Neil's mistress, his eyes narrowing. "And as Layla just pointed out, he's much more calculating than any of us had realized."

"*Layla?*"

Oh. God. Somehow he had just made it worse. What had Neil told her?

Blair put her hands on her hips and turned her murderous gaze on Neil's girlfriend. "You want him? You can *have* him." She took a step closer. "But right now, you better get the hell out of my sight, or I might not be responsible for what I do."

Layla's eyes widened, then she scooped up her clothes off the floor and hurried out the door. She cast a worried glance to Neil on the way out. He gave her a slight nod before she ran down the hall.

But Blair missed their silent interaction because she'd turned her attention back to Garrett. "And you . . . you worthless, disgusting excuse for a man."

"Blair," he pleaded. "Please listen to me."

Blair rushed toward him and shoved his chest. "There's not one damn thing I want to hear from you. I've heard enough to last a lifetime."

The pain in her eyes seized his heart, squeezing tight. How was he going to fix this? "It's not how it looks."

Contempt washed over her face. "Do you have any idea how many times I've heard those exact same words from the couples filing into my office? Do you think I'm an idiot?" She released a harsh laugh. "Oh, wait. I think this proves you do. Screw stupid Blair—then laugh about it with your cheap girlfriend."

She was killing him. "*Blair.*"

Neil put an arm around her shoulders, but she shoved it off. Garrett expected him to flinch from the rejection—instead, he grinned. "Blair, don't listen to him. He screwed you last night, and he didn't even wait for the hotel staff to change the sheets before he invited his girlfriend back over. I warned you that his room had a revolving door."

Blair shook her head in disgust.

Garrett took a step toward her. "He's doing this to get back at me, Blair. Layla's *Neil's* girlfriend. Not mine."

She put her hands on her hips. "And she just *happened* to be half-naked in your room?"

"It's not how it looks. I love you, Blair. You have to believe me. Nothing has changed that."

She glared at him, her face wrinkling in disgust. "You're right, Garrett. Nothing *has* changed. You're still the lying, cheating bastard I thought you were five years ago. You're not man enough to be in a relationship. I can't believe I was stupid enough to fall for your bullshit. *Again.*"

Neil put his hand on her arm. "Blair, let's go. You need to rest before the wedding."

She turned her gaze on him, venom in her eyes. "You think we're still getting *married?*"

Neil rolled his eyes. "Of course we're still getting married. Everything was fine until he showed up. Now that his true colors have shown through, there's no reason we wouldn't proceed with the wedding. Just like we planned."

Blair looked at Garrett, and he watched as the anger on her face faded, replaced with dismay.

"I don't know that woman, Blair. Neil sent her here to break us up." Garrett's voice cracked. "You have to believe me."

"I don't *have* to do shit." She spun around and stomped down the hall. "I don't ever want to see your sorry face again. Go to fucking hell!"

"Blair!" he shouted, trying to run after her.

Neil blocked his path and gave him a stone-cold smile. "I

told you not to screw with me, Garrett. I warned you that I *always* win."

Horror washed through him. "Oh, my God. You would hurt her like that to get back at me?"

Hate filled Neil's eyes. "I put it together after we started dating. It wasn't too hard. She went to the same law school you did, at the same time. She was dumped by a guy who slept his way through the school. So did you. It was a nice bonus, knowing I was seeing your old girlfriend. But then Nana insisted you come to the wedding, so I put an insurance policy in place to encourage her to keep our engagement. Just in case."

Oh, God. "Your friend is the junior partner who told her about the potential partnership or firing. He made it all up." He felt like he was going to throw up. "What the fuck, Neil?"

"Knowing how much she holds a grudge, I figured she'd castrate you on sight. But I had to make sure you wouldn't screw this up for me, so I convinced Ben to tell Blair the story about the partnership. She holds her job sacred, so I knew that even if she were still attracted to you, she'd never act on it. She'd offer up her firstborn child to stay at her firm. I never thought she'd consider dumping her job for *you*."

"Why are you trying to keep her so badly? Is this really all about you and me?"

"God, you really are a narcissist. Stealing something you want is a bonus. The thing I don't understand is why *you* want her. She's perfect for me. We'll live our mostly separate lives, but we'll both have the professional spouses we need. Do you know how hard it's been to find someone as detached as her? I'm not about to let that go."

Garret shook his head, speechless. Then he remembered his original plan. "I'll give you Nana's farm if you don't marry her."

Neil's smile fell. "You can't promise me that. It's not yours to give."

Garrett took a step toward him. "Nana told me she's giving me the farm. The entire thing."

"She's giving it to *you?*" He spat in disgust. "I *knew* it."

Garrett held up his hands. "But I'll give it to you. Everything except the land with the house and the barn."

Neil's eyes narrowed. "You would give all that up for *her?*"

Garrett took a breath, trying to hide his relief that Neil was listening. "I'm in the process of having a contract drawn up."

Neil studied him for a moment, then laughed. "That's a good one. You think I'm going to fall for this bullshit?"

"It's not bullshit. My friend is working on it now."

"How *convenient* that it's not ready yet. You think I'm just going to cancel the wedding on your word?"

"I'm telling you the truth, Neil."

Confusion clouded his eyes. "You'd really give up millions to keep her?"

Garrett shot him a glare of contempt. "I would ask 'wouldn't you?' but the fact we're still discussing it speaks for itself."

Neil rubbed his forehead, then looked up at Garrett, an ugly smile spreading across his face. "Okay. I'll do it. But . . ." He paused for long enough for hope to bloom in Garrett's heart. "You can't have her either."

"What the hell are you talking about?"

"If you can produce a contract before my wedding, I'll sign and call it off. But you have to agree you won't pursue her. The two of you are over."

Garrett shook his head in disgust. "You idiot, I can't put something like that in a contract."

"I know." He waved off the issue. "But you can prevent me

from releasing indiscreet photos of Blair that could cost her not only this job, but kill her career."

The blood rushed from Garrett's head. "What photos?"

Neil smiled, but evil filled his eyes. "I have a tape and photos of Blair. Having sex. I'm sure she would hate to have those get out."

Horror washed over Garrett. He could barely stand the thought of them having sex, let alone having it recorded for anyone to see. "Blair agreed to film a *sex tape?*"

Neil laughed. "Agreed? God no. But it shows her in several very compromising situations. And it's *very* clear it's her."

Garrett shook his head, still in shock. "You would do that to her?"

"I can't believe you have to ask me that, cousin. You really *don't* know me." He laughed. "But don't worry. This setup." His hand waved a circle around the room. "This pretty much makes sure you don't stand a chance, but just in case . . . I have my insurance."

"You really are a prick," he spat in disgust.

Neil smirked. "Tell you what. I'm going to continue with the plan as it stands. But if you show up with a contract before I say I do, you have a deal."

"You're presuming Blair will still marry you."

He grinned. "She will. Now that she's lost you, her job is the only thing she has left." Neil spun around and walked down the hall. "See you at the wedding."

BLAIR STOOD in the lobby of Garrett's hotel, trying to piece everything together. There was no denying there had been a half-naked woman in Garrett's room. And there was no denying the horrified look in his eyes. The real question was who was Layla and why was she there?

And then there was the inexplicable fact that Neil really expected her to still marry him. Why was he acting so calm and rational? She'd be furious in his shoes, and she didn't even love him. He claimed to love her, and yet he was acting like sleeping with his cousin was a crime on par with purchasing the wrong toilet paper brand.

But something else was nagging her, something she couldn't quite put her finger on.

She replayed their conversation in the bakery . . . and then it struck her like a bag full of bricks.

"Blair." Neil called her name from across the lobby. She turned to face him, newly amazed by how collected he seemed after the ugly scene upstairs. But that's what she'd wanted, right? Someone calm and rational.

Neil stopped in front of her and gently put his hand on her arm. "Are you okay, darling? I know that had to be humiliating."

She cringed. "You have no idea."

His face softened. "I meant what I said, Blair. I still want to marry you. I love you enough to overlook all of this."

She shook her head. "I just don't see how you can feel that way."

"I'm not like you."

"Thank God for that, right?" she asked dryly.

He placed a kiss on her mouth. "We'll go through with the wedding to save your job. Then we'll sort everything else out later. Okay?"

"That's right, we're going to save my job." It was all she had left. Her gaze narrowed. "I want you to propose to me again."

His eyes widened. "What?"

"I've heard another man's proposal and accepted it since last night, Neil. You need to propose again."

"Okay . . ." He took her hand in his. "Blair Hansen, you are perfect for me. Will you marry me?"

She smiled and took her hand from his. "I'll see you at the wedding." Then she turned and started for the door.

"But you don't have your car. Don't you want me to take you home?"

She looked back at him. "No. I have so much to do to prepare for the wedding. I want everything to be *perfect*."

Chapter
Twenty-Nine

GARRETT LOWRY WAS A DESPERATE MAN. He'd spent an hour repeatedly calling and texting Blair until Megan finally answered and told him that Blair had never picked up her purse. She still didn't have her phone.

The rest of the day was spent trying to get the contract for Neil put together, emailing documents back and forth between a law school friend who was a practicing estate law attorney in Missouri. But his heart was in his throat when he asked Nana to meet him in the hotel bar.

He sat at a table, nervously tapping his pen on the file sitting in front of him on the bistro table. As he watched her approach, hobbling toward him with her cane, he realized Neil might get his inheritance sooner than Garrett would like, and not just because he didn't want his cousin to have possession. She was walking slower than ever. She had more wrinkles, and her eyes were deeper set than usual. She looked older than her years, and it scared him.

When she neared the table, he stood to help her with her seat, and she waved him off. "The day I can't sit my ass in a chair is the day I'm checking into Sunnybrook Retirement Home."

"I already told you I wouldn't let that happen, Nana."

She eased herself onto the chair and looked up at him as he

sat across from her. "What are you going to do about it? Put me in your fancy California apartment?"

He shrugged. "I could move in with you."

She laughed. "Claiming your inheritance before my body's even cold."

His eyes flew open. "No, Nana! I—"

She laughed again. "Relax, boy. I'm teasing ya. That's not your style." She shifted around in her chair, leaning her hand on her cane. "But from the way you look, I presume there's still a wedding today."

He sighed. "It's a long story, but basically Neil tricked Blair into thinking I was about to sleep with another woman after she and I . . . had already gotten back together. She went to break things off with Neil, and he sent his girlfriend to my hotel room. She started stripping . . ."

"And Blair showed up?"

"Yeah, with Neil."

"Aww . . . and he made sure to paint you as the devil incarnate."

He didn't respond. The answer was obvious.

"So did you invite me here to lick your wounds for ya? 'Cause you know that's not *my* style."

"No, Nana." He swallowed. Jesus, this was hard. "I want to ask you for a favor."

"Go on."

"Neil is willing to be bought off."

"What the hell does that mean?"

"He's agreed not to marry Blair if I'll give him something in return."

Sadness filled her eyes. "So you give him my land in exchange for canceling the wedding."

He nodded, part of him dying inside.

"I thought that girl had some sense in her head. Why can't she just tell him no?"

"She doesn't know he's been cheating on her."

"Well, why not?"

"Uh . . ." he stammered. "It would hurt her. Badly. I couldn't bring myself to tell her."

"The girl I met at that spectacle of a wedding shower was no wilting flower. She's made of sterner stuff. She's not going to fall to pieces if she finds out, so what were you thinking?"

She was right. God, he was an idiot. Ever since he'd found out, he'd danced with the idea of telling her, but the time had never seemed right, and he'd never managed to force out the words. "Obviously, I wasn't."

"So tell her before the wedding and be done with it. If she chooses to marry the fool, let her accept the consequences."

"That's not all, Nana. He has something else up his sleeve."

"What?"

He grimaced. He hated to even think about Blair having sex with Neil, so the last thing he wanted to do was talk about it.

"Out with it, boy."

"He has photos of them . . . in bed. He says he'll make them public."

"Sex photos?" She shook her head and gave him a look of disgust. "You kids these days. No sense whatsoever." She put her hand on the table. "If she chose to take dirty pictures, then she shouldn't be ashamed of 'em. Let her accept the consequences of that too."

"That's just it, Nana. She didn't approve of the photos. She doesn't even know they exist, and they could destroy her career."

"So Neil is threatening to release them unless you sign over your inheritance?"

"Once he realized how far I was willing to go, yeah."

Her eyes were blazing. "I take it you need me to sign something to make this nice and legal."

He cringed. "Yes, ma'am."

She sighed, looking even older. "Well, where is it?"

He slid the paper out from the file. What was he doing? He was asking his grandmother to sign her life's work away to his maniacal cousin. And this was all his fault, because he was the one who'd spilled the beans about getting it all and setting the wheels in motion. "The document says I'm going to inherit everything except the house and the barn."

"I told you that you're going to get it all."

"It's safer this way. Give it to Kelsey. Then Neil has no chance at it."

She peered into his face for a long moment, her gaze as penetrating and sharp as ever. "You're really willing to give up everything for this woman?"

"Yes, ma'am. I'll do anything to protect her. Even if she never forgives me."

She picked up the paper and ripped it into two.

"Nana!"

"I raised ya right, despite your mother's influence. We're going to make this right, but we're not about to reward that ferret for his bad behavior. You're going about it all wrong, boy. Time to draw up a new set of papers."

He looked down at his phone, and his heart started racing. It was already three o'clock, and the wedding was at five. "I don't know if there's time."

"You just get the papers and show up at the church. We'll deal with the rest there."

"And what will these new papers say?"

She grinned. "It's time you learned from the master."

BLAIR STOOD in the nursery of the First Presbyterian Church, looking at her reflection in the mirror. Her wedding dress was on a hanger behind her. She'd never been like most girls, Megan and Libby included. She hadn't thumbed through bridal magazines and picked flowers and wedding colors when she was in high school. Blair wasn't a romantic kind of woman —at least not the capital "r" type of romantic many women went in for—yet she'd had some ideas of what her wedding would be like.

And this was so not it.

"Why are you doing this?" Megan pleaded for what had to be the millionth time. "Why are you marrying him?"

"I have my reasons."

Her friends had been so dismayed when she called to tell them the wedding was still on, Libby most of all. In fact, she still hadn't shown up. It was vaguely reminiscent of Megan's wedding. Only Blair had been the hold-out then.

And Megan and Josh had been in love.

Blair sucked in a deep breath. "The wedding is in twenty minutes. I need to get dressed."

"You don't want to wait for Libby?" Megan asked in dismay.

"She's not coming. Not that it matters."

"How can you say that?"

She shook her head. "It doesn't matter. Are you going to help me or not?"

The door opened, and Libby walked in, already wearing her red taffeta gown. "You should be in a Hallmark commercial. One for anti-romance."

"Zip it, Libby," Blair said, stomping over to her dress and pulling it off the hanger.

Megan grabbed her arm. "Blair! It's obvious your heart's not in this. And how could it be after your night with Garrett?"

Blair closed her eyes and fought tears. After the events of the morning, she was certain the relationship was unsalvageable. But she couldn't let herself think about that now. "I don't want to talk about Garrett."

"It wasn't how it looked, Blair," Libby said in disgust. "If you would get off your self-righteous high horse, you might be able to see that."

Blair sucked in a breath and turned to her. "You have to trust me, Libby. Can you *please* just trust me?"

Libby shook her head. "I'm here as your friend, because I love you, but this is without a doubt the single worst mistake of your life."

"Libby!" Megan shouted.

"You know it's true, Megs," Libby shot back. "You're just too busy trying to pretend everything is okay to point it out."

"This is Blair's decision. We have to respect it."

Blair ripped off her robe and grabbed the waist of her dress and started to step into it.

"Blair," Megan protested. "Let us help you."

"I don't need your help. I can do it by myself."

She poked her right arm through the sleeve while Megan stood in front of her. "But you don't have to do it yourself. Asking someone for help isn't a weakness."

If only people would stop telling her that. Blair shoved her other arm through the sleeve. "My mother taught me that depending on someone too much is a recipe for self-destruction. I will never make that mistake." Again. She was dangerously close to losing it. Well, all she had to do was make it through the service. *Then* she could fall to pieces.

A familiar voice called out from behind her, "I hope that isn't the only lesson I've taught you."

Blair spun around and gasped. An attractive blonde woman stood in the doorway, worry filling her eyes. She looked like an older version of Blair. "Mom."

Marla Hansen took several steps into the room. "Girls, I think I need a moment with my daughter."

Megan and Libby shot each other a look and hurried out the door as Blair's mother moved toward her.

"Oh, Blair. You're as beautiful as a bride could be, but you look absolutely miserable."

To Blair's horror, she started to cry.

"You're a difficult woman to find," her mother teased. "No one knew where you were all afternoon."

"I lost him, Mom."

"Who?"

"Garrett Lowry. I found him again, and then I lost him."

"Megan told me." Her mother pulled her over to a sofa, then wiped the tears from her cheeks. "Do you love Garrett?"

She let out a sob. "Yes."

"Then why are you marrying Neil?"

She sucked in a breath, trying to get control. "Because Garrett . . . There was a woman in his room this morning. Wearing only her bra and panties. Just like before. But Garrett was fully clothed, and he knew I was coming back to the room, so there was no way he was part of it. It didn't matter. I wasted no time ripping him apart and blaming him."

"Blair, that's the reaction any woman would have had."

She shook her head, crying harder. "You didn't see the look in his eyes. I was beyond awful. I ripped his heart out. He begged me to believe him, and I didn't."

"So all you need to do is apologize and give him time. You don't run into the arms of a man you don't love."

She shook her head.

"I did the same thing with your father, Blair, and all three of us were miserable. Don't make the same mistake."

Blair took a deep breath. "Neil is not a good person. I know that now. Maybe marrying him is what I deserve."

"No. Blair."

She stood and moved to the mirror, trying to reach around her back to zip up her dress. Her mother brushed her hand away and finished the job. She rested her chin on Blair's shoulder, staring at their reflections in the mirror.

"You deserve love, Blair. I know you have a hard time believing it. You think your father's rejection means you're unlovable, but it's not true. Libby and Megan love you unconditionally. Even Garrett Lowry is proof of that."

Tears filled her eyes again. "I hurt him. I drove him away five years ago, and I just did it again. Maybe I'm not meant to be loved."

"That's bullshit if I ever heard it. Everyone deserves to be loved, Blair. Don't give up on yourself. Not now. Not ever."

Blair stared at her reflection. She might be wearing a wedding dress, but her red eyes and nose looked better suited to a commercial for seasonal allergy medication. She grabbed her veil and jammed the comb into her head. "I'm going to set things right."

"By marrying Neil? I already told you—"

Blair stomped over to a table stacked with flowers and grabbed her bouquet. "You better take your seat. I'm ready to do this."

"What?"

Blair looked into her mother's eyes. "Trust me, Mom. I know what I'm doing."

"I want you to be happy, Blair."

To her irritation, she started to tear up yet again. "This is part of that plan, Mom. You know me—I always have a plan."

Her mother cupped her cheek and searched her eyes for a long moment. Then she pulled back and said, "When you were a little girl, I always knew when you were up to something from the look in your eyes." She kissed her cheek. "I trust you."

Blair nodded, trying to swallow the lump in her throat. "Thank you."

She walked to the door and flung it open, not surprised to see her two friends huddled outside. "The wedding's still on. Get your bouquets."

"But—!" Megan exclaimed.

"Let's go." She swept down the hall, her small train flowing behind her, until she reached the lobby of the church.

Melissa stood by the closed doors to the sanctuary. Her eyes widened in surprise when she saw Blair. "You aren't supposed to be out here yet. People will see you. I'm supposed to call you, remember?"

"I didn't want to wait."

Melissa looked her up and down, worry in her eyes. "Are you okay?"

"I'll be better once this is over."

"Blair, don't—"

Blair put her hand on Melissa's mouth. "Don't *you* start."

Melissa nodded, and Blair removed her hand. "Okay."

"Let's get this going immediately."

"But we have four more minutes."

Blair stomped her feet anxiously. "If I don't do it now, I might lose my nerve."

"Maybe you should listen to that inner voice, Blair," Libby said from beside her.

"Good to see you two are joining me," she snipped back.

Melissa looked flustered. "But people are still being seated."

"Okay, two minutes. Then we go."

Blair's mother, who'd trailed her out of the lobby, kissed her cheek. "Be kind to yourself, Blair. Then you're more likely to be kind to others. And stop lashing out at your friends. They only want to help you."

Kindness wouldn't help her now. She needed all her bluntness and all her anger. Her grief would ruin everything. But she nodded. "I love you, Mom."

"I love you too."

As her mother entered the sanctuary, Megan and Libby shot her looks of disappointment as they waited. Every time they started to say something, she cut them off.

Finally, Melissa lined them up and cued the pianist to begin the wedding processional, and Dena came running from the church offices.

"No one told me it was time!" she said, her face puckered in irritation. "I don't even have my bouquet."

"You don't need it," Blair snapped.

"I'm not going without my flowers!"

Blair thrust her bouquet at Dena's chest, and the woman scrambled to keep the flowers from falling. "Here. Now get going." She gave Dena a little push toward the now-open doorway.

The woman stumbled several steps before recovering and then paused for long enough to shoot a glare over her shoulder.

Oh, if you think you hate me now, just wait.

"Blair, what's going on?" Libby asked, her previous antagonistic attitude gone.

"I asked you to trust me. Can you do that?"

Libby searched her eyes. "Yeah. Why do I have a feeling this will be a wedding we'll never forget?"

"Because you know me well." She gave Libby's arm a small push. "See you after."

Libby started down the aisle wearing an ear-to-ear grin, leaving Blair alone with Megan and Melissa.

"Blair, I'm sorry," Megan whispered, tears in her eyes. "I should have trusted you."

"I've made some really stupid mistakes lately. I can see why you wouldn't." She smiled, her eyes filling with tears again. "Thanks for not giving up on me."

"Never." Megan gave her a kiss on her cheek.

"Megan," Melissa whispered. "It's time."

Megan started down the aisle, and then it was just Blair and Melissa. "Melissa, no matter what happens tonight, I want you to know you still have a job at Sisco, Sisco, and Reece. I talked to Mary in HR, and she said the other attorneys would be lining up to work with you."

"I'd rather stay with you. At least you believe in your cases. You're trying to help those women." She paused. "And you believe in me."

"There's more." Blair grimaced. "I made some calls this afternoon. Ben Stuart lied about the partnership. But I still might not have a job after what I'm about to do."

"You know I stand behind you no matter what." The music changed, and Melissa smiled. "It's time. Are you ready?"

She sucked in a deep breath. "Time to raise some hell."

Chapter Thirty

NANA RUBY HAD GONE to the church with his aunt and mother. They'd fought over who was stuck taking her, so Nana told them they both got to ride with her in her old pickup truck. With the windows down.

At first Garrett's friend wasn't too thrilled by the prospect of drafting a brand-new document, but he changed his tune as soon as he heard the terms, which gave him a good maniacal laugh.

"I owe you, man," Garrett said, rubbing his hand through his hair. He had just sent the document from his laptop to the printer in the hotel business center, and his heart was working double time. Would this actually work? "Seriously, send me a bill."

"Nah, just make me the best man in your wedding to this girl and we'll call it good. I'm happy to be an emissary for true love."

"Let's not put the cart before the horse." Garrett sighed. "One step at a time."

He hung up and pulled the three-page document off the printer, one page at a time, but the third page caused a paper jam. He tried—and failed—to open the printer. Panicked, he ran into the lobby and skidded to a halt at the front desk. "Can someone help me? The last page of this document is stuck in the printer, and I need it like five minutes ago." He glanced at the clock on the wall. 4:30. Blair would be walking down the aisle in just half an hour.

The startled hotel employee looked him up and down. "Someone will come around to help you in about ten minutes, sir. We're short-staffed."

Garrett leaned over the counter, desperation filling his words. "You don't understand. My entire *future* depends on that page. I need it to stop a wedding and save the bride-to-be from a terrible mistake." He knew he sounded like a crazy person. He found he didn't much care. He *was* a crazy person at this point.

"Oh, isn't that romantic," an older woman said behind him. "He's trying to stop a wedding."

"How's that romantic?" a man grumbled. "He's breaking up a wedding."

"I bet he loves the girl." She tapped Garrett on the shoulder. "Do you love the girl, young man?"

"Well, yeah . . ." he mumbled, then turned back to the bewildered desk clerk. "Please. Is there any way you can send someone sooner?"

The elderly woman approached the desk. "Can you send someone? This boy is trying to win his woman."

"With a paper?" the desk clerk asked, incredulous.

"Please," Garrett begged. "Just trust me."

The clerk shrugged. "Sorry. I don't know anything about the printers, and the guy who does just left the building. But he should be back in less than ten minutes."

"The wedding's in twenty-five minutes."

The older woman walked away from the desk, heading toward the busy lobby. "Excuse me," she asked in a voice as loud as an umpire's, "does anyone here know how to fix a printer? This young man is trying to stop a wedding and win his girl, but he needs a particular paper to do so, and the printer is jammed."

The entire lobby, which had been buzzing with activity moments before, came to a halt. The guests and employees began to murmur as they all stared at him.

"Isn't that sweet," a woman gushed.

"Do you love her?" another woman asked.

"Yes," he said, his face flushing. "I love her. Can anyone help me?"

A middle-aged man called out, "Why do you need the paper?"

Garrett put his hand on top of his head. "I just *do.*"

A woman hit the man on his chest, giving him a disapproving glare. "Roy! What kind of question is that?"

"It's a logical question, Bev!"

She scowled and gave his arm a slight shove. "Give him your printer."

"What?"

"Let him print off his paper thingamajiggy on your printer." She glanced over at Garrett. "Roy has a portable printer in his bag here. He can set it up and print off your paper."

"Thank God." Garrett hurried over to the couple and watched as the man slowly pulled his printer from a bag and set it on a coffee table in the lobby.

The man glanced around. "I need an outlet."

Garrett took the cord and plugged it in, then proceeded to watch the man set up the machine as slowly as humanly possible. A crowd gathered in a tight circle around them as he waited for the printer to warm up.

"Can I do anything to help?" Garrett asked, running his hand through his hair and glancing up at the clock.

"What time is your wedding, dear?" Roy's wife asked.

"At five. In fifteen minutes."

"Look out. Get out of the way!" a man shouted as the crowd parted. He appeared in the opening, wearing a hotel uniform, and handed a paper to Garrett, gasping for breath. "I heard about your situation while I was standing in line at the bakery. Is this what you need?"

Had the desk clerk called him? Garrett didn't care how he'd heard, only that he had what he needed. He snatched it from the man's hand and scanned it. "Yes. Thank you!" Then he grabbed the man's face and kissed his cheek. "Thank you!"

The employee grinned from ear to ear and blushed profusely as Garrett let him go and turned to the elderly gentleman who was still working on his printer. "Thanks for your help, Roy."

"Go get 'er!" his wife shouted, punching her fist into the air.

It was only as he ran toward the front door that he realized he'd parked valet. He'd have to wait several minutes for them to get his car.

"I need a taxi," he told the valet parking attendant.

"He's about to stop a wedding!" a young woman shouted out to the employee. "Make it snappy!"

The employee glanced at his hand. "With a *legal document?*"

Garrett released a groan. "It's a long story."

The attendant shook his head, warily eyeing the papers. "I don't know, dude. I'm not sure I should get involved."

Realization washed over Garrett, and he held them closer to the man. "You don't understand. I'm trying to *save* the bride. The groom is threatening her, and this will protect her."

The attendant's eyes widened. "Well, why didn't you say so?" He looked around the drive, a frown wrinkling his forehead. "It might take several minutes to get a taxi though."

"I don't have several minutes!" Why hadn't he thought to

have his car pulled out of the garage while he waited on the printer?

A hipster-looking guy in his twenties, a beanie cap on his head despite the August heat, tapped Garrett's arm. "Where's the wedding?"

"Uh . . ." Garrett shook his head. "The First Presbyterian Church."

A murmur went through the group of twenty-some-odd people who had gathered around him.

"We can drop you off," the young guy said. He turned to the woman next to him. "Can't we?"

She nodded enthusiastically. "Yeah! But I want to watch."

"Sure. Whatever." Garrett nodded and waved his arm. "Just get me there."

"Let's go," the guy said, leading him out to a tiny compact car parked in front of the hotel. His female companion climbed into the back while Garrett slid into the passenger seat, his knees tucked under his chin. He was surprised to see a small crowd of people following them.

A young woman leaned into his open window, her eyes bright with excitement. "He said the First Presbyterian Church, right?"

"Yep!" Garrett's new driver said, starting the car. "See you there."

To Garrett's horror, several people were hopping into the cars parked around them. "Oh, my God. Are those people following us?"

"Well, yeah," the woman in the back said with a laugh, huddled over her phone. "You always hear about this kind of thing, but who ever gets to see it? Shoot, people are tweeting about it. There are hashtags even."

"*What?*"

She laughed. "Yeah, there are two—#legalweddingcrasher

and #fixtheprinterstopthewedding. The second's kind of long, but it seems to have the most tweets. A hotel employee even tweeted that he was racing back from his break to help."

"You've got to be kidding me."

She laughed again. "You're going viral. What's your name?"

"Uh . . . Garrett. Why?"

She grinned, took a photo of him, and then started typing on her phone. "No reason."

"Stop tweeting about me!" Garrett didn't use Twitter much, but he dug his phone out of his pocket and pulled up the app, trying to remember his password. He looked up at the road and didn't recognize the route. "Do you know where you're going?"

"Yeah, I grew up around here. We're only about five minutes away."

Garrett glanced at his phone. His worthless Twitter app was open, but it was unusable without the proper password. "It's five minutes 'til. I should barely make it." Neil would be up at the altar already. Since he thought Garrett had a contract that would guarantee him a few million dollars, Neil wouldn't mind getting pulled away, but Nana Ruby had a part to play in this new scheme. How would he know where to find her?

"Oh," the woman in the back murmured, sneaking a glance up at him. "They have a good point."

"Who does? What are you talking about?"

"People think you look like shit. We need to clean you up if you're going to crash a wedding."

He let out a groan and looked down at his jeans and T-shirt. "I've spent an hour trying to hunt Blair down—"

She frowned and cringed. "Uh-uh. Don't put it like that. You sound like a stalker."

He shook his head. "And then I've spent the last three

hours trying to draw up a legal document to get my cousin to agree not to marry my ex-girlfriend. I didn't have time to change into my tux."

"Wait. Tux?" the driver interrupted. "You're in the wedding?"

"*Was.* My grandmother made me a groomsman, but after this morning, I doubt anyone wants me there."

"What happened this morning?" the guy asked, leaning closer.

"Uh . . ." What was he doing? He was spilling his guts to complete strangers. He looked over his shoulder—and saw that the woman behind him was tweeting a play-by-play. He snatched the phone out of her hand and scanned the screen. When he saw the photo of him littering the stream—his eyes half closed and his mouth open, his body twisted at a weird angle as he leaned over Roy in the hotel lobby—he understood her previous comment.

"I took another one." She grabbed the phone and swiped the screen. "Here."

The new photo showed him sitting in the front seat, his eyes wide, making him look crazed. He wasn't sure it was much better. "What are people saying?"

The woman beamed. "They love you. You're a trending topic."

Oh, shit. Blair was going to flip out. "You have to stop them."

"Dude," she laughed. "I couldn't stop it if I wanted to— which I don't. Helping something go viral is like my lifelong dream come true."

"You need new life goals."

She laughed again.

The car slowed down, and Garrett looked up to see a traffic jam. "Why's everyone stopped?"

"If I had to guess . . ." The guy sat up straighter, then looked out his side window. "I think there's a bunch of people going to the church."

"Wait. All the guests they invited would already be parked."

"Dude, you went *viral*. Don't you get it? These people found out about it on social media."

The blood rushed from his head. "All these people are going to Blair's wedding?" he asked in horror.

"Of course not," the guy laughed. "Some of these people are just driving. I guess about fifty percent are planning to go to the church."

"I'll find out," the woman said, typing furiously on her phone. Seconds later cars started honking.

"Huh," the guy said, twisting his mouth as he concentrated. "I'd say it's more than fifty percent."

The car came to a dead standstill. Based on the seemingly endless line of cars ahead of them, Garrett suspected they weren't moving very far, very fast any time soon. "How far is the church from here?"

"Uh . . . about three blocks up and one to the left."

Garrett opened his car door, holding the papers in his hand. "Thanks for the ride." He looked at the woman in the back. "I think."

"Go get 'er, Garrett!" the woman said with a wide grin.

He shut the door and walked around the front of the car to the sidewalk and started jogging. As he ran, people leaned out their car windows, shouting his name.

"It's him!"

"Go, Garrett!"

"Get your woman!"

After two blocks, he glanced at his phone, horrified to see it was five o'clock. He still had two blocks to go. It was a hot and humid summer day, and he hadn't dressed for a summer afternoon run. Perspiration beaded on his forehead, sending streams of sweat down the side of his face and his neck.

People were leaning out their windows, chanting his name. "Garr-ett! Garr-ett!"

A teenage girl ran up to him and handed him a bottle of water, then jogged beside him for several paces. "What you're doing is *so* romantic!"

Shit. Blair hated romance. Would she see it that way?

People were lined up on the sidewalk in front of the church, chanting his name. How in the hell had so many people heard about this in thirty minutes? He reached the top of the steps leading to the church and leaned over his legs to catch his breath. Then he looked at his phone. 5:10.

Dammit.

He was greeted with silence when he pushed opened the door leading to the foyer. Based on the rehearsal the night before, they probably hadn't reached the wedding vows yet, but what if it was running fast? The double doors to the sanctuary were straight ahead.

Garrett sucked in a deep breath, wiped his forehead with the back of his hand, and pushed the sanctuary door open.

Blair stood at the altar next to Neil. She looked beautiful in her close-fitting lace dress, but her veil was crooked, and she wasn't holding a bouquet. Neil stood next to her wearing his black tux and an arrogant smile that nauseated Garrett. Or that could have been the full bottle of water he'd gulped down as he ran. Probably both.

No one seemed to notice him except for Blair's assistant, who was sitting in the back row. Her head turned, and her mouth dropped into an O, but otherwise she remained motionless.

Given all his recent bad luck, something must have finally

turned his way. The minister turned to look around the church, his head jutting back in shock, and his eyes widening when he saw Garrett standing in the back of the aisle. His look of surprise quickly turned to concern as he uttered the line that every minister in every wedding had to be terrified to say.

"If any of you has a reason for why these two should not be married, speak now or forever hold your peace."

A loud, vehement chorus of "I object" rang out through the church, but the one that shocked him most was from the bride. And from the look of fury on her face, Neil had to be shitting his pants.

Chapter Thirty-One

GARRETT TOOK several steps down the aisle, but he stopped in his tracks when he realized Blair hadn't noticed him yet. She'd turned her cold fury on Neil, and he wasn't about to interrupt her. He wanted to see this. He slid into a pew to watch the show.

"Neil, I've dealt with many cheating, lying men over the past four years, but you are hands down the most despicable, pathetic excuse of a human being I've had the misfortune to meet."

"Blair." He reached toward her. "You're embarrassing yourself."

She slapped his hand away. "I embarrassed myself by staying with you for the past two years. I embarrassed myself by agreeing to marry you. But I am *not* embarrassing myself right now. I'm finally taking control of a situation I've allowed to coast along for far too long."

"Blair!" he grunted in a low voice. "Now is not the time to air our dirty laundry."

She tilted her head, her eyes icy blue. "So when exactly *is* the best time, Neil? After the wedding? Should we have Reverend Baker speed this up so we can go to a private room and discuss in *private* how you're *cheating* on me and have been since we met?"

The arrogance bled from his face.

"Oh, yeah. I know about Layla." She turned, and her gaze scanned the crowd. "And isn't that a surprise. She didn't come to the wedding, even though Neil added his *girlfriend's* name to the guest list to *our wedding* along with all his other co-workers." She turned her attention to the groom. "That took a lot of fucking balls. Where'd you dig those up? Off a corpse in the hospital?"

The rattle of coins interrupted the silence. Debra stood, holding out the battered cat jar. "That's five dollars, Blair."

Blair slowly turned her cold gaze to Neil's mother, the look in her eyes terrifying. The woman sank back onto the pew without uttering a word.

"I'm surprised Layla's not here." Her eyebrows rose in mock surprise. "You and I know it's not because she's *shy*," Blair said in a coy voice. "She had no problem stripping to her *underwear* in Neil's cousin's hotel room this morning."

Several people gasped, including Garrett's own mother. He would have some explaining to do later.

"Little Layla must get around, because she was busy screwing Neil earlier in the week. I'm pretty damn sure you were too busy banging the nurse you worked with that you couldn't be bothered to wonder why I didn't come home Monday night."

"Blair," Neil pleaded.

She pointed her finger at him. "I'm just getting started with you." She took a breath. "But I'm not here to talk about Layla. I'm here to honor Neil."

"Blair. *Stop this.*"

She snatched the bouquet out of Megan's hand and hit him in the chest, sending several roses flying. "*You* will be *quiet*. I'm talking right now." He made a move toward the steps, and she whacked him again. "Don't even think about it, asshole. I'm not done with you yet."

His jaw set, and he looked furious.

"One would expect a man who has a girlfriend *and* a fiancée to be a man of confidence, and why not? He had the world by the tail, right? Yet he was so worried about his cousin coming to the wedding and stealing me away from him that he convinced his friend, a junior partner in my firm, to *lie* to me and tell me that my job at the firm was dependent on my wedding. If my wedding went *perfectly*, I'd make partner. But if I didn't go through with the wedding, I would be fired." She scanned the crowd until her gaze landed on the guilty man. "And Ben Stuart was so convincing I fell for it." She began a slow clap, the stems of the bouquet muffling the sound. "Bravo, Ben. You deserve a Tony nomination for that performance."

"Blair," Neil pleaded. "I didn't know that Ben—"

"Don't you *even*." She hit him in the chest with the bouquet again, a shower of roses flying every direction. "Yeah, I figured it out, even if I admit to missing it last night when you mentioned my ultimatum from work without me having told you about it."

"Blair."

"Then you mentioned it again this morning when you realized that I truly intended to break up with you. So when you failed to talk me out of dumping you, you sent your slutty girlfriend to Garrett's hotel room, then insisted that we go back to talk to Garrett *together*. But here's your mistake with that one, Neil: What are the odds of me finding my fully clothed boyfriend with a lingerie-clad woman *twice*? Because, call me a fool—and I've rightly earned the title—but I can't imagine Garrett would ask me to marry him and then invite a skanky woman to his room twenty minutes later."

Neil's face had turned as red as the bridesmaids' dresses.

"Maybe if you knew how to satisfy a man, I wouldn't have to go elsewhere for sex."

A horrified gasp spread throughout the crowd.

She put her hands on her hips and eyed him with distaste. "Neil, you wouldn't know how to satisfy a woman if she supplied her own vibrator."

Debra and her daughter gasped, but the sounds were practically drowned out by the crowd's collective laughter. Neil's fury increased, and he took a step toward her.

Garrett had heard enough. "You need to back away from her Neil. *Now.*" The command in his voice was unmistakable. He started down the aisle, the papers in his hand. "Have you listed your grievances, Blair? Because I have a few of my own."

At the sound of his voice, she twisted to face him, her mouth dropping open in surprise. "Garrett."

He approached the altar, trying to keep his rage at bay. "Neil, you self-righteous prick."

Neil pointed to the back door. "Get the hell out of here, Garrett! None of this concerns you!"

"When you send your girlfriend to strip in my room, it concerns me. When you hurt and try to humiliate Blair, *it concerns me.*"

Neil leaned closer and lowered his voice, motioning to the papers in his hand. "I thought you were bringing me an *offer*, cousin. Do you really want to do this?"

Garrett sneered, "You mean the deal where I was going to pay you to call off the wedding?" He looked over at Blair and smiled. "Looks like I don't need that deal anymore."

"What about the *other?*" Neil asked, his tone hateful.

"The other?" Garrett asked, feigning innocence. "I think Nana Ruby has something to say about that."

Neil's face paled. "Nana Ruby?"

"I've had enough of your bratty behavior," Nana said,

standing up from her seat toward the front of the church and shuffling past several people to get to the aisle. "I should box your ears, Neilson Allen Fredrick."

He clenched his hands at his sides. "Stay out of this, Nana."

Aunt Debra rose up and rushed over to her mother. "What's going on here?"

"What's going on, Debbie Sue, is that your son is a liar, a cheater, and apparently an extortionist. You should have raised him better."

"They're lying!" Debra shouted. "My little Neil wouldn't do any of this!"

Nana Ruby waved to him. "The proof is in the pudding." She looked up at him. "What do you have to say for yourself?"

"I'm innocent."

"Then I guess you won't mind signing this paper Garrett's made, ensuring you *stay* innocent."

Neil glanced around the church at all the curious guests. The back of the church was now full of over a hundred people, who from the state of their attire, were social media onlookers. "This doesn't seem like the right time." He took a step down from the altar, and Nana smashed his foot with her cane. He stumbled back onto the altar as fast as he could manage.

She gave him a scowl. "Now seems like the *perfect* time. You were blackmailing your cousin over this wedding and this girl, so you might as well wrap up all your unfinished business at the wedding. Because from the looks of things, that's all that's getting finished here."

Neil's eyes narrowed. "What does it say?"

Garrett lifted the papers. "Perhaps you should read it."

"If you want any kind of inheritance at all from me, you'll sign it." Nana held a pen toward Neil. "Give him the papers, Garrett."

Garrett handed them to his cousin, knowing his cousin

would sign. Nana Ruby had offered him one-fourth of the land —his expected inheritance, but only if he not only agreed to never release the video and photos of Blair, but also gave Garrett any hard copies Neil might possess.

Neil jerked them out of his hand, and gave them a good shake before he started to read. It was all the opportunity Garrett needed to sneak a glance at Blair. Megan and Libby flanked her now, and he wasn't surprised by her defiant stance. Yet she snuck a glance at him, and their eyes locked. He saw sadness and regret in her gaze, and his heart sank to his feet. Had he really lost her?

"I'm not agreeing to this." Neil flapped the papers at Garrett. "I bet you drew these up yourself. How do I know they're legal?"

"They're legal," Garrett said in disgust. "And if they aren't, then you'll have your out." Garrett's voice tightened. "But I assure you, if you let them leak, I'll come after you faster than white on rice."

"Sign it," Nana barked.

Gritting his teeth, Neil awkwardly bent over and signed the papers on his leg, then tossed them back at Garrett as he rose. "Can I go now?" Then he looked around the church and went slack-jawed as if finally realizing he was acting like an ass in front of over three hundred people, including two hundred of which were his family, friends, and colleagues—not to mention the hundred or more strangers that filled the back of the church, most with smart phones in their hands, recording the entire fiasco.

Dr. Neil Fredrick was about to become a viral sensation of his own.

Nana stepped out of the way, and Neil hurried down the aisle and out the back doors.

The minister, who had stood behind the altar with an

admirable poker face throughout all the commotion, finally spoke. "Well . . . in all my twenty years of officiating weddings, I've never had anyone object, let alone half the church." He turned to Blair and gave her a sympathetic smile. "Looks like you dodged a bullet, young lady."

Blair's gaze turned to Garrett. "I guess I did." Then she took a deep breath and started to say something before stopping.

Garrett took a step toward her. "Blair. I'm sorry."

Her eyes widened in surprise. "Why?"

"For not telling you about Layla."

Shock covered her face and she choked out, "She . . . you slept with . . ."

"No!" Horror filled his words. "God. No. I meant I'm sorry I didn't tell you about her and Neil. When I went to the hospital a few days ago to ask him if he loved you, and the two of them were together in his office, Neil admitted he was sleeping with her and intended to keep her as his mistress after your wedding."

"But why didn't you tell me that?"

He grimaced. "Because I knew how much it would hurt you. I hoped I could get you to end it another way, so you'd never have to know."

"You were trying to protect me?" she asked, incredulous.

"Yeah."

She smacked his arm with Megan's nearly destroyed bouquet, and the last few remaining flowers flew out. At this point, it was little more than a collection of pointed green spikes. "Well, don't do that. I don't need protecting. I can handle it."

"Yeah, Nana Ruby pointed that out this afternoon." A sheepish grin spread across his face. "But you have to understand—I love you. Wanting to protect you seems to go hand in hand with that."

"You still love me?" she whispered.

His smile spread. "Yeah, I do."

"Even after the horrible, hurtful things I said?"

"You were shocked and hurt, Blair. I would hope you'd be that upset if I were actually screwing around on you. *Of course* I still love you. I've loved you for years."

She reached out to him, and he pulled her into his arms, lowering his lips to hers for a soft lingering kiss. "I'm starving. Know of any place we can get something to eat?"

She grinned and glanced back at her assistant. "As a matter of fact, I do." Then she turned her attention to the guests, most of who were now standing and filling the room with the roar of their voices.

"If I could have your attention!" she shouted.

When the ruckus continued, Nana Ruby stuck her fingers in her mouth and released a whistle so loud it shocked everyone into silence. When they realized the bride was about to address them, they gave her their enraptured attention.

Blair took a deep breath. "First of all, I'd like to apologize for the spectacle you just witnessed, although from the looks of some of you," her gaze landed on Kelsey, who bounced a baby on her shoulder and wore a wide smile, "you enjoyed every minute of it. In that spirit of celebration, and if it's not too awkward for you, there's a reception with food and music that's already been paid for . . . so I invite you to come on over and join us."

Garrett took her hand and led her down the aisle to a chorus of cheers and whistles. A loud cheer rose above the rest, which was when Garrett realized the couple who had given him a ride to the church were sitting in the back pew. The woman was furiously typing on her phone, and the man gave him a thumbs-up.

"Say, Garrett," he said with a huge grin. "Where exactly is that reception?"

Garrett squeezed Blair's hand and gave her a sheepish look. "There's something I have to tell you."

Her eyebrows rose. "And that is?"

He cringed. "We *may* have become a social media sensation."

"*What?*"

"Blair," a man called out from behind them. They turned to see an older, distinguished-looking man approaching them. Blair's back stiffened, and Garrett instinctively put his arm around her.

"Mr. Sisco."

He grimaced. "On behalf of the firm, I would like to extend my apologies for Mr. Stuart's behavior. We do not condone what he's done, and the partners will meet next week to discuss an appropriate punishment."

"Thank you," she said briskly.

He leaned closer. "But I can tell you that there was a nugget of truth to what he told you. We *are* considering you for partnership."

Garrett expected her boss's statement to make her relax, but she only seemed to get more tense. "I see. Are you sure I'm partner material? Are you sure I'm not too much of a bitch?"

"What?" he asked, his face turning red.

"You were right, there was some truth to what Ben said. Several truths. I made a few phone calls this afternoon, and it turns out I've been considered for partner before, but one of the senior *married* partners refused to vote for me because I wouldn't sleep with him."

Her boss's face grew even redder. "I assure you that's not true." He paused. "And even if it was, you don't have proof."

She gave him a cold smile. "And that right there is proof enough."

"Blair," he gushed. "I know we'd love to make you partner and offer you a nice signing bonus."

"I'm sure you would." Her eyes sparkled with the look of a predator about to devour its prey, and Garrett found himself incredibly turned on.

"Mr. Sisco, you can take your partnership and shove it up your ass. You'll find my letter of resignation on your desk on Monday morning."

"Blair, I'm sure we can work something out."

"The only thing we're working out is how quickly you can get out of my sight."

His jaw clenched with anger, and he stomped out of the sanctuary.

She took a deep breath and let it out. "That felt good."

"I bet it did."

"But I don't have a job. And Melissa . . ."

"Blazer, I want you to be happy where you work. But for the record, if you *had* accepted, we might have had words. There's no way I want my wife working for a bunch of sexist pricks."

She spun around to face him, lifting her hands to his face. "Your wife?"

A lazy grin spread across his face. "I know. It's going to take some getting used to."

"In a bad way?"

"In the best possible way." He pulled her to his chest and kissed her, thankful that she didn't pull back, even though they were in a church full of people. "I think I'm underdressed for this reception. How about we swing by my hotel room and pick up my tux?" He grinned. "And do a few other things."

"Impatient again?" she laughed.

"Are you kidding?" He shot her a look of disbelief. "I almost lost you forever. I'm scared to death to let you out of my sight for one minute."

She tensed. "You're not going to be one of those clingy husbands, are you?"

"I've thought of you nonstop for five years, and this morning you turned your back on me to marry my asshole cousin. You're going to have to give me at least a couple of hours of clinginess to calm my anxiety."

"Then if you want to be clingy, I have the perfect idea for how we can make use of a few of those hours."

His hand dug into her hip, his eyes full of longing. "I need to find a car."

THEY SHOWED up at the reception about an hour later, arriving to the cheers of Blair's friends and family and some of Garrett's family. Blair was still wearing her wedding dress since she didn't have anything else to change into, but she'd let her hair down and removed her veil. "I like the idea of you not having a wardrobe," Garrett had teased while he nuzzled her neck in his room when they were supposed to be getting dressed, "but it might not be a bad idea to keep a few articles of clothing around."

He wore his tux, and she warned him that this was the only wedding reception they would get, so he'd better dress the part.

They ate and danced, and she found herself feeling more relaxed than she'd been in years. She looked up into the face of the man who had refused to leave her side all night, amazed that he was really there with her.

He glanced down at her, a warm smile spreading across his face.

"When you look at me like that," she said, smiling coyly, "all I can think about is you naked."

His eyebrows rose, mischievousness dancing in his eyes. "Is that so?"

"What are you doing next week?"

He brushed his lips against hers, and that was all it took to make her blood hot. "Hopefully spending every minute with you."

She tilted her head. "How about spending the week with me in Costa Rica? I paid for a week at an all-inclusive resort for the honeymoon. Non-refundable."

His eyes twinkled. "So this is a *practical* invitation?"

"I'm a practical woman."

"Only one of *many* things I love about you." He lowered his head to kiss her, then he pulled back to look into her eyes. "So . . . if we're going on a honeymoon, I think we should actually be married first."

Her breath caught, and she tensed. This was getting very real, very fast. Somehow the prospect of marrying Garrett was so much more frightening than her engagement with Neil had been. She had so much more to lose.

But for once, she was going to ignore the voices of caution in her head. They had kept her from living for the last ten years, and Garrett had been the only one to truly quiet them. It was time to let her heart take the lead for a while.

"Okay."

"*Really?*"

"You thought I'd say no? You already proposed this morning. Trust me, that'll be hard to explain to our kids if we have them."

He laughed. "When I proposed this morning, we didn't discuss dates. I know how you like to plan things out. We can wait if you'd prefer. The last thing I'd want is for you to feel pressured."

"No." She shook her head. "No more waiting. We've wasted five years, and we've got some making up to do."

"Then how about we get married on the beach in Costa Rica? Just you and me. Are you okay with that?"

"That's exactly how I want it," she murmured as she kissed him. "But I want a different ring. This ring has been nothing but trouble."

"I'll get you a new ring, but I'll be forever thankful for my family heirloom. I wouldn't be here right now if not for this stupid ring."

He wrapped an arm around her back and pulled her close. "Mrs. Blair Lowry. Or maybe Mr. Garrett Hansen." His eyes twinkled. "Or is it Myers? Who can keep up?"

"Shut up and kiss me, player."

"Gladly."

The Gambler (Libby's Story)
The Wedding Pact #3
Available now!

About the Author

Denise Grover Swank was born in Kansas City, Missouri and lived in the area until she was nineteen. Then she became a nomad, living in five cities, four states and ten houses over the course of ten years before she moved back to her roots. She speaks English and smattering of Spanish and Chinese which she learned through an intensive Nick Jr. immersion period. Her hobbies include witty Facebook comments (in own her mind) and dancing in her kitchen with her children. (Quite badly if you believe her offspring.) Hidden talents include the gift of justification and the ability to drink massive amounts of caffeine and still fall asleep within two minutes. Her lack of the sense of smell allows her to perform many unspeakable tasks. She has six children and hasn't lost her sanity. Or so she leads you to believe.

denisegroverswank.com

www.ingramcontent.com/pod-product-compliance
Lightning Source LLC
Chambersburg PA
CBHW030530190726
48283CB00006B/1844